Malevolent Hearts

Book 1 of The Malevolent Trilogy

By Carrie Dalby

Book designed and published by Olive Kent Publishing
Mobile, Alabama

Cover art by Amanda Herman

www.carriedalby.com

*For all who have lost a loved one to illness
and the city of Mobile, Alabama*

One

The hired carriage pulled to a stop in front of the stately home on Chatham Street. I stood from the bench and descended to the curb. While the driver went for my luggage, I untied the leash of my German longhaired pointer.

"Come on, Tippet. Let's go see Aunt Ethel and Uncle Andrew."

The driver left the cast iron gate in front of the house open, and I met him halfway up the walk on his return.

"It's all on the front porch, Miss Hall."

From my reticule, I retrieved the fare to pay for my trip from the train station to here on the west side of Mobile. "Thank you."

The gate clanged shut behind him.

In the afternoon heat, I took a moment to appreciate the shaded yard which was surrounded by camellia and azalea bushes for privacy, all within a decorative fence. Large for a city dwelling, the property ran the length of the block facing Washington Square Park. The branches of the sprawling oaks reached for each other over the shrubbery, linking the house, stable, and shed in a secret web of protection from the world.

Glass shattered to my left. Startled, my gaze went to the remnants of a bottle at the base of an oak. Tippet's hackles raised, and he gave a low growl.

"Drat!" someone muttered from the tree canopy before a leg with a torn stocking dropped into view.

"Hello?" I called, stepping closer with Tippet at my heels. "Could I be of assistance?"

A childish face hung upside-down a moment later, braids falling away from her round cheeks. "Cousin Merritt Hall of Grand Bay?"

"Yes, and am I to guess you're cousin Winifred Ramsay?"

She laughed. "Give me a moment."

My uncle's niece was the reason I was there on the tenth of September 1897. After being orphaned, Winifred traveled from Charleston in June to stay with Uncle Andrew and Aunt Ethel. They did their best with the girl, but her "unsettled nature" they hoped she'd outgrow had increased as the summer progressed. Aunt Ethel wrote my mother in August, begging for me to visit. "Merritt's good sense and firm convictions will surely be a stabilizing influence on the girl," is what she had written.

Winifred jumped to the ground, straightening her black cotton dress and pinafore—much more suited for a girl half the age of her fifteen years. She stood two inches taller than me and was rounded everywhere I wasn't. Her brunette braids crowned what would have been a wholesome look were it not for the too-short skirt and her womanly measurements that practically burst the seams.

"You brought a dog! Aunt Ethel said you might." Her head bent over Tippet, whose fur, like my own hair, was a shade darker than her locks.

"I had to bring Tippet. The rest of my family is in Mississippi this week visiting Aunt Ethel's other sister. Tippet is trained to hunt with my father and brother, but he stays with me around the house."

"How lovely!" Winifred rubbed Tippet's silky ears and kissed his head. "You'll grow to love and protect me, won't you?"

Tippet licked her face in response, giving a soft bark of agreement.

"Shall we collect the glass and report to Aunt Ethel?" I motioned to the fragments amid the tree roots.

"I suppose." Her blue eyes darkened as she looked up to a hanging bottle. "I wish I had more than one, but it will have to do until tomorrow."

Winifred gathered the chunks of glass into her handkerchief as I stared at the empty bottle of cooking oil dangling on a length of twine from the tree. Curious. I followed her to the front porch. Patches of peeling paint were evident on the clapboard sides and the shutters running the length of the long, narrow windows needed tightening, but Uncle Andrew was never one to spend a dime until something was falling apart.

As soon as we passed into the foyer, Winifred shouted, "Aunt Ethel, she's here!"

My aunt emerged from the parlor in a stiff black dress. She looked small under the high ceiling—a sad, aged doll in her fifties. Unfortunately, my features mirrored hers; a sharp, narrow nose and a brow that tended to look angry unless smiling.

"Don't shout, Winifred. It isn't proper to introduce a guest as such." Aunt Ethel's pinched scowl softened as she reached for me. Despite her weariness, my aunt's frame was solid beneath her embrace. "Dear Merritt, it's been too long."

I had last visited along with my parents and brother over Mardi Gras, though we were forbidden from participating in the celebrations the city offered. Uncle Andrew and Aunt Ethel had no living children and owned a general store on the outskirts of town. We had free range when we visited, much like we had within our father's own store in Grand Bay.

"Thank you for inviting me, Aunt Ethel."

Winifred continued to the kitchen to deposit her broken glass in the rubbish can. Once she was down the hall, our aunt sighed.

"She's smiling for the moment," Aunt Ethel remarked. "That's more than I've seen her do for weeks within these walls."

"I'll be of service however I can," I said, though I doubted my effectiveness. At the age of nineteen, I was to be placed over the care of a distant cousin, when several years before I had failed in a similar situation to horrific results.

"Get Tippet off that leash. You know he's welcome anywhere."

"Thank you, Aunt Ethel."

"I hope you won't mind sharing a room with Winifred. We have the cook staying with us now that her husband has passed on, and I want to keep the other bedroom available for guests."

I removed Tippet's leash, but he stayed by my side. "That's no trouble. I'll collect my luggage off the porch."

"The front bedroom, adjacent the sleeping porch. Winifred's been sleeping out there the past month. She even repainted the ceiling."

I hung the leash on the coat tree. Winifred silently joined me, taking my smaller bag after I hoisted the larger suitcase under my arm. Tippet followed us up the stairs and into the sparsely furnished room. Setting my bag on the bench at the foot of one of the four poster single beds, Winifred looked around anxiously.

"I'm glad you're here," she said, "but I stay outside most of the time, unless the gardener is working in my favorite area."

"Would you like to bring Tippet?"

"Yes, thank you." She showed me my appointed drawers and wardrobe space before turning for the door with Tippet.

I unpacked before joining Aunt Ethel in the parlor. Patting the spot on the stiff settee beside her, she took my hand as soon as I sat.

"I must tell you while she's out. Winifred has been nothing but trouble since she came—just like most of the others in Andrew's family—but the Ramsays are even worse than the Allens. And there's a boy that's been hanging around. I've told him not to call, but he meets her by the back fence rather than come to the door. He even brought her the paint for the porch, but I can't very well keep track of her every minute."

"Surely a young boy is—"

"He's seventeen if he isn't a day—one of those Catholic rascals who can do no wrong so long as he's first in line at confession. It's absolutely disgraceful what their society groups subject the city to during Mardi Gras. Mark my words, that one will be just like the rest in another year or two, drinking and cavorting with unspeakable women during Carnival. It's shameful! I don't know what he's thinking with trying to take up with little Winifred."

"She's not so little, Aunt Ethel. The clothes she's wearing have the opposite effect of making her look young."

My aunt stared, dumbfounded. Not knowing if I shook her delicate sensibilities, I decided to lay it all out at once to prove I had Winifred's best interests at heart and didn't hold with her bigotry to Catholics. My new neighbors in Grand Bay were a lovely young couple of that faith, and I always enjoyed seeing the beautiful cathedral when downtown.

"She's fifteen, Aunt Ethel, much too old to be showing so much of her legs. She needs ankle-length skirts. And her blouse is scandalous. She might have gone through a growth spurt since she arrived, but her chest is—"

"There's no need to discuss things like that. I'll speak to Andrew."

When Uncle Andrew arrived home, he spent time in his study until joining us at the supper table. He always looked old to me on my seasonal visits, but his gray hair and beard was fading to white—a shocking change from how he had looked that spring.

After several minutes of enjoying roast chicken and greens, Uncle Andrew caught Winifred's attention. "Ethel tells me a shopping trip is in order for you. That will be just the thing for you and Merritt to enjoy together on her first full day here. Don't worry about prices. It's long overdue."

"Thank you, Uncle Andrew." Winifred smiled at him.

"Ethel seems to forget about growing young ladies, though she was one once."

"I only had our sons a handful of years before they returned to their Maker." Aunt Ethel sniffed. "And girls these days are so different than I was—except dependable Merritt. But even she hasn't grown an inch since she was fourteen."

"I'm not immune to follies, Aunt Ethel." I pushed the limp greens around my plate. "I've failed at my responsibilities before. I'll never forget what happened to Di—"

"That wasn't your fault, Merritt," Uncle Andrew said with a rare show of force.

"Of course it wasn't," Aunt Ethel added. "Your time with Winifred will be much different than with Diamond. We have faith in you."

But with the thought of my deceased cousin, my appetite was gone. Winifred continued eating.

"Bartholomew, my assistant manager, was pleased to hear you arrived today." My uncle's voice was back to his soft tone, deep and soothing. "He looks forward to meeting you."

Aunt Ethel actually smiled. "Is he coming to supper tomorrow, Andrew?"

"Naturally."

Winifred frowned at the news, but finished off her chicken before looking expectantly for dessert.

Keziah, the old cook, soon arrived with a peach cobbler and a dish of heavy cream. My mother couldn't stand anyone in her kitchen. She hired a few local girls twice a year when it was time to give the house a good scrubbing top to bottom, but otherwise she did it herself, with me helping since I was old enough to hold a broom. I was always uncomfortable being waited upon, even by friendly, old Keziah.

The final chatter around the table consisted of me answering Uncle Andrew's questions about my father's business and how he was training my brother, Ezra, to eventually run things.

After supper and readying for bed, I followed Winifred onto the sleeping porch. She waited until I settled in a hammock before she blew out the candle, as the porch didn't have gaslights. My thin cotton gown clung to my damp body despite the breeze. A chorus of cicadas buzzed from the nearby oaks while my cousin murmured church hymns from her own hanging bed.

Mulling over the words of my aunt—her worries that Winifred was troublesome—and the sallow look my uncle had at the supper table, I had difficulty falling asleep.

As I was finally drifting off, Winifred began to cry. I fell to my knees, almost landing on top of Tippet who slept beneath my hammock. In the light of the moon, I made my way to Winifred.

"What is it?" I felt for her hand as Tippet came to a stop beside me. "What can I do?"

"You're already doing as much as I can hope for." Winifred scratched at her bare arm. Even in the pale light, I could make out reddened welts from mosquito bites.

"Don't scratch or you'll scar." I straightened. "I'll fetch the chamomile from—"

"No! Don't leave me."

"But—"

"I'll stop scratching, Merritt."

I smoothed her ruffled hair and agreed to stay on the porch, but it was another hour before I fell asleep.

Come the first ray of morning, I found myself staring at the pale blue of the porch ceiling. It was too dark to see it clearly when we went to bed, but in the sunlight I saw it for what it was: haint blue. A color meant to keep a home safe from evil spirits.

Two

Saturday morning consisted of a trip to Gayfer's Department Store where Winifred glowed amid ribbons and lace. My cousin happily tried on ready-made outfits of all types and colors, though Aunt Ethel decided on black for the majority of Winifred's clothes. A few blue dresses—to match her striking eyes—did make it onto the receipt.

Back at the house, I took noon dinner with Aunt Ethel and Winifred. Outfitted in a new black skirt that reached her buttoned boots and a properly fitted matching blouse, Winifred topped the mature look with an up-do. The melancholy color and style caused her to appear older than me.

"I'm going to rest," Aunt Ethel informed us when we finished eating.

We watched her leave and Winifred rose from the table. "Could I bring Tippet into the yard?"

"You needn't ask. He's yours as much as mine while I'm here."

Winifred threw her arms about me when I stood. "I love you, Cousin Merritt."

I watched from the window as Winifred ran across the lawn. Tippet raced beside her and then jumped into her lap when she sat on an iron bench beneath the far oak. As I exited the screen porch and crossed through the miniature orchard of satsuma trees, a cheerful whistle of three distinct notes carried through the heavy air.

Tippet barked as a young man with a mop of brown hair bound over the short fence in the narrow space between two azalea bushes, rattling the bottles in the crate he carried. Eyes only for Winifred, he set the box on the grass and went to his knees before her. Tippet wiggled free, examined him, and then licked his grinning face—the ultimate approval.

Laughing, Winifred leaned over and kissed the stranger's other cheek. "You remembered!"

I stopped a few feet away, captivated by his broad shoulders and fluid grace.

"I always keep my promises, Winnie. You should know that by now."

He looked like he was going in for a kiss, so I cleared my throat. The young man jumped to his feet as Tippet bound to me.

"Sean, meet my cousin and her dog, Tippet."

I joined them by the bench.

Unruffled by my lack of a commanding presence, his youthful grin returned, and he shook back a lock of hair that hung over his forehead as he looked down at me. "Hello, Cousin."

Winifred giggled. "Her name is Merritt Hall. Merritt, this is Sean Spunner."

I offered my hand, and he brazenly brought my knuckles to his lips. "Miss Hall, it is a pleasure."

The flutter in my stomach over the attentions of a handsome young man left no room to fault Winifred's obvious delight. Aunt Ethel was right in thinking him a rascal. Surely he left a trail of girls in his wake with his amber eyes and ear-to-ear grin.

I curtseyed to match his ridiculous introduction. "Mr. Spunner, might I ask what brought you into the yard in such an ungentlemanly way?"

He motioned to the crate. "Bottles for Winnie. She requested as many as I could gather, and I'm happy to say my friends helped me empty a few last night."

"Sean, you shouldn't have." Winifred clasped her hands behind her back. The motion accentuated her new ensemble.

Sean's gaze raked over every inch. "Miss Hall is here one day, and you already look more like the young lady you truly are. Whatever will you do with me when you surpass my boyish ways?"

"Oh," she sighed and took his hand once more. "I never will."

He soaked in her adoration and gave her another charming smile. "Good. And remember, I'd do anything for you, Winnie, even polishing off the rest of my uncle's whiskey so I could bring you an extra bottle."

In an attempt to break their too-familiar stares, I nudged closer. "Why do you need whiskey bottles, Winifred?"

Her eyes dropped to the toe of her boot, which she drug through the thick grass as she bit her lip. Surely she knew our uncle and aunt kept a dry house and would frown on liquor bottles.

"I'll fetch the twine," she muttered before turning for the house.

I caught Sean's steady gaze.

"She hasn't told you?" he asked.

"I've been here twenty-four hours, Mr. Spunner. What do you think?"

"I think you need to call me Sean, Miss Hall."

Matching his smile, I tried not to laugh. "Fair enough."

"Winnie thinks she's haunted. A spirit comes to her in her sleep that somehow relates to the fire her family died in." He angled closer. "Despite her parents' Baptist beliefs, her old Mammy in Charleston raised her on Gullah superstitions. I'm doing all I can to ease her worries."

"The paint for the porch's ceiling?"

Sean nodded. "And bottles in the trees to catch evil spirits. But I got the best ones I could find so she'll at least have something nice to look at."

The earnest gaze in his golden brown eyes melted my concern. No matter his flirtations, he did care for Winifred. "May God bless your efforts, Sean."

Winifred returned, clutching a ball of twine in her right hand and scissors in her left.

"With that hairstyle and your new clothes," Sean said, "I insist on being the one to climb the tree. I don't want your aunt fussing at you for spoiling anything before you make it to the supper table."

"I did rip my stockings yesterday when I hung that one."

He stuffed the twine into the pocket of his trousers and took the scissors. "Where do you want them?"

Winifred pointed up. "Some here, please, and the rest in the trees by the back porch."

Sean rolled his white sleeves and deftly pulled himself onto the lowest branch from the bench to begin his climb.

"How can we get the bottles to you?" Winifred called up to him.

In response, he unwound several feet of twine and wiggled it above her head. She jumped to catch the end.

Sean tugged playfully. "Looks like I caught a keeper!"

Winifred's laughter filled the yard.

"Have your cousin tie on one of the bottles. Then I'll raise it until you tell me it's high enough."

After seven bottles were hung from the oak, Sean returned to the ground and surveyed his handiwork.

"Are you sure your uncle won't knock his head on that one?" He pointed to an amber glass that hung lower than the others.

"Uncle Andrew doesn't come out here, and the gardener is a stumpy fellow." She looked at him through her lashes. "And I want that one where I can easily see it."

He raised his dark brows questioningly.

"It's the color of your eyes," she whispered.

I half expected Sean to crow, but he merely hoisted the crate and swaggered across the yard toward the copse of satsuma trees. Tippet bound after him.

Winifred took my arm. "Isn't he wonderful?"

"He's very attentive."

After collecting a stepladder from the shed, Sean hung bottles with our assistance. The assorted cobalt and green glasses swayed on their cords, little nooses set to capture ghosts where once a different spirit resided.

While Sean carried the ladder back to the shed, Aunt Ethel stormed out of the kitchen. Hands on her hips, she stared at Winifred first and then me with disapproval.

"What's the meaning of this?"

"It's only a bit of whimsy, Aunt Ethel," I said as she came onto the lawn.

"Whiskey and brandy and scotch! Dear Lord, what will the neighbors say?"

"You can't see it from the front walk, Aunt Ethel," Winifred said. "You can't see any of the bottles from the road. I did think of that."

"What are you planning to do with all this?"

"I—"

Sean came up behind us, and Aunt Ethel set her sights on him. "You! I should have known! Leave it to a Catholic to—"

Winifred took her hand. "It was my idea! He only brought what bottles he could find when I asked him. Don't be mad."

"If it was a different day of the week, I'd march down to your uncle's office and give Patrick Finnigan a piece of my mind, Sean Spunner! Get these vessels of the devil off my property this instant!"

Winifred broke into sobs and ran for the far bench.

"I meant no offense, Mrs. Allen. I only tried to help." Sean followed Winifred's path and sat beside her, a comforting hand going to her shoulder as Tippet laid his head on her lap.

"First whiskey and now touching—that boy is brazen trouble!"

"He's good for her, Aunt Ethel. I've never seen her smile like she has since he appeared. Not even when trying on that blue dress this morning. I've been out here since he arrived and he's done nothing improper."

"I don't trust him an inch." Her brow creased further. "You'll chaperone them?"

"I'd be happy to."

Aunt Ethel sighed and motioned to the nearest satsuma tree. "But what of these bottles? I remember some of the Negro communities sticking them on trees. I don't fancy them in our yard."

Choosing my words carefully, I tiptoed around their grim purpose. "It's a tradition along the coastal communities. I've seen it down in the bayou and apparently they did it in Charleston as well. It's cloudy today, but when the sun shines, you'll see it's really quite striking."

She huffed. "I wash my hands of that rascal. If anything happens to Winifred, I'll hold you *and* him responsible."

Three

I allowed Winifred and Sean a few more minutes before approaching the bench. "It's time Sean went home."

Winifred's arms went about his waist, and she buried her face in his chest. A bittersweet smile curled Sean's lips, and he enfolded her in his embrace.

"He can stop in tomorrow after church or any other time that's convenient."

Her head jerked up. "Aunt Ethel—"

"She said he's welcome to visit if I chaperone."

"Merritt, you're an angel!" Winifred launched from the bench, nearly knocking me backward as she hugged me. "I wish you had come sooner."

I caught Sean's eye as she clung to me, and he flashed his devilish grin.

When Winifred let me go, he kissed my hand. "Thank you for looking out for Winnie, Miss Hall."

"Don't make me regret this," I retorted.

"Never. I'll see you both tomorrow." He kissed Winifred's cheek, collected his empty crate, and strolled to the gate for a proper exit.

"You look peaked from the excitement, Winifred. Why don't we rest until Uncle Andrew returns?"

Fear clouded her blue eyes.

"I'll stay with you, and we'll use the hammocks on the sleeping porch," I added.

"So long as Tippet comes."

"Of course."

We settled on the porch; I with my copy of Kipling's *The Jungle Book* and she with her daydreams of Sean. We were both down to our underclothes and barefoot in the summer heat. Around the side of my book, I studied Winifred. A hand was tucked under the soft lines of her rounded cheek that echoed the curves of her developing body. Sean was right in calling her pretty. In another few years, she'd be a gorgeous woman while my sharp angles shouted of a lady who preferred books and a dog over human companionship.

I managed to finish a short story in the Kipling collection before the sound of a wagon pulling into the back gate snagged my attention.

"Forgive me for not helping, Bart," Uncle Andrew called. "I'll see you inside."

Winifred groaned. "I'd forgotten he was coming today. Bartholomew Graves is as boring as his name. Uncle Andrew must feel sorry for him. He comes for supper most Saturdays."

"Has he no family?"

"Not that I know of, but I don't pay attention when he's here except to play the piano after supper."

We redressed in our shared bedroom—Winifred accomplishing the task much slower because she stopped to lavish Tippet with scratches and petting.

When we reached the foot of the stairs, Aunt Ethel called out. "Winifred, please help Mr. Graves with anything that needs unloading."

"Not if she's wearing one of those new outfits," Uncle Andrew countered.

Winifred laughed and danced into the parlor. "I am, Uncle Andrew. And thank you!"

"It's good to see you happy, Winifred," Uncle Andrew said. "You look just like your mother when you smile, God rest her soul."

She leaned over his chair to kiss Uncle Andrew's cheek above his beard before taking the settee.

"I could help unload," I offered from the doorway.

Uncle Andrew shook his head. "It isn't much today. Bart is probably done by now."

I took a seat beside Winifred.

"I'm glad you girls rested," Aunt Ethel said. "You shouldn't have been out in the heat so much this afternoon."

"I love the outdoors," Winifred said. "Maybe Merritt and I could go on walks together."

Down the hall, the guest bath door clicked shut.

"We'll discuss that later." Aunt Ethel straightened her skirt and adjusted her stature in the armchair.

We waited in silence for the visitor to appear. Uncle Andrew's eyes closed with apparent exhaustion and Winifred's in boredom. My curiosity over the man my cousin found repulsive kept my attention high as my clasped hands tried not to fidget.

When Bartholomew Graves appeared in the doorway of the parlor, I muffled a gasp. The shock wasn't for what I saw, but what I didn't. Expecting comical features or even looks that were a bit obscene, his neatly combed brown hair topped a body that was far from hideous. He could have come from New York or San Francisco, except for a bronzed complexion, typical from the southern sun. There was nothing to distinguish him in any certain region or demographic in his functional business suit and basic eyeglasses. But compared to Winifred's Sean, there was no doubt a lack of charisma.

"Welcome, Mr. Graves," Aunt Ethel said. "I'm glad you could join us. Do sit with the girls."

His face glistened as though he didn't properly dry it after washing. Taking a handkerchief from his pocket, he dabbed it across his high forehead before looking to us.

"Miss Winifred."

She was polite enough to nod in his direction.

"And our other niece, Merritt Hall, from Grand Bay," Aunt Ethel said. "We've spoken to you about her."

Bartholomew came to my side and offered his hand. "It's good to meet you, Miss Hall."

"Call me Merritt, please." I shook his hand and smiled.

"Of course, Miss Merritt."

When he sat beside me, I looked to my cousin. Winifred shrugged and picked at her fingernails.

"Do you think we'll escape Yellow Jack this year?" Uncle Andrew asked no one in particular.

"The newspapers say there are no cases," Bartholomew said matter-of-factly.

"There were quarantine officers on the train inspecting the passengers yesterday," I offered.

"Why didn't you tell us, Merritt?" my uncle asked.

"I didn't think of it until now, but they're common enough in summer."

"Good heavens!" Aunt Ethel wrung her hands. "I'm glad Winifred arrived before yellow fever season. That would have been terrible for her to be subjected to medical inspection by a stranger."

I crossed my ankles and tried not to feed on the anxiety permeating the room. "There have been guards on the Bayou La Batre bridge the past several days too."

"That's never a good sign. The officers will keep creeping in closer until the city is a prison of death and disease!"

"Enough, Ethel." Uncle Andrew's sharp tone cut the room with a palpable snap, bringing to mind the fact that their two sons died from the fever when they were boys.

Handkerchief to her nose, Aunt Ethel rushed from the room.

"Please excuse her," Uncle Andrew said to Bartholomew. "I forget how anxious she gets this time of year."

As though shrouded in her own worries, Winifred's mouth tugged down at the corners. Her parents and sister were lost in a house fire that spring. Perhaps it was thoughts of that horrific event that haunted her—had her seeking bottles to collect the memories that plagued her night and day.

***

Sunday afternoon found Winifred and I on the bench beneath the oak. Above our heads, the glass bottles sparkled in the oppressive heat like dew on a headstone. I aired myself with a folding fan decorated with gleaming cranes, wishing my dress was thinner than the light-weight summer frock already was. Winifred wore a new blue dress that matched the summer sky, a black mourning band for her family tied around her upper arm since she wasn't in mourning garb.

As soon as the cheerful three-toned whistle floated into the yard, she was on her feet. Despite his permission to come, Sean hopped the fence like he had the day before, but this time he was as silent as a swan.

"Winnie, you look stunning." He fell to his knees in the grass before her, hands clasped. "Run away with me, dear lady! End this torment of looking upon you without knowing you're mine."

Giggling, Winifred took the sides of her dress and swished them as she looked down at him. "You'll have to catch me first!"

She dashed for the far corner of the yard. Stumbling to his feet, Sean gave chase. Coming around the front of the house as he disappeared behind it, Winifred leapt onto the bench and was about to climb the tree when I grabbed her wrist.

"Not in your new dress! You're too old to play about like this, especially with a young man."

"But we always—"

"He likes you Winifred. He's…" I paused as Sean ran to us, but decided he needed to hear it as well. "It isn't proper for the two of you to keep on with these games."

His hand reaching for hers stopped midair as he looked at me with wide eyes.

"How old are you, Sean?" I asked.

"Seventeen."

"Then you're old enough to know you shouldn't be chasing girls about like you did when you were in short pants. If my parents saw my seventeen-year-old brother chasing a young woman like you're doing to Winifred, they'd tan his backside for being fresh."

"How dare you say that, Merritt? Sean's an orphan like me and has no—"

"From what I've heard, you both have been taken in by uncles who have your best interests at heart. You needn't carry on in ways that could bring shame to either family. We'll see you another day, Sean. Goodbye."

He bowed his head and turned for the gate.

Following, I stopped him on the front walk. "I hope I wasn't too sharp with you."

"No, Miss Hall. You're right. I spent too much time with some younger fellows over the summer—a last hurrah before my university studies begin in earnest. My uncle needs my help at his firm, and I'm on a fast track to get my credentials though I'd rather still be running around." His eyes brightened. "From the moment I saw Winnie in the yard, I've been mesmerized. She was so sad, I had to try to help her through the heartache. I was twelve when my parents died, but it took me several years to come to terms with it all—plus the change of living with my uncle's family. And that was without thinking a ghost was haunting my dreams."

"I'm glad you found her."

His straight teeth flashed with his broad smile. "So am I."

Taking a deep breath, I readied for a talk I didn't know would be needed when I agreed to help with my cousin. "I might be stepping out of line, but since I've come to keep an eye on Winifred, I need to ask. What are your intentions with her, Sean?"

"I love her. I truly do. I don't aim to string her along."

I crossed my arms. "She's young and impressionable."

He glanced to the bench across the yard where Winifred sat with her head resting on Tippet's. "I know she won't be ready for anything until she settles down from her loss, but I want to be here for her as much as possible. Maybe in a few years, when I'm steady at my uncle's office and she's finished schooling, I'll be able to speak for her properly, but I'd never say that to her now. I don't want her beholden to me when she might mature beyond these playful weeks and decide I'm nothing but a gnat floating in her iced tea."

A laugh blurted out. "Don't try to charm me, Sean. I've already been warned about you."

He ran a hand through his shaggy hair, grinning more. "I'd be remiss if you hadn't."

"Ethel Allen doesn't like you hanging around here." I placed a hand on his shoulder. "But let's prove her wrong, shall we?"

Four

Unbeknownst to me, my jurisdiction with Winifred included the role of governess. The following day—and every Monday through Friday—Aunt Ethel expected me to tutor my cousin in etiquette, French, history, and literature, as well as oversee her piano practice. History was the easiest since it was my favorite subject, but Winifred had little patience for refined behavior when moving daintily slowed her down.

The first few days of the schedule had me questioning my aunt's intent. Surely two weeks would do little to set Winifred on a new path if her schooling would disappear when I returned home.

Wednesday afternoon, around the same time the sun sank low enough to provide a touch of relief and the weekly laundry delivery had been made, Winifred talked me into sitting under the oak for a spell. Sean whistled from the road a few minutes later, letting himself in the gate. I raised my eyebrows at Winifred.

"He often stops by on Wednesdays." Winifred met him in the middle of the yard, exchanging a few words before dashing through the back screen door.

Tippet followed Sean over.

"Good afternoon, Sean. Winifred failed to warn me you'd arrive today."

"I can't always finish my studies in time to make it, but I do my best." His eager grin widened when Winifred crossed the yard carrying a tray with glasses of lemonade.

"Refreshments are served," she declared, holding the tray first to me and then Sean.

The three of us squeezed onto the bench, Winifred in the middle and the empty tray at her feet. Sean held his drink in his far hand and his left rested on her skirt at the knee. Leaning forward, I turned to him with my eyes narrowed. He pursed his lips and languidly moved his arm to rest around her shoulders—taking a moment to tug at my bound hair first. I laughed.

"Isn't your cousin's pretty when she smiles?" Sean asked Winifred. "I think she wants us to think her stern, but she's really quite jolly when she isn't scolding."

"Merritt is the best," she replied.

"*Merritt.* Even her name demands one to behave." My cheeks heated as he peered around Winifred to study me. "We should call her 'Merri' instead."

"Merri Hall!" Winifred laughed. "It sounds like an excellent place for a party."

"Merri it is. Merri and Winnie, the best cousins in the state of Alabama."

"Your own cousin is delightful." Winifred clasped her hand around his. "You should introduce Megan to Merri sometime."

"She's off with the Easton twins on their grand European tour to prove their cultured education is complete. They won't be back until Thanksgiving."

"I hope to travel like that someday." Winifred sighed. "But I don't think Aunt Ethel would approve."

"Then you'll have to wait until a man sweeps you off your feet and carries you around the world for a honeymoon."

I changed the subject to redirect their adoring attention. "Do you know if the Easton twins are any relation to Susan Easton, who recently married David Shepard?"

"I'll say! There are ten siblings, but Susan is the next oldest from the twins. I always thought the Easton sisters the prettiest girls in town until Winnie arrived. How do you know Susan?"

"The Shepards moved into the house next door when they married. They shop at my father's store. We've hosted them for supper a few times since they have no family nearby."

We finished our lemonade and walked Sean toward the gate, Tippet running circles around us.

Sean paused at the satsuma tree bedecked with his bottles. "Are they working?"

"I think so," Winifred whispered.

Sean took her hand. "I'll be back Saturday afternoon, Winnie, if that's fine with you."

"Of course."

He kissed her cheek and turned to me. "And Saturday afternoon is good for you, Merri?"

I tried to hide a smile and nodded.

"Good." He kissed my cheek as well before turning back to Winifred. "Keep Merri out of trouble."

A cooling rain started at nine that night, lulling me to sleep quicker than usual. I awoke several hours later. The rain dripped off the eaves, spattering on the stoop of the covered porch below. The chorus of frogs swelled, the cicadas joining as the rain slowed.

Whimpering interrupted the night song.

Thinking Tippet dreamed, I dropped my hand from the hammock and reached for his fur. My fingers met raised hackles. Tippet shifted and growled.

"No, please," Winifred whispered. "Don't come any closer."

The skin on my arms prickled

"No!" Winifred's word clattered through the charged air.

I sprung from the hammock. The persistent dampness from the lingering summer humidity painted the bottom of my feet with condensation.

"Winifred!" In the dark, I took the sobbing girl by the shoulders. She clung to me and wept.

As her crying slowed, she spoke in broken sentences. "She hates me. Madder than ever."

I led her to the rocking chair, forcing her to sit. "Shush, Winnie. It was just a dream."

She wiped her nose on the end of her nightgown. "Tippet doesn't bark at dreams."

"Tippet responds to your unrest."

Winifred shifted uneasily. "She doesn't like the bottles or Sean."

I froze, one hand on my cousin's back and the other gripping the chair. "Who?"

"Nancy. She doesn't want me happy."

Keziah and Aunt Ethel were the only other females in the house. It must be her nightmares Sean mentioned.

"I want you happy, and Sean does too." I hugged her until she calmed.

***

Saturday, September eighteenth, Sean joined us in the yard after our midday dinner. He greeted Winifred and then shook a stick at Tippet to get the dog's attention before he let the stick fly. Tippet bolted to the discarded limb and happily carried it back to Sean.

"Now that you know his favorite game, he won't leave you alone," I said.

"I'll never get tired of throwing when the company is fine." Sean tossed the stick again and settled beside Winifred.

"Could we go on a walk?" she asked.

Sean removed his hat and fanned himself. "It isn't too hot for you?"

"Walking and sitting are equally miserable at the end of summer."

"Maybe if we went to get a cola it would help."

"That would be wonderful." She looked to me. "You know Aunt Ethel never lets us have any."

"The drug store is only a ten minute walk," Sean added.

I agreed to the plan and told Aunt Ethel we were going for a stroll.

Before we reached Government Street, Sean had introduced us to half a dozen people in the neighborhood. Several invited us in for iced tea—which we politely refused because the call of fizzy drinks was stronger.

His shortcut into town led us through back streets and side alleys like stray cats—save we didn't have to climb any fences. Sean's commentary on what places were the best for purchasing candy, pens, and every other notion Winifred could want kept the journey engaging.

As soon as we were through the drug store door, Sean offered us both an arm. At the soda counter, he took the stool in between.

The soda clerk—a young man who looked about my age—turned to us from behind the counter.

"Good afternoon, Mason," Sean said. "Allow me to introduce these two young ladies. Miss Merritt Hall of Grand Bay and Miss Winifred Ramsey, who recently moved here from Charleston. Ladies, this is Mason Remington. He creates the best colas in town. Don't bother trying any of the other locations selling. See Mason for all your refreshing drink needs."

"Yes, please do." The young man gave me a precursory nod before turning to Winifred. "It would be a pleasure to serve you."

Sean slid his arm around Winifred's shoulder long enough to get his attention. The clerk immediately broke his smile and stepped toward me.

"What will you have, Miss?"

"We'll all have the same thing," Sean said. "Your special and a peppermint stick for each of my ladies while we wait."

Mason opened the penny jar and removed two sticks, handing Winifred's to her with a wink and mine without so much as a smile.

Seeing the slight, Sean bumped my elbow with his and whispered, "You're too refined for the likes of him."

Halfway through our colas, an older couple came into the store and started talking with the pharmacist. I was too busy watching Winifred and Sean to pay attention to the happenings across the store, but when a few more customers arrived, the conversation over the druggist's counter grew heated.

"Mark my words," the first gentleman to arrive said. "That man they pulled out of the boarding house last week hasn't been heard from since. I'd lay my life that Yellow Jack's caught him."

"But the notices from the Board of Health in the newspapers—"

"Those officials don't say nothin' 'til it's too late," another voice replied.

"They'll be calling out the Can't-Get-Away Club as soon as tomorrow if that foreign man's got the fever. "

"I need to start packing my family tonight," a woman said before rushing out the door.

"Don't start a panic in my store, Mr. Paterson," the owner said. "Only the authorities can declare an outbreak and you having leave to inspect a ship doesn't amount to medical training in my book."

Sean and Winifred heard the last bit of the conversation—as it appeared the whole town did. On our walk back, we promenaded through flurries of chatter as the cola churned within my stomach.

When we were beyond the crowds on the south side of Government Street, Sean took Winifred's hand. "You have nothing to fear, Winnie. You're much too pretty for old Yellow Jack."

"What do looks have to do with illness?"

"Sickness can alter us. My cousin has scars from the pox on her arms and torso."

Winifred reached for her skirt. "My knees are so banged up—"

"No!" I barred her hand from lifting her clothing.

Eyes wide, she looked around the street. "It's just us, Merri."

"Sean has no right to see your legs."

"Before you got here, he—"

"Listen to your cousin, Winnie. Merri knows best." Sean's rosy cheeks could have been from the heat, but I knew a guilty blush when I saw one.

It was clear her upbringing was much different than mine. Did she go around showing her legs to whoever she wished? Did Sean take advantage of her naivety to indulge in intimacies? The familiarities they had enjoyed before my arrival had to be stopped, and Winifred educated about impropriety.

Five

Bartholomew was pleasant company at our Saturday evening supper, even if it was mostly talk about the store's business between him and Uncle Andrew. Still, it helped me forget my concerns over the behavior between Winifred and Sean.

Then I woke in the middle of the night to Tippet growling. The hair on my arms stood at attention. I dropped an arm to Tippet, fingers caressing his raised fur.

"Shh, Tippet. Good dog," I whispered.

"I'm scared, Merritt." Winifred's desperate plea tugged at my heartstrings. "She's in my dreams, but can't reach me on the porch."

I followed the sound of my cousin's sniffling. As soon as I was within reach, her arms were about me. I sat on the rag rug with Winifred, Tippet between us. When Winifred no longer heaved with sobs, I pulled my blanket to the floor to cushion our heads. Tucking the girl to my side, my dog snuggled around our bare legs.

That morning, church was a flutter of fans as people chattered about leaving town as soon as they packed their fried chicken. Even the minister seemed to feel the panic in the air. He cut his sermon short by thirty minutes and the congregation surged for the door in their haste.

"No small talk today. We need to get away from Yellow Jack." Aunt Ethel called over her shoulder, referencing the confirmed case of fever listed in the morning newspaper.

Uncle Andrew fetched the buggy and met us at the sidewalk. Aunt Ethel hastily climbed onto the front bench, and Winifred and I took the second row. My cousin clutched my hand the whole ride home.

Keziah served a hot meal when we returned, ignoring Aunt Ethel's constant fussing as she came and went from the dining room.

"Are we leaving town?" Winifred asked.

"No," Uncle Andrew answered.

"We must keep the girls safe!"

Uncle Andrew tucked away the roast beef like nothing was wrong. "They'll be safe enough here, Ethel. Just keep them home."

She paled under the weight of her memories.

Seeing her unable to eat, I went to Aunt Ethel's side. "You look like you could use a rest. Allow me to escort you to bed."

Aunt Ethel shivered despite the heat as we made our way upstairs. After seeing her settled in the bedroom, I turned for the door.

"Keep an eye on Winifred," she called as I left.

Upon returning to the dining room, I met Uncle Andrew's grim face with a forced smile. "She's resting."

He nodded and stood from the head of the table. "You girls aren't to leave the yard. It would be better if you stayed inside, but I won't force that issue yet."

"Yes, Uncle Andrew." I looked to Winifred and she nodded.

He went to his study and Winifred shoveled the rest of the potatoes from her plate into her mouth.

A few minutes later, we sat beneath the oak with Tippet at our feet. On the other side of the azalea bushes, horse hooves clattered and wheels rumbled near continuously in the street. Curious, I went to the nearest gap in the foliage and watched as families with cargo packed around them rolled toward Government Street—a mass exodus. Wishing I could bring Winifred to my home during the yellow fever scare, I turned away from the lucky ones leaving and returned to the bench.

"Any sign of Sean?" she asked.

"No, but it looks like the whole neighborhood is heading out. His family might decide to leave town."

"I hope he wouldn't leave without saying goodbye."

Sean's whistle carried through the muggy air as he entered the front gate. Tippet ran to his side and Winifred jumped to her feet, reaching for him.

Sean swung their joined hands. "I half expected you ladies to be gone. I'm glad I caught you."

"Are you leaving?"

"No, but Uncle Patrick is bringing Aunt Cecilia to her cousin in Montgomery for safe keeping. They take the train before dawn tomorrow. What about you?"

"Uncle Andrew won't send us off. He says we'll be fine if we stay home." Winifred gazed at Sean. "What do you think?"

"I think I'll have to check in on y'all as much as possible. How about it, Merri?" His eyes sparked like a cat's.

"I suppose it would be okay." I winced when Winifred inched closer to him. "But I don't think there should be any physical contact. You know, with the disease spreading. I wouldn't want either of you passing along yellow fever."

"Oh." Winifred dropped her hands to her side. "I'm sorry Sean, but I feel fine."

"That's good to hear. I do as well." He planted a quick kiss on her cheek. "Cheer up, Winnie. I've brought a riddle book to keep your mind sharp rather than fretting about fever."

"And Nancy."

Sean pointed to the nearest bottle. "They aren't stopping the dreams?"

"They're back. I think we need more by the house."

"I'll bring some, Winnie." Sean climbed the oak branches above the bench and tucked in the crook of a limb just high enough so his dangling boot wouldn't graze our heads. He pulled a book out of his shirt pocket and read in a voice much like a professor, "Which of the feathered tribe would be supposed to lift the heaviest weight?"

Leaving them to their harmless play, I paced the yard as I kept an eye on the street. Washington Square—the tree-dotted community park across the road—had a sinister tone. Typically a popular Sunday afternoon destination, the green space was deserted. The traffic was now sparse, the neighborhood quiet except Sean's words and Winifred's giggles.

After half an hour, I returned to the bench. "I think it's time Sean went home."

Sean swung down in a jiffy. "No frowns, Winnie. Merri knows best." He claimed her cheek with a parting kiss.

"And I said no contact."

"My humble apologizes, Miss Hall." He gave a deep bow.

Winifred giggled.

He winked at her. "It was worth it."

"Don't make me change my mind about you," I warned.

Six

Monday morning, Aunt Ethel was still in bed from the afternoon before. After Uncle Andrew left, she sent word for us to continue studies as normal. I gathered Winifred and her books on the back work porch after breakfast. Time crawled by until Sean whistled from the sidewalk. Winifred was out the door in an instant, bare feet rushing down the path.

Sean held a bottle in each hand and Winifred's adoration forever.

"I had to slip out when the cook was busy. Althea, our cook, has been tasked to keep an eye on me while my uncle is gone," he said as he went for the citrus trees. "I know my Winnie needed more protection. I'll rig them up right quick."

"Just on the end of some branches is fine. Don't bother with string. I'd feel awful if you got in trouble for coming over."

"No worries for me, Winnie. I'm always glad for a study break. Uncle Patrick laid out a schedule more advanced than the college to keep me occupied during the epidemic." He looked to me. "It is one, you know. Newspaper and word of mouth are reporting all sorts of ill people."

Sean handed Winifred one bottle and jumped, grabbing a satsuma branch with his empty hand. He jimmied the bottle onto the end and gently released it. With a wink and a smile, he retrieved the second bottle and repeated the process.

"No trouble last night?" His voice and eyes were soft. After Winnie shook her head, he fingered her cheek. "Good. And none will happen tonight either. You need rest to stay healthy."

An ache filled my chest at the tender exchange.

Sean looked to me and smiled. "No need to chase me off, Merri. I'm leaving, but I'll do my best to stop by tomorrow."

Winifred walked him to the gate and then returned directly to continue her assigned reading, smiling to herself over the book.

I wrote a letter home. My mother, father, and brother, Ezra, should have returned the day before from their visit to Aunt Gladys's in Mississippi, and I expected to hear from them soon.

Aunt Ethel joined us for dinner at noon, and then we all napped during the afternoon heat.

The pattern of a quick morning visit from Sean, Winifred's studies, noon dinner with our aunt, and then supper with Uncle Andrew lasted through Wednesday.

"The mail never came today," Aunt Ethel told her husband that evening.

"Mail strike," Uncle Andrew replied. "Carriers are refusing to bring things in or out of the city, even with fumigating the letters."

"No doubt, with those filthy mail bags. Simon and James always collected the mail. Do you think that—"

"Enough, Ethel. I'll hear nothing of previous experiences. This year is different. There have been medical advancements. We'll all come through fine."

Later, under the darkness of night, Winifred softly sang hymns in her hammock. Barely audible above the chorus of frogs and cicadas, I strained to hear her angelic voice. Was it fear or tiredness that caused her words to quake?

"Winnie?" I whispered. "Are you okay?"

"I can feel him praying for me. Sean is praying on his knees as he clutches those beads with the cross. Aunt Ethel thinks he's wicked, but he isn't. He loves God and prays to Mother Mary to help me."

"We pray too," I reminded her.

"But there's power in love. I love him, and I think he loves me too." I saw the outline of her form in the hammock turn toward me. "Why doesn't he tell me he does, Merri?"

Thinking back on the conversation I'd had with Sean the previous week, I recalled his plan to speak for her in a few years. "Some boys like to do things proper. Despite his unorthodox ways, I believe Sean Spunner is a gentleman when it counts the most."

"He is, Merri. He truly is. One day soon, he'll kiss me on the lips."

"Not during an epidemic." My voice of reason sounded harsh.

"I will accept true love's kiss whenever it is presented to me."

As though startled by her reckless declaration, the chirps and hums of the creatures hushed like a blanket was thrown over them. The atmosphere shifted with the silence, rushing outward to escape the approaching doom, which I hoped didn't end like it did with my other cousin.

***

After over-sleeping the next morning, Winifred and I hurried through breakfast before gathering on the back porch for study time. She worked silently as I read from a Louisa May Alcott novel. Every ten minutes, Winifred would pause and look to the clock before gazing in the direction of the front gate. She never spoke, but her words were there.

Where is Sean?

At half-past ten, Keziah brought us each a glass of iced tea. "That's the last of it, Miss Merritt. No ice was delivered this morning. I'd tell your aunt, but she's too distracted sewing those fever cloths to worry about ice."

I nodded. "We'll tell Uncle Andrew this evening. Maybe he knows someone outside of town that could deliver to his shop."

Keziah returned to the kitchen and Winifred looked to me. "I'm glad you're here. I'd hate to be stuck with a bunch of old people during a scare like this."

We fell back into our separate reading—Winifred still watching the clock.

The familiar whistle sounded just before noon. As though too startled to move, Winifred didn't meet Sean until he stood at the base of the back stoop with a little sack slung over his shoulder.

He took a moment lift his cap and wiped the sweat from his forehead with his handkerchief before speaking. "I had to act as errand boy at Uncle Patrick's office this morning because his regular clerk didn't show. There's hardly any streetcars running, so I raced about on foot all morning."

"Do you need a drink? We're out of ice, but—"

"Thank you, but I'm headed home for dinner. I just wanted to let you know I won't be over tomorrow if I have to work again, but you can be sure I'll be by this weekend to see my girl and her best cousin." He smiled and leaned to the side to meet my gaze through the screened porch with his dashing smile. "Take care of her, Merri."

"But—"

"Shh!" Sean interrupted Winifred, head cocked toward the little grove.

He fished about in his pocket and retrieved a cork before rushing to the nearest satsuma tree. Jumping, he snatched one of the cobalt bottles from the end of a branch and shoved the cork in it when he touched the ground.

"Caught one!" Seeing the mix of fear and relief on Winifred's face, Sean spoke quickly as I exited the porch. "I've trapped a spirit!"

"You have?" Winifred took my hand when I stopped beside her, eyes never leaving Sean's glistening face.

"As sure as my name is Sean Francis Spunner!" He gripped the neck of the bottle, a thumb over the end of the cork, and shook it. "Do you think it's Nancy?"

"She's the only one that comes to my dreams." Winifred drew a step back.

"I'll go down to the river before I return to the office and toss her into the water."

"What if a barge knocks the cork loose?"

Sean rattled the bottle more. "I'll make her so dizzy, she won't know which way to look to find her way back here."

Winifred peered at the blue glass. "I hope you're right. She'll be awfully sore if she makes it back. Perhaps you should bring one of your priests here to—"

"I'm sure Sean can see to things himself, and you know Aunt Ethel would never allow that."

She shrugged and returned her attention to Sean. "And you're sure you caught her?"

"I've caught something. I can feel it in my bones."

Winifred smiled, the worry lessening around her blue eyes. "Thank you."

"It's my pleasure, Winnie." He removed the sack from his shoulder. "I brought you my favorite book I told you about to keep you company. I'll see you and Merri soon."

Winifred's smile lasted all afternoon, making me appreciate Sean humoring her with his attempts to put her at ease.

Before supper, I helped Aunt Ethel bring her teetering stacks of fever cloths to the upstairs linen cupboard. Over the course of two days, she'd gathered every imaginable piece of cotton fabric from worn petticoats to holey sheets, cut them into six-inch squares, and sewed the edges straight on her Singer machine. Three stacks of the folded swatches, each two feet high were the result of her efforts. Why she bothered sewing them, I didn't understand. Once they were used to cool a fevered body, they would be burned—not laundered. Maybe Aunt Ethel needed a task to keep her hands busy and her mind off the growing number of fever cases in the city. One house across the park had the dreaded yellow flag hanging from it. Yellow Jack was here, no doubt about it.

Uncle Andrew, pale and sweaty, staggered up the stairs.

"Andrew!" Aunt Ethel went to his aid, an arm about his waist to support him.

I came forward to help.

"No, Merritt, stay back." She steered him toward their bedroom.

"It's nothing," Uncle Andrew said. "The heat got me today, that's all. I overworked because our stock boy didn't come in. It was a bumper day. Bartholomew proved himself invaluable."

"Not too invaluable if he let you work like an ox while he was safe at the counter."

"No, Ethel. Bart did all the loading. I was on my feet at the register all day. No dinner. No time for a pipe."

I watched from their bedroom doorway as he eased into the corner rocking chair. Aunt Ethel poured some of the water from the pitcher into the wash basin on the dry sink, soaked a fresh cloth in it, and then rang it out before bringing it to him to wash his face.

"Shall I fetch some tea?" I asked.

"No, but tell Keziah to ready a supper tray for him. He needs to get his feet up."

I relayed the message in the kitchen and found Winifred in the parlor.

"Uncle Andrew won't be down for supper," I told her as I stepped between armchairs to reach the settee.

"He looked awful when he came in the door," Winifred remarked. "I hope it isn't fever."

"You saw Sean today, tired out from the heat. It's ten times worse for a man Uncle Andrew's age."

"I wanted to grab Sean's hand and run for the nearest creek. I'd jump in fully clothed in a heartbeat."

I narrowed my eyes.

"It'd be better than hearing you fuss at me if I got down to my petticoat first."

"You need to learn more decorum, Winnie. We agreed last night that Sean is a gentleman. You need to be a proper lady to match him. A lawyer is a highly respected professional, and Sean's uncle has him set on the path toward that. Before you know it, young Mr. Spunner will be suited daily and attending the courthouse regularly. He can't have the weight of running about with an unruly girl marring his character."

Fists clinched and splotches of red on her cheeks, Winifred stood. "That's the meanest thing you've ever said, Merritt Hall. Take it back!"

"I won't because it's true. I like Sean, and I love you. I want what's best for the both of you."

She trembled a moment before flinging her arms around me. "I love you too, Merri. Don't ever leave."

I hugged her back, knowing I'd do whatever I could to give my cousin support during her dreadful year of loss and change.

Seven

To Aunt Ethel's consternation, Uncle Andrew readied for work Friday morning. He looked better than he had the evening before, but the sheen of sweat lingered on his brow. After he left, Aunt Ethel started wiping down everything in the pantry, tossing flour sacks around like a disgruntled dock worker as she organized the already clean storage.

Winifred and I took our books and hurried through the kitchen to the porch. We passed the day with our typical studies, meandering through the yard, plus an afternoon nap during the worst of the heat. Even without Sean visiting, Winifred was peaceful—possibly because she carried his copy of *Frankenstein* everywhere.

The supper hour came and went while the three of us looked at each other in the parlor.

Keziah appeared for the fourth time, wringing her hands in her apron. "Shall I serve, Mrs. Allen?"

"Never in thirty years of marriage have I eaten supper without Andrew," Aunt Ethel declared. "I don't intend to start now."

Winifred rubbed her stomach and silenced a vocalized complaint. Keziah paced the hall but didn't mention her meal spoiling, though the chicken and dumplings smelled wonderful.

Long after the mantel clock chimed eight o'clock, the sound of the horse and buggy rolled through the screened windows.

Aunt Ethel rushed for the back and I followed. Driving Uncle Andrew's single horse buggy into the open stable was Bartholomew Graves. His glasses glinted in the light from the nearby lamp post.

"Mr. Graves!" Aunt Ethel crossed the yard like a woman half her age.

Bartholomew hopped off the buggy seat and went for the floor board of the backseat. There he moved a few sacks and lifted a blanket to expose Uncle Andrew.

Aunt Ethel gasped and clutched her heart. I took her elbow to steady her as we neared them.

"I had to wait until dark to smuggle him past the city's checkpoint. I knew you'd be worried and want him here, Mrs. Allen. I tried to get him to go home at noon, but he wouldn't budge. I had to lay him out in the office an hour later."

"The stubborn fool!" She touched her husband's head, but he was unresponsive. "Thank you, Mr. Graves, for bringing him at your own peril."

"Allow me to get him inside."

"I'll ready his bed." Aunt Ethel turned for the house. "Merritt will show you the way."

Bartholomew shifted a few more items and pulled Uncle Andrew toward the edge before lifting the gray man over his shoulder.

I held the screen open and led the way past Keziah and a crying Winifred.

"If you need to rest before the stairs—"

"Please don't stop, Miss Merritt."

Impressed with the strength of the quiet man, I increased my speed and waited for him at the top of the stairs. "It's the room with the light on."

Aunt Ethel fluttered about as they came into the room. "Run along, Merritt, and fetch a stack of cloths, wash basin, and quinine."

When I returned with the requested supplies, Bartholomew held my uncle upright on the side of his bed while Aunt Ethel removed his garments. Several red welts that looked similar to Winifred's mosquito bites marred his arms.

"See that Keziah feeds you girls and Mr. Graves," she spoke to me as she worked. "Send coffee up for me later."

"Yes, ma'am."

I returned to the parlor to calm Winifred. "Aunt Ethel is seeing to him, and we are to eat supper with Mr. Graves."

I patted her back until Winifred's crying slowed.

A minute later, Bartholomew entered the room. "Mrs. Allen has asked for me to go for the doctor. Please don't hold your meal on my account."

Winifred stood and wiped her nose with a lace-edged handkerchief.

"Wash up and I'll be in shortly, Winifred." I watched her go for the half-bath in the hall before turning to Bartholomew.

"Mrs. Allen told me to come to the kitchen door when I return," he said.

"I'll let the cook know."

After passing word to Keziah and washing at the kitchen sink, I settled with Winifred in the dining room. She immediately blessed the food and ate. Wrestling with worry over Uncle Andrew's poor health, I fed most of my dinner to Tippet under the table.

Winifred perked up when Keziah carried in a pan of pear cobbler. "There's no cream for it, but it's still warm."

"It smells lovely." Winifred dished for herself without pause. As soon as the cook left the room, she looked to me. "Am I expected to entertain Mr. Graves when he returns?"

"I can't very well sit with him by myself."

She sighed. "How long is he to stay?"

I forced my voice to stay level. "I don't expect it to be too late. It shouldn't matter though. It's not like you have a previous engagement."

"I wish I did, for I'd rather be anywhere else than with Mr. Graves."

"There is nothing wrong with him, Winifred. He's very kind."

"But as boring as dry toast." She took a bite of cobbler.

"Sean's company has you spoiled."

She smiled around her mouthful and swallowed. "Admit that you prefer Sean as well."

"You cannot compare a peacock to a quail. Just because one is all show and the other plain, doesn't mean the plain one isn't good in its own right." I dished a scoop of cobbler onto my plate. "Mr. Graves did our family a great service this evening, and you need to show him respect."

After helping herself to more dessert, Winifred looked to me. "May I be excused?"

"Yes, to the parlor."

Tippet followed her out of the room, and I brought our dishes to Keziah.

"Mr. Allen looks bad. I've never seen him like that in my dozen years here."

"Hopefully the doctor will come before long. Please be sure Mr. Graves eats as soon as he arrives."

In the parlor, Winifred was curled in the corner of the settee. She clutched Sean's worn leather copy of *Frankenstein* to her chest, and Tippet's head was on her knee. Before I could question her, a knock sounded on the front door.

Bartholomew stood on the porch with a dark-haired, mustached man who was almost as tall as him. "I brought Dr. Sherard, Miss Hall. I thought it best to bring him to the front door."

"Of course, Mr. Graves, and thank you. Keziah is waiting for you in the kitchen." I nodded to the doctor. "If you would follow me, I'll bring you to my uncle."

Aunt Ethel waited at the top of the stairs, hands clasped. "I'll take the doctor from here, Merritt."

In kitchen, Bartholomew ate at the corner table but immediately stood, the napkin from his lap clutched in his large hand.

"Don't mind me, Mr. Graves. I just wanted to be sure you had everything you needed."

"Thank you, Miss Merritt. I have all I require. Miss Keziah is a fine cook. I always enjoy my meals here."

"I'm glad to hear that." I smiled and he dipped his head a fraction of an inch. Unsure if he was being shy or eyeing his uneaten food, I hurried to excuse myself. "Unless you'd prefer company, I'll wait in the parlor."

"Miss Winifred might need your companionship more than me."

I laughed softly. "She has my dog and a book, Mr. Graves."

Bartholomew adjusted his glasses and pulled out the nearest chair. "Then join me."

I took the seat and tried not to be wary of Keziah at the sink. She did her best not to appear to listen, but she crossed the kitchen more often than necessary as she put away dishes. Not wanting to impede Bartholomew's meal, I didn't attempt conversation. Instead, I noticed his precise manners and the calculated way he savored each bite as though to enjoy the chicken and dumplings as long as possible.

As he drew closer to finishing, he met my gaze with his brown eyes. I blushed at being caught.

"I spoke with Dr. Sherard on the drive over. Cases of yellow fever are growing all over the city, but the Eighth Ward has the highest numbers."

"Where's the Eighth Ward?" I asked.

"Right here."

An oppressive silence filled the room. Bartholomew finished his supper, and Keziah collected his dishes as we left the kitchen.

He stopped midway to the parlor. "If you don't mind, Miss Hall, I'd like to stay until the doctor is done. There are a few things I need to ask Mrs. Allen about the store."

"Join me and Winifred while we wait."

I had to clear my throat to get Winifred's attention from the book when we entered.

"Oh." She straightened from her corner perch, tucking her skirt around her legs as her feet went to the floor. She continued to hold the novel though she no longer read. "Thank you for bringing Uncle Andrew home, Mr. Graves."

"I'm happy to be able to repay a fraction of the kindness your family has shown me, Miss Winifred."

After I sat beside my cousin, Bartholomew relaxed into the armchair.

Winifred looked between us and her blue eyes brightened. "Merri is very thoughtful."

"Merri?" He looked me over a moment. "That does fit."

Winifred hugged the book to her chest. "You must call her Merri from now on."

He shook his head and looked at the rug. "I couldn't, Miss Winifred."

"Why not?"

Bartholomew sat forward as though uncomfortable. "A man calling a lady by her Christian name is something reserved for close relationships. It's even more so for a familiar shortened name."

"But Sean calls her Merri."

"Sean, is *your* close friend, Winifred." I looked to Bartholomew. "Call me what you're comfortable with. You're almost family to my uncle and aunt."

"Thank you for your confidence."

From up the stairs, a wailing cry sounded.

"Miss!" The doctor called. "I could use your assistance."

Bartholomew stood before I could and offered a hand to steady me as I passed him. "I'm here if you need me, Merritt."

I didn't have time to dwell on his kindness as I flew for the stairs.

Dr. Sherard stood in the hallway outside Uncle Andrew's bedroom. "Your aunt has suffered a shock. Her husband has yellow fever."

I caught my breath and went to pass into the bedroom.

"I wouldn't if I were you."

"But Aunt Ethel will—"

"She's in the bathroom. Give her a few minutes to collect herself."

Sobs came from behind the closed door.

"I will report the case to Mr. Burke, chairman of your ward, and check in on Mr. Allen tomorrow. Everyone living here needs to be quarantined."

"I understand, Dr. Sherard."

I walked him downstairs. On the front porch, he set his bag on the floor and unfolded a yellow piece of fabric over a foot square. The echo of the hammer nailing the flag onto the side of the house pounded through my soul.

Eight

I grimly closed the front door and returned to the parlor. "It's yellow fever," I announced. "I'll see what we can do and pass along information."

Winifred buried her face in Tippet's scruff and Bartholomew frowned. Upstairs, Aunt Ethel was still closeted away, so I checked on Uncle Andrew from the doorway.

Quiet as death.

"Merritt," Aunt Ethel said as she exited the bathroom. "He will surely die."

"We'll do our best to help him." For the first time in my life, I felt my aunt lean completely on me. "Mr. Graves is still here. He'll need instruction for the store."

"Allow me to see him so he can go home."

I escorted her to the parlor.

"Mr. Graves, I can never repay you." Aunt Ethel hugged him. "I wanted to thank you and put your mind at ease. I'll not leave Andrew's side after this moment."

"I'll do whatever I can for you and Mr. Allen."

She stepped back and looked up at him, one hand still on his arm. "I trust you with all the affairs of the shop, Bartholomew. Andrew has done nothing but praise your work and clear thinking the past year. I know hiring you is the best thing he could have done."

"I'm pleased to have your trust, Mrs. Allen."

"You must take the horse and buggy when you leave. We would have too much trouble trying to care for the mare."

He nodded. "Miss Keziah informed me the ice and milk are no longer arriving. With your permission, I'll use the horse to bring you supplies as often as possible."

"Talk it over with Keziah before you leave to secure a list of the household's needs. I have to return to Andrew now." She turned to Winifred. "Winifred, listen to Merritt in all matters. My last direct request is for you to bring me a cup of coffee."

"Yes, Aunt Ethel." With the book tucked under her arm, she hurried for the kitchen.

"Keep her safe, Merritt."

I nodded and caught Bartholomew's eye after Aunt Ethel left. "Thank you for easing her worries."

"And yours too, I hope."

"Yes, Mr. Graves."

"Call me Bartholomew, Merritt. I'll speak with Miss Keziah and be on my way."

Not wanting to crowd into the kitchen, I waited before the empty fireplace. Minutes later, Bartholomew stopped in the doorway.

"Is there anything you would like on the supply list, Merritt?"

"No, thank you. I trust Keziah knows best."

He smoothed the tuft of thick, brown hair directly atop his head that tended to pouf rather than lay straight. "I told Keziah my deliveries will most likely be after dark as the checkpoints might prove troublesome."

"Don't risk anything serious in our behalf."

"I won't leave you ladies without help."

"Will the horse be too burdensome for you with work and your home to care for?"

"The stable behind the store is well equipped, and I inhabit the apartment over the shop, if you didn't know."

"I didn't." I gave him a little smile. "I suppose it will work out."

Bartholomew straightened his glasses. "It will, Merritt. Send word whenever you need help."

"How? The post stopped running days ago, and Aunt Ethel never allowed a telephone line to be installed."

"There's usually some boy about ready to make a bit of coin, epidemic or not, but I'll return in a few days."

I walked him outside and waited by the gate to close it after he left.

Keziah removed the apron from her plump figure and hung it on the kitchen hook. "I'm going to bed now, Miss, but wake me if I'm needed before breakfast."

I turned down the gaslights on the way to the parlor. I stopped for Winifred, and the cook warily climbed the stairs.

"It's time to get ready for bed," I told my cousin.

She kept Sean's book in one hand and the other on Tippet's head. "I don't think I'll be able to sleep."

"Nevertheless, rest is needed."

***

I woke before Winifred. In the golden sun, she looked like an angel with porcelain skin and rosy cheeks. *Frankenstein* was tucked under her arm and a smile like the ones when Sean was in sight graced her lips. She probably dreamt of him.

After dressing, I found Aunt Ethel leaning over her husband.

"Can I get you anything?" I asked.

"I need fresh water and fever cloths." She carried the partial bowl of water to the window, opened the screen, and tossed the remnants into the yard.

I carried the dry sink pitcher to the bathroom to refill and brought it back before going for the cloths.

Winifred stood in the doorway to our room when I returned with the massive pile.

"I guess Aunt Ethel did need to sew all those," my cousin whispered.

Keziah stood outside the bedroom, listening to orders from my aunt.

"Give everything I've asked for to Merritt to bring up. There's no reason for you to wear yourself out on the stairs," she concluded.

I handed the cloths to Aunt Ethel and watched Uncle Andrew from the doorway while she took a few minutes in the bathroom. She reappeared with a scrubbed face though still looking exhausted.

"When you deliver the tray from Keziah," she told me, "bring the dinner bell from the credenza in the dining room. I'll ring if I need help."

Winifred looked to be on task as she prepared for the day, so I rushed down to let Tippet out. After delivering the stocked tray to Aunt Ethel, I took my embroidery project depicting a coastline and a small sewing basket from my drawer to have downstairs.

Winifred joined me in time for breakfast. Decked in her Sunday best that matched the color of her eyes, she glowed with anticipation as she set *Frankenstein* on the table. My annoyance with her grew the longer I looked.

"You shouldn't be wearing that, Winifred. Aunt Ethel wouldn't approve unless you're on your way to church. You don't even have your mourning band on."

"She's too distracted to notice unless you point it out to her, but you don't want to worry her, do you?"

Winifred didn't understand what a flirt she was, and it shouldn't be my place to educate her in those regards, but there appeared to be no other choice.

"*You* are worrying me," I said in a snappish tone as I took my seat at the table. "I know you're excited over the possibility of seeing Sean, but we're under quarantine. Sean's uncle won't want him over here when he hears Uncle Andrew is on the list of the infected. What if he picks up the fever when he stops by?"

"He'll never get sick, and neither will I. Sean told me I was too pretty for yellow fever."

"It's nothing to jest over. We're under serious threat. Uncle Andrew might die."

Winifred jumped to her feet, knocking the raspberry preserves onto the white tablecloth. "Don't you think I know it, Merritt Hall? There's death everywhere I look! Allow me to hold to what good I have while I'm able."

She ran out.

Perhaps I was too hard on Winifred. She was still reeling from the loss of her parents and sister. Not to mention a haunting of sorts. She most likely understood the horrors of death better than me. But it didn't give her an excuse to ignore our uncle's illness or dismiss her mourning to look pretty.

I silently finished my simple breakfast. Afterward, I cleared the table and brought the soiled tablecloth to the back porch to soak in the washing tub. There was no chance the laundry would be picked up from an infected house. Plus, the yardman didn't show up the day before. He would also stay away when he saw the warning flag. Feeling the weight of what the days ahead would bring, I sighed.

Winifred sulked on her favorite bench with Tippet at her feet. I brought my embroidery to the back porch to watch over her. A few minutes later, Aunt Ethel's bell rang. I set my coastal scene aside and hurried for the stairs.

Before I could speak, my aunt barked orders from the bedside.

"Burn that sack with yesterday's clothes and cloths." She pointed to the laundry bag on the floor just inside the room. "There's a barrel in the stable. Haul it into the yard. You'll need to burn things at least once a day, maybe twice."

"Yes, Aunt Ethel."

In the yard, I dropped the bag in the open area beyond the citrus trees. I rummaged through the stable, picking over tack and feed bags to locate the barrel in the far corner. A patch of sweat between my shoulder blades added to my discomfort as I shimmied the barrel until it was free of the rut it had settled into. After resting a few seconds, I continued the awkward waddle across the length of the stable, growing wetter by the second in the harsh heat of the enclosed space.

Once I got to the fresh air of the doorway, I leaned against the exterior wall in defeat.

Sean hopped the gate at the driveway, white shirtsleeves rolled over his elbows. "Are you all right, Merri?"

"Stay back!" I held up a hand. "Uncle Andrew has the fever."

"But what—"

"I have to burn everything that touched him yesterday." I wiped my forehead with the hem of my apron. "Aunt Ethel told me to haul this into the yard."

"Allow me to help."

I stepped back and Sean immediately turned the barrel on its side and rolled it with his boot toward the yard. The laughter that slipped out felt good. "Don't I feel like a ninny!"

Sean's grin was as kind as ever. "I'm sure you never had to move a barrel before. Your mind has plenty of other things to worry over rather than the easiest way to get this from one place to another." He continued to nudge the metal container. "How is Winnie handling the news?"

"Not well. We got into a disagreement at breakfast. I'm afraid our ways of coping are vastly different, but I'm trying to understand her methods."

"What do you mean?" His gaze darted from the path of the barrel to me.

"Aunt Ethel caring for Uncle Andrew and being under quarantine means more work for us. Keziah is good with the kitchen and some cleaning, but the yard and laundry service have stopped. Not to mention we've already lost the ice and dairy deliveries. But what does Winifred do? She wears her Sunday best—a statue lording over me, too good to help."

"Differences aren't such a bad thing, Merri, but it would be difficult for a young lady to be more sensitive to needs of those around her than you. Your commitment to duty is unshakable."

"And your way with words is beyond reproach, Sean." I nodded ahead. "Out by that laundry sack is where I need the barrel. I'm sure you can guess where Winifred is."

His gaze immediately switched to the far oak. With his cheeky grin larger than ever, he gave the barrel a strong push. "It brings me joy to see her."

"See only. We don't want to infect you."

"I want to ease your burdens, not add to them, Merri."

"Then keep your distance."

The same time we came to halt at the linen sack, my dog ran for us. Tippet jumped at Sean as he stood the barrel upright. He rubbed the dog's ears and then took off running. Tippet followed, barking excitedly on a lap around the yard. Sean took an elaborate stumble several feet in front of Winifred's bench, and Tippet playfully pounced on him.

I dropped the laundry sack into the barrel and turned for the potting shed to gather some wood from the pile stacked beside it.

"Hold on, Merri!" Sean called. "I'll get that."

He grabbed an armful of split logs before I could reply. I followed him back to the barrel where Winifred waited for us.

"It all has to go?" She poked at the sack with a stick.

"Every day. There's much we need to do to stay safe."

Sean built a pyramid with the logs on top the bag and then dug through his trouser pockets. He tossed a crumbled piece of paper in between the wood and also a filthy handkerchief before retrieving a matchbox.

Winifred leaned closer. "What else do you have in there?"

"I might possibly have a lock of my lady's hair, folded within a lace hanky close to my heart." He patted the breast pocket on his shirt and winked as he stepped away.

My cousin blushed and angled in once more, but Sean danced to the far side of the barrel. "Why do you keep moving?"

"I love watching you, Winnie, and the view is even finer from a short distance." Sean dropped a lit match upon the paper.

Winifred smiled and began prancing around the barrel, circling wide beyond Sean.

"'She walks in beauty, like the night

Of cloudless climes and starry skies;'"

Sean recited the lines of Lord Byron as Winifred increased her efforts.

"'And all that's best of dark and bright

Meet in her aspect and her eyes:

Thus mellowed to that tender light

Which heaven to gaudy day denies.'"

Winifred continued to dance in rhythm to the poem, arms out as though welcoming his invisible touch. The intensity of his voice was electric, even to me as he said the final words. At the close, Sean bowed and my cousin curtsied. Sean motioned to the bench, and accompanied Winifred across the lawn, keeping several feet between them.

Sighing, I turned for the house.

Keziah was kneading bread dough. Aunt Ethel stared at her husband, a glazed shroud over her sight as though she couldn't tolerate the thought of reality. Not wishing to disturb her numb state, I returned to the kitchen and collected a tray of room temperature sweet tea before crossing the yard to the shade of Winifred's oak. I would chaperone until the fire in the barrel burned down and then urge Sean to leave so I could focus my cousin on chores.

Nine

After my bath and hair washing that night, I sat in the hallway to keep Aunt Ethel company while Winifred took her turn. We didn't speak, but I hoped my aunt felt a bit of comfort knowing I was there on the straight back chair from the guest room.

A cough wracked Uncle Andrew and set him trembling. Roused from his rest beside me, Tippet lifted a shaggy head.

"No, Lord, please." The words escaped my aunt with pure despair as the cough continued until he choked in his prone position.

Choking turned to retching.

Winifred stood beside me as black vomit gurgled from our uncle.

"Aunt—"

"Keep her away, Merritt!" Aunt Ethel worked to roll her husband onto his side.

His new position brought the bile to the floor like fouled mud. I swallowed my instinct to gag and turned away, circling Winifred with an arm to ease her toward our room as she quaked with unshed tears.

We sat on the edge of the closest bed, and I hugged her. The anguishing sounds continued down the hall.

When the silence came, I decided that was worse.

I pointed to Winifred's blue dress hanging from the footboard on her bed. "Be sure that gets hung properly for airing."

She nodded and turned away, wiping at her eyes.

"I'm going to see if—"

"Don't leave me, Merri."

"It will just be a minute. I can't leave Aunt Ethel if she needs help." I patted Winifred's shoulder and motioned with my other hand for Tippet to stay by the bed. "Think about how Sean looked on the grass with Tippet licking his face."

She sniffed. "Have you ever heard a boy recite poetry?"

I paused in the doorway. "He's more man than boy—despite his capricious ways. Sean is an educated gentleman, on his way to a grand life."

"I want to be a good match for him." Winifred looked like a child in her white nightgown and braided hair. "Promise you'll teach me, Merri. I never listened to my sister, but you're my second chance. Instruct me on how to be proper."

"What do you think I've been trying to do the past two weeks?"

I stopped outside my uncle and aunt's bedroom. The vomit was wiped away, but the stench lingered as Aunt Ethel laid a wet cloth on his forehead.

"Can I do anything?" I asked in a voice not much louder than a whisper.

"He's burning with fever and his pulse is racing. The doctor said this afternoon those were sure to come next. Not that he needed to remind me. I'll never forget those days with James and Simon. God rest their souls."

Uncle Andrew lurched with a convulsion, triggering a new round of retching.

"Keep Winifred calm. I'm blessed you're here, Merritt."

Winifred was hugging Tippet. I turned down the gaslight. "Come on, Winifred. We might as well try to sleep."

We moved onto the porch with only the light from the hallway behind us. Before I could settle in my hammock, Winifred grabbed my hands.

"Let's pray for Uncle Andrew." We went to our knees on the rag rug between our hammocks, cotton nightgowns touching. Still gripping my hands, Winifred spoke. "Oh, Lord, forgive us our trespasses as we come to thee in our time of need. Help heal and comfort Uncle Andrew from the fever and give Aunt Ethel strength to support him, and Merritt and I the means to help her. These things we pray, Amen."

"Amen."

"And God bless Sean for being so wonderful. Please let him visit tomorrow." Winifred kissed my cheek before springing into her hammock. "Goodnight, Merri."

I scratched Tippet's head before trying to get comfortable for the night. The wet air weighed me down as the buzz of cicadas threatened to overpower my nerves. Only when my cousin stopped her whisperings about Sean did my mind slow from the activities of the day. But worry over Uncle Andrew caused restlessness before I fell into exhausted sleep.

***

I woke to Winifred's cry.

Climbing out of the hammock, I went to her. "What happened?"

"Nancy can gloat over her brother's eminent death, but didn't like Sean's attentions to me yesterday."

"Nancy's *brother?*"

Winifred sobbed, unable to answer. I left Tippet with her and walked the hall. Aunt Ethel, head down and eyes closed in exhaustion, sat beside her husband amid the stench of the dying.

Could Nancy—the figure from Winifred's nightmares—be his sister?

I knew more about Aunt Ethel's family as my mother was her sister, but it was commonly known that Uncle Andrew was raised in Charleston. After the war, he retired from the army and moved to Mobile. He started the store and married Aunt Ethel, a decade his junior. But a sister beyond Winifred's mother is someone I didn't recall hearing about.

I left the fear of the unexplained behind to deal with the horror of certain death.

By the time I had a decent flame licking at the soiled linens in the barrel, I was sweating in the morning sun. Afraid to think through the perils of the circumstances, I rolled up the brown gingham sleeves on my work dress. I stepped back as the flame increased and tackled my hastily made knot of hair at the nape of my neck. Hair loose, I racked my fingers through the mass streaming over my shoulder all the way to my waist.

"I followed your smoke signal but never expected to catch you disarrayed, Merri," Sean said as he came through the bushes. "How are things?"

Turning to Sean, I gave him a small smile in greeting as I began a fresh braid. "It was a trying night. The burning seemed like a respite after what I've witnessed. I need this moment to prepare myself before dealing with Winnie."

"She's distraught over your uncle?"

"The black bile started." I wrapped my braid into a bun and secured it on the back of my head with a few hairpins from my apron pocket. "And she thinks her nightmares have something to do with it."

"I have an idea. You don't need to tell Winnie you saw me, but I'll be back later today." Sean was over the fence as quick as he arrived.

Once the fire burned down a safe distance from the rim, I returned to the house and washed up to my elbows with lye soap in the sink on the back porch.

Keziah motioned to a food tray when I stepped into the kitchen. "For your aunt. Breakfast for you and Winifred will be in fifteen minutes."

"Thank you."

Upstairs, Winifred was in the bathroom and Tippet lay in front of the closed door. Aunt Ethel lifted her weary head when I came to the doorway.

"Shall I bring it in?"

"Don't cross the threshold, Merritt. You girls are in enough danger as it is." Aunt Ethel's hands trembled slightly as she took the silver tray from me.

"Were you able to rest?" I whispered.

"Yes, he's been quiet for several hours. I hope Dr. Sherard comes early today."

"Will he come on the Sabbath?"

"There is no day of rest in times like these." She sighed and sank into her chair. "The Can't-Get-Away Club members work tirelessly until the epidemic is over. Did you bring in the newspaper?"

"I didn't think of it."

"I would like to know the numbers."

"Yes, Aunt Ethel." The words were automatic though obsessing over the yellow fever statistics was the last thing she needed to do.

I snapped my fingers, and Tippet left his post to follow me downstairs and out the front door. The newspaper lay all the way at the gate with a note attached.

LAST DELIVERY

Even the paper boy was afraid of our house, but I decided it was for the best—for Aunt Ethel's sake. I laid the thin bundle on the side table in the parlor before going for the dining room. As soon as I took my chair, Tippet stretched before the unlit hearth.

Winifred arrived a few minutes later with a scrubbed face, pale and innocent, and solemnly took a seat. "I'm sorry I'm late. I'm going to work hard today, I promise." She picked at the corner of her napkin before she laid it in her lap. "I'll do anything to keep my mind off Uncle Andrew and my dreams."

Keziah brought in a small platter of biscuits and sausage plus a coffee pot and gravy boat. "It's not much, misses, but I'm doing the best I can."

"No—"

"No butter, milk, or cream, Miss Winifred."

"For once, I'll be happy to see Mr. Graves if he ever returns with a delivery." She smothered two biscuits with watery gravy.

I would be happy to see him as well—he represented a rational voice amid the hysterics of my cousin and aunt.

Ten

Despite it being Sunday, Winifred and I worked around the house. We swept the main floor and did the downstairs linens. I scrubbed the kitchen and dining room laundry on the washboard and passed the items to my cousin to run through the wringer.

Sean arrived when we were on the last of the washing.

He waved to us from the back stoop.

"We'll be out in a few minutes," I called.

"I would gladly help if you'd allow it."

"It's not me setting the rules, it's Yellow Jack," I replied.

Sean nodded and switched a small book between his hands. Tippet gave a soft yip at the door and I let the dog out to keep Sean busy.

Through the screened porch, Winifred watched him meander in the shade of the citrus trees with Tippet as she turned the crank on the wringer. That morning, Sean had worn work clothes, but now he was dressed in a navy blue suit. His red cravat was loose about his neck, top shirt buttons opened beneath the jacket. Cufflinks winked in the sunlight, and his pants were pressed to perfection above his shiny black shoes.

"I can imagine him in a courtroom when he's dressed like that," she whispered. "But I'd much prefer to see him in a tree with me."

Smiling, I fed the last napkin into the wringer. "I'm sure he'd rather be there with you as well."

Winifred collected the final piece and added it to the wicker basket on the counter. I opened the screen door as she lifted the load.

"Allow me, Winnie." Sean tucked his book and jacket into the crook of a satsuma tree. He took the laundry basket without touching her and stood beside the clothesline I'd rigged between a satsuma tree and the corner of the shed.

I fished clothespins from my apron pocket and passed them to Winifred so we both could hang the linens.

"You look pretty, Winnie." Sean smiled as we each took a napkin.

"In my wash dress? Don't tease when you look spiffy in your suit."

He raised his brows and bit his lip, watching her in silence as she hung two more napkins. "You always look beautiful."

She smiled. "Did you bring me another book? I'm not quite finished with *Frankenstein*, but it's most tantalizing. I don't think Merri would allow me to read it on the Sabbath. She thinks it scandalous enough the rest of the week."

His gaze shifted to mine as I took a hand towel from the basket and clipped it to the line. "I'm afraid the book I brought today isn't for your reading pleasure. I do hope it will ease your worries, though."

I stepped back to allow them a moment while Winifred hung the last towel.

"What is it?" She went to the tree he left his things on and retrieved the leather book, flipping through it. "Why, it's in another language! What's this about, Sean?"

He set the basket at the base of the trunk and gently took the book from her. "Something to be treated carefully. It's very special to the owner. I must return it in pristine condition."

Sensing trouble, I joined them. "If it's of such value, why was it loaned to you?"

Sean failed to meet my eye. "It's only temporary. Father Quinn won't mind when he finds out."

"You stole it from a priest?" The question came out louder than expected.

Sean's cheeks heated. "Borrowed, without permission. He will get it back this very day. And if he knew the purpose, he'd find no fault. He's not as staunch and set in his ways as the other priests."

"That's why you dressed up," Winifred declared. "You needed to look your best to go to the cathedral. It's magnanimous, isn't it? I peeked in one day when I was downtown with Aunt Ethel. She was furious I dared enter the gates."

"Don't try changing the subject," I scolded. "What Sean did was—"

"It's a book of Rites. There's one in here to bless a house." Sean clutched it. "I'm going to recite it and drive out the spirit haunting your dreams."

"How can you when it's written in gibberish?" Winifred asked.

"Latin." He smiled at her. "I've studied it in school and am well-versed."

"I'll never be good enough for you, Sean. I'm no young lady of accomplishment. I don't even recognize Latin when I see it."

"My uncle chose Latin for me to help with my law studies. *Habeus corpus* and all those other terms, not to mention it gives me a keen edge during Mass to know what the old words mean. And as for accomplishments, I've never seen the superior level of tree climbing skills you display or the sheer magnitude of your sparkling exuberance. Those mean a great deal more to me than embroidery talents or finishing school manners."

Winifred threw her arms around Sean.

He looked to me. "I'm more worried about Winnie feeling secure than catching yellow fever. Have you ever heard of Dr. Nott? He wrote articles published in medical journals about mosquitoes being the cause of infection but couldn't prove his theory before his death."

Kissing the top of her head, he set her on the bench beside me and stood back once more. "I want to bless the house—to protect you from your haunting dreams and the disease. Your aunt won't allow a priest, so I'm going to try it myself."

"You can't come inside, Sean."

He looked to me. "I'll risk the fever to see this through."

Recognizing his determination, I changed my tactic. "You can't go inside in the middle of the day. Even if you stay away from our aunt and uncle, Keziah will see you."

"Could you return after supper?" Winifred asked.

"I don't think that's a good idea," I said. "Aunt Ethel would have a fit if she knew you were doing Catholic prayers in her house. She's already worried about Uncle Andrew. I don't want to add to her concerns."

"I won't be able to sleep until something is done," Winifred declared.

I thought of the paint on the porch ceiling and the bottles on the trees. Each brought Winifred peace, though it was short-lived. Would the risk of being caught outweigh the possible benefit of the prayers?

"Merri, he went to all that trouble to filch the book," Winifred whined. "The least we can do is let him to bless the house. I'd hate for Sean to get into trouble over something he did in my behalf."

"Don't worry about me, Winnie. Anything I do in an attempt to help you is never a wasted effort."

"Please, Merri." She squeezed my hands, blue eyes watery. "It might even help Uncle Andrew."

"Come to the back porch between nine and ten—no earlier and no later. But if you see the doctor here or Aunt Ethel about, stay away."

"Of course. I'll return under the cloak of darkness, ladies."

Winifred brought the empty laundry basket to the porch, and we entered the house.

A minute later, a knock sounded on the front door. I admitted Dr. Sherard, and he slowly made his way up the stairs. While he examined Uncle Andrew, Aunt Ethel hastily washed and changed, passing on to me her towel bundled with her previous outfit so I could burn them.

While I sweated over the second fire of the day, the driveway gate opened. Expecting to see Sean up to some mischief, I was met by the sight of Uncle Andrew's buggy being driven toward the stable by Bartholomew.

I poked the items in the barrel with a long stick so they sat lower before leaving my post.

"I didn't expect to see you in daylight hours."

He lifted his hat and wiped his brow with a handkerchief. "I thought to try the Sunday afternoon guards at the checkpoint. They appear a tad more relaxed than the weekday ones. How's your uncle?"

"The doctor is with him now, but he's not doing well."

"I'm sorry to hear that. I did manage to bring a good bit of supplies." He motioned to the back of the buggy. "At least you won't go hungry anytime soon. If you'd be so kind as to allow me to wait until the doctor leaves, I'd appreciate it. The fewer people who see me here the better."

"I'll shut the gate and get you something to drink."

As soon as I was in the kitchen, Winifred rushed in from the hall. "There you are! The doctor wants to speak with you."

"Then could you take a glass of tea to our visitor in the stable?" I whispered.

Winifred's blue eyes brightened with her smile. "Yes!"

Not having time to explain it wasn't Sean, I hastily washed my hands and hung my apron on the wall hook before going to the parlor.

"Thank you for seeing me, Miss Hall," Dr. Sherard said as he smoothed his dark hair over his receding hairline. "Mrs. Allen told me she relies heavily on you. I want to be sure you understand the dire situation your uncle is in—and therefore your aunt. Perhaps we should sit down."

I nodded and sat on the nearest armchair. The doctor took the closest end of the settee.

"Your uncle is in his final days—possibly hours. Your aunt, as I understand, knows the progression of the disease from her experience with her sons several decades ago. At times, knowledge is beneficial, but I am afraid in your aunt's case it is detrimental. Her nerves are already on edge, and she is showing early signs of hysteria. I fear when the grief strikes, there will be only one thing we can do for her."

I leaned forward, grateful for his insight. "What is that, Doctor?"

"Lock her up until she returns to normal."

My shoulders drooped under the weight of his words. "I beg your pardon?"

Not registering the shock in my voice—or politely ignoring it—he continued. "It would be difficult to secure a location to take her as you will all still be under quarantine a minimum of ten days after Mr. Allen passes, but if she gets too much for you to handle, it will be my moral obligation to have her removed to seek treatment. The cook lives here, from what I have gathered, and you're old enough to make do, and I would continue to check in. Of course, the need may not arise, but I'm seldom wrong in these areas."

In direct opposition to my instinct to huddle into myself, I straightened my posture and met his judgmental stare. "Thank you for your concern."

He smiled, mustache lifting with the movement as he stood. "I will see you tomorrow, Miss Hall."

I walked him to the front door and hurried up the stairs, dreading what he might have told Aunt Ethel. She held her silent post at her husband's bedside, eyes closed in prayer. Uncle Andrew was almost unrecognizable with the veins of face distended and a lemon hue to his skin.

Sighing, I turned back to the main floor and out the back door.

Winifred stood upon the buggy in the stable, her arms extended as she recited Shakespeare. Bartholomew smiled up at her, and Tippet barked over the spectacle. My fists clenched and my pulse raced. Confused at my anger, I looked on as Winifred angelically completed Juliet's lines, and our guest offered his hand to help her down. Only when Bartholomew's polite smile turned to a grin as he met my eyes did I realize I was jealous.

"I kept Mr. Graves entertained," Winifred said as she collected her apron from the top of a feed sack and tied it around her middle. "Now that you're here, I can leave him in your capable hands."

"We need to bring the groceries to the kitchen first."

"I'm happy to help, Miss Merritt." Bartholomew adjusted his spectacles.

"It's too dangerous—both in exposing you to the infection and if someone were to see you. You need to be free to run the store."

His long face set in a grim line and he nodded. "Allow me to unload the goods, at least."

Winifred and I accepted armfuls of food stuffs from Bartholomew, which we carried to the back door. Tippet ran laps between the locations.

Keziah, delighted over the fresh supplies, sent me back to the stable with a hunk of cornbread for our deliverer. The kitchen was soon stocked. I returned, Tippet at my heels in the darkening afternoon. Bartholomew sat on a low stool just around the corner of the doorway, finishing off the remainder of the food and drink provided him.

Thunder rolled, rattling the walls.

"Have my seat." He stood, brushing the crumbs from his brown trousers.

"I wanted to thank you for taking such risks for us."

Another deep clap of thunder boomed, followed almost immediately by a streak of lightning.

"You'll be here for a bit, like it or not." Bartholomew pulled a bale of hay close and perched upon it after I sat on the stool.

After discovering my envy of Winifred's time with Bartholomew—and therefore my feelings for the man—I shyly lowered my chin. "It's a good respite, and I like your company."

"I enjoy your company too, Merritt. And I'm glad to see you rest a moment." His smile turned him into an extraordinary sight. "Before she started performing, Winifred told me how much you've been doing for the household. I'm grateful you came so you're here for the Allens and Winifred. What was the news from the doctor?"

I looked to my folded hands as lightning lit the sky and rain began to pour. "Uncle Andrew has hours, maybe a day or two, but Dr. Sherard is more concerned with how Aunt Ethel is handling things," I said loud enough to be heard over the rain. "The doctor is expecting to have to lock her up when he passes—says she already exhibits signs of hysteria."

"I'm afraid I don't have knowledge in that regard, but I have utmost faith in you handling things around here, no matter what happens." Bartholomew leaned forward, elbows on his knees. "Your uncle and aunt often praised you during my suppers here and they aren't the type to puff people up. They have my esteem, and in turn, you have it as well."

I was trapped in a house of terrors and surrounded by people who expected everything of me, but for the first time, I felt I could handle it with some degree of proficiency. Lightning illuminated the gray yard, and I spoke my next words without looking upon the face of my companion.

"Thank you, Bartholomew."

"I'll help however I can." He stood and rested a hand on my shoulder. "As soon as the lightning is through, I'll leave. Rain will be a good cover."

He pulled the oiled tarp over the back of the buggy and secured it against the weather. Hearing him work behind me produced an odd sense of comfort as I counted the growing space between the thunder and lightning. Bartholomew had the buggy turned about and hitched to the mare when he next spoke.

"I think I'll be fine now, Miss Merritt. Be sure to thank Keziah for the cornbread and tea." He pulled on a rain slicker and smiled when I turned to him. "Send word if you need something, otherwise I'll do my best to check in by midweek."

I nodded and managed a smile. "Thank you again."

He lifted his hat and gave me a subdued grin. "Take care of yourself, Merritt."

Before he could stop me, I rushed out to open the gate. After latching it behind him, I trudged to the back porch in my damp clothes.

Eleven

Winifred and I spent the rest of the afternoon and evening downstairs so my cousin wouldn't hear the sounds of Uncle Andrew's sickness or Aunt Ethel's despair. Frequent trips to the upper hall kept me apprised of the worsening situation. Come nightfall, Winifred was blissfully unaware with her nose in Sean's copy of *Frankenstein* beside the soft glow of the gaslight.

Keziah stopped in the parlor doorway, causing Tippet to sit up. "The kitchen is tidy, Miss Merritt. I'm taking these bones to bed."

"Thank you. We'll see you in the morning."

My dog lay back down, and I returned to my needlework. The beige stalks of seagrass blurred before the blue background threads. I closed my eyes against the heat, stress, and exhaustion.

"Are you unwell, Merri?" Winifred's voice was filled with anxiety.

I opened an eye to show her I was alert. "Hot and tired is all."

She looked to the mantel clock. "I think I'll be finished with the book by the time Sean arrives."

Setting the embroidery hoop on the side table, I closed my eyes once more. "That's good."

"I want to experience everything he loves." With a sigh, she settled back in the armchair.

I envied her simplistic view of the world. Why couldn't I turn off my concerns as easily as Winifred?

Fatigue must have won the battle for Winifred soon nudged me awake. "It's nearly nine," she whispered. "We should wait on the porch for Sean."

"Have you heard anything from upstairs?" I straightened and rubbed my neck.

"Not a thing since Keziah went up." She set the book on the credenza in the hallway. "I finished reading."

"If only you could see to your studies as readily as you did that novel."

"If my studies were as thrilling as *Frankenstein*, I would."

We smiled at each other and stole through the unlit kitchen to the open door, meeting the rough floorboards of the porch with our bare feet.

The inky blue of the night beyond the screen outlined the dark shape hunched over the porch steps. Winifred crept toward the door.

"Sean, you're early," she whispered.

He raised his head and turned. "I needed a few minutes to collect myself."

She caught her breath and released the latch on the door. "Are you all right?"

He nodded and stepped in.

"Did the priest catch you when you went back?"

"I confessed before returning his book." His voice was soft in the dim porch. "Father Quinn holds nothing against me, though he reminded me it was foolish to be dishonest for anyone—even a pretty girl. I assured him it was my own idea. I'd do anything for you, Winnie."

Tippet scratched his pant leg while whining. Sean looked crestfallen, but absentmindedly stroked Tippet's head.

"Mr. Graves brought us groceries today. We're stocked up on everything except milk and ice. And I finished *Frankenstein*. It was riveting," Winifred gushed, not picking up on his mood.

"Why don't you get the book and place it by the back door so Sean doesn't forget to bring it home," I suggested. When Winifred disappeared into the kitchen, I looked to Sean. "What's wrong?"

He crossed his arms and looked to the ceiling. "I was going to go to the Eastons' house after I saw Father Quinn to ask Peter's opinion on blessing the house. He's only eleven, but he's settled on joining the priesthood. I know he's been studying about things and thought he'd know as well as anyone else about blessing things, no matter his humble age."

He sniffed and wiped his nose on a handkerchief from his pocket as Winifred returned.

She carelessly set the book on the edge of the wash sink when she noticed Sean's upset. "What is it?"

"I was just explaining to Merri about the sad news I received. My friends, the Eastons, have been struck with the fever. When he was done talking with me, Father Quinn was off to give the last Rites to Rebecca," his voice hitched. "Peter, Aaron, and Lucy are sick too—all the younger ones except the baby."

"How awful!" Winifred cried.

Sean blinked rapidly, eyes glistening in the dim light. "At least one brother is safe at boarding school and the twins are in Europe with my cousin. The oldest two are married with families of their own. Your new neighbor is one of the Eastons, Merri, remember?"

"Yes, but they must be worried to distraction."

"And you as well, Sean," Winifred said. "You often spoke of them as you stopped by on your way to and from their house this summer—the battles with the boys and the fair-headed maidens."

"Mrs. Easton never fussed when the yard got tore up like other mothers would, and she helped the cook make a passel of cookies each time friends were there. She must be in agony with her little ones suffering."

"Do they live in the Eighth Ward as well?" I asked in a hushed tone.

He nodded. "Our area is the worst hit. Mr. Burke is our chairman for the Can't-Get-Away Club. He's keeping as busy as a doctor these days."

We stood in a triangle of hushed silence the better half of a minute.

"I'll pray for them, Sean," Winifred whispered. "Your dear friends won't be forgotten."

He squeezed her in a tight embrace. "Thank you."

Knowing an attempt to stop any contact would be futile, I turned away a moment. The night hid the flush on my cheeks, and I tried not to second guess either of their motives beyond giving comfort. No matter his previous claims of not trying to attach himself to Winifred, everything Sean did and said laid another line of stitches between his soul and hers. Neither would escape unscarred.

I calmed my breathing and turned back. "It's time, Sean."

He kissed Winifred's temple before separating. Reaching into the pocket of his black shirt, he retrieved a folded piece of parchment. "I believe I have it memorized, but I want to be sure I don't skip anything. Shall I recite the Rites here or in the parlor?"

Winifred took Sean's arm. "Our bedroom. That's where she comes in my dreams."

"We can't bring Sean upstairs. It's not fair to get him closer to the fever, not to mention how we are supposed to get him upstairs without Aunt Ethel or Keziah noticing?" I was too emotionally exhausted to deal with a disappointed Winifred, but I knew it had to at least be attempted for there to be any peace between us. "Sean may try it here first."

Sean tucked the paper back into his pocket. "Both of you cross yourselves like this."

We followed his lead in doing the sign of the cross. I felt my aunt's judgment bearing down on me with each of the four points. I was now marked by the stain of papacy in her eyes.

Sean spoke with reverence, and the strangeness of the foreign words wove through the air, building up until they loomed like a wave. But their crash settled about us with a warm calm. Tension an unseen power struggled around the space.

A rush of movement set my skin tingling. Tippet gave a low growl and sniffed every corner and the dark shadows.

"She's here," Winifred whispered. "Sean, you have to stop her."

"Holy Mary, Mother of God," Sean said as he clutched a rosary in one hand before he returned to Latin with a wavering voice.

"Please don't stop." Winifred's grip tightened in mine and she tensed against the energy in the air.

Sean's voice rose to a crescendo before he uttered "Amen."

Absolute silence lasted three agonizing seconds.

Aunt Ethel wailed in anguish, followed by a gasping cry of "He's dead!"

Sean's face gleamed pale with fright. "The prayer somehow—"

"Think nothing of the sort." I turned to Winifred and took her by the shoulders. "Get him out of here as soon as I'm gone."

She nodded, tear stained face iridescent in the half-light.

At the kitchen door, I turned back once more. "It wasn't you, Sean, but you have to leave."

Keziah was already in the doorway to my aunt and uncle's room. I nudged around her and entered the death space without permission. Placing a hand on Aunt Ethel's back, I let her know I was there though she was unseeing with her face on her husband's still chest.

It was going to be a long night.

Twelve

After an hour of weeping, Aunt Ethel was forced to remove herself from the bedroom as Dr. Sherard and two men arrived to claim the body.

Clinging to the doctor's arm, she heaved out the words. "How did you know to come for Andrew?"

"Your concerned neighbor, Mr. Finnigan, telephoned me."

"Mr. Finn—" Her shocked look melted into grief once more.

Taking pity on the doctor, I escorted my aunt to the guest room, setting her in the wingback chair near the window.

"Would you like tea, Aunt Ethel?"

"No, Merritt. Please see to the doctor."

Uncle Andrew's body and the men who accompanied the doctor were already gone from the second floor.

Dr. Sherard stopped me at the top of the stairs. "Your house has guardian angels, Miss Hall. If your aunt had been left to cling to a corpse all night, I would have had to tear her away from it in the morning."

"Thank you for coming promptly."

We went halfway down the stairwell and he paused, a hand at my elbow. "Patrick Finnigan is a friend of mine. He's the best sort, but if something were to happen to his nephew, he would not be forgiving. He has high hopes for the young man."

"I understand, Dr. Sherard. Winifred and I have nothing but gratitude for Sean's generosity."

"Please return that appreciation by keeping the lad away until you are out of quarantine."

He resumed descending the stairs, leaving me on the landing between the pull of responsibilities and feeling cursed no matter what I did. I shook off the numbness and hurried down the last of the stairs in time to open the front door.

"Remember to burn everything from the bed area, Miss Hall. I'll see to your aunt tomorrow."

I closed the door, resting my forehead on the back of it.

Five seconds of blessed silence passed. I closed my eyes, hoping for an uninterrupted minute of peace.

"Merri, are you all right?"

I exhaled and turned. "Yes, Winifred. I need to see to Aunt Ethel. You may wait for me on the sleeping porch."

"I'm not setting foot upstairs alone. I'll wait down here with Tippet."

"Suit yourself."

Upstairs, I readied the taps and turned the water on in the bath. As the tub filled, I gathered the soiled linens from Uncle Andrew's bed into a basket. Also added were the fever cloths—used and unused—stacked in the room and any handkerchiefs I saw lying about.

In the guestroom, I offered my hand to Aunt Ethel. "A bath will help you relax. I'll collect your dirty clothes and bring you a fresh nightgown."

"You're good to me, Merritt." She clung to me a minute.

"The water, Aunt Ethel." I stepped away to shut off the taps. "Leave your clothes by the door, and I'll collect them in a few minutes. Dr. Sherard says we need to burn everything."

Keziah watched me from her doorway as I came and went with my aunt's clothing—the pile in the basket growing larger.

"You need some help, Miss Merritt?"

"I've got it, but thank you. Please go back to bed so you'll be fit to handle the meals tomorrow. We'll all need nourishment come morning." I hefted the laundry, feeling the weight of death with the burden.

"I won't wake y'all for breakfast. You tell me when you're ready."

"Thank you, Keziah."

I brought the basket straight out the back door and set it on the ground. Ignoring my cousin's stare as I passed back through the downstairs hall, I climbed the stairs. I turned down the guestroom bed while waiting for Aunt Ethel to complete her bathing. When she opened the door, I immediately steered her to the unoccupied room.

"The air is fresher in here. I think you'll sleep better."

"I wanted to keep the room clean for guests. If your parents come for—"

"We'll have no visitors while we're under quarantine, Aunt Ethel. The post isn't even leaving the city to send word."

She sat on the side of the bed. "It isn't fair to Andrew to have no services. He was a good man."

"We'll give him a memorial service. He won't be forgotten." I motioned for her to put her legs on the bed and then guided her onto the pillow. "Now try to rest. We'll see to plans in the morning."

She gripped my hand. "Don't allow Winifred to hear me cry. Keep her away."

I sniffed back tears of my own. "She knows death and grief as well as any of us. She'll understand your sorrow."

"Go, Merritt. I'll be fine."

I left her in the guestroom with more than an ounce of reluctance. Thinking of Dr. Sherard's warning, I didn't want Aunt Ethel to slip into melancholy when alone, but I had much work ahead of me in cleaning the sick room.

Grabbing the bare mattress off the bedframe, I drug it down the hall, careful not to knock any portraits off the walls. I fought the floppy mattress all the way down the stairs—a controlled slide in which I barely managed to keep upright with me beside it.

"Merri!" Winifred exclaimed from the parlor doorway as I careened to a halt to catch my breath at the bottom.

"It must be burned. Would you help me get it to the barrel?"

"But it's too big to fit."

"I'll have to cut it up." I looked at her over the top of the mattress. "I'll be out there a while. If you need company, sit with Aunt Ethel. I have her in the guest room."

"I can't come?"

"You need to stay inside and listen out for Aunt Ethel. She needs you more than I do."

Winifred solemnly nodded. "You bring Tippet, then. I don't want you out there alone in the dark."

It took several minutes to relocate the mattress outside with Tippet running playfully around us. I walked Winifred back to the house, took a drink of water, and collected the kitchen shears because they were stronger than anything in the sewing basket. After gathering firewood and moving the laundry basket to the burn area, I started a blaze in the barrel.

The smoke kept the bugs away. Tippet—smart enough to stay clear of the heat—settled by Winifred's bench under the oak while I fed linens into the barrel. I packed in as many sheets as possible, stepped back, and wiped my sleeve across my forehead to clear the sweat before it could run into my eyes. Then, I tackled the mattress. The ticking cut easily enough, but the filler crumbled like chaff.

Scooping up a handful, I dropped it into the barrel. Flames shot out to capture the fuel, blazing white hot and singeing my fingers as a breeze caught a few loose bits. I gave a startled cry and jumped back, nearly twisting my ankle as I stumbled over the corner of the mattress.

Tippet barked.

"Merri, are you all right?" Sean emerged from the bushes with a hand on Tippet's head beside him.

"Does your uncle know where you are?"

He shook back his wave of brown hair. "Since when do you care about Uncle Patrick?"

"Since Dr. Sherard practically accused me and Winifred of luring you here against your uncle's wishes. I've never been so embarrassed in my life, especially since I tried to keep you away myself." I sat on the ground without finesse, drawing my knees to my chest. "I don't know why I bother with anything."

I tucked my head between my knees and allowed a few tears to escape. Once set free, my emotions flowered in a torrent of despair.

Sean's hand went to my back as I wept. My sniveling kept all option of conversation at bay, but he managed to communicate his concern.

"Cry all you need to, Merri," he soothed when my weeping calmed enough to be heard over. "No one can be stalwart forever."

I wiped my face on my apron and glanced at the young man sitting between me and an infected mattress. "You shouldn't be here. You shouldn't be exposed to all this."

I gestured broadly to the soiled linens and ticking, but he caught my nearest hand and kissed my knuckles. "I told you I wasn't afraid of catching anything. If I placed a bet, my money would be on mosquitoes, as I mentioned before. Sit there while I get this mattress cut into manageable pieces."

"Be careful. It practically exploded when I added some of the stuffing to the fire."

"Dried cotton is extremely flammable. You're lucky you didn't get burned."

Sean reached in, grabbed a handful, and sauntered to the barrel. With a flourish, he tossed the bedding into the flames. Knowing what to expect, his cat-like reflexes kept him out of harm's way. He quickly gathered more.

"Thank you for sending word to the doctor, though I'm worried about his warning. He says your uncle will blame us if you take sick."

"Uncle Patrick and Dr. Sherard are old mystic society brothers and chatter like women when together—no offense, Merri." Sean flashed his typical grin, but it looked more mature in the firelight. "They'll complain about anything and everything to let off their cares, but they know better than to pin a sickness on one household during an epidemic."

For several minutes, I watched Sean's steady movements as he worked between the burn barrel and the shrinking mattress.

I stood and brushed my backside clean. "Why did you come back tonight?"

"To make sure the doctor came. I told Uncle Patrick y'all were afraid Mr. Allen wouldn't survive the night and that Dr. Sherard had been seeing to him. He closed himself up in his study, but I heard him on the telephone and hoped he had called his friend. I'm glad one thing I set in motion went well."

"We couldn't have asked for more than what you've done for us these past days."

"Please don't shut me out. I need to do all I can for Winnie, especially after the trauma of the blessing I gave."

We both fed the fire, setting an unspoken rhythm of tearing, tossing, and standing back while the other did the same. Twice, tears rolled down my face. The first time, Sean handed me his handkerchief when his arms were free. I used it several minutes while he continued on without me and then tossed it in the fire. The second time, he caught my eye and shook his head.

"My pockets can no longer support you, Merri."

I gave a choked laugh and used my sleeve to dry my face.

We stood side-by-side as we watched the last of the linens burn.

"Thank you, Sean. I didn't realize how much I needed someone tonight."

"I'm always at your service, Merri. I'll check in as soon as I can. Keep Winnie safe in the meantime."

"You've more than proven yourself. I hope she waits for you as she matures."

A grin was his reply before he ran for the space in the azalea bushes and bound over the fence—causing Tippet to race to the spot he disappeared.

"Come on, Tippet. He'll be back another day."

Before leaving the barrel, I untied my apron and fed it to the dying flames. Next went my simple work dress. I ran to the back porch in my chemise.

I washed at the kitchen sink, but the odor of smoke clung to my underclothes and hair. Listening for crying or movement, I found the downstairs empty. The second floor was still as well. All the bedroom doors were open save Keziah's at the end of the hall. On the guestroom bed, Aunt Ethel hugged Winifred to her bosom, both with dried tears on their peaceful faces. I turned down the gaslight and crept to my room, falling exhausted into my previously unused bed as the hum of cicadas through the screen lulled me to a dreamless sleep.

Thirteen

I woke peacefully in the morning. Staring into the hall through the open door, I strained to hear what was going on in the rest of the house. I sprung from bed, reaching the hall as my head registered my movements. Holding the doorframe, I closed my eyes a moment to regain my balance before venturing to the guestroom.

Aunt Ethel dozed in the chair, pulled close to the bedside where Winifred slumbered. I refused to linger at the sick room, but Keziah's door was open and the bed made. Pausing at the top of the stairs, I finally heard the typical morning noises coming from the kitchen. Satisfied all were accounted for, I gathered fresh clothing and did what I should have done the night before—bathe.

By the time I was presentable with braided hair and wearing a simple red calico dress, Aunt Ethel prowled her bedroom. She absently fingered the dresser and caressed the footboard of the empty bed.

"You cleared everything," she stated.

"Everything exposed, as the doctor recommended, Aunt Ethel."

"What time did you finish? You were in bed when I woke at three."

"Not long before that. I'm glad you got some sleep."

"Dear Winifred asked if she could lie down with me. I couldn't turn her away after she lost the last member of her family."

"We'll be her family."

"Yes, yes we will." Aunt Ethel took me in a tight hug. "We'll be family to each other, my dearest girls."

I didn't wish to be too harsh in reminding her I wasn't there forever. After consoling her a few minutes, I tried to prepare her for the day. "How about breakfast? Mr. Graves brought plenty of supplies yesterday."

"I'm not hungry."

"You've barely eaten for a week, Aunt Ethel. Please try something. It will be nice to sit with you. Winifred and I have been lonely at the big table."

She patted my hand and stepped to the back window, gazing at the brightening sky. "Maybe next hour."

Smiling with relief, I went for the kitchen to ask Keziah to have breakfast ready at seven-thirty.

"I'll have a feast, Miss. And look what arrived—a bottle of milk! I saw that scamp deliver it."

"Scamp?" I crossed to the sideboard where the cook motioned to a piece of paper. On a thick sheet of stationery, written in the most elegant and gentlemanly hand, was the following.

Mrs. Allen,

I am sorry to hear about the passing of your husband. Andrew was a fine neighbor and man. He will be missed. I am under the impression that you currently have two nieces residing with you and your delivery services have refused contact while you are under quarantine. My nephew, Sean, has my blessing to deliver one of our milk bottles to your back step each morning until your household is cleared from the shadow of the yellow flag. Please accept it as a humble gesture from one neighbor to another.

Sincerely,

Patrick Finnigan

I ran the note upstairs in hopes of convincing Aunt Ethel that Sean and his family were respectable. She sat at her post of the past days, staring at the bare bedframe.

"Look what came, Aunt Ethel." I handed her the letter.

Winifred joined me, wearing one of her simple black day dresses. "What's going on?"

"A note," I whispered. "It's from Mr. Finnigan, but I know Sean is behind it."

Our aunt's shoulders sagged and she held the paper out for me to take. "It's another excuse for that boy to run about."

I passed the note on to Winifred and stood before my aunt. "It's a kindness they're doing at their own peril, Aunt Ethel. Something no one else save Uncle Andrew's employee has ventured to do. That's the second act of kindness from Mr. Finnigan in less than twelve hours. Where have your other friends been these past days?"

"Using their common sense, that's where." She crossed her arms. "I don't need charity from a Catholic."

"Then don't drink the milk." I couldn't keep the scorn from my voice. "Keziah will put it to use in her baking, and Winifred will enjoy a glass with her breakfast." I put an arm around my cousin and steered her out of the room.

We stopped on the stair landing.

Winifred held the letter to her heart and smiled. "Aren't they thoughtful, Merri? I don't think I could ever love a man more than I do Sean. His uncle must know something of what we feel for each other to allow him a daily visit. What time does the milkman come to the neighborhood? I'll wait for—"

"You'll do no such thing." I took her arm and continued our journey to the first floor. "Mr. Finnigan gave permission for Sean to quickly drop the milk. We're under quarantine and need to be cautious to protect others."

"But he gave his blessing! Who needs a blessing to deliver milk? Sean must have told him how he feels about me. Why else would a blessing be needed other than for courtship?"

"Sean is forever crossing himself and speaking of blessings and prayers. Don't you remember what he attempted last night?"

Winifred shivered. "But for his uncle to knowingly send him here daily—"

"I have it on good authority that Mr. Finnigan is concerned over Sean's safety. I'm sure he would not permit him to come if he suspected we would confront him."

"You act as if I'd lie in ambush to infect him!"

I narrowed my eyes at her. "Have you ever met Mr. Finnigan?"

"No, but—"

"Then don't claim to know his thoughts when you know nothing of the man or the situation."

Winifred stomped down the hall, Tippet at her heals.

I followed her to the kitchen and called out as she reached the back door. "Breakfast at the bottom of the hour—don't be late."

With both Aunt Ethel and Winifred at odds with me, breakfast was a quiet affair. We ate sparingly, but Winifred made a point of drinking the milk with exaggerated enjoyment.

"You mentioned a memorial service, Merritt," Aunt Ethel said as I rose from the table.

"I thought it only proper as there won't be a church or graveside service, but if you aren't up to it I understand."

"It's a lovely idea. I'd like to have one tomorrow at sundown." She looked to my cousin. "Winifred, choose two hymns to play on the piano. Merritt will be in charge of the display and singing at least one solo."

"Display?"

"Mementos from Andrew's life," she said. "Portraits, medals from the war, diplomas, and the like. Arrange the mantel in the parlor with them, please." Her dark gaze clouded and she appeared to look through me. "I'm going to rest now."

Aunt Ethel staggered out. I caught her at the foot of the stairs and escorted her to the guest room.

"No, not here. I need to be in our bedroom."

"But there isn't a functional bed, Aunt Ethel. You need rest."

She pointed an accusing finger at the mattress she'd slept half the night on. "Bring it over. This room can be barren, but not the space I shared with Andrew for thirty years."

I set to work stripping the bed of its linens so they wouldn't drag across the floor. Winifred arrived in time to help me relocate the double mattress. We remade the bed in record time, but Aunt Ethel set her heavy soul in the chair instead.

"Come on," I whispered to Winifred. "We can work on the memorial service plans. I'll check on her in a little while."

Downstairs, Winifred sat on the piano bench. I continued to the next door and paused before the closed room I had only entered once, when I was a curious six-year-old who wanted to know what mysteries my uncle kept in the space he inhabited every evening after supper while on one of my visits from Grand Bay.

Just as before, the odor of Uncle Andrew's tobacco surround me when I stepped inside. The room was smaller than I remembered—and messier. Stacks of papers overflowed the opened roll-top desk, the only light spots amid the paneled walls and dark furniture beside the sheer drapes over the small window. The bookcases had several random piles on the floor before them as well, making the room feel cramped. The only other furniture beside the desk, chair, and shelves was a brown wingback chair by the fireplace. The leather was worn and sagged in the middle from decades of use.

Choked by emotions, I stepped backward. My heel met someone's foot.

"Oh!" Winifred jumped but put a hand on my back to steady me. "I'd never thought to look in here before."

I turned to her. "Would you get one of the gathering baskets from the kitchen? I'd like to keep what I find together."

Winifred returned a moment later with the requested basket. "May I help you?"

"You need to decide on your hymns and practice. You haven't touched the piano since Uncle Andrew took to bed."

"'Abide with Me' and 'The Lord is My Shepherd.' I already know the psalm by heart. I'll practice 'Abide with Me' later. I don't want to wake Aunt Ethel if she's asleep."

"All right, but don't go digging for trouble. If anything needs to be moved, I'll do it."

She twirled in the middle of the small space. "We should ask Aunt Ethel if we can turn this into my school room."

"We'll do nothing of the sort." I took Winifred's arms to stop her dance. "She's deeply grieved, Winnie. We need to humor her, not force change."

"You were forceful with her about that letter in calling out her unjust feelings toward Sean and his uncle."

I lowered my head in shame. "I shouldn't have caused trouble over that in her present state. The disappointment over her not being moved by the kindness offended me, but her prejudice against Catholics isn't going to be cured while she's grieving her husband."

"I think that would be the best time. Sean and Mr. Finnigan are the only ones reaching out."

"And Bartholomew," I reminded her.

"But he's paid to."

"If you're passing judgment on good deeds based on payments, I'm sure Sean would heartily agree seeing your smile is payment enough."

Winifred huffed but was immediately drawn to the desk. "What all do you think is in here? Store records? Bills?"

"Please don't touch anything. You're likely to start an avalanche."

She clasped her hands behind her back before perusing the wall of shelves. "Do you think he read all these? I never saw him with a book, and I've been here months."

I looked over her shoulder and scanned the titles. "It's mostly nonfiction and these plain ones might be ledgers of some sort."

Taking the top of one spine, I pulled the leather volume down along with a sprinkling of dust. I opened it and found store records from 1891.

"Boring." Winifred turned toward the crowded mantel. "What about the war medals Aunt Ethel mentioned?"

"I've never seen them—or heard Uncle Andrew talk about the war. He was young and forced into service for the Confederacy. He hated violence and detested war." I pulled out the top desk drawer and refiled through the assortment of fountain pens and wooden stamps with things like PAID and PAST DUE written backwards at the end of them.

"Uncle Andrew was the oldest and my mother the baby of the family. She didn't remember much from the war years, but her two sisters apparently had beaus involved."

"Tell me more about Uncle Andrew's family. Aunt Ethel just referred to them as the 'crazy Allens.'"

Winifred giggled. "My mother was flamboyant, and apparently the most mellow out of the lot. Meda Winifred Allen was the belle of Charleston when she came of age the decade after the war, though said not to have been as pretty as her oldest sister, Diana. Diana married her soldier after the war ended but they died in a house fire the following year."

She paused, mulling over her own words as I tried to look busy while not ruffling too deep into my uncle's secrets.

"I suppose the Allen family is cursed with fiery deaths. All the sisters have died in house fires because Nancy was at Diana's house when it happened."

The name brought chill bumps to my arms. "Nancy?"

"Yes, Nancy Emila Allen," Winifred whispered and looked about as if we might be watched. "Some people think she started the fire."

I took Winifred's hand and led her to the settee in the parlor. "But why, Winnie? Why would she do that?"

"Burn all her sisters and herself? I don't know, but she's scaring me in my dreams. I pray she doesn't do more."

I refused to believe that because it was bad enough accidentally causing the death of someone. "There is no sense in a young lady destroying her family. What would cause her to do that?"

We sat in silence as horrific thoughts spiraled about. Hatred. Jealousy. Wretchedness. All those were possible because of the single, strongest emotion a human can experience. Love.

"Winnie, how did you survive the fire?"

"I wasn't in the house when it started."

"It happened at night, didn't it, while everyone was sleeping?"

She blushed and looked to the clasped hands in her lap. "I'd stepped out a few minutes before. I was in the barn."

"Were there babies animals to see to?"

"No." She hesitated. "I was visiting with the stable hand."

I starred, mouth gapping, at my brazen cousin.

"It was nothing—nothing like what I feel for Sean. A few stolen kisses is all."

"Winifred, did your parents know? Your sister?"

"No, and it was nothing more than a rush, Merri. Looking back, I see it was only surface deep. What I feel for Sean is real."

"It seems like your nightmares are worse the nights after you and Sean express your feelings for each other. Do you think these dreams about Nancy could be guilt over your relationship?"

Eyes large with fright, Winifred shook her head. "I have no guilt over Sean, and I'll never give him up."

Fourteen

Aunt Ethel refused to leave her room to eat at noon. I brought her a tray and was told to leave it. When I returned an hour later with Dr. Sherard, Aunt Ethel was in the same position in the rocking chair, the tray untouched on the bed beside her.

The doctor took in the scene from the door and turned to me. "How long has she been like this?"

"I brought her here this morning after changing out the mattress and linens with the ones from the guest room."

"You burned the old things?"

"Yes, sir."

"However did you manage all that?"

A rush of indignation flared within. "I might not look like much, Dr. Sherard, but I *am* resourceful."

"Girls like you are usually more than capable of handling difficulties that would break a weaker woman like that angel-faced cousin of yours. Your aunt is typically tough as nails too. Let's see if I can keep her from hysterics by appealing to her logic." He patted my arm condescendingly and entered the room without a backward glance at my reddening face.

"Mrs. Allen, you don't look well."

Aunt Ethel raised her chin at the harsh tone, showcasing swollen eyes and a red nose.

"It is as I feared. You must take fresh air and eat to keep your strength. These nieces of yours need looking after. And your husband's affairs will need to be settled speedily for your financial wellbeing." He fingered the pulse in her wrist and felt for fever on her brow. "Do you need a draught to help you sleep at night?"

"No, Dr. Sherard, I'll be fine. Merritt is excellent help. She brought my dinner to me, though I was too sad to eat at the moment. I'll do so now."

I couldn't watch her pathetic attempt to swallow the stale toast and room temperature soup so I paced the hallway until Dr. Sherard exited the bedroom.

"Settle down, Miss Hall. We cannot have you brooding as well. I will return in the morning. If she does not rest tonight, I will force a sleeping draught. Unless, of course, she is in active hysterics—then I will have to take her away."

I wanted to shove him out with his final words, but managed to convey my thanks before closing the front door behind him. Hurrying back to my aunt, I found her with the soup still in hand.

"I'm not hungry."

"It's all right, Aunt Ethel. I'll take the tray. Would you like to sit in the parlor or on the back porch?"

"No."

"How about lying down to rest a bit?"

"All right." She left her shoes on the floor and stayed on top of the covers.

"I hope you'll be able to join us for supper," I said before leaving.

Winifred practiced the piano, so I dropped Aunt Ethel's tray in the kitchen and stole into the study to further explore. The next drawer I tackled was filled with banking booklets and deposit receipts for what appeared to be Uncle Andrew's personal account. It was tidy compared to everything else I had seen and would be easy to direct Aunt Ethel there when the time was right.

The bottom drawer—deeper than all the rest—held a box brittle with age concealing what I believed to be the objects of my search. As I straightened, Winifred entered.

"I think I have it. Why don't we take it to the dining room table so we can spread out a bit? It's stifling in here."

"It's like a treasure party!" Winifred said as we approached the table. "Shall I ask Keziah to fix us tea?"

"No, but tie back the drapes to try for a bit more breeze."

"There's not much luck in that. It's awful today." When she returned from the task, Winifred settled next to me, our backs to the door so we could use the light from the window.

The corner of the lid crumbled when I lifted it off, but the body of the container kept its shape. A black scrapbook tied with faded satin ribbons was on top. Opening it between us, we leaned over until our foreheads nearly touched to study the daguerreotype on the first page.

"Granny and Grandpa!" Winifred leaned closer. "We had a similar portrait in our parlor. Oh, I miss my home and family."

"So these are Uncle Andrew's parents?"

"Yes, Papa passed away when I was about seven and Granny not long after my tenth birthday."

I squeezed her hand and nodded for her to turn the page. It was, after all, her family.

Uncle Andrew had worn a beard for years and it was difficult to recognize his young, clean-shaven face in his Confederate uniform.

"I didn't know he was so handsome, did you?"

Winifred laughed. "Granny kept one of his soldier portraits on her mantel. Besides, he had to be handsome enough to capture Aunt Ethel's attention, being so much older than her."

"That's common enough, especially after a war when there's not as many young men about."

"I hope there's never another war, ever again. I couldn't handle losing Sean." She pointed to a young couple on the next page, the man in uniform. "That's Aunt Diana and Uncle Jack. Of course, I never met them, but Mama and Granny had lovely stories about Diana."

"You're teaching me today, Winnie. I'm glad I'm here with you and Aunt Ethel." And for that moment, I truly was.

Then Winifred turned the page. There was another portrait of Uncle Andrew, this time in uniform atop a horse.

"Calvary is always dashing." Winifred smiled and turned the page.

Her gasp let me know who it was holding a nosegay in the next daguerreotype. The young woman was the height of early 1860s fashion with her hair done in ringlets, lace gauntlets on her hands, and an off-the-shoulder crinoline dress. Nancy Allen would have been beautiful were it not for the scowl that pressed her lips into a thin, angry line. Her face was long and solemn, not at all like Winifred's round face.

"Mama told me Nancy was upset over a soldier who didn't make it home. Some boy she said Diana swore would never give her a second glance, but she was smitten with him nonetheless."

"Unrequited love," I whispered.

Winifred held my gaze, understanding. "*Lost* unrequited love—the ultimate disappointment because you would never know if you could have turned his heart."

Bartholomew came to mind. How would I feel if I didn't get the chance to see if he might be interested in me because of this epidemic? I nodded.

"I feel sorry for her." Winifred sighed. "But it's no excuse for her to torment me. I wasn't even alive then."

Meda was on the next page, brightening Winifred's spirits once more. She looked very much like her mother, and I envied their soft features.

When we were done, she fingered the edge of the bound pages and looked to me. "Do you think Aunt Ethel would allow me to keep this after the memorial service? Or at least a few of the photographs?"

"I think so, but allow me to ask about it when the time is right."

"Because she likes you more?"

"Because you tend to be rash and emotional and Aunt Ethel responds better to level-headedness."

Winifred rolled her eyes, pulled the box closer, and removed a handful of knickknacks—marbles, rocks, and a few random buttons. "These must be childhood things."

I took one of the brass buttons and studied it. A capitol C distinguished the front—not a letter from his name, but of service.

"Cavalry." I handed it back to my cousin. "I bet that's all that's left of his uniform."

"I wonder where his sword is."

"Possibly buried," I remarked. "He was a pacifist as long as I've known him. Have you ever known a man more quick to lend a calming voice when anger is stirred?"

"But swords are romantic, bringing to mind daring escapes from pirates and—"

"Do stop with your fancies and look for medals or something to appease Aunt Ethel. I doubt a button will do."

In the end, it was all we had to offer—besides the portraits of young Andrew Allen of Charleston in service during the Civil War. We presented our paltry findings to Aunt Ethel in the parlor before supper.

"I haven't seen this book since Andrew showed the boys, one sitting on each knee the spring he acquired it on our trip to Charleston. They died later that summer. Papa is with you now, dear boys." She sniffed as she leafed through the thick, black pages. "Well done, Merritt. And Winifred. I heard you practicing earlier. It sounded lovely. Tomorrow night will be special."

As we finished supper, Keziah came into the dining room.

"There's a caller at the back door, Mrs. Allen."

Her face clouded. "It's not that young rascal, is it?"

Winifred looked pained at the harshness.

"It's Mr. Graves."

"Bring him in, by all means, Keziah. You know better than—"

"The quarantine, Aunt Ethel." I rose as I said the words.

"I did have him come inside the porch so the mosquitoes wouldn't get at him," Keziah said.

"It wouldn't be safe for him to come in the house," I reiterated. "Shall I escort you to greet him?" I caught Winifred's eye over our aunt's shoulder and gave her a little smile to encourage her to finish her meal. Then I motioned Tippet to stay when I passed him where he sprawled in the hallway.

Bartholomew stood in the middle of the screened porch holding a bouquet of assorted flowers that were difficult to see in the waning light.

"My deepest sympathies, Mrs. Allen." He offered the flowers, the gesture stilted compared to the flourish Sean would have seen to, but heartfelt. "I'm at your service."

"Thank you, Mr. Graves. Merritt, do take the flowers and set them in water."

"Miss Merritt." He nodded to me, oval face as solemn as ever.

Our fingers touched when I took the bouquet, and I knew in an instant he was concerned for me as much as my aunt—at least I fancied it so.

"How did you know about Andrew?" Aunt Ethel's voice carried into the kitchen where I saw to the flowers.

"Sean Spunner arrived at the store this morning with the news. I came as soon as I completed my duties for the day."

"Will we ever be rid of that rascal?"

"I hope you won't."

I set the flower vase on the counter and hurried back so I wouldn't miss a word.

"Did he tell you of the message system he arranged?" Bartholomew asked when Aunt Ethel didn't respond.

"No." Aunt Ethel crossed her arms.

"He'll stop at the store by noon each day to collect any correspondence that I need sent to you. In return, he said you could leave any messages on the back stoop for him to collect when he brings your milk each morning. He's extremely clever for his age."

I smiled at Bartholomew's kindness in defending Sean when it was clear Aunt Ethel couldn't stand him. "I've tried to explain his goodness, but she's blinded by his charm, thinking it false."

Bartholomew laughed and my heart gave a leap at the sound. "He's a charmer by no small means, but he's sincere. You're in good hands with him."

Winifred rushed onto the porch, Tippet at her heals. "He's the dearest boy I've ever known!"

"Well this is awkward," Sean's smooth voice said from the back stoop. He tipped his hat toward us. "My apologies for this unannounced visit, but I failed to leave word about an evening pickup for the empty milk bottle. Was one enough or do you need two bottles, Mrs. Allen?"

"One was plenty." Aunt Ethel turned crimson in the light coming from the kitchen door. "Please thank your uncle for us. Winifred, fetch the bottle."

"Thank you again, Sean," I said stepping closer to the door.

"It's my pleasure, Merri."

Winifred returned with the bottle, heading straight for the door.

"Step back, Mr. Spunner," Aunt Ethel said, "and Winifred will set the bottle out."

"Yes, Mrs. Allen." He exited the rectangle of light on the stoop for the green of the lawn.

Winifred hesitated before the screen before kissing the mouth of the bottle and leaning over to place the glass outside. Sean bit his lip as he moved closer, eyes never leaving Winifred's figure as she shifted away from the door.

"Thank you again, but you may go now." Aunt Ethel said once Sean had the bottle in hand.

"Uncle Patrick had one more message for you. He felt it unsympathetic to add in his note this morning, but didn't want to go another day without offering his services. Should you need help with any legal affairs, he is happy to assist without compensation."

Aunt Ethel straightened. "Andrew has used Mr. Crawley, and I don't plan on changing lawyers because my husband passed on."

Sean climbed onto the top step, the rim of his bowler touching the screen. "That's the thing, Mrs. Allen. Mr. Crawley left town at the first hint of fever. Word is his health isn't the best, and his daughter he went to visit in Birmingham might insist on keeping him with her. My uncle doesn't want you to fret over anything. He's here through it all and is friends with the firm's owner, Mr. Melling. He could easily access Mr. Crawley's files without issue should you need him to."

"That is beyond generous," Bartholomew said to fill the silence from Aunt Ethel's slack mouth. "Mrs. Allen appreciates it, but she's had a trying day."

"Yes, of course. Leave any messages for my morning delivery if needed. My sincerest condolences." Sean descended a step and his tone softened further. "The Easton family lost little Rebecca today, but the others are hanging on for the moment. So much sadness in the city. Well, goodnight, ladies. Mr. Graves. Thank you for helping the household."

Sean jumped back another step and bowed.

"Goodnight, Sean. I'm sorry about your friends," Winifred called.

Aunt Ethel turned on her in a flash. "Go prepare for bed, Winifred."

"Yes, Aunt Ethel. Goodnight, Mr. Graves." She slipped into the house.

"If that sly Catholic thinks he can weasel his way into stealing me as a client—"

Bartholomew caught my aunt's gaze. "Mr. Finnigan is doing you a favor, not looking to trick you. As a business owner, your husband will have left behind a paper trail that needs to be seen to in order to keep the store open so you have a source of income. I suggest you gather what you can find here, and I'll see what are in the files in the office, and then we can compare, perhaps over the weekend. You might need legal assistance in the end, but don't worry about that yet. For now, use the Spunner mail system to send word if you need me."

"Thank you, Mr. Graves. I'll see what we can find this week." She entered the kitchen and we listened to her heavy footsteps fade into the hallway.

"Don't wait on her if you think I need to be made aware of something," Bartholomew whispered. "We can correspond no matter how trivial you think the situation."

"I appreciate it. I'm not sure what tonight will bring between Aunt Ethel and Winifred."

Bartholomew shoved his hands into his trouser pockets. "Write me if you need anything. Goodnight, Merritt."

"Goodnight." I sounded hoarse with emotions and watched him leave.

At the corner of the house, he turned and lifted a hand in farewell. The small gesture fortified me to face the night with my haunted relatives.

Fifteen

Upstairs, Winifred was in her nightgown, and Aunt Ethel sat on the edge of her bed, fully dressed and staring at the floor.

"Why don't you freshen in the bath and ready for bed, Aunt Ethel?" I suggested.

"I suppose I must."

"Do you want to go on to bed, Winnie?"

"I don't want to be alone."

"Not even on the porch?" I whispered.

She shook her head.

Unable to reason with Winifred, I set about tidying the guest room. Winifred followed me around, her attempt at helping vague at best.

Aunt Ethel exited the bathroom in her cotton nightgown, buttoned to the wrists and neck. Her eyes were unfocused and swollen from tears. She must have cried while the water was running so we wouldn't hear. I took her arm and brought her to bed.

"Rest, even if you can't sleep," I encouraged as she lay back on the pillow.

She gripped my forearm before I could step away. "You'll see to Winifred, won't you?"

"Always, Aunt Ethel. Don't worry about us."

"Andrew brought her here to do his duty to the family he left behind after the war, but he loved her—loved both of you—like his own. And your brother. Be sure to tell Ezra that Uncle Andrew was as proud of him as he was about his sons he lost. We lost. I've lost everyone."

"You still have me and Winnie, Aunt Ethel. We're not going anywhere."

"Dear girls. Dear, dear girls," she said between tears.

"Shall we stay with you?" I asked.

Aunt Ethel shook her head. "Go on to bed. I'll see you in the morning."

Winifred came for her as I went for the door. "I'm sorry if I've been wicked. I'll do better, I promise. Merri is teaching me decorum and manners as well as my academic subjects. I'll be a proper young lady in no time."

"You are a beauty." Aunt Ethel embraced Winifred even tighter. "I fear you need no improvements. You're already catching the eyes of men and will be a well-kept woman by the time you're Merritt's age."

Though I knew it was not meant to be an insult, my stomach soured at the words. In the shared bedroom, I pulled my hair from its confining bun and shook it until it hung like a brown veil down my back. Taking my brush from the drawer, I tackled my hair with all the energy I had. The tresses turned glossy with the attention but my sharp nose and chin never softened.

"Your hair is beautiful," Winifred said upon entering. "You know, I think Mr. Graves likes you."

"Why would you say such a thing?" I removed my dress and folded it into the basket in the corner I placed my dirty clothing.

"I watched from the kitchen before I came onto the porch and heard what you said in Sean's defense. And then Mr. Graves laughed. I've known him since my first week here and I've never heard him laugh like that. He's quite handsome when he smiles."

I collected my nightgown. "I'm going to wash."

When I finished, Winifred sat in the doorway of Aunt Ethel's room, head leaning against the doorframe. Our aunt was curled on the bed, facing away from us. Not wanting to bother her in case she slept, I motioned to Winifred. I turned down the gaslight in the hallway, then our bedroom.

The moon was a tiny sliver, but the sky was clear enough to provide a safe path to the sleeping porch. Winifred hurried in front of me with Tippet. We settled in our hammocks and I stretched my arms over my head to keep them from sticking to my sides.

Worry over Aunt Ethel being restless and the faces of Uncle Andrew's dead family members from the scrapbook had me sleepless amid the buzz of the cicadas and peeping frogs.

Winifred groaned and fidgeted in her sleep, causing Tippet to whimper and sniff the air.

Sleep must have come, for I woke when Tippet's claws tapped across the floorboards after stealthy Winifred. The sky was indigo with a faint golden blush on the horizon beyond the oak trees.

"Trying to meet Sean when he brings the milk?" I asked.

Winifred looked back with a sheepish grin.

"Be sure to dress first and stay on the porch."

"Yes, Merri." She rushed into the bedroom.

I slowly stood from the hammock. Winifred pulled her black skirt over her petticoat and buttoned on a black shirtwaist.

Black on black.

Mourning dress appropriate for the memorial service we were holding that evening.

At least she was prepared for it with proper fitting clothes. I went to the closet and removed the only black ensemble I possessed—a Sunday dress for church or funerals I packed at the last minute though it wasn't ideal for summer. A premonition? I would have to skip housework to wear it, but a day off to keep a closer eye on Aunt Ethel might be for the best.

I washed my face in hopes of improving the stain of a restless night on my countenance, but it did little to help my sallow complexion or camouflage the dark shadows under my eyes. Giving up, I descended the stairs without redoing the braid I'd slept in.

Winifred stood near the back screen door, shamelessly brushing her hair in the rectangle of light that poured onto the porch from the open kitchen door.

"You should have completed that upstairs," I stated.

"Seeing you with your hair down last night gave me the idea. Sean has never seen mine loose. It's becoming for a lady to expose her hair—an instant infusion of allure and beauty."

"Are you always so fanciful early in the morning?"

"I'm not sure. I don't often wake early."

"Then you must have slept well."

She paused, tapping her brush on her chin. "I think I did, though I have a vague memory of a fiery nightmare."

"You did seem troubled at one point, but you didn't wake up from what I could tell. Even Tippet was concerned."

"I don't remember any of that. And Tippet is happily sniffing about the yard right now. He's a good lookout for Sean. I know he'll give a—"

Tippet's quick bark denoting excitement broke the early morning stillness, causing me and Winifred to laugh.

Sean crossed the ever lengthening grass glistening with dew. His white shirt and pale blue pants contrasted against the greenery of the yard making him appear larger than life. His usual jovial face was grave. Even Tippet was subdued—not jumping around him.

"Oh, Sean!" I feared Winifred would crash through the door the way she leaned on the screen. "I wish I could hug you right now."

"That would be heaven, Winnie." His smile brightened his face a moment and he set the milk bottle on the bottom step. "I miss your soft touch."

"Any more word on your friends?"

He shook his head, causing his brown hair to flop over his forehead in a boyish way. "Not since the news of Rebecca yesterday evening. I'm dropping a note of condolences to the family next."

"I wish I could go with you." Winifred placed her right palm flat against the screen. "I'd hold your hand the whole way there and back."

"I'd love that." He hopped up the steps and placed his palm against the door from the other side before I could think to pull Winifred away. "I'm weak today."

"Are you getting sick?"

"No, dearest Winnie." He brought the hand from the screen to his chest. "I'm weak in spirit."

"Poor Sean," Winifred lamented.

He returned to the lawn and spread his arms. "'Can death be sleep, when life is but a dream,

      And scenes of bliss pass as a phantom by?

      The transient pleasures as a vision seem,

      And yet we think the greatest pain's to die.'"

The words of "On Death" by John Keats echoed over the hush of sunrise.

      "'How strange it is that man on earth should roam,

      And lead a life of woe, but not forsake

      His rugged path; nor dare he view alone

His future doom which is but to awake.'"

Sean once again mounted the stoop and leaned his forehead against the screen, Tippet keeping behind him as a silent sentinel. "Angels should not be in black. How may I help you ladies?"

"We're having a memorial for Uncle Andrew this evening," Winifred said. "We'll light candles, and I'll play a few hymns on the piano that Merri and I will sing."

"Hearing that would fortify my heart."

"But you can't—"

Sean interrupted me. "Which window is it?"

"The one by the hydrangea bush on the opposite side," Winifred was quick to reply.

"I'll listen quietly from the yard when I pick up the milk bottle." Sean met my gaze with hope. "That's all right, isn't it, Merri?"

I smiled in relief. "Of course, Sean."

"I look forward to hearing you tonight—the both of you." He ruffled Tippet's fur before going for the gate.

Sixteen

Two hours later, Aunt Ethel sat at the breakfast table with us though she didn't eat. Afterward, Winifred and I rearranged the parlor to her specifications. Extra chairs were brought in from the dining room and all seating done in a semicircle around the piano. There was space for a dozen souls—enough seats for us and those Nancy had apparently done away with.

Winifred looked pale against the harsh black clothing, her eyes vivid blue pools amid her snowy skin. I uttered a silent prayer for her safety as she set the plant stand away from the window—most likely to clear the view from the yard to the piano.

A knock sounded on the front door a minute later, and I invited Dr. Sherard inside.

He looked about the parlor, stroking his mustache. "Don't tell me you expect visitors while you are under quarantine, Mrs. Allen."

Her red-rimmed gaze was unfocused. "One never knows who will stop by for our memorial service this evening. Andrew was loved."

"His name and address were in the newspaper this morning with the other fever victims. Anyone with a lick of sense will stay away." He set his black bag on one of the empty chairs and advanced. "How much sleep did you get last night, Mrs. Allen?"

Aunt Ethel shrugged. "I might have been up after midnight, but the girls saw me to bed. They take good care of me."

"But they can't force you to sleep." He felt her forehead and neck. The pulse in her wrist. Then he retrieved a bottle of elixir from his bag and turned to me. "Two spoonfuls before bedtime tonight."

"Yes, sir." I slipped it into my pocket.

"No devil's fire for me and my house, Dr. Sherard!"

He looked at her with an amused smile. "I'm not handing you a bottle of whiskey and telling you to enjoy yourself, Mrs. Allen. I am entrusting a medicinal amount of a sleeping draught to be sure you stay fit enough to run this household. Surely you don't wish to fail Andrew after all his years of toil to provide for you and your family."

Her hand trembled, then her lips. Even Winifred looked up in alarm.

I could have let loose a thousand ill-mannered thoughts on the doctor for needlessly scaring my aunt and cousin in their delicate conditions, but I smiled politely instead. "Thank you for stopping, Dr. Sherard. I'm sure you're busy and need to be on your way."

"I'll be back in the morning and expect a report of a restful night."

Aunt Ethel managed to nod, eyes still large with fright.

The doctor pointed to the yellow flag when he reached the porch. "That is a sign for no visitors, Miss Hall."

"Yes, Dr. Sherard."

"If your aunt is delusional enough to believe visitors will come, she is further gone in her head than I expected. It doesn't bode well."

"Aunt Ethel understands, but it's too painful for her to think of her husband not being shown the respect she wants to display for him. Not to mention being left alone by all her friends. It's a lonely time for her."

He gave a curt nod. "Until tomorrow, Miss Hall."

Returning to the parlor, I immediately went to Aunt Ethel's side. "Don't worry, Aunt Ethel. You'll get along fine if you only rest."

"Mr. Graves must have the legal papers. Only the papers will save the store."

"We still have time for that," I reminded her. "Let today be for rest and remembering."

"I need to lie down. Will you start on the files for me?"

"If that's what you want." I escorted her to her room.

"Don't wake me for dinner if I manage to sleep, but wake me an hour before supper so I can look presentable."

I agreed, tied on an apron, and met with Winifred in our uncle's study.

"You don't have to help with this."

"I want to. Tell me what to do."

I looked over the bookcases and pointed to the one filled with store ledgers. "Go through those. See that they are in chronological order and affix date labels so they can be read without pulling each book out."

"Yes, Merri." Winifred collected the stepstool from the kitchen and set to work.

***

By the time I roused Aunt Ethel, the store ledgers in the study were labeled, Uncle Andrew's desk organized, and all the loose stacks on the floor gone through. I had to take a damp cloth to my dress to clean off the dust before I could present myself at supper, but the day's efforts were well worth the trouble. The only things left to see to were the books.

I brushed and reset my hair in a chignon before descending the stairs. Winifred and Aunt Ethel waited in the parlor for me. They were on the settee amid the awkward arrangement—a painful reminder of our aloneness.

Supper of canned fish loaf and greens was a silent affair. After barely a week of quarantine, I was already tired of tin goods. Only Winifred cleaned her plate.

The three of us gathered in the parlor. We waited until Keziah tidied the dining room and joined us before we started. Winifred, looking mature in her black silk, rose from her chair to light the candles. Candlesticks had been placed on the side tables and piano, plus photographs of Uncle Andrew were arranged on the mantel. I went to the wall switch and turned off the gaslights after Winifred completed her duties.

When the room dimmed, the yard through the opened windows came into focus. Two figures in black stood beyond the blooming hydrangea in the dusk. The giant periwinkle blossoms obscured the furthest visitor, but Sean eagerly stood within three feet of the window. I smiled at him before taking my seat with Aunt Ethel.

"In memory of Andrew Daniel Allen, my uncle," Winifred said with a steady voice. "We honor your Christian life, this night and always."

She sat at the piano and started playing the twenty-third psalm. On the second round, she sang "The Lord is My Shepherd" in a soft alto to her own accompaniment. Before she started the tune the third time, I left Aunt Ethel to stand beside the piano bench. My soaring soprano joined my cousin's voice.

By the end of the song, Aunt Ethel was in tears. "Don't mind me girls, it's lovely. Keep going."

Winifred and I exchanged glances and she began playing "Abide with Me," singing the first verse. We switched off singing the different verses, closing together with the final.

Winifred stood and spoke to Aunt Ethel loud enough to be heard outside. "Uncle Andrew took me in as his own. I looked forward to loving him as a father, but he was taken away too soon. He was kind, stubborn, and resilient—that much I witnessed in my short time here. But he will always be my dearest uncle as well as the bridge from my past life to my future."

She went directly to Aunt Ethel and threw her arms about her.

Keziah quietly excused herself. The distant sound of her cleaning the kitchen soon started. A minute later, Keziah motioned to me from the parlor doorway.

My cousin and aunt were still nursing their sorrows, so I stole from the room.

"Callers at the backdoor, Miss Merritt," Keziah informed me when I reached the hall.

Expecting to be introduced to Mr. Finnigan, I straightened my dress and dabbed at my cheeks with my handkerchief, hoping I'd make a good impression on the distinguished lawyer. I didn't wish to do my family a disservice by appearing ill-kempt.

I went through the kitchen, back straight, knowing they could see me before I could see them as I stepped through the open door onto the porch.

"You have a stunning voice, Merri," Sean said as I came close to the screen door.

"Thank you, Sean. It was a comfort to Winifred to know you were there. You and—" I faltered as my eyes adjusted to the darkness in the yard to recognize Bartholomew Graves, black hat in hand. "Bartholomew, what a surprise! I assumed Sean would have brought his uncle when I saw a second figure."

"Sean came to the store this morning to tell me what you ladies had planned. I felt it the least I could do to offer a show of support to the Allens. Mr. Finnigan did welcome me to their home for supper. He was most hospitable."

"That was very thoughtful."

"It was no trouble," Sean said. "I thought with Bartholomew running the store, he'd be the person to discuss business with if Mrs. Allen needs help."

Surprised at the forethought—and a niggling of Aunt Ethel's fear of Mr. Finnigan wishing to steal her as a client—caused me to look at Bartholomew in shock. "Did you speak of the Allens' affairs to Mr. Finnigan?"

"Only in general terms. I let him know what I was doing at the shop to be sure I wasn't breaking any laws by running things after Mr. Allen died."

"And are you?"

"I'm in the right, so long as Mrs. Allen is agreeable to it and I'm keeping the books and drawing the salary previously agreed on."

"I'm glad to hear that. She's getting anxious about finding the proper papers. Winifred and I are in the process of going through Uncle Andrew's study. We have all the store ledgers from 1867 through 1896 labeled and in chronological order."

"And I have this year's, January through the current September." Bartholomew gave a shy smile.

"You'll get things worked out in no time," Sean remarked.

"I'm sure you were hoping to speak to Winifred," I said.

"If it's possible."

"She and Aunt Ethel were consoling each other, but I think Aunt Ethel would like to know there were more in attendance at her memorial service. It might lift her spirits. Give me a minute to check on them."

In the parlor, my aunt and cousin were still holding each other but they were no longer sobbing.

"Aunt Ethel?" I came around the grouping of chairs. When she looked up, I judged her to be in a peaceful mood. The shared grief had been a relief. "We had two more in our memorial audience than you knew about. Mr. Graves and Mr. Spunner joined us from outside the window. They're at the backdoor and would like to pay their respects, if you're up to it."

She looked to Winifred who had straightened and smiled at the words. "I won't keep this one from greeting them, but I would like to ready for bed. Please tell them I appreciate their kindness, but send them home."

She lumbered to the hall and then paused. "And inform Mr. Graves all we have accomplished in the record hunt."

"Yes, Aunt Ethel."

Winifred hurried before me and reached the screen as I passed through the kitchen doorway.

"You sing and play the piano wonderfully, Winnie—much better than me," Sean was quick to say. "Will you practice each evening so I may hear you when I collect the milk bottle? I'd happily listen to you every day."

"Then I'll do it for you, Sean. Tomorrow I'll play and sing for your dear little Easton friends. What hymns do they like?"

"Rebecca was always singing Christmas carols."

"Then I'll fill the air with the Christmas spirit though it's three months before the day. It's the least I can do to help you through your pain when you've been so attentive to ours."

I stood beside my cousin and looked into the night. "Aunt Ethel sends her thanks, but is overly tired. Get the milk bottle, Winnie, and we'll say goodnight."

We said our farewells to Bartholomew and Sean and watched them disappear into the dark.

Seventeen

Winifred woke me the next morning as she rummaged around the bedroom.

"Did you sleep well?" I asked.

She smiled and continued arranging her hair in a loose bun. "Yes, and I dreamt of Sean. We were walking along the bay with Tippet as our chaperone. Of course, that meant we could kiss as often as we liked." She giggled.

I ignored her brazen confession and crept down the hall. Aunt Ethel was asleep, complete with a light snore, proving the medicine had worked.

When I emerged from the bathroom, Winifred was already gone. I pulled on my brown skirt and buttoned my puffed-sleeved shirtwaist on the way down the stairs to save time. The kitchen lights were off and my bare feet across the tiles allowed me to enter the dark porch unannounced. Winifred stood on the stoop, hands on her hips.

"I told you I'm fine." She spoke to Sean with a saucy tone.

"It's just, I—"

"What could be more important on the opinion of how I'm feeling than my own self?"

"I had a dream last night. You were—"

"I dreamt of us too!" She grabbed his hands. "We were playing at the bay. Tippet chased us as we ran together, holding hands. It was glorious."

"I hope to do that with you some day, Winnie dearest." He kissed her knuckles before releasing his hands from her grasp.

"But not today." She folded her arms and turned away—looking directly at me on the porch. She shrieked and then laughed. "Merri, you gave me a fright! I feared it was Aunt Ethel at first, but she wouldn't be wearing white."

I advanced to the door. "My wardrobe is limited."

"Since you're here, you can collect the milk from Sean. I don't fancy speaking to someone who doesn't think I can talk intelligently about my own feelings." She opened the screen and disappeared into the house.

Sean moved back a few feet when I exited.

"I'm sorry I upset her."

"It was a disappointment compared to her fanciful dream. She'll be over it in no time."

"She wouldn't let me explain." Sean looked down as he moved the toe of his boot through the grass. "I have these dreams every so often. I didn't understand until after the second time it happened."

"What dreams?"

"Warnings. I saw my granny die in one, and years later, my parents. Megan thinks I have the second sight, like an Irish witch."

My knees buckled, but Sean took my elbow and helped me to sit on the step. I caught my breath then looked up at him with visions of the raging creek that took my other cousin in my mind. "What happened to Winifred?"

Sean jabbed his boot into the lawn. "This grass is getting too tall. You'll have snakes moving in. Not to mention more mosquitoes."

"Sean, the dream."

"That yardman isn't coming back. He was old anyway. I'll cut it myself this evening and find you a new boy once you lose the yellow flag."

"Sean Spunner, if you don't tell—"

"The fever." His voice cracked. "She was burning with it and delirious, but you were with her, comforting her how you could."

"And Aunt Ethel?"

"Just you, but I came and did what I could as well. You had her down here on the porch. There was a pallet against the interior wall. You were doing the washing, burning, and cooking. Everything."

My eyes widened. "Where was Aunt Ethel? Keziah?"

"I don't know. I'm sorry, Merri."

"I'm glad you didn't explain to Winifred." Not heeding my own advice, I took his hand. "Please don't tell her."

"She'll see the truth in my eyes eventually." He squeezed my hand. "Don't let Winnie play out here until I cut the grass."

I promised I wouldn't and collected the milk on my way inside.

Winifred pounced as soon as I was in the kitchen. "What nonsense did he tell you?"

"Nothing whatever."

"You exchanged several words."

"But Sean doesn't speak nonsense. Haven't you told me that yourself?"

Winnifred turned with a huff and flopped onto the settee in the parlor as Keziah came down the stairs.

"Good morning, Miss Merritt. I take it the milk is here."

"Yes, Keziah. Did you notice Aunt Ethel about?"

"She's still sleeping like a baby. I'll have breakfast ready in an hour."

***

Before Sean arrived that afternoon, I had to chase Winifred inside. She'd taken Tippet into the yard but didn't meet any snakes as Sean feared, though she did collect several welts from mosquito bites. Winifred forgot her annoyance with Sean and happily played Christmas tunes while he mowed the lawn before supper. I sat near the parlor doorway, where I could hear a visitor come to the back door while keeping an eye out the window across from me. Periodically, Sean passed as he pushed the long handle of the grass cutter. Winifred watched him until he was out of sight, scratching at her bites in between hymns.

Aunt Ethel slouched on the settee. Still exhausted from grief, she barely passed another medical inspection by Dr. Sherard. Nausea over Sean's words from the morning swept me. What would Aunt Ethel do if Winifred took ill? She was missing from Sean's premonition. Was she ill as well or locked in an asylum?

In a lull between Christmas carols, Sean whistled an Irish tune as he strode past the window, Tippet bounding behind him.

"I do hope Mr. Dudley comes back," Aunt Ethel said.

"Sean doesn't think he will," I replied. "But he'll find you a new yardman once we're out of quarantine."

"I don't need that rascal poking his nose around here anymore than I need his uncle taking over my business affairs."

"Mr. Graves advises us to accept all help from Mr. Finnigan and Sean. He's worried about you, Aunt Ethel, and has confidence in their support."

She sighed. "I do respect Mr. Graves's opinion, but—"

Winifred exuberantly pounded out "Hark! The Herald Angels Sing" on the piano to silence our aunt. She followed it with a rousing rendition of "O Come, All Ye Faithful," to which she sang along.

Throughout supper, Winifred kept her head cocked toward the window, and our aunt stayed silent as she picked at the chicken and greens.

"May I stretch my legs in the yard?" Winifred asked Aunt Ethel as soon as she finished everything on her plate.

"Not alone."

"Tippet is outside."

"A dog is not a chaperone."

Winifred's blue eyes sparked with what I knew to be the memory of her dream. She urged me to eat faster, but I kept to my regular pace.

When we carried our dishes into the kitchen, Keziah motioned to the counter. "The milk bottle is there. You'll find your young man on the stoop, enjoying some of my cornbread and a glass of tea."

Winifred skipped out with the bottle, a peculiar sight of jubilance in mourning garb.

"Walk with me, Sean Francis Spunner."

Sean bowed and motioned her to choose the path they would take about the yard. He mirrored her steps from a two foot distance and I trailed them, Tippet at my side.

"Your music was invigorating. I wasn't expecting to hear the Christmas songs. Have you forgiven me, Winnie?"

"I could never stay mad at you." The smile she turned on him was glowing. She touched his forearm below his rolled shirtsleeve and he drew instinctively closer, quickly kissing her ear before resuming their distanced stroll.

Within a few minutes, Sean took the lead, keeping them out from under much of the tree canopy and away from the foliage as twilight turned to dusk. I shadowed them for quarter of an hour, noting Sean's protective ways while he chatted about poetry. He only touched her to take her arm when she went too close to the bushes.

She scratched a bite on her wrist and Sean stopped his speech on Edgar Allan Poe to question her. "When did you get those mosquito bites?"

"I was only at the bench with Tippet for a minute this afternoon before Merri forced me indoors."

"For the sake of all things holy, Winnie, keep away from thick shade and don't scratch the bites you already have!"

It was the sharpest tone I'd ever heard him use. I recognized the fear, but Winifred only registered the admonishing. Her lip trembled as she turned to him.

Sean immediately softened his voice and took her wrist. "Dearest, you're the sweet thing ever—to man or beast. The mosquitos can't resist you any more than I can. Don't allow the bugs an opportunity to feast. It isn't healthy to get so many bites. Remember Dr. Nott?"

"I remember everything you say, Sean."

"Then apply the knowledge, you stubborn creature." Sean kissed the top of her head.

As though sensing Sean's time was coming to an end, Tippet went to him. He rested a hand on the dog's head as they made their way to the back stoop. Sean's dishes were cleared and he retrieved the milk bottle before turning to us.

"Thank you for chaperoning, Merri. I look forward to seeing you both tomorrow. Stay out of trouble, Winnie."

"Anything for you."

Sean's grin filled his face, but it didn't reach his eyes. Fear was settled in the amber depths, and it made my blood chill.

Eighteen

It was another peaceful night for Aunt Ethel, and Winifred suffered no ghostly dreams about Nancy. After breakfast, I set Winifred to accomplish her daily schoolwork in the parlor and entered Uncle Andrew's study to finish going through the bookshelves. Since the section with the store ledgers was complete, I was left with a bookcase of random nonfiction with a few novels mixed in. I started at the top of the five shelves and pulled out each volume, flipping through the books to make sure no important papers were stashed within the pages.

Biographies and religious texts accounted for most of the first shelf. I marked with slips a few volumes that would be a good fit for Winifred's education. Halfway across the second shelf, my cousin pranced into the room.

"I completed the history studies, Merri. May I help you?"

I glanced at the clock. "I want you reading for another hour. You've lost a lot of education time this week with all the work you've helped with already."

"Then may I read from the book Sean left this morning?"

Pausing a moment at the thought of her impressionable mind being subjected to the flirtations of *Daisy Miller*, I decided it would keep her engrossed and out of physical trouble. "Don't let Aunt Ethel catch you reading Henry James."

"She's in the parlor. I'll read on the back porch."

As Winifred went for the kitchen, I paused in the entry to the sitting room. Aunt Ethel was in her husband's armchair, staring at his cavalry photograph on the side table. She appeared peaceful, so I turned back to the study.

I worked without interruption and soon found myself reaching for an unmarked book. It was slightly taller than its neighbors though the thin spine left no room for words. Filled with illustrations, the book struck me as odd compared to the rest of my uncle's collection. Then the subject of the visuals registered, and I knew the omission of a title was purposeful.

People.

Without clothing.

Naked male and female couples connected in more ways than I ever dreamed possible. I had been told the basics about coupling, but nothing like what those images showed!

Was it shock that kept me turning the pages or curiosity?

When I got to the end of it, I hugged the volume to my beating breast. The tantalizing drawings of beautiful depravation had my body tingling. I needed it out of the house to safeguard Winifred against this awakening, but who would help me?

Bartholomew?

Wrapped in an erotic embrace with—certainly not when just thinking of him with those pictures set my face burning. He was trustworthy, but this book was a different matter. I didn't want those acts in his mind—especially linked with me. Though his capable hands touching…oh, I was a fallen woman now with such ideas. Winifred must never see them!

I couldn't start a fire in the house as it was still too hot for all but the cooking stove, and using the burn barrel would only cause questions.

Dr. Sherard wouldn't be embarrassed by naked bodies, but he already lorded over us. The book would give him more power to wound Aunt Ethel, for he was not discreet with her feelings.

Sean!

Surely an imp like him was already subjected to the ways of the world. It would be no shock to him to know of the book's existence, except for the fact that it was in the Allens' home. Sean was my only hope to dispose of it.

I tucked it on the top shelf and completed my search—haphazardly shaking books and not bothering to mark any more of interest.

Crouched on the floor as I searched the bottom shelf, I jerked when Winifred touched my shoulder.

"I didn't mean to scare you, Merri. Dinner is ready."

I nodded and stood. "I didn't hear you come in. Where are your boots?"

"Since I'm not allowed in the yard, I didn't bother to put them back on after removing them to curl up to read."

I wiped the dust from my hands on the underside of the apron. "How is the story?"

"Delicious! I can't help but think of Megan Finnigan and those Easton twins causing such stirs on their European travels." She paused in the hall. "Sean assured me I would be prime pickings for men over there looking for a quick romance. I doubt I'll ever get to travel before marriage, but I hope to see the world afterward. It would be safer to do so with a husband than a chaperone at any rate. No offense to you, Merri, but I think European men would be too smooth for even your level head. They're well-versed in sweeping women off their feet."

"A continent full of Sean Spunners? There would be a plethora of swooning."

Winifred giggled. "It's a glorious thought, don't you think?"

"I believe one young man like Sean is all the world could handle." I left my cousin smiling in the doorway and crossed the parlor to collect Aunt Ethel. "Dinner is on the table."

She closed her eyes and slouched. "I'm not hungry."

I looked to the mantel clock. "It's a quarter past noon, Aunt Ethel. You need to eat a little bit of something since you didn't take more than half a piece of toast at breakfast and we'll need to give a truthful report to Dr. Sherard when he arrives."

"I wish that man would leave us in peace."

"He's concerned about you. We all are. I'll see you to the dining room now."

Aunt Ethel held my arm on the way to the table. I tried not to notice the way her hand trembled or the jerky movement of her head when the sound of an empty tray clattering to the kitchen floor rang through the house.

Winifred kept quiet as she ate, and I was happy to see at least one of us had her full appetite. I swallowed half my usual amount of grits and fried okra while watching my aunt aimlessly stir her grits. She only took two bites but drank all her tea.

As we finished the midday meal, the doorbell rang. Winifred didn't bother to answer it as Sean never used the front entrance, and Aunt Ethel was unmoving. I went for the door myself.

"Good afternoon, Dr. Sherard."

"How is your aunt today, Miss Hall?" He stepped into the foyer and looked at me with his condescending gaze.

"Much the same, though she does sleep at night. We have enough medication for one more dose."

"Tomorrow is the pivotal day, but it's good she's lasted this long."

I motioned to the dining room. "We just finished dinner. Aunt Ethel is still at the table."

Winifred had conveniently disappeared. Dr. Sherard noted the full bowl before my aunt and shook his head. "Food, Mrs. Allen, is necessary if you want to have strength for your nieces."

"Nothing tastes right anymore."

"Like it or not, it must be consumed. Add more salt or pepper if you must." The doctor set the shakers beside her dish and watched her dutifully add more seasoning to the grits. "Now try it."

Holding the spoon limp in her hand, she scooped and raised the now tepid and lumpy meal to her mouth. She swallowed and her spoon clanged to the place setting.

"Mrs. Allen, I must—"

Aunt Ethel rose from the chair, fists on the table. "I am not a child, Dr. Sherard. I am a grown woman who has the right to grieve when her husband of thirty-one years is taken from her."

He took a step back. "Naturally, but—"

Aunt Ethel placed a hand on her middle. "My solid form assures me I will not waste away in a matter of days. I'll eat when I feel like it, not at your command."

"Very well." He drew his shoulders back and nodded to me. I followed him to the front door. "Be sure she receives the sleeping draught tonight. I shall return to see if she will stay or be sent away, Miss Hall."

"Yes, Dr. Sherard."

As soon as he was gone, I rushed to my aunt. She still stood beside the table.

"I should have scolded him days ago. I'll take no orders from anyone who isn't my Andrew. Wake me for supper."

Winifred and I climbed the stairs behind Aunt Ethel. I settled on the chair in the corner of the porch with a lap board to pen a letter to my mother. It was my fourth note since the quarantine. Though no mail was coming or going from the city, I wanted a record of everything to share with her whenever I could send word.

After two pages, I decided to rest on my bed. Tippet raised his head, and then Winifred leaned over to get a better look from her nest in the hammock.

"Join me if you wish," I called to both.

Tippet pattered over and with one snap of my fingers, jumped onto the foot of the bed. He circled three times before curling into himself with a pleased moan—the padding a luxury to his old joints.

I reached down to scritch behind his ear. "Good boy, Tippet. Enjoy yourself."

Stretched out properly for the first time in days, tightness in my shoulders and neck I didn't realize I had loosened with the support of the solid surface beneath me. Tippet shifted and rested his head on my foot.

My mind drifted. Images from Uncle Andrew's forbidden book undulated in a hypnotic orgy of sensual delight. I never had a beau or even been given a stolen kiss on the lips, but a base carnal memory I shared with humanity stirred deep within. Until that day, I had accepted my lot in life as a spinster without bitterness. Now, I ached for companionship. Craving to experience love—physical and emotional—I shifted my legs and folded my hands on my stomach. Thoughts of being filled with the seed of a lover and experiencing the growth of womanhood brought forth the image of Bartholomew Graves.

Our moments in the stable during the storm and in the dark of the porch were chaste, but now that I knew the possibilities between a man and a woman, I reimagined those private minutes in a passionate light—and the world seemed a beautiful place despite the shadow of yellow fever.

***

Winifred roused me from my scandalous slumber at five o'clock. I washed the sleep from my face, set my hair into a chignon, and redressed. Aunt Ethel and Winifred were already in the parlor. *Daisy Miller* was on the corner of the grand piano and my cousin played a Beethoven piece off the sheet music before her.

"You look rested," I told Aunt Ethel as I took the space beside her. "Your coloring is improved."

"And there's a rosy glow about you, Merritt. I hope you haven't been too overworked."

Heat burned my cheeks at the memory of my dreams. "I have plenty of energy, Aunt Ethel."

We listened to Winifred's playing until the tinkling of the dinner bell sounded above the soft chords.

Aunt Ethel took my cousin's arm and walked with her to the dining room. "I do love to hear you play. I haven't the heart for it myself these days, but music does soothe the pain."

Smiling, Winifred kissed her cheek. "I'm glad you find peace with the music."

If I focused on my cousin and aunt, supper appeared to be a near-cheerful meal. But internally, anxiety plagued me—or rather my uncle's book tormented me. How to get a private word with Sean was my highest priority of the evening. As soon as he arrived for the milk bottle, Winifred wouldn't leave his presence without being forced, but I couldn't make it too obvious I had a secret to share because she would dig until she found the truth.

I worried all the way through the banana pudding.

Winifred happily played and sang "It Came Upon a Midnight Clear" while I carried the last tray of dinner dishes into the kitchen for Keziah. Through the open door, Sean waved from the back step. I rushed out before Tippet could sense his arrival and give the welcoming bark that would signal to Winifred her sweetheart was there.

Sean jumped out of my way when I barreled out the screen door. Without question, he jogged after me until I stopped in the stable. I leaned against an empty stall and caught my breath before speaking.

"I need your help with something, but Winifred can never find out about it."

Gaze intense, he gave a solemn nod. "I'd do anything for you, Merritt Hall."

"You have to swear to me, Sean."

"I swear on my life, Merritt." He crossed himself. "What is it?"

"Uncle Andrew had a naughty book in his collection." I rushed out the words. "I need it out of the house before Winnie or Aunt Ethel finds it. Winnie would be ruined and Aunt Ethel severely pained to know her husband had such a secret."

To his credit, Sean didn't laugh. He even managed to keep his smile mostly hidden. "It was a shock finding something like that, wasn't it?"

I nodded.

"Poor, Merri. I bet you immediately flung it—" He must have seen the guilty look on my face for a chuckle slipped out. "You looked! That's nothing to be upset over. You're curious. All of us are at some point in our lives."

Hand clutching at an empty feed sack hanging by the stall, I held back my embarrassment as I shared the truth. "I couldn't stop looking. It was debauched, but I never knew coupling was so engaging. I wasn't told the half of it."

Sean momentarily bit his lip, eyes wide. "I've seen a few books like that. Basic anatomy and simple sketches of couples."

"There's nothing simple about it. These drawings were scandalously detailed—colored even."

"Color illustrations." Sean whistled. "That must have cost a bundle."

"Sean Spunner, that's not the point. I don't want you running off to sell it if I give it to you. It needs to be kept away—"

"From Winnie. I understand."

Tippet barked from the house.

Not wanting to be caught in the stable with him, I hurried out. "I'll place it in that feed bag before nine tonight. Collect it any time after," I said over my shoulder.

Sean kept pace with me around the yard. "I'll keep it safe."

I knew my words would be dismissed, but I had to speak them for the wellbeing of my soul. "Destroying it would be a better option."

The final strains of "The First Noel" drifted out the open windows of the house as we approached the back porch.

Tippet waited at the screen and I let him out. The dog bounded to Sean in the twilight, followed by Winifred. Sean pulled a peppermint stick out of the handkerchief in his pocket and tossed it to her. I couldn't help smiling over their simple joy of sharing and being together.

Quarter of an hour later, I called to them across the yard. "It's time to go in, Winnie."

Sean accompanied her to the house. "Until tomorrow, dear Winnie."

"Oh, your book!"

Sean and I blanched at her words when she hurried inside. Winifred returned half a minute later with *Daisy Miller,* and I exhaled in relief as Sean smiled.

"Done already? Did you enjoy it?"

"It was clever, though it does make me worry over your cousin and her friends."

He laughed and tucked the book under his arm. "They're well-chaperoned by three respected ladies—one for each of them. Besides, Megan wouldn't do anything without a friend to spur her on, and Cora and Emma would be too worried about scuffing a boot or staining a gown to do anything remotely adventurous. They aren't as fantastically daring as you, Winnie."

She clasped her hands before her and looked up at him. "No climbing trees?"

"Nothing of the sort in the last decade from those three. You must never lose your whimsy."

Winifred blew him a kiss and went inside. The sadness Sean had over his dream the previous day descended on his countenance once more. I handed him the bottle.

"I don't want her to be forever young," he whispered. "She needs to live and mature."

"I'll watch over her. Don't forget your mission tonight."

He flashed a grin. "You'll never know I was here."

Nineteen

The golden glow of sunrise struck my eyelids the moment before Winifred's humming met my ears. Prepping for the day, she tied a jaunty blue ribbon in her hair. It looked ridiculous with her black ensemble, but I didn't say anything.

I set about topping my underclothes with a gingham wash dress. It was completely countrified, but I didn't expect to see anyone other than Sean and Dr. Sherard that day.

A few minutes later, I joined Winifred and Tippet outside the kitchen. My cousin fingered the cobalt bottles hanging in the citrus trees, and Tippet sniffed around the azalea bushes.

Tippet barked his greeting to Sean, who strode to Winifred.

"Here is your milk and a dash of something extra." He passed her the bottle and retrieved what looked like a small pillbox from his pocket. "Pour the contents into a cup of milk and stir it in."

"What will happen?"

"Magic!" He grinned. "It will turn the milk chocolate."

"However is that possible?" She flipped the tin open and sniffed it.

"It's a mix of cocoa powder and sugar. Althea experimented with the recipe to get just the right amount of sweetness. Remember, one cup. Nothing more, nothing less, dear lady."

"I'll do it right now!" Winifred dashed inside.

Sean laughed and turned to me. "How's that for clearing a path to privacy? I figured you'd want a few minutes to follow through with your instructions to me."

"Did you destroy it?"

"I can't destroy a book, especially one that's a work of art. It's more detailed than any other I've seen. I'm keeping it safe in my personal collection."

I opened my mouth to protest, but he cut me off.

"I have an extensive library in my bedroom. Only the housekeeper comes in to tidy things. She'll never notice one book out of hundreds when I'm employing your uncle's mode of secrecy."

Crossing my arms, I scowled at him. "What's that?"

"Hiding it in plain sight. It will be for my eyes only—and maybe a few select friends at the right price."

"Sean Francis Spunner, you're a rotten cad!"

The screen door snapped shut.

"You must try it, Merri." Winifred handed me the glass. "But what has you yelling at Sean?"

"She's been under too much pressure lately. I told her she needs to take time for herself more often. Let down her guard."

I tried to ignore the pull of his tender touch when he stroked my arm. I knew he didn't mean it in the way my body felt it.

"Mr. Graves is coming tomorrow," Sean reminded me. "Allow him to see you like this, simple and carefree without the fuss of puffed sleeves and ruffled collars."

I knocked his hand away and stepped back. "I don't need wishful thinking and romantic notions to cloud my mind. The house is under quarantine—a fact you keep forgetting—and I have my grieving aunt, not to mention her aging cook and my cousin to see to."

"Don't do this to yourself."

"Do what?" I turned for the house.

"Hide yourself away when you have something glorious within your reach." He took me by the shoulders and turned me around. "You were in quarantine long before you arrived here. Don't be afraid to live, Merri. Open yourself to love and adventure."

"I'm the oldest. I have to be the responsible one." A hot tear streaked my face as I forced the memory of the raging creek back into place.

"Your family needs to see you live, not continue in drudgery as if you're serving a life sentence."

"It's what I'm called to do. I can't let them down."

"You won't." Sean took me in a brisk hug that squeezed the breath from me. "You'll be able to do even more for others after you care for yourself."

"But I've failed before." I pulled away and went for the bench.

Winifred sat beside me as I gathered my courage.

"Merri, what can I do to help?" Winifred's hand settled on my back.

"Nothing. Everything Sean said was true. I've failed an aunt and cousin before," I whispered. "Aunt Gladys, Aunt Ethel's youngest sister. She no longer comes to visit—not since that summer seven years ago. That's where my parents and brother went when I came here. Aunt Gladys doesn't like to look at me, so they put me on the train coming here when they left for Mississippi."

"What happened that summer?"

"My cousin died." I sniffed. "They say it wasn't my fault, but I was in charge."

"Seven years ago, you were only—"

"Twelve, but I was the oldest." I straightened with the remembered mantel of responsibility. "Ezra was barely ten, and Diamond was eleven. My mother claims Diamond was naughty, but if I was sterner, she would have obeyed. I should have locked the doors when the rain started back after I heard her bragging to Ezra she could jump the creek. She was always showing off, thinking she was better than us Alabama cousins because her daddy owned more land in Mississippi than we had in our whole town."

"You were just a girl, Merri. How could they expect you to handle a wild one practically your own size?"

"She was bigger than me—taller and stronger. She pushed me to the ground the year before but said if I tattled, she'd tell her mother I started it. Since she was the guest, I never told."

"You must have hated coming here to be stuck with another wicked cousin. They thrust me on you without warning."

"I think this was supposed to be my second chance." I stood and turned away. "Uncle Andrew is dead, and the doctor is looking for any reason to send Aunt Ethel away."

"Uncle Andrew wasn't your fault."

"Dr. Sherard seems to think I'm in charge, giving me the medication to disperse."

"If something happens to Aunt Ethel, it will be the grief, not your improper care. And anything that afflicts me is my fault, not yours. I'm sorry if I've been wicked. I'll be good now, I promise."

"I know you're trying, Winnie, but it's too late." I went to the porch and tied on an apron. I relished the momentary escape the soap flakes and scrubbing board offered—being in control while washing away flaws.

Sean left Winifred at the bench and crossed the yard. I refused to look up from my work when he stopped on the other side of the screened wall.

"I'm sorry if I added to your troubles, Merri," Sean said through the haze of the barrier. "And I'm even sorrier that you didn't feel you could confide in anyone before now. Winnie is devastated for being the means of reliving your pain. Tell me what we can do to help."

I wrung a kitchen towel and lifted it to the sunlight to check for stubborn stains. Seeing nothing amiss, I set it aside and submerged another towel.

Scrubbing commenced.

"We've only known you a few weeks, but she loves you like a sister, Merritt Hall. And like annoying siblings, we'll not leave you alone."

"One obnoxious brother is enough for me, Sean Spunner. And as for a sister, I fear I'd be little use for her."

"The hell you wouldn't!" He gripped the horizontal support beam, rage in his eyes. "And no, I'll not apologize for swearing in front of a lady. Not when the lady is acting addle-brained! You've done nearly as much for Winnie this month as anyone besides her mother has done in her whole lifetime. Don't discredit yourself to those who love you."

I hung my head.

Sean hurried through the door and embraced me. "Merri, can't you see you're no longer that twelve-year-old girl? I knew you were bitter about something, but I had no idea of the pain you carried."

It felt good to cry and be held. I continued on shamelessly. Winifred joined us, quietly rolling her sleeves to finish the washing. Sean kept me in his arms until my tears slowed. Then, he helped me to the cast-off kitchen chair in the corner of the porch.

"You don't need to say anything, but hear me out. I'm going to visit Mr. Graves and let him know of the situation. He's concerned about you and needs to know your pain." Sean dropped to his knees and brought his hands to my face, wiping the residue of the tears with his thumbs on each cheek. "It's nothing to be embarrassed about. You did all you could and there's no blame, but the ones who care about you need to know so we can better support you. And he cares about you, Merri. Don't ignore his efforts or any feelings you might have, all right?"

I managed to nod, and he looked over his shoulder at Winifred wringing the towels.

"Don't watch, Winnie," he called. "I'm going to kiss your cousin."

Sean leaned in, soft lips brushing my cheek before he landed close to the corner of my mouth. "I'll see you this evening."

The tingly sensation running through my body kept me alert to Sean's goodbye with Winifred—which included a hug and kiss of her own. Then she followed him into the yard, pinning the towels to the clothesline after he disappeared.

Upon her return to the porch, she cleaned Tippet's water bowl and took my arm. "Let's eat breakfast."

"I need to check Aunt Ethel. She was still sleeping when I came down."

"I'm seeing to her today," she insisted. "No extra worries for you."

Twenty

After our midday dinner, I sat in the parlor with Aunt Ethel. Her peaceful review of the Allen family scrapbook was interrupted by the chiming of the doorbell.

Winifred, hard at work sweeping the hall, answered the door. "Good afternoon, Dr. Sherard. Aunt Ethel is in the parlor."

He entered the room with a backward glance at Winifred before turning to his patient. "How are you today, Mrs. Allen?"

She set the book on the side table and lifted her pointy chin. "As well as can be expected."

"I'm sure you will all be glad to hear you are halfway through your quarantine. Wednesday you will be free to accept callers or go out, if everyone is still healthy."

Winifred let out a little squeal of delight in the hallway.

Dr. Sherard laughed and smoothed his mustache. "I'm sure I can guess who will be first in line to greet her."

I smiled, knowing the doctor would be mortified if he learned his suspected caller had already hugged and kissed both me and Winifred that morning. I flipped through a magazine while my aunt was inspected, ignoring his baited comments as well as Aunt Ethel did.

"Well," he said as he straightened, "I'd like you to go until Monday without the sleeping draught to see how you do, if you're comfortable with that."

"I never wanted it to begin with."

"We shall see if your demon draught, as you call it, proves to be more heavenly than hellish for you, Mrs. Allen. I will check in with you Monday unless I'm summoned before then."

"Two days without him," I told her as Winifred saw the doctor out. "He must have found you very well."

"Perhaps he's learned not to pester me daily."

That evening, Winifred settled down with a hymnal and played Christmas tunes. Aunt Ethel attempted a cross-stitch sampler but spent more time staring out the window than working. Still, it was progress.

Tippet gave his single bark announcing Sean's arrival, and I followed Winifred onto the kitchen porch. She set the empty bottle on the step and ran into the twilight for a game of tag across the yard. Tippet jumped and barked at both. A few minutes later, Winifred took refuge with me by the citrus trees. Sean fell to the ground before us. He had lost his hat and Tippet licked his face.

"Not now, Tip." Sean laughed and pushed the dog away so he could sit up. "I have an important message to deliver."

My cousin smiled and watched every movement Sean made as he stood and straightened his clothing. He slapped his derby against his leg before setting it on his head.

Sean's grin was as wide as his hat brim. "Mr. Graves sends his thoughts and prayers for the inhabitants of the Allen home. He has advertised that the store will be closed tomorrow and plans to arrive here at nine in the morning to discuss business matters with Mrs. Allen, though he hopes to see Misses Merritt and Winifred as well. Mr. Graves also asked that, should my schedule allow, for me to stop by midday and see if there are any messages that need to be carried to the appropriate persons. I assured him I will be happy to do so."

"That all sounds fine, doesn't it, Merritt? Maybe Mr. Graves would stay for dinner. Let me go ask Aunt—"

"We can't host anyone in the house."

"But we could have a picnic. The weather's been cooler and it would be lovely to sit under the trees. He could have his own blanket." She rushed inside before I could protest further.

"I suppose Aunt Ethel will have to come outside to speak with him anyway." I looked to Sean. "Winnie will invite you too, if she has her way."

"I'd be happy to come—if I'm invited." He winked. "As for Mr. Graves, his unspoken message was one of deep concern for you. Be sure to grant him a private audience tomorrow, Merri."

"Is he expecting to kiss me since you did?"

He looked to the grass, blushing. "I didn't tell him about that. Mr. Graves may look as placid as his name, but he's strong from lifting supplies at the store. I don't want to give him an excuse to knock me flat."

I laughed, causing Tippet to come to me, and then sobered at the thought of another recent concern. "Did you tell him about the book?"

"That's our special secret." Sean squeezed my hand a moment before stepping back. "Even among those who might eventually see it, no one will ever know where I acquired it."

Smiling with relief, I scratched behind Tippet's ear.

Sean bit his lip and watched Winifred exit the house. I could imagine the thoughts he had—visions of Winifred in positions like the women in the book. But there was no greed in his stare, only love.

"We shall welcome Mr. Graves in the yard tomorrow morning for business, followed by a picnic dinner," Winifred announced. "Aunt Ethel leaves it to us to decide on the placement of chairs and other needed things. And there will be room for you, Sean."

"With your aunt's permission?"

She gazed into his eager face and smiled. "That will be forthcoming."

***

In the dead of night, I startled awake from a shuffling sound in the bedroom. A pale figure stared onto the porch from the doorway. Sitting upright, I gasped in alarm. Tippet sat up but didn't growl.

Aunt Ethel.

Crossing to her, I reached out a hand. "What is it? Do you need help?"

She tucked her arm around mine and led me into the room so we wouldn't disturb Winifred.

"Why do you girls still sleep outside when the nights are cooler?" She clutched my arm and in the dim light coming from the hall, I noticed the anxiety in her gaze.

"We like hearing the frogs and cicadas. And if we talk too much before sleep, it won't bother you or Keziah."

"Then you aren't scared? Winifred doesn't fear anything?"

I opened my mouth to speak, but she continued.

"I feel something in here." She motioned around the room with her free hand. "A restless resentment is festering."

"Winnie often has nightmares. Apparently, they were worse when she slept inside."

"Go back to Winifred. I trust you to keep her safe."

"I'm trying, Aunt Ethel, but I don't know if I can."

"Diamond was a thousand times naughtier than Winifred, if that's what you're concerned about. Gladys spoiled her, and her father's people were as uppity as they come, a disastrous combination." She hugged me. "And you were a meek soul. Gladys and Octavia were to blame for leaving you with her. Yes, Octavia too. Your mother isn't innocent. If you've felt guilty all this time it's because those women allowed you to do so in an attempt to appease their own responsibility in the accident."

"My mother always told me not to worry—that it wasn't my fault," I said around a welling lump in my throat.

Aunt Ethel shook her head. "But she didn't tell you to place the blame from your shoulders onto her own. You never gave it away, not even to the Lord."

"I try to let it go."

"You need to, Merritt. Life will be gone before you know it and carrying a burden like that is no way to live."

She swiftly went for the door and disappeared into her own room. I stood looking after her until Tippet whined from the porch. A check on my cousin proved her slumbering so I climbed back into my hammock, mulling over Aunt Ethel's words until the sky lightened.

Dressing silently, I took Sean's advice and pulled on a simple calico work dress rather than one of my fashionable—and stiff—shirtwaists. As the day before, I wore no corset, only a full-length chemise and my underdrawers. I brushed through my hair and twisted it into a loose bun. Aunt Ethel and Winifred slept on, so I brought Tippet with me to the kitchen.

Sean was already on the back step, sitting with his head down. I gave Tippet the hand signal my father used when hunting to keep him from barking. When we got to the screen, I heard the young man crying. Unable to witness him suffering, I unhooked the latch, let the dog out, and dropped onto the wide stoop beside Sean. My arm was immediately around him. He turned to me without shame, crying on my shoulder.

"Did the fever claim another of your Easton friends?" I asked once his crying stopped.

"Peter *and* Aaron. There'll be no more games in that yard after this loss. Lucy is still down with the fever, but appears to be making a recovery. I pray she does. The Eastons have already lost so much."

I smoothed his hair as though he were a little boy. "I'll pray for her too, Sean."

"She's thirteen, the oldest of the ones at home since Eddie is at boarding school. She's just as likely to be up a tree or running with the boys. Two Halloweens ago, she got me with molasses, feathers, and flour."

"When this fever business is over, you can introduce her to Winnie."

"They'd get along swell." He wiped his eyes. "I don't want Winnie to see me upset, but tell her I'll stop in before noon like we discussed."

"I will." I smiled up at him when he stood.

"Thank you for allowing me the use of your shoulder. You look extra pretty today, Merri. The print on your dress brings color to your face." Sean leaned over and left a peck on my cheek. "So does a kiss."

"You're still a rascal, even when you're being sweet."

He winked, scratched Tippet behind his ears, and was gone.

Winifred didn't come down until Keziah was cooking breakfast. My cousin flopped beside me on the settee, and I closed the book I was reading.

"Did you see Sean?"

"Yes."

"Why didn't you wake me?"

"Because you need sleep, and he didn't wish you to see him upset. The two Easton boys passed away, but he said he'll be back before noon and looks forward to seeing you then."

Aunt Ethel arrived in time for breakfast looking almost like her typical self, though still a tad too pale.

After eating, Winifred and I set out four dining chairs amid the satsuma trees. Winifred, who had no interest in the business talk, would ready the luncheon area for the midday dinner.

The sound of the gate opening sent Tippet running around the house and my heart fluttering. I calmly went toward the driveway, pausing to shut the gate while the dog followed the buggy into the stable.

"Good morning." I stayed in the doorway feeling woefully underdressed before his brown day suit.

"Miss Merritt." He nodded and seemed to take in the length of me with a sweeping glance.

I reached for the bucket hanging on the wall. "I'll fetch the water for the horse."

He crossed the space in a second, reaching for it himself. "Allow me. I know my way around here as well as anything."

Not wishing to trail him, I waited while he set Uncle Andrew's horse with feed and water. He retrieved a satchel from the buggy seat and then a crate of supplies. I turned to leave and he followed, carrying the goods from the store.

"I'd offer my arm if I could."

Smiling, I lowered my head. "Four more days of quarantine. We're to sit together in the little grove near the kitchen for you to discuss things with Aunt Ethel."

Bartholomew stayed a few steps to my right, both of us glancing sideways as we made our way around the yard.

"I'm glad to see you looking well, Merritt." He stopped walking, and I paused too. "I hope it's all right that I've been asking Mr. Spunner for a daily update. Not just of the household, but of you."

"Sean said as much, and it's brought me comfort this week. Thank you for your concern."

"You mean you're happy I'm asking about you?"

His gaze burned me in such a way I could no longer ignore him.

"Yes, Bartholomew. I'm pleased you care. I've enjoyed your company since we were introduced." My face warmed with the admission.

"You've brought me much happiness, Merritt."

Winifred ran to us. Seeing his smile, she giggled. "I hope I didn't interrupt anything. Aunt Ethel said to get her when Mr. Graves arrives, but if you two need a few—"

"You may tell her he's here," I said quickly. After she scampered off with the message and Bartholomew's delivery, I started for the chairs. "You'll be invited to stay for dinner. Winifred is helping Keziah plan a picnic."

Bartholomew kept pace with me. His smile caused me to want to laugh and sing and run. It was no wonder Winifred and Sean were so boisterous around each other if this is what they felt. I forced the energy in my legs to hold steady as I led us the last dozen feet.

"This one is for you." I motioned to the chair furthest apart.

"Thank you." He leaned his satchel against the chair and stood beside it.

Only when Aunt Ethel and I were seated beneath the bottle trees did he do the same.

"We've found no will." Aunt Ethel clasped her hands in her lap and got straight to business. "Did you?"

"I'm afraid not, but that might be something he had his lawyer keep."

"It appears Mr. Crawley is out of town indefinitely," Aunt Ethel said. "What can we do?"

"You need to take Mr. Finnigan up on his offer, Mrs. Allen. I took the liberty of asking Mr. Spunner to stop by later this morning in case we should need his assistance with messages. I believe you should request Mr. Finnigan to step in on your behalf and secure your husband's file from Mr. Crawley's office."

She shook her head. "Begging a Catholic is not something I wish to do."

"You needn't beg, Aunt Ethel," I said. "Mr. Finnigan has already offered those very things in friendship."

"I've never said more than two words to that man."

"Then it's high time you did." Bartholomew's tone was respectful though it carried authority. "You have requested my help—which I gladly give—but I can do nothing for you on the legal front. You need a professional, a man who has the right connections, and that's Mr. Finnigan."

"Fine. When that boy shows up, send him away with the message."

"It needs to come from your lips, Mrs. Allen," he reminded her. "I have no power to do your bidding other than at the store."

"And how was that this week? Is business good during this fever crisis?"

"Things slowed a few days after the news of Mr. Allen's illness, but it's back to normal."

"Closing on a Saturday can't be good."

"Seeing the paperwork and legalities through is more important than a day's income." He inclined his head and softened his tone. "It will all work for the best, Mrs. Allen, and I'll do what I can for you in the meantime."

Aunt Ethel sniffed into her handkerchief. "I don't know what I'd do without the two of you. I know I've been blessed though my Andrew was taken away. Now, Merritt, run in and get the list of papers you found in the study and we can compare with what was at the store."

When I got to the back steps, I heard my aunt's voice behind me. "Haven't I always told you she's a treasure, Mr. Graves?"

"Yes, and she is."

Smiling, I hurried past Winifred's preparations in the kitchen and collected the master list from my uncle's desk.

"I'll bring out tea in a few minutes," Winifred told me on my way back outside.

Bartholomew and Aunt Ethel sat in silence. He stood— smiling—when I returned. Passing him the paper, I sank onto the chair and willed myself to stay calm when I wanted to throw my arms about him as wantonly as Winifred did to Sean. Bartholomew cared for me! I had hoped so for weeks, but there was no denying his affections when he looked upon me like no one ever had in my life. Nor did I want such regard from anyone but Bartholomew Graves.

As he read my list, I plucked a leaf from the nearest satsuma tree. The oblong smoothness of the green kept me from reaching out to Bartholomew. I imagined the veins of the leaf were tendons of his hands that rippled with each movement beneath his skin as he held the paper. Would I ever find out if his fingertips were smooth or calloused? I never understood what is was like to crave a touch, but now it consumed my every thought.

Bartholomew's gaze met mine. A momentary glint of sun off his glasses sparked a fire that ignited a trail to mine. How did I breathe before today without this connection?

"Well, Mr. Graves?" Aunt Ethel urged. "Is all the information you need about the store there? You look upon Merritt as if she forgot something."

"Miss Merritt is thorough and her penmanship is neat. I would like to see the ledgers from a year ago to compare sales with our current market."

Glad to expel my energy, I was on my feet in an instant and went for the house.

Soon, Bartholomew sipped a glass of tea as he looked over the daily reports from September 1896. Aunt Ethel held her cup silently, eyes closed. I left the grouping when Winifred came out with an armful of blankets and followed her to the shade of the oak further back in the yard.

"We'll each get our own blanket," she explained as she deposited the load on the bench. "Aunt Ethel said she's too old to eat on the ground, so she'll have this seat. Sean gets the yellow one, and I'd like the blue. You may choose between the other two which you prefer for yourself and Mr. Graves."

"Couldn't you and I share? It'll be one less to clean up afterward."

Winifred shrugged. "If I sit on the side closest to Sean's blanket and—"

"We will all be within easy talking distance. Besides, Sean doesn't even have an invitation yet."

"That's forthcoming." She took a red blanket from the stack and marched back to the house.

Twenty-one

As Bartholomew finished his study of the ledger, Sean whistled his way up the sidewalk. Winifred left the jars in which she was arranging flowers and ran for the gate.

"Winifred Alene Ramsay!" Aunt Ethel's use of her full name brought Winifred's dash to a respectable stroll, and she stopped several feet from the fence.

Bartholomew looked to his pocket watch. "Half past ten. He's early."

"Come in!" Winifred called.

Sean entered the gate and gave Winifred a jaunty bow, keeping his hat in his hand as he followed her to our gathering.

"Good morning." Sean greeted us with a smile. "How might I be of assistance today, Mrs. Allen?"

"We have yet to locate a copy of my husband's will. Do you think that would be something in his file at Mr. Crawley's office?"

"Most assuredly, Mrs. Allen," Sean answered. "Is that the only thing you need?"

She looked to Bartholomew.

"The store records are in order, as well as the household accounts," he said.

"Then you're in better standing than many people who find themselves in this situation. I'll go to my uncle now so things can be acquired as soon as possible."

"On a Saturday?" Aunt Ethel questioned.

"On any day for a widow in need, Mrs. Allen. You and your nieces must be seen to, the sooner the better." He returned his hat to his head.

"Mr. Spunner, another moment of your time." Aunt Ethel spoke in a wavering voice. "We are to picnic at noon with Mr. Graves. You are welcome to join us."

"Thank you, Mrs. Allen. I hope my circumstances allow a speedy return." He flashed a wicked grin at Winifred before exiting the yard.

"That boy will be the death of me." Aunt Ethel shook her head.

Smiling, I snapped my fingers. Tippet was immediately at my side. "I'm going to walk him around the yard to stretch my legs," I announced.

"Do you mind company?" Bartholomew's warm gaze was expectant.

"Not at all." I turned to my aunt. "Do you need anything while I'm up?"

"No, dear. Enjoy your stroll."

Bartholomew left his suit jacket hanging over the back of his chair and allowed me to set the pace. Tippet walked between us, something I'd never known him to do. Perhaps dogs could feel connections between people and he was jealous. I grabbed the next stick we passed, hurling it toward the driveway.

Tippet caught up with us before we turned into the shadowed walk between the bush-lined fence and the stable. Bartholomew took the stick and tossed it straight ahead, and then fell behind me for the narrow path. Rather than run back through the azalea bushes, Tippet waited at the end of the building for us to emerge.

Before I reached the corner, Bartholomew brushed my shoulder with his hand. His light touch sent a quiver through my soul.

"Merritt, would you be opposed to me calling on you this Wednesday evening?" He stepped back when I turned to him.

"When our quarantine is over?"

Nodding, his dimples flashed with a shy grin. "I have a hankering to hold your hand. Would you allow me to do so when I call?"

The silliest of smiles filled my face, but I managed to speak. "Yes, Bartholomew. I think I'd like that very much."

I could only image I'd enjoy holding hands with Bartholomew because I had wanted to embrace him since he arrived. Hug him and more, as I battled the residue of thoughts planted in my mind from that book. His tall body would—

"Are you all right?" he asked.

I blushed as I returned my eyes from perusing his form to looking at his face. "Yes."

"I felt as though you laid me bare."

"Don't worry, everything was fine." I heated further and rushed for Tippet before Bartholomew could process my words.

He caught up to me when I was beyond the oak in the farthest corner of the yard. I felt his previous caress on my shoulder like a brand and refused to turn around.

"Merritt, you're the most alluring creature I've ever met. Watching you these past weeks without being able to express myself and waiting for word of your safety has been torturous."

I stepped to the oak and put a steadying hand on the trunk, watching a wood ant scurry through the crags rather than look at the man who spoke to me.

After a minute of silence, he spoke again. "Have I offended you with my declaration?"

"No." I gathered my courage and raised my head to Bartholomew's earnest gaze. "I'm not as bound to sensibilities as my aunt, though neither am I as uninhibited as my cousin. You will find me firmly in the middle, naïve but expectant for all the glories of courtship. If I seem aloof it's because I don't know how to trust these feelings. I think they're strong enough to break the chain tethering me to reality, and I'm unsure if I can be entrusted with the power. Does that make sense to you?"

His smile was one of relief as he laughed. "I feel similar concerns. I'll tread carefully."

Bartholomew and I resettled in our respected chairs under the satsuma trees with Tippet lying in the grass between us. Aunt Ethel gave us a knowing look that almost caused a guilty blush. As though unsure what to say, Bartholomew picked up the year-old ledger and flipped through the pages.

Winifred carried her flower jars to the chosen picnic spot beneath the oak and spread three blankets before the bench. Each blanket and the iron seat received a jar before she ran back to the house. She returned to the yellow blanket with four more jars and arranged them in an arch across Sean's space.

"A girl shouldn't be so obvious about her affections," Aunt Ethel remarked. "She's much too young to be serious about a suitor, especially one I'll never approve of."

"Winnifred is trying to cheer up Sean because two of his friends passed away yesterday," I replied.

"Yellow Jack?"

"Yes, the third loss from the Easton family."

Aunt Ethel sighed. "It's a terrible season."

"New Orleans has it worse," Bartholomew remarked. "Their numbers in the newspaper are higher than anywhere else, including Mississippi."

"What towns?" I asked. News of the outside world and thoughts of my family's safety caused a wave of unease. "My parents and brother were headed to Jackson for a visit when I came here."

"Just the coastal ones have reports. Scranton, Biloxi, Gulfport."

"I'm sure they're fine," Aunt Ethel remarked. "Gladys never mentioned any fever issues in all her years there."

"I know it's difficult, but try not to worry," Bartholomew said.

"Do you have family nearby?" I asked.

"Not anymore. The last of my family, an uncle and cousin, moved last year from McIntosh Bluff to Texas, where my mother went to live with my older sister after Pa died. That's when I decided to move towards the city. I had enough saved to relocate and tide me over until I found work. Your uncle hired me straight off because my family ran the general store up north. I was raised doing it all from sweeping floors to loading supplies. Once I finished schooling, they put me on the ledgers because that was their weakness. My father and uncle had them so messed up they might as well have tossed dice to see who owed what on their accounts. I cleared it all out, and they were able to sell the business for a good profit before they left."

"Andrew kept the tidiest records."

"That he did, Mrs. Allen. He was a fine shopkeeper and an even greater gentleman."

Only if you didn't know what lurked on his bookshelf! Confirmation of my ruination from looking at it shone through again when Bartholomew stretched his legs in front of him. Imagining his long limbs entangled around me...

I started humming "Onward, Christian Soldiers" to stop the image.

Bartholomew tilted his head to study me, but Aunt Ethel began to clap to the beat.

"Sing if you must, Merritt. Your voice will ring through the neighborhood."

"No, I couldn't." I cleared my throat.

Tippet barked once and bound to Sean as he came through the gate.

Aunt Ethel wasted no time. "I didn't expect you until much later, Mr. Spunner."

Unphased by the sharp edge in her voice, he smiled. "If you give me half a chance, you'll find me competent and precise, Mrs. Allen. My uncle was able to catch Mr. Melling on the telephone at his home. Mr. Melling is sending a clerk to meet my uncle at the office next hour to help him locate your husband's file. Uncle Patrick plans to arrive here at two o'clock with everything you need."

"No questions asked?" Aunt Ethel asked.

"As I said, my uncle and Mr. Melling are friends."

"But why does Mr. Melling not wish to keep my business at his establishment?"

"With all respect to your husband and family, Mrs. Allen, I will say this as bluntly as possible. George Melling has raised the caliber of Melling & Associates since his father opened the doors. The original Mr. Melling welcomed business of all levels, but the current Mr. Melling has singled out the wealthiest clientele since his father retired. He has no interest in keeping the affairs of men like Mr. Allen that Mr. Crawley acquired decades ago as they profit him very little in the long-run."

Hand to her heart, Aunt Ethel shifted to the edge of her chair. "Then where are people like me to go? Who will help?"

"Patrick Finnigan is of the same mindset as Mr. Crawley. My uncle does not discriminate a case based on the person's status. He has pledged to help all law-abiding citizens and does his best for each one. You'll be in good hands, Mrs. Allen. I promise."

Aunt Ethel humbly lowered her head. "Thank you, Mr. Spunner."

Just before noon, we gathered under the oak. Keziah had worked wonders on our limited fresh supplies, disguising canned goods into fruit tarts, meat pies, and vegetable soufflés, all baked into bite-sized morsels so no silverware was needed for our picnic.

Sean appreciated Winifred's jarred botanical offering, fashioning two nosegays out of the arrangements. He tucked one through a buttonhole of his shirt—his jacket long since discarded—and placed the other over Winifred's right ear when Aunt Ethel wasn't looking. Then, he set about naming all the flowers with their common and Latin names in a dizzying rush that Winifred could only smile and nod over. The yellow lantana against his equally sunny blanket attracted butterflies by the dozens, and we dined as though on a nature expedition.

Aunt Ethel sat above us on the bench, looking solemn. Several times she smiled over Sean's pleasantries as he entertained Winifred with dramatic retellings of lighthearted humor that had us all laughing. I could tell she tried to stay sour, but Sean appeared to be winning her over with his vast collection of memorized lines, from poems to riddles.

And Bartholomew! I had never spent an extended period of time with him. Our morning hours blended into an afternoon of brightness that defied the autumn sun. Laughing and grinning were his typical expressions as we followed Sean's antics. Bartholomew ate heartily on his blanket to my right. The natural light was kind to his countenance, giving him a glow to accompany his glorious smile.

We all benefited from the entertainment and fresh air—Sean most of all. The sadness he carried that dawn was nowhere to be seen. Vivid eyes, flamboyant moves, and that impish grin imprinted on my heart as the perfect example of charm and wit. I loved him, both for Winifred's sake and my own, as he had personally lifted my spirits multiple times. No matter what might become of me and Bartholomew, 1897 would be remembered as the year Sean Spunner waltzed into my life, all thanks to Winifred Ramsay.

When everyone finished eating, Winifred and I carried the dishes to the kitchen while Bartholomew and Sean shook and folded the blankets. Begging for attention, Tippet jumped at Sean until he gave chase, leaving Bartholomew to carry the blankets to the back porch.

I met him on the stoop and took them from him. "Thank you."

"It's my pleasure, Merritt. I've enjoyed every moment of my time here today." Bartholomew stepped back, glanced about, and then dropped his voice. "I like your relaxed style for a day in the outdoors. That red is pretty on you."

Thinking of Sean's peck on my cheek, I stared at Bartholomew's mouth. What would *his* lips feel like on my skin?

"Thank you," I managed to reply. "You look nice today too."

The five of us were settled in an expanded circle of six chairs when a gentleman of the truest sense entered the front gate. His suit and coordinating derby were a perfect blend of summer and autumn—navy blue but lightweight. The gold cravat at his throat was held in place with what appeared to be a diamond tie pin, glinting in the sunlight as he shifted the brown briefcase from his right hand to his left.

Sean rose from his chair and crossed the lawn. "Uncle Patrick."

There was little to show a family connection between the two beyond their stature. Patrick Finnigan had pale skin and auburn hair, but they both carried themselves with confident ease.

The man removed his hat and stopped ten feet from Aunt Ethel, offering a slight bow in which his immaculate locks did not move an inch. "I hope my condolences have reached you, but I must tell you in person how sorry I am for your loss, Mrs. Allen."

"Thank you, but I had no idea you were acquainted with my husband."

"We conversed a few times a month along the way, enough to appreciate his neighborly greetings and miss them now they're gone. A trifle compared to you and your family."

"Thank you for your kind words. Allow me to introduce my nieces, Merritt Hall and Winifred Ramsay."

We stood from our chairs on either side of her when she introduced us.

Unable to shake hands, Mr. Finnigan looked to me and Winifred in turn, nodding a smile at each of us. "Ladies, I'm glad to meet you both and even more happy that you are here with your aunt at this time. I don't know what I would do without Sean's companionship with my wife and daughter gone from home."

"Sean has been wonderful to us as well," Winifred said. "Thank you for sending the milk, Mr. Finnigan."

"Sean doesn't like anyone to go without. After meeting you all, I better understand his heartfelt concern."

Winifred glowed with the words as she sank back to her chair.

The lawyer nodded a greeting to Bartholomew. "I'm glad to see you here as well, Mr. Graves."

Aunt Ethel cleared her throat and motioned to the two empty seats. "Please, gentlemen."

Mr. Finnigan went to the seat directly across the grouping from Aunt Ethel and set his hat under it. Sean returned to the chair closest to Winifred, on his uncle's right.

"Would you care for anything to drink?"

"No, thank you, Mrs. Allen." He opened the briefcase he'd sat on his lap. "I'd prefer to get right to business as this is already overdue."

"As you please," she responded.

"Through the generous hospitality of Mr. Melling, I was able to acquire your husband's file from Mr. Crawley, as well as your own. I have the sealed will, but also the notes for the draft of it. This document replaced the previous one—two to be exact. Andrew wanted the basic details of the previous wills recorded so there would be no confusion over the apparent changing of his wishes. I admit that I'm curious to see the full document."

"Andrew never said a word to me about any of it beyond me drawing up my own will earlier this year."

"Most men don't worry their wives with legal and business matters, Mrs. Allen. It's nothing against you." He looked around the circle and held up the large envelope. "With your permission, I will open the document and read, cementing myself as your new legal counselor."

The battle appeared fierce in her mind as she stared at Mr. Finnigan. He lowered the envelope and sat stoically, allowing her to decide if prejudices would rule over common sense. Aunt Ethel looked to Bartholomew a moment before refocusing on the lawyer.

"In a show of gratitude for your kindness, I accept your offer, Mr. Finnigan."

"Thank you for your confidence, Mrs. Allen. I will do my best for you and your family." His hand smoothed over his hair before he slipped a capped fountain pen under the red seal. Paper unfolded, Mr. Finnigan began. "I, Andrew Daniel Allen, being of sound mind on this day, July 16, 1897, do hereby present this Last Will and Testament, nullifying the previous documents which noted my sons, now deceased, as joint heirs, and then my wife as sole heir."

Concern lit Aunt Ethel's eyes when the lawyer paused.

"To my wife, Ethel Taylor Allen, I leave my house at the corner of Chatham and Palmetto Streets, including the property and all the items in residence. Should she no longer be living or is incapacitated, the home will be placed in the joint ownership of our nieces, Winifred Alene Ramsay and Merritt Hall, to live in or sell as they see fit."

Winifred gasped and covered her mouth.

"He loved you both," Aunt Ethel said.

"But Ezra!" I said. "I couldn't possibly—"

"He will inherit your father's store and house, Merritt." Aunt Ethel turned to me. "Surely you realize that. Andrew is looking out for you girls."

Mr. Finnigan held up a finger and continued reading. "To my sole living nephew, Ezra Gordon Julius Hall III, I leave fifty percent of my stock market holdings. The other fifty percent, as well as all private cash and bank account balances, go to my wife, Ethel. Should she no longer be living or is indisposed, those assets, as well as the house, are to be divided between Merritt and Winifred. Finally, I hereby bequeath all real estate, licensing, and property associated with Allen's General Store to Bartholomew Hutkee Graves, my assistant manager."

All eyes turned to Bartholomew as he noticeably paled. "There must be some mistake."

"No," Aunt Ethel said. "He's appreciated all you've done for him since he hired you last year, and Andrew was always one to reward hard work."

"But the whole business? Mrs. Allen, I couldn't! My own family didn't give me a cut when they sold in McIntosh. You'll need the income to—"

"No, Mr. Graves. Andrew knew I would never want to be bothered with the details of retail finances. I'm sure there's plenty in the bank to see me through the rest of my life. I don't need much." She turned to Winifred and then me. "And girls, when I am no longer here, all that is left goes to the both of you, and only you. Ezra, as I said, will have your father's legacy, Merritt. Do not feel that it's unjust or playing favorites. The only thing I let Andrew know was that I wanted to care for the girls in the family when my time was up. I'm pleased to see he saw to that."

Winifred threw her arms about our aunt. "Then I'll never be homeless, will I? My father's cousin received his assets after the fire. All I had was the clothes on my back. I had to get my dresses from the church's charity barrel."

"Dear girl," she said as she hugged Winifred, "you will never be without again. I'll see to it, and if not me, Merritt or a man in your future."

"I had high hopes when I read the draft," Mr. Finnigan said, "but one never knows what could be changed between that and the final. I'm pleased to see it worked out well."

Sean's ear-to-ear grin smiled upon Winifred, but Bartholomew wiped his handkerchief across his brow and leaned back like a man contemplating a tremendous amount of responsibility.

Mr. Finnigan addressed Aunt Ethel. "I should like to give you a few days to think everything through. Shall I return Monday?"

"Monday is fine."

"I'll be here about four o'clock." He stepped toward Bartholomew. "And you, Mr. Graves. There will be papers to sign and other formalities, but for now, keep running the store as you have been since Andrew took ill. I'll be in touch as soon as possible."

"Thank you."

Sean walked his uncle to the gate and Bartholomew began pacing the yard. Tippet followed him, whining. I traced Bartholomew's path to the stable. His suit jacket was thrown over the back of the buggy, and he braced himself against the nearest stall, Tippet staring at him from the door.

"Bartholomew."

His head jerked at my voice. "Why are you here after what you learned?"

"I learned that my uncle and aunt were very considerate to me and Winifred."

He motioned to himself. "And what your uncle said about me."

"He rewarded a valued employee he relied upon."

"He called out my full name, Bartholomew Hutkee Graves."

"As is proper for legal documents, though I don't have one, neither does my mother or any of her sisters. Did you notice my aunt was addressed as Ethel Taylor Allen? Taylor is her maiden name. You have an odd middle name, but it's nothing to be shy about."

"My middle name comes from Tustunnuggee Hutkee, a close relative of my maternal grandmother. You probably know him by his white name, William McIntosh."

"The Creek Nation warrior chief from the Indian Wars?"

"Yes, and he was successful until he surrendered much of the Indian lands to the United States and suffered a traitor's death."

"But that's not you."

"It is, Merritt. I'm mixed blood. What do you think your family will say to me when your aunt can't stand the thought of a Catholic helping her out?"

"If you were willing to come to me as Bartholomew Graves, the same should hold true to Bartholomew Hutkee Graves because you're one in the same."

We stared at each other. I felt my gaze soften into a longing I couldn't disguise. I wanted to touch him—to hold him as I nestled against his broad chest and kiss his tight mouth until he smiled.

"Come to me Wednesday as you promised," I told him, "or you'll be hard-pressed to earn my forgiveness in the future."

Twenty-two

Saturday afternoon turned into a quiet Sunday. After reading The Holy Bible and listening to Winifred play hymns on the piano, I was left staring at the porch ceiling in the autumn night.

I dropped my hand, and Tippet licked it. I continued to stare at the pale ceiling. After this summer, I'd always relate haint blue to the color of devotion.

After midnight, the floorboards inside the house squeaked. I lifted my head and looked through the open door. Backlit from the hall, Aunt Ethel entered the bedroom. I swung my feet to the floor, and Winifred's hand jerked out.

"It's Nancy," she hissed. "Straight from my dreams."

"It's Aunt Ethel. I saw her cross the threshold in the hall light. I have a clear view from here."

"Merritt, don't—"

Tippet's nails clicked across the hardwood boards as he rushed ahead of me. Aunt Ethel was on her knees in the bedroom.

I dropped beside her as Tippet frantically sniffed around.

"Are you all right?" I stood, pulling her with me. Aunt Ethel broke away from me and began ripping apart the neatly made beds. Blankets went flying.

I tried to catch her, but she screamed about being left alone because her husband was gone. Winifred stood in the doorway, eyes wide. A minute later, Keziah looked on from the hallway. I struggled to calm my aunt. Nothing I said reached her.

"Winifred, you need to run to Sean's house and ask Mr. Finnigan to telephone Dr. Sherard. Tell them we need immediate help. Stop for shoes and a wrap on your way out, nothing more."

While she laced on her boots, I took one of the discarded blankets from the floor and lunged at Aunt Ethel. Wrapping the blanket about her torso, I nudged her toward Winifred's bed and fell on top of her. My cousin snatched her shawl from the dresser and hurried out.

"Shall I help you with her or make tea?" Keziah asked.

Older than my aunt, the cook would have been a liability to the situation with her potential for injury. "Tea, please, Keziah."

Aunt Ethel continued to yell and moan, but she thrashed less as I waited endless minutes. What would we do when Aunt Ethel was taken away?

Sitting upright beside her, I turned her on her side and kept a hand on her shoulder. She stared into nothingness.

Footsteps pounded up the stairs. Sean, followed by Winifred and Mr. Finnigan ran in. Despite wearing a cotton pajama set, Mr. Finnigan commanded the room. The lawyer assessed the situation in a second and snapped his fingers at Sean.

"Get Miss Hall downstairs. Miss Ramsay will help me watch her aunt until the doctor arrives."

Sean put his arm about me. When we made it to the bottom of the stairs, I stopped. His arm tightened around my thin nightgown.

"A little further, Merri. Would you like to sit in the parlor or the kitchen?"

"The parlor. We'll be able to let the doctor in quicker from there."

Sean sat beside me on the settee in the dark room, an arm still about me. The heat from his body seared my left side with the contact. Looking at where our thighs touched, I gasped at noticing his striped nightshirt.

I immediately tried to pull away, but his arm hugged me to his side.

"Calm down," he said. "I pulled on trousers before leaving home. Besides the length, it's no different than me wearing my shirt untucked."

I sighed. "What will Winnie and I do when Aunt Ethel is taken away?"

"Mr. Allen saw to that. 'Should she no longer be living or is indisposed, those assets, as well as the house, are to be divided between Merritt and Winifred.' That means it would all be yours and Winnie's."

"I wouldn't feel right living here with Aunt Ethel locked away."

"Winnie couldn't stay here without you, Merri. She's not of age, but with you and Keziah here, it could work."

"How do you process all the information so readily?"

"I've been acting as a junior law clerk for my uncle for two years, and you can be sure I always keep Winifred Ramsey's best interests at the forefront of my mind."

"You're a scoundrel."

He stretched, hand reaching around my shoulders and his face nuzzling to my ear. "Which is why Uncle Patrick sent me away from Winnie, her being in that pretty flowered nightgown."

I pinched his arm and jumped off the settee with the knock at the front door.

Dr. Sherard eyed Sean behind me when I opened the door. "This situation isn't ideal," he said in way of greeting.

"It was an emergency," Sean replied.

"We're grateful for Mr. Finnigan's and Sean's assistance," I said briskly. "Aunt Ethel is upstairs."

She still laid on Winifred's wrecked bed, my cousin sitting at the foot of it and Mr. Finnigan watching over the prone woman from the other side.

Dr. Sherard felt her pulse and tested reflexes. "What happened to her?"

"She was wandering about and grew hysterical. When I couldn't calm her, I sent Winifred for help."

"It's a self-induced trance, common for hysterical women. The best place for her is the asylum ward of the hospital."

"No!" Winifred's eyes filled with tears as she clutched the doctor's coat sleeve. "Don't take her away."

"My dear girl," he said with softening features, "your aunt will be properly cared for. I don't wish you or your cousin the stress of caring for her when she's prone to fits. Mr. Finnigan informed me he is your family's legal counsel now. Don't you think this is for the best, Patrick?"

Mr. Finnigan looked from Winifred to Aunt Ethel and then to me before meeting the doctor's gaze. "Yes, Dr. Sherard. The young ladies have been through enough these past weeks. Miss Hall is quite capable and their cook can chaperone. I'll stop in regularly as well. I'll telephone the hospital in your behalf and the first order of business for me tomorrow will be arranging for telephone lines to be run to this house from the pole out front."

"But Aunt Ethel didn't want the buzzing lines in the house," Winifred said.

"Your aunt will not be here for some time," Dr. Sherard said. "And I fully agree. You girls need to be able to call for help without running across the neighborhood in your nightgowns."

Winifred blushed and Sean winked at her as though *he* wouldn't miss the sight.

"I'll see you tomorrow, Miss Hall and Miss Ramsay," Mr. Finnigan said.

"Be sure to bring Sean with you," the doctor said. "There's no need for him to stay any longer. To be safe, both of you need to wash and change your clothes. This house is still under quarantine."

I walked Mr. Finnigan and Sean downstairs. "Thank you for coming so promptly."

"You are most welcome, Miss Hall. I will be in touch tomorrow."

"Goodbye, Merri." Sean left a quick kiss on my cheek. "Try not to worry."

"Tea is ready," Keziah said after I closed the front door. "Will Mrs. Allen want some?"

I shook my head. "But Winifred and I will. My aunt will be brought to the hospital soon."

"The poor lady. Might I say farewell to her?"

"If the doctor says it's all right. And ask Winifred to come down, please."

In an attempt to bring comfort, I arranged a cozy tea setting at the little table in the kitchen, complete with a cookie plate filled with the goodies from the jar Keziah kept on the counter. When Winifred entered, I hugged her.

"Keziah is staying with the doctor," she whispered.

"That's good. Do you think you could eat something?"

Winifred nodded and I brought her to the table. We were on our second cup of hot tea, and had each eaten a couple cookies when I heard the horses arrive. Winifred and I held hands as Dr. Sherard orchestrated the orderlies with their cot to collect Aunt Ethel and load her into the enclosed wagon.

After the conveyance pulled away and Dr. Sherard said goodbye, Winifred and I huddled together on Aunt Ethel's bed for the rest of the night.

Twenty-three

Come morning light, I was able to slip away from Winifred. After making the beds in our room, I pulled on a simple wash dress before twisting my hair into a bun.

Sean waited on the back stoop when I entered the kitchen.

"Good morning," I called as I crossed the porch.

Smiling, he held out the milk bottle as I opened the latch on the screen. "Good morning, Merri. Uncle Patrick said to tell you he'll stop by on his way home from the office to update you. Most likely sometime after five."

"Thank you." I took the bottle and set it on the counter inside the door before going outside to embrace him. "Thank you for everything. You've been a great friend."

"I'd do anything for you and Winnie. Always remember that." He rubbed my back before letting me go. "Do you have any messages that need to go out?"

"No, I'm not sure what to think right now. I'll most likely have several questions when your uncle comes this evening."

I brought the milk into the kitchen, placing it next to Keziah who was kneading bread dough. "I'm surprised to see you up this early after the night we had."

"You girls have to eat."

"Thank you for your service, Keziah. I don't remember a visit here without your wonderful meals."

My cousin woke before breakfast, and we spent a quiet day doing chores to present a clean home. I wanted to show we could run things without our aunt. Laundry was washed and hung to dry before dinner, floors swept and scrubbed after the noon meal.

We were showered and dressed respectfully in skirts and shirtwaists when I let Mr. Finnigan and Sean into the house. I took their hats and led them into the parlor. Winifred set down her novel and smiled at her beau as I took the space beside her and the men settled in the armchairs opposite.

"Ladies, I have good news this evening. Your aunt has settled in her ward at Providence Infirmary without any agitation."

"Is she responsive?"

Sean grinned. "I told you Merri is bright. There's no need to hide the full truth from her, Uncle Patrick."

The man's freckles blended into his blush. "You certainly called the facts, Sean. I meant no disrespect, Miss Hall, but I try to point out the good in any situation. Your aunt is indeed still comatose. Whatever it is she experienced last night shocked her senseless, but the fact that she isn't violent is great news. That means she is not being restrained."

Winifred let out a cry of alarm. Sean went immediately to her side and took her hand into his own. He met his uncle's narrowed gaze and held his spot standing beside the settee, clasping Winifred's hand.

"I will check on her daily until you are able to venture out. The Sisters of Charity who run the hospital are wonderful."

"Sisters of—Mr. Finnigan, I'm not sure if you're aware, but Aunt Ethel has an absolute loathing for Catholics. How will it be for her when she awakens from this stupor and finds herself surrounded by nuns?"

"Surely she knows you cannot take two steps in Mobile without running into a Catholic."

I smiled, pleased he wasn't offended. "I'm sure, but she's avoided all dealings with them as much as possible."

"Until now," he said with finality.

"Yes." I stretched out the word, unsure how to progress.

"Providence Infirmary is the best—a modern sanitarium. She will be able to have her own doctor in attendance as well as her pastor. They do not exclude anyone the patient wishes to consult with. I knew you would want the best care for her, and Dr. Sherard and I agree she will receive that there."

"Thank you, Mr. Finnigan."

"Telephone workers will be here at the end of the week to run the wires from the pole to the house and install a box for you. Where would you like it located?"

The swiftness of the events was dizzying, but I paused for a minute to think it through. "The study, please. That will keep the telephone tucked away from Aunt Ethel's view."

"Very well, Miss Hall. Tomorrow, I will see to your financial needs, having your name added to your aunt's account as I have Mr. Allen's name removed. How much cash should I withdraw for you to tide you over for any immediate household needs?"

"Five dollars should be plenty. We've received several deliveries from Mr. Graves in the past few weeks. We'll need to set up an account with him now that he's the owner rather than Uncle Andrew. Please inform Bartholomew of my wish, Sean."

He nodded.

"Store accounts can be managed monthly with a check for the amount owed. I'll secure you the five dollars in various denominations so it will be easier for you to use it as needed." Mr. Finnigan looked to his nephew. "It's time we go home, Sean."

***

Winifred and I passed a second peaceful night in Aunt Ethel's room. After she greeted Sean and collected the morning milk from him, I set my cousin at the dining room table with studies for the day, breaking for meals and some yard time with Tippet.

When Sean returned before supper, we met him under the swaying bottles in the tiny grove.

"Your cash and coin from my uncle." He presented me an envelope with the First National Bank logo on it from his messenger bag.

"Thank you, Sean."

"And for Winnie." He pulled out a small box. "From the gentleman whose heart you hold."

Her cheeks pinked as she pulled the blue ribbon and opened the lid. "Sean, it's beautiful!"

She tilted the box toward me, showcasing the intricate piece of chocolate shaped into a heart.

He leaned over her shoulder to kiss her ear. "You're the keeper of my heart, Winnie."

She threw her arms around his neck. "What can I give you to show my affections?"

"Cookies." Sean grinned. "I've walked miles since dinner and supper is still an hour off."

As soon as she ran for the house, he looked to me. "Don't be mad. I had the same dream about Winnie last night. I decided I can't *not* tell her how I feel."

"You said Winifred was too young."

"She needs to know in case…if anything were to happen to her, I'd—"

The screen slammed as Winifred rushed out, hands cupped around the sweets. Sean bit his lip as he watched her every move. I would have to force a corset on her daily if she insisted on running about like that.

"Here!" She poured the handful of cookies into his open satchel. "Eat some now and the rest on your way home."

"You're lucky I just delivered my final message or I'd be in a heap of trouble for getting cookie crumbs all over important documents." Sean fished out two cookies and stuck one in his mouth.

"There isn't a message from Mr. Graves?" Winifred asked.

He shook his head, still chewing.

"He's been silent for days. And you gave him Merritt's message about the charge account this morning?"

Sean swallowed and glanced at me before turning back to Winifred. "I did, and he looked mad about it, but didn't say anything."

"And he heard about Aunt Ethel? Is he going to break his friendship with us because he got what he wanted—Uncle Andrew's store? Was he only being nice to—"

"No." I interrupted Winifred's ridiculous ideas. "He's not like that. You should be ashamed for even thinking such things."

"Then what is it?" she asked.

"Mr. Graves was just given a massive responsibility. He's thinking things through on how best to handle the store and—and everything."

"Like you?" Winifred gave me her wide-eyed stare.

"I'm sure I'm at the bottom of any potential list he has."

"Not if he's smart," Sean said.

I shrugged. "It is what it is."

Winifred stepped closer to me. "But you like him, don't you?"

"Yes." I closed my eyes and pictured his typically serious face laughing as he was Saturday morning.

I slowly walked into the house and counted to thirty before picking up the milk bottle. When I reached the back door, I stared at Sean holding Winifred. One arm low around her waist, his other hand cupped her cheek as they gazed into each other's eyes. Sean's lips were moving but I couldn't hear the words, though I knew what they were.

He loved her.

She would never be alone in this life.

He would wait for her as long as necessary.

When his face lowered to hers, I rested my forehead on the screen. I still loved Sean—for his kindness and all he stood for—though he was thoroughly kissing Winifred after promising me he wouldn't. His hand on her face caressed to her neck, then her shoulder, moving still lower.

"Goodbye, Sean!" I called. "We'll see you tomorrow."

He wrapped his arms around Winifred, lifting her off the ground as they kissed again.

"She's my girl, Merri!"

"I never doubted it."

Twenty-four

Now that Sean held nothing back, I couldn't allow Winifred to meet him unchaperoned. Wednesday morning, I almost had to pry her away from him. Getting her to focus on studies was a lost cause, so I instructed her to sweep and mop the upstairs to expel her giddy energy while I beat the rugs.

After dinner, Winifred finally settled enough to read from her assigned history book. I stepped out the backdoor to shake the bedroom rugs once more before bringing them inside. Tippet settled in a sunny patch the lengthening grass. Minutes later, Sean's whistle announced his approach. I quickly signaled to Tippet to stay quiet so he wouldn't announce the arrival, and dashed for the gate to bar Sean from entering.

"Good afternoon, Merri." He looked around at the deserted street before kissing my cheek.

"You smell like you've been rolling in a fish boat."

He held up a sack and then hung it from a spoke on the fence. "Uncle Patrick was getting tired of canned meat. He sent me to the docks to buy what I could. I got you ladies a half dozen Spanish mackerel while I was there."

"That's extremely generous of you."

Sean's hand went to the latch.

I pressed against the gate so he couldn't swing it inward. "But it's not going to allow you entrance."

"Merri, it's Wednesday. Quarantine is over."

"It doesn't give you license to waltz in here and distract Winifred whenever you wish. I finally got her reading this hour after your shameless display with her this morning. I may not be as old and stern as Aunt Ethel, but I need to retain some control over this household. I hope I don't need to remind you that you recently said Winifred wasn't ready for a full kiss, yet twice now you've swept her away."

"It was wrong of me to promise that."

"I can't have you putting her head in the clouds multiple times a day."

His eyes flashed a dangerous gold. "If our time with her is limited, do you really want her wasting hours on school work? Why not let her live?"

"She might survive, Sean."

"None of the others have." He looked to his shoes.

"She's younger and stronger than the ones you've dreamt about before." I poked him in the chest, causing him to look up. "And if you get any harebrained ideas about taking advantage of your sway over her and attempt to make her woman, so help me Sean Spunner, I'll—"

His mouth opened in shock before it set into a grim line as his eyebrows narrowed. "I can't believe you'd think that of me, Merritt Hall. Have I been so feral that I've lost your trust or is that all *you* can think about since looking at that book?"

The words stung with their truth, and he saw it in my eyes.

"Forgive me, Merri." He laid a hand over mine on the gate. "I know what that awakening feels like, but I swear to you I've never acted fully on it. Winnie isn't a conquest, but my first love. The thought of her not being my *only* love has me in a tizzy. I want to share as much as possible with her, memorize the sight and scent of her. Yes, the feel and taste of her too."

"I need to instruct her and run the household as if she has a full lifetime. Winifred's ruination would serve nothing but guilt and—"

"Is that all you think of me as, a man set out to ruin women?"

"You told me you wouldn't speak for her until you were settled in your profession and she had finished school." I fisted my hands and put them on my hips in hopes of looking stalwart.

"The vision changed everything, can't you understand?"

"Visions, ghostly nightmares, death. Everything was straightforward before coming here. I got on fine with my life."

"No you didn't. You needed this experience to put aside your childhood fears and guilt." He retrieved the sack from the fence. "Take the fish and enjoy a fresh meal. I'll see you after supper."

Sean walked away with as much swagger as ever, irking me to no end.

"You smell like a ship's slop bucket, Sean Spunner! Don't comeback until you bathe!"

With a hearty laugh, he turned. "I love you too, Merri Hall!"

Tippet barked his own farewell.

Winifred hurried out the front door as I came up the walk. "Is Sean here?"

"He's gone now but will be back after supper. Be sure to complete your studies."

***

Keziah happily cooked the Spanish mackerel, balled cornmeal to fry along with it, and warmed a can of green beans for supper. Winifred settled at the piano after eating, playing Beethoven while I cleared the remains. On my last trip to the kitchen, Sean peered in the screen door.

"Get to the front like a proper suitor," I called to him.

He whooped and jumped off the steps. I paused in the parlor to see Winifred's face when the knock came. Blue eyes bright, her smile stole the light from the meager lamps in the room.

"Sean Francis Spunner is here to call on Winifred Alene Ramsay."

"You are welcome—this time."

He kissed my cheek and swept into the hall. Falling on a knee beside the piano bench, Sean took Winifred's hand and gazed up at her.

"'Gentle and good and mild thou art,

    Nor can I live if thou appear

    Aught but thyself, or turn thine heart

    Away from me, or stoop to wear

    The mask of scorn, although it be

    To hide the love thou feel'st for me.'"

He pressed his lips to her knuckles.

"I'll never hide my love, Sean, but that was lovely."

He stood and slipped onto the bench beside Winifred. "The cunning words of Percy Bysshe Shelley, for his lover, Mary, who later wrote *Frankenstein* that you enjoyed."

"You know everything, don't you?"

"I know that I adore you." He kissed her nose. "That I'd give anything to see you smile—especially at me."

She shifted against his side, and his arm went about her as his lips lowered to her smiling face. I couldn't help but stare as the kiss continued, and Winifred seemed to be absorbed by Sean's lips and hands.

Knocking at the front door brought us all back to reality. Expecting the doctor or Mr. Finnigan, my mouth gaped when I saw Bartholomew.

Hat in hand, he wore a humble expression and his brown eyes were sincere. "Good evening, Miss Merritt. I've come to call on you, like we discussed Saturday."

After placing his hat on the credenza, I swallowed my fear. "Come in and help me chaperone Sean and Winifred in the parlor. I don't dare leave them another minute."

"Mr. Graves! I thought I'd never see you again." Winifred played a few happy chords on the piano, cherubic cheeks as rosy as her lips.

I looked between Sean and Bartholomew. "Have you both had supper?"

Sean nodded.

"I didn't stop to eat after I closed the store," Bartholomew admitted though he looked pained to do so.

"Let me check the kitchen."

Keziah washed dishes.

"Mr. Graves arrived without having eaten supper. Is there anything we could quickly fix for him?"

"There's one more mackerel. Tippet would have got it, but I'd rather it go to Mr. Graves. I'll fix up a few more hushpuppies— for the dog and the man. Give me a quarter of an hour, Miss Merritt."

"Mr. Spunner is here as well. I'll fix a coffee tray with cookies and—"

"You go be the hostess and be prepared to bring everyone to the dining room."

"Thank you, Keziah." I straightened my skirt and returned to the parlor.

Expecting to have to chase Sean off the piano bench, he instead had pulled an armchair to the side of the instrument so he could gaze upon Winifred as she played.

"We'll be called to the dining room shortly for food and drinks," I announced before crossing the room to Bartholomew. He had risen when I entered and didn't sit on the settee until I was comfortable in the spot beside his.

"I'm sorry for the trouble," he said.

The light chords of a dreamy song continued on. I spoke freely knowing the two across the room wouldn't notice anything short of the call for food.

"You're no trouble, Bartholomew. You've helped keep this household going since Uncle Andrew took ill."

"That message you sent about a charge account, I hope you know I dismissed it immediately. After all your family has done for me, I can't accept money from any of you."

"And we cannot live with you buying our food and supplies. At least charge us cost if you won't accept retail price."

His brown eyes bore into mine, his tight lips creeping into a smile it looked like he wasn't ready to share. Then he laughed and took my hands his both of his—warm and secure. "Merritt, you were made for me. From your patience to being raised with shopkeepers, not to mention your alluring face and...."

"Yes?"

His touch trailed to my shoulders. I'd never noticed how large he really was. Solidly built—his big hands felt as though he could crush my slight frame. As his face lowered to mine, he caressed across my shoulders and down my back, gently pulling me toward him.

"I just want to hold you, Merritt. Protect and love you," he whispered.

"Kiss her, you fool!"

I could have clobbered Sean for his timing.

Bartholomew immediately straightened and dropped his arms. "Forgive me, Merritt."

"I won't." I crossed my arms and glared at Sean before looked back to Bartholomew. "I'll not forgive the interruption either. I want you to kiss me."

Winifred giggled and Sean whistled.

Bartholomew looked over his shoulder toward the piano and then back at me with the sweetest expression—shy smile and hopeful eyes. "Later, Merritt. I don't wish an audience for our first kiss."

I nodded and relaxed into the cushions of the settee, putting more space between us as we talked of the store and him keeping the mare until Aunt Ethel returned.

"How is Mrs. Allen doing?" he asked.

"Well enough, according to Mr. Finnigan and Dr. Sherard. I hope to be able to visit her tomorrow. When she returns, we'll find out if she wishes to keep the horse and buggy," I continued with a halting voice.

He linked our hands and tucked them between us. "I'd buy them if it comes down to it."

"If you need any supplies from the stable, bring them with you tonight."

"Thank you, but I'll wait until next time. I plan on coming back soon—if you'll have me."

"Better wait and see how he kisses before answering, Merri," Sean joked.

I ignored him. "I'd enjoy that, Bartholomew. Which day is best for you?"

"Saturday afternoon or Sundays. I've decided to close Saturdays at noon so I have a bit more time to myself—at least until I hire on someone else."

"I'm sure you'll find your stride in no time." I looked to Sean, who was switching his cat-eyes between us and Winifred. "When you're ready to hire, be sure to tell Sean. He seems to know everyone and can send people your way."

Bartholomew smiled. "Our friend is resourceful."

We sat in silence, holding hands, and watched Winifred sing for Sean. His rapt attention was as entertaining as the music, which he joined in, turning a few songs into duets.

When Keziah rang the bell, I motioned the young couple out of the room first. Bartholomew offered his arm. His lips met my cheek for a brief second before we stepped out of the parlor.

Entering the dining room with a broad smile, I tried not to look surprised that Keziah had set the plate with Bartholomew's supper at the head of the table. No one had used Uncle Andrew's place beside Andrew Allen. Ever. Sean helped Winifred into a chair, standing behind the empty seat beside it until Bartholomew escorted me around the table to my typical place.

He looked from me to the plate of food. Having taken supper here countless times, he knew the significance. "Shall I move my setting to sit beside you?"

"No, it's fine. I'm sure Keziah was tired and wasn't thinking straight."

Sean gave an impressive prayer over the food. Thoughts of Aunt Ethel worried me as he and Winifred helped themselves to the cookies and coffee set in the middle of the table. What would she do if she knew a Catholic prayed over the food at her table? How would she take the news of me and Winifred hosting two young men in the house with only Keziah to chaperone?

"Are you not hungry, Merri?" Winifred asked a minute later.

"Not much. The fish was filling." I forced a smile at the couple across from me as I took the coffee pot.

The men discussed their Gulf favorites the next few minutes, Winifred chiming in about the catches in Charleston.

"Merritt, are you well?" Bartholomew's voice was deep, full of concern.

"Yes, just worrying too much." I set my full cup down but didn't let go of the handle as the steam rose.

Bartholomew caressed my knuckles and then touched my cheek. How his strong hand could deliver a gentle touch that sent a shiver down my spine was magical. "What can I do to help?"

Two other pairs of eyes were on us, but his gaze was only concerned with me. The pad of his thumb trailing my jaw nearly sent me into convulsions of pleasure as I gripped the cup tighter.

"Pray. Pray for Aunt Ethel's healing—and for all of us."

Bartholomew nodded and leaned back in his chair. His plate only held thin bones, so I passed him the cookie platter and poured fresh coffee into his cup.

"How about a few more songs before I go?" Sean asked Winifred.

She nodded and looked to me. "May we be excused, Merri?"

"I better hear singing within thirty seconds after you leave this room."

Sean's eyebrows rose at the challenge. "It shall be done."

He escorted Winifred from the table, stopping in the doorway to kiss her before they dashed to the parlor.

Laughing, Bartholomew helped himself to a few more cookies. "They're charming."

"Trouble wrapped in a bundle of cuteness is the worst type, like a mischievous kitten." Winifred started on a jaunty tune and Sean's rich baritone joined in. "That means they aren't kissing."

Bartholomew chuckled. "Relax for a minute, Merritt."

Keziah came to the door at the same time the piano paused in the other room.

"Thank you, Keziah," I said. "We're finished."

"Did you get enough, Mr. Graves?"

"I did, thank you. Everything was great."

"Before anyone says it, I placed you at the head on purpose," Keziah told him. "With Mr. Allen gone and you being in control of his store and the oldest man in attendance, well, that puts you in charge in my mind, and I don't know another man more suited to that role than you."

The piano picked up again, but faltered on a C flat.

"Thank you, Keziah. Please let me know by Friday morning what supplies you'll need the next month so I can bring them when I next come. Stock is running low all over town."

"Thank you, Mr. Graves. I'll work on a list with Miss Merritt tomorrow."

"Excuse me." I stepped around them and went toward the sound of giggles in the parlor.

Winifred nuzzled against Sean's chest as he kissed her neck while they snuggled together on the piano bench. "It's time to bid Sean goodnight, Winifred. Sean, you may collect the milk bottle from the kitchen on your way out."

Bartholomew stopped mere inches behind me, placing his hand on my elbow—the touch of his tall body hot and strong against my back.

"Come on, Sean." His breath heated my right ear with the words. "I'll give you a lift home."

"Did you kiss her thoroughly after we left you alone?"

"No," Bartholomew answered. "Though a gentleman never kisses and tells."

Sean grinned. "Then allow me to drop the title for a moment to exclaim that Winifred's lips are sweeter and more delectable than any fruit known to the world—and those kisses are all for my harvesting."

"Goodnight, Sean," I said with annoyance over him stealing my moments with Bartholomew.

Twenty-five

After breakfast the next morning, I completed a shopping list with Keziah. To be safe, I factored in Aunt Ethel's return and the possibility of hosting Bartholomew and Sean a few times a week so we wouldn't to have to scrimp to offer hospitality.

As I went to join Winifred in the parlor, a knock sounded.

A courier boy handed me a note and hurried off the front porch as though he knew a yellow flag had been nailed there as recently as two days ago. The letter was from Dr. Sherard, stating there were fresh cases of yellow fever near Providence Infirmary and advising us not to visit our aunt that week. I had chosen my best red day dress that morning to bring a bit of cheer to Aunt Ethel, and the thought of another day trapped at home after weeks of isolation was depressing.

"Winnie." She looked up from her book, eyes as blue as her dress. "Dr. Sherard doesn't think it wise for us to visit Aunt Ethel just yet. How would you like to go to Unc—Bartholomew's store? We could leave our order and see if anything else strikes our fancy."

"That would be lovely! I'll get my boots."

"And I'll have Keziah fix us a travel dinner. We'll picnic while we're out."

"You're wonderful, Merri!" Her bare feet pattered up the stairs.

Half an hour later, Winnifred and I walked toward Government Street. I carried the picnic basket though we agreed to switch it off along the two mile journey. Expecting to see traffic—wagons, pedestrians, and streetcars—we were met with continued stillness on the main thoroughfare.

"It's eerie." Winifred looked up and down the street, fingering the black mourning band around her upper arm that matched the velvet ribbon around my own sleeve.

"Let's cross and start walking. If a streetcar happens along, we'll take it."

Two supply wagons passed going either way along with what looked like a doctor in a buggy rushing across town, but nothing else for five minutes. The warm autumn day offered crisp blue skies and the canopy of oaks shaded us from the bright sun. If it wasn't for the unease of the epidemic and Aunt Ethel's health, it would have been a perfect outing.

Halfway there, Winifred took the picnic basket from me. She chatted about Sean and rummaged through the basket's contents when she was quiet. We continued up the sidewalk, crossing the side roads until we were beyond where the vacant streetcar tracks looped back toward town. We walked the final block without word.

"I haven't been to the store since July," Winifred remarked.

"It's been since last year for me." The exterior trim was newly painted along with the ALLEN'S GENERAL STORE sign. "Everything looks cheerful."

"It looked like this when I was here before."

"No wonder Aunt Ethel told Bartholomew he'd done much to help the business. Uncle Andrew never liked to spend money on appearances. He was all about functionality."

Winifred took the lead and dashed up the wooden steps and through the screen door—another new addition. "Mr. Graves!"

He came around the counter, tucking something into his apron pocket. I stepped to the side of the door, suddenly unsure if coming was the right thing to do.

"Miss Winifred, is everything okay? Is Merritt—"

"We're fine. Our visit with Aunt Ethel was cancelled and we wanted an outing after our weeks in the house."

I opened the screen door and joined my cousin. Bartholomew met my eyes and smiled. "I'm glad to see you, Merritt. It was quite a surprise when Winifred rushed in like that."

He briefly took my hand, squeezing it before stepping back a polite distance.

"I brought our shopping list." I handed it to him. "If it's too much, reduce it as necessary. I might have over-estimated things."

Bartholomew scanned the paper and nodded. "I should be able to fill most of it."

"Thank you." I wanted to hold his hand again, but controlled myself.

"We're out and enjoying the day, Mr. Graves." Winifred waved the basket at him. "Could we set up a picnic in the stretch of shade along the railroad tracks behind the store? Keziah fixed plenty. You're welcome to join us."

"That sounds nice, thank you. My stocker didn't show today so there's no need to work around his break." He looked at his watch. "I've been closing up for half an hour around noon when it isn't busy. If you give me about ten minutes, I'll lock things up for a spell."

"Wonderful!" Winifred smiled at him. "Do you have something we could use as a rug?"

"The blanket out of the back of the buggy should work. It's in the stable, but if you ladies wait here. I'll collect it for you."

"Thank you, Mr. Graves."

He stepped out the backdoor, and I grabbed her elbow. "What do you think you're up to, Winnie?"

"Giving you a romantic picnic with Mr. Graves." She giggled. "He sure looked concerned when I arrived."

"It's not funny."

"It was a test. He passed."

I crossed my arm. "A test for what?"

"His love for you. Be flattered by his sincerity, Merri, but there's one more test to complete."

Bartholomew returned with the snap of the rear screen door. He removed his eyeglasses and wiped them on a hanky he pulled form his apron pocket.

"It's warmed up today," he remarked as he set them back on his nose. "I went ahead and spread the blanket for you."

"Thank you. I'll start setting the picnic." Winifred hurried through the store without permission to use the employee door.

"I haven't visited the store since Spring '96. The improvements you've orchestrated are terrific."

"Thank you, Merritt."

The front door opened and a man entered with two children in tow. I moved to the wall of fabric to browse while Bartholomew made small talk as he helped the family. A woman who looked to be in her twenties arrived before he was done waiting on the man.

Bartholomew greeted her but finished adding the family's purchases to his ledger before turning to the lady.

"Sorry for your wait. How may I help you, ma'am?"

"I'm afraid to venture to my regular store on Dauphin Street, but I'm in desperate need of soap and night cream." She clutched her reticule and looked about at the simple shelving and displays.

Bartholomew gave a reassuring smile. "It doesn't look like much, but we do stock the best to help folks who don't wish to travel downtown for everything. Do you have favorite brands in mind for either item?"

She blushed, looking to Bartholomew with a too friendly gaze. "Ivory, and I saw an advertisement for a new cream, but I can't recall it now."

"Browse a moment over here. Perhaps one of the jars will look familiar. I've heard good things from customers about…"

I tried not to listen to his sales pitch, but he was so calm and helpful, it was difficult not to get a little jealous of the attention he gave her. Fingering a green calico bolt as though contemplating a purchase kept me from looking totally dejected.

I heard the register ring and the woman laugh.

"I'm glad you ventured in this morning, ma'am."

"So am I, Mr. Graves. I doubt I'll travel into the city for anything now that I know you stock all my favorites."

He held open the door and set out a CLOSED FOR DINNER sign he had waiting behind a nearby shelf, locking the entrance. Brown eyes intense, he crossed the store to me.

I rubbed my palms on the side of my skirt. "You have a way with people. It bodes well for business."

A primal look flashed in his eyes and a quiver in my middle tingled as he stopped, our boots nearly touching.

"Merri—"

Unsure if he shortened my name on purpose or if his need was so great he clipped the word from his mouth as he pressed my lips with his. One of his arms went low about my waist, tugging me closer, and the other around my shoulders holding me in complete support.

Hands momentarily trapped on his chest, I trailed them over and around his torso, memorizing the feel of him as we continued to kiss. I both cursed and blessed his apron as it prevented me from being that much closer to his skin. Never having explored a man, I marveled at his strength—the solid, unwaveringness of his stature. How could anyone consider him average, unremarkable?

Heat—whether it was from me or him, I didn't know—encompassed the moment. His hands spanned my waist before they traveled my slight hips and tugged me against him with his hot touch on the small of my back.

I moaned into his mouth, startling my common sense back to life. Eyes opened, I stepped out of his arms. I must have looked as shocked over the situation as I felt about my behavior because Bartholomew paled.

"Merritt, forgive me. I didn't mean to—"

I closed the gap and hugged him, tucking my head against his solid form. "Don't take it back, Bartholomew. It was wonderful."

Then we were at it again, noisier as our kisses now attempted to express rather than convince the other of our passions. Gasping breaths and moans of surrender I could imagine accompanying the acts within that book filled our corner of the store. Coming out of the haze, I realized I was sandwiched between the back wall and Bartholomew. The intense stare in his dark gaze widened with realization of our shameless actions.

"I wanted this moment with you," I whispered. "Don't feel guilty."

"I don't want to take advantage, Merritt." He held me so tight it almost hurt. Bartholomew's kisses traveled to my left ear, and his hand migrated to my backside. "I love you."

Electricity surged from each connection our bodies made and settled in a pulsing mass within my core. I wanted him in a way I didn't understand but knew it related to the physical feelings. And the book—those cursed pages! Clinging to him, I felt the swoon strike as he shifted me away from the wall. I couldn't speak or stand on my own. He walked me to his stool behind the counter. Perched on the edge, I gazed at Bartholomew.

"I'm sorry if I did or said too much. We should get outside. The fresh air will be good for you and Winifred will be wondering about us."

Winifred! I jumped off the stool, glad for Bartholomew's steadying arm.

"You have nothing to worry over," I told him as he held the screen open for me. "I on the other hand forgot my cousin and decorum."

"Mr. Graves," Winifred called from the blanket under a live oak. "Do you have any ice? Our jars of juice are warm."

"I do," he said, keeping hold of my arm.

"I've got it from here." I stepped to the side and smiled at him. "But hurry back to us."

Winifred looked from my rosy cheeks to my well-used lips when I reached the picnic. "It's the genuine deal with Mr. Graves."

"What?"

"I know you wouldn't allow a man to kiss you like that unless you loved him. That was my second test—leaving you alone with him. And don't feign shock. I looked in the door a few minutes ago to see what was keeping you. I never would have thought he was that brazen."

"Winnie!" I dropped to the blanket and folded my legs under the skirt of my dress. "That's no way for a young lady to speak."

She poked me in the ribs. "And no way for a young lady to behave. And you call yourself a chaperone. I wish Sean could have seen you two."

"I'm glad he didn't."

Giggling, she looked to the store and watched Bartholomew exit the backdoor. "It feels wonderful, doesn't it? To be held and kissed by a man who loves you."

I nodded, refusing to trust my voice with him coming nearer.

Winifred accepted the jar of ice. "Thank you, Mr. Graves. Keziah knew what she was doing when she packed—three jars of juice, three sandwiches, and plenty of cookies and dried banana chips." She opened each jar and shook a fraction of ice bits into each of them before dispensing the hand-squeezed satsuma juice. "Merri made the cookies yesterday. She's just as good of a cook as Keziah. She grew up without servants and knows everything about keeping house. I'm glad Sean will earn a fine living because I'm near hopeless, though Merri is teaching me things. She's clever, resourceful, *and* pretty."

"That she is." Bartholomew's gaze met my eyes with a smile. After a minute of quiet chewing, he balanced his food on his knee.

"This is the most pleasant dinner break I've ever had. I'd welcome a weekly visit like this, if you ladies would enjoy it as well."

I nodded but before I could speak, Winifred clapped her hands together. "We would love to, Mr. Graves. Thank you for the invitation."

"Miss Winifred, as I hope to be seeing more of you and your cousin, I'd be happy to have you call me Bartholomew as she does."

Her blue eyes widened in delight. "What about Bart or Barty?"

"No one but my granny has ever called me Barty, but Merritt may call me anything she wishes."

They both looked to me. I blushed behind my juice jar.

After several seconds, Winifred poked my knee. "Well, Merri?"

I cleared my throat. "I like Bartholomew's name. It's—"

"Romantic, isn't it?" Winifred giggled.

It was Bartholomew's turn to redden.

"I was going to say distinguished, but romantic works as well." I folded my used napkin into a smaller square and tucked it under the basket's edge. "Though I will probably shorten his name at some point, like to call him over for help or—"

"In a cry of passion."

"Winifred!" Completely embarrassed, in part because the images from the book immediately came to mind, I covered my face with my hands.

"I'm sorry," she said, though she sounded nothing of the sort. "My mouth runs away without thinking. I didn't—"

"I think you've said enough, Winifred," Bartholomew spoke with a direct tone that left no room for her to swindle her way out of anything. "Please go sit on the back step a few minutes and think about the consequences of your naughty words."

"Yes, Bartholomew." Her voice held a sincere sadness.

A few seconds later, Bartholomew gently took my wrists and lowered my hands from my hot face. Bringing them to his heart, he then dipped his head to kiss my knuckles.

"Don't be embarrassed, Merritt." Our linked hands settled between us. "I hope we do have passionate moments together."

"I'd like that."

"Good." He kissed my cheek and stood, bringing me with him. "Was I too harsh with your cousin?"

"Not at all. I try to be stern, but it isn't the same as a patriarchal figure."

Without being asked, Bartholomew helped me pack the remainder of our picnic and fold the blanket. He took both the blanket and the basket, stopping at the stable to drop the blanket and then offering his arm to escort me to Winifred.

"I'm sorry, Merri."

"It's all right, but try to avoid inappropriate subjects in the future." I led her through the door Bartholomew held opened for us.

He stopped at the counter and retrieved two peppermint sticks from the penny jar, tucking them into the basket before passing it to Winifred. "For your walk home."

"Thank you, Bartholomew. May I hug you? It's much nicer than a handshake among close friends. Sean hugs Merri."

"Do I need to speak with him?" Bartholomew crossed his arms and narrowed his eyes.

Winifred laughed. "No, he loves Merri as a friend. He's even kissed her."

"Don't expect that from me. My kisses are for one woman only."

He put an arm around her for a half hug, his awkwardness showing in the stilted movement. But Winifred dropped the picnic basket and threw both arms about his neck, practically hanging off him.

"Thank you, Bartholomew! You've been so kind to the family and Merritt deserves all the happiness in the world after putting up with me this past month." She stepped back and looked up at him. "And I'm sorry I ever thought you dull."

Laughing, he shook his head. "What could I have done during those suppers with you while I wished you were the other niece I'd heard so much about?"

"You wished I was Merri?"

He nodded. "I don't know if they did it on purpose, but your uncle and aunt shared many stories and spoke of Merritt's kind ways from the beginning. I was captivated by the thought of her and then enchanted with her dear face when I was shown a photograph."

"What photograph?" I blurted.

He motioned us into the office and pointed to the desk inside the small room. "Mr. Allen brought that in this May."

It was me in a white dress on the porch of the church in Grand Bay after the Easter cantata I soloed in that spring. A wreath of flowers crowned my head and my smile was joyful because I was happy to be out of the spotlight.

"It's lovely, Merri! Why don't you wear that dress?"

"Because I didn't pack it. It's at home."

"Home?" Winifred frowned and her voice dropped. "I forget you aren't home with me."

"I'm not leaving any time soon, Winnie. Come on."

Bartholomew watched me steer Winifred back into the store, dark eyes thoughtful. Then he leaned in, kissing me solidly on the lips. After patting Winifred's shoulder, he smiled. "Don't give your cousin too much trouble."

"I won't." She laughed. "At least not on purpose."

Twenty-six

As we approached the gate, the smell of fresh-cut grass filled the air.

"Sean!" Winifred ran across the manicured lawn.

Keziah was hanging kitchen linens to dry on the clothes line when I reached the back. "I told Miss Winifred he was gone, but she rushed to the stable to check. How was your dinner?"

"Wonderful, thank you. Bartholomew enjoyed it as well."

"I figured he might. Leave the basket in the kitchen. I'll see to it."

Calling Winifred, I encouraged her to rest so she'd be fresh for Sean's post-supper visit. We were soon lying in the hammocks on the sleeping porch during the height of the afternoon heat, Tippet between us on the floor. My mind raced in deafening circles, all revolving around the minutes alone with Bartholomew. I could no longer fault Sean or Winifred for acting too familiar or taking liberties when I was willing to give Bartholomew so much at the first opportunity.

Two restless hours later, we washed for supper. The jambalaya was excellent, but we didn't converse much. As we finished, Tippet gave a bark from the hall just before a loud knock sounded at the front door.

Winifred rushed to answer it.

"I missed you when I was cutting the grass." Sean did a strongman's pose. "It was so warm in the sun, I took off my shirt while working."

She laughed and fell into his arms. "I'd ask you to remove your shirt right now so I might see what I missed, but I promised Merri I would try to avoid scandalous topics."

"Feel the strength coursing through me and imagine my muscles."

Face angled up, she kissed him and he immediately reciprocated. When their hands began roaming, I interrupted.

"You may sit together in the parlor."

Winifred hung his suit jacket and hat on the coat rack and hurried ahead to ask Keziah for a tea tray. Offering his arm, Sean leaned close as we entered the parlor.

"You have the air of a woman who's been thoroughly kissed, Merri. Did you and Bart have a moment today?"

I nodded, cheeks warming.

"Good," he proclaimed, hugging me before we took seats—him on the settee with room for Winifred and I in the armchair. "Uncle Patrick will be here in a few minutes to discuss legal matters. He thought you'd prefer him coming here rather than going to his office."

Winifred flounced in and dropped beside her beau. "Tea and cookies will be here soon."

"So will Sean's uncle. Please ask for another setting to be included."

When she left, Sean struck with another round of banter. "Did you get a feel for any of the positions from the book while you were at it with Bart?"

"Sean Spunner, you—"

"What did he say?" Winifred tucked herself under his arm and left a kiss on his neck that caused him to re-cross his legs.

"Nothing fit for polite society," I quipped.

"I asked after her and Bart. Merri having time with him is the only reason I'm not upset you missed me mowing the lawn."

"Will you come back tomorrow?" Winifred asked.

"Unfortunately, I can't. Today was the only day this week I could squeeze in the time to do it. Uncle Patrick has me booked solid with studies and errands. I even have work to do Saturday."

"All day?" Her eyes were dewy.

Sean fingered the tip of her nose and flashed his toothy grin. "Possibly, but I don't want to spend what time I will have pushing the grass clippers. Not when you're here with ready lips."

"I love you, Sean."

"Dearest Winnie." He kissed each cheek and then her forehead. "I'll love you always."

They held each other in the most natural, relaxed embrace I'd ever witnessed. No flirting, no grab for more. Just love, pure love. I wanted to throw my arms about them both and savor the moment.

Knocking on the front door pulled me from the fog.

Winifred sat back. "I'd like to answer it, Merri, to show Mr. Finnigan what a proper young lady I am."

Sean stood beside her and watched her leave, but slouched in resignation when she disappeared. As soon as his uncle stepped into the room with Winifred, he straightened.

"Miss Hall." Mr. Finnigan took my hand. "I hope you are well."

"Yes, thank you."

He came to the end of the settee closest to my chair, Winifred taking the other end with Sean in the middle.

Mr. Finnigan placed his briefcase on the floor by his shiny black shoes and frowned at his nephew's jacketless state and close proximity to Winifred. "Sean, you seem to have made yourself right at home here."

"Yes, sir."

The lawyer turned to me. "As this situation is most unique, I wanted to update you personally because I'm sure you'll have questions."

"I appreciate it, Mr. Finnigan, especially if you have news of Aunt Ethel. Dr. Sherard advised us not to visit her and we had hoped to do so today."

"She is stable, comfortable, though not speaking. But she is also not violent or agitated, so the doctors consider her in a good place—for the time being. It is her body's way of protecting itself, but the longer she stays like this, the darker the projection becomes."

"What can we do to help?"

"Keep up with the household and each other, and continue to pray for your aunt." Mr. Finnigan smoothed a hand over his immaculate auburn hair. "If you remember, your uncle's will touched on many things including instructions for difficult situations. One of those was if Ethel was unable to care for things, the house and private accounts would go to you and Winifred."

"But she's alive! I couldn't possibly—"

He placed a calming hand on my forearm. "No one thinks of you as an opportunist, Miss Hall, but the fact of the matter is this house needs a mistress and your cousin is in need of a guardian."

A boulder of unease rolled down my torso and settled on my stomach. "I—I was only to be here temporarily. I packed enough things for two weeks, and I'm already over twice that, Mr. Finnigan."

"You'd leave me, Merri?" Winifred's voice quaked with unshed tears.

"No, Winnie, but I wasn't prepared for an extended stay. I haven't heard from my parents or been able to send a letter to them since my first days here. I don't even know if they returned home or are stuck in Mississippi. They must be worried about me, though I've refused to dwell on it because there was nothing I could do to remedy the situation. And now with Aunt Ethel in the hospital, though we are out of quarantine, I don't think it wise to leave town in case she should need something."

"I want your permission to do two things, Miss Hall." Mr. Finnigan spoke with conviction that soothed my upset. "First, I would like to hire a private deliveryman to carry word to your family in Grand Bay. Send any correspondence you wish, including a list of personal items you might need. My hire will have instructions to wait until he secures a reply from your parents and any requested supplies before returning. Second, I would like to file the paperwork setting you as guardian of the Allen estate and Winifred. I could do that next week, to see how Mrs. Allen does the next few days, but I think it would be best to get word to your family as soon as possible."

Seeing my hesitation, Sean spoke. "Merri, the papers would be written declaring temporary ownership and guardianship, pending a reevaluation of the situation in a certain amount of weeks. You wouldn't be stealing from your aunt, you would be doing her a service in seeing to the welfare of her home and Winnie."

"Yes, Miss Hall. I'm afraid by law, you could not stay here much longer without her consent—of which there is no way of knowing when—and if—she would be able to give it. Processing Mr. Allen's wishes will secure all three of you ladies with a home and the means to upkeep it. I must advise you to not delay beyond Monday on that matter."

I looked from Sean to his uncle and back again.

"You can trust Uncle Patrick to do right for you and Winnie, not to mention your aunt. He's gone to the hospital every day this week to check on her."

"Thank you for your concern—the both of you."

Feeling the tension in the room, Keziah silently delivered the tea tray and retreated to the kitchen. Winifred went to work pouring, glancing at Mr. Finnigan to see if he noticed.

"I had forgotten the old cook," Mr. Finnigan remarked. "Doesn't she require wages? There would be no way to pay her without accepting."

I sighed. "She works more for room and board these days, but yes, Aunt Ethel gave her a bit each week."

"There you have it." The lawyer sat back and accepted the teacup and saucer with a cookie from Winifred as if everything was settled. He took a bite and then another. "She is an excellent baker."

"Merri made those," Winifred remarked. "But Keziah does well too."

"These are quite extraordinary, Miss Hall. Your domestic skills are a credit to you."

"She's teaching me everything she knows," Winifred blurted as she discretely scratched her ankle with her other foot. "I've learned ever so much from her in our time together."

Mr. Finnigan's eyes swept between her and his nephew. "I'm sure you have, Miss Ramsay."

I smiled at my cousin, wishing I could put her at ease.

"I started Mr. Graves's paperwork yesterday." Mr. Finnigan smiled. "If he keeps the store up like it's been going this past year, he'll be in a great place to settle down to start his own family in half a year's time. He'll want to see how it weathers through the fever epidemic, of course, but the end of winter, it should be fine for him."

"Is that all you look at in deciding a man's personal happiness—how well he can support a family?"

Everyone in the room turned to Winifred.

"My dear," Mr. Finnigan sounded slightly put out, "I may sound harsh, but I was once as big a dreamer as Sean. It's in our blood. Our family sailed from Ireland with hopes so romantic it would make a girl blush, but reality must strike at some point. The Finnigans went through their hell after my father arrived on this soil, and my purpose is to make sure none of us suffer needlessly again. Sean might not have our name, but I'm raising him as my own. I allow him his poetry and romances because he works and studies hard. He's ahead of his peers by two years in schooling and will be plenty young enough once he's settled in the profession to enjoy a full life with an equally vivacious wife, should that be his desire."

Her mouth, rounded in surprise, shifted into a smile, and she motioned to the piano. "Shall I play and sing for you?"

"No, but I thank you. It would remind me too much of Cecilia. I miss her while she's away, especially in the evenings. She sings and plays the piano wonderfully, though Sean fills in when needed. Cecilia taught him when he came to us."

"Winnie is much better on the piano than I am, Uncle Patrick," Sean said as he stroked her hand.

"Perhaps next time, Miss Ramsay." Mr. Finnigan reached for another cookie. "Sean is but seventeen. Most would say it's folly for a man to marry before the age of twenty-five, and I would agree. Many more would say thirty is best, but I think it depends on the man's temperament. A young man needs freedom to mature and decide on his tastes before settling with a wife. Too much pressure to provide a certain lifestyle at a young age leads to bitterness. Of course, those without don't know anything different than a life of toil. To them it's a comfort to have a ready bedfellow not needing funds other than those to purchase food to cook for him."

Sean reddened.

"Mr. Finnigan," I said, "I really don't think this is appropriate conversation for our tea."

He had the audacity to chuckle. "Forgive me, Miss Hall. I've been too much in the company of men these past weeks and forgot myself."

"We should go, Uncle Patrick."

"Not until I have Miss Hall's answer."

"I accept your advice, as long as it's temporary control."

"Very good. Securing a deliveryman will be my first item of business in the morning. I'll take note of your home address now so I might have that information when selecting a candidate." He opened his briefcase and retrieved paper and pen, taking down the information for Grand Bay, as well as my parents' names. "Have your letter ready by nine tomorrow morning, Miss Hall."

We made our way to the front door.

"Miss Ramsay," Mr. Finnigan said as Sean pulled on his jacket, "I believe I understand the root of your questions this evening. Your cousin or your aunt will have plenty to keep you until you're of age, and then you'll have your own percentage of the estate. You don't need to rush to capture a husband to support you. You're a pretty girl and will continue to mature into a striking creature. You'll be able to marry well when the time comes."

Sean placed his hat on and stepped close beside her, starring at his uncle as though he'd grown horns. "Because I'll be waiting for her, Uncle Patrick."

He laughed. "I wouldn't doubt it. You have as sharp a mind as I've ever met, and I don't say that because you're my nephew. Good night, ladies. Look for word from me tomorrow."

Twenty-seven

Winifred still slept while I dressed in a ruffled-neck shirtwaist with mutton chop sleeves and a plaid skirt. I opened the bedroom curtains before nudging her shoulder.

Groaning, Winifred turned away from the window. "My head aches and it doesn't feel like I slept more than two hours between all my nightmares about Nancy."

"You had a restless night, but you did sleep." I pulled back the covers. "A hot breakfast will help. I'll do your hair for you if that will ease your burden."

I brushed and braided Winifred's brunette hair loosely to reduce scalp strain. Her skin looked pale against the black outfit, almost sallow. A cloud of unease attempted to settle in my middle, but I pushed it aside with a smile.

After breakfast, I compiled all the letters I'd written to my mother into a larger envelope and added a cover letter explaining the current situation with Aunt Ethel and my need to care for Winifred, as well as a list of clothing and books to be sent to me. As a post script, I added:

> P.S. I'm in love, Mama. His name is Bartholomew Graves and he is now the owner of Uncle Andrew's store. He is a hard working country man with fine manners any gentleman would be proud of. I hope you will be able to meet him soon.

Letters all sealed in a large envelope from Uncle Andrew's desk, I found Winifred lounging on the settee. I suggested she sit in the yard for fresh air while I picked satsumas. Tippet at her feet, she slouched on her favorite bench under the oak, Sean's bottles swaying above her in the breeze.

At a quarter to nine, a wagon stopped before the gate. Showing me his contract of service with Mr. Finnigan to secure my correspondence and travel to Grand Bay in search of my family, the man glanced about the yard nervously.

"I didn't need to see your papers. I would have trusted your word."

"I ain't never been hired by a lawyer before, Miss Hall, nor had to sign my life on a promise of delivery. I reckoned I'd need to flash these documents to all involved to get the rest of my payment."

"Very well. I'll be right back." I went inside and returned with the envelope and a shiny quarter as a bonus for him. He accepted both with a tobacco-stained smile and tipped his hat in parting.

Winifred's dullness continued at lunch, though I tried not to let my concern show.

As Mr. Finnigan had promised days ago, the telephone workers arrived to string the wires from the street pole to the house. The hammering and drilling drove Keziah outside, but I watched from the parlor as the lines were snaked the length of the hall ceiling and run down to a box installed on the wall of the study.

"And how do I settle the bill?" I asked the lead man after he showed me how to ring the operator.

"It's being billed to Mr. Patrick Finnigan. He a relative of yours, Miss?"

"He's our lawyer."

His eyes wandered my most fashionable ensemble—making me glad I'd opted to wear it that day. "Of course, Miss. A fine lady like you would have one. Good day."

Left alone in the house, the hum of the wires grew louder. I imagined Aunt Ethel's horror when she returned. If she—no! I couldn't think that.

Should my first call be to Providence Infirmary to check on her or to Mr. Finnigan's office to thank him? Winifred shuffled in with Keziah to see the new addition to the household. A call to Dr. Sherard might be in order, but I couldn't dwell on that. It threatened to make Winifred's poor health a reality. She took to her hammock and slept until I woke her for supper.

There was a slight improvement in Winifred that evening. She ate more than she had at the previous two meals, but not her typical amount.

The shrill ring of the telephone pierced the closed study door as we finished eating. I looked at Winifred before standing, expecting her to follow me for the occasion of the first call but she stayed at the table.

I lifted the receiver to my ear and leaned toward the mouth piece set in the oak box. "Hello?"

"How are you enjoying the telephone, Miss Hall?"

"I didn't know who to telephone, so you're my first caller, Mr. Finnigan."

"If your family has a telephone, you could ring them to let them know you have a line."

"Aren't out of town calls expensive?"

"The price would be worth piece of mind, if it's needed."

"I'll wait to see if there's word from your courier first, Mr. Finnigan."

"Practical to a fault you are, Miss Hall. Sean should arrive any moment. Please see that he stays no more than an hour today."

"I will, and thank you for your help, Mr. Finnigan. And for sharing your nephew. Winifred and I are very fond of him."

"As he is of the both of you. Do telephone if you need anything. Finnigan Law Firm on Dauphin Street during the day or my residence on Palmetto in the evenings. The operator will put you through."

"Thank you again. Good night."

The knock sounded on the front door as I hung the receiver. I welcomed Sean inside.

Grinning from ear to ear, he hugged me. "Don't expect me to telephone when I'd much rather be here in person."

"Thank you and you know we'd both miss you if you failed to visit, Sean."

Winifred stood in the dining room doorway, her face brighter than it had been all day as she looked upon our guest.

"What's the matter, Winnie?" He kissed her. "Are you feeling all right?"

"I've been tired and haven't had an appetite, though seeing you helps me feel better."

His playful air switched to one of concern. "And did Merri telephone Dr. Sherard? That's one of the reasons the telephone was installed."

"It's no bother, Sean. Can't a girl feel poorly without a fuss being made?"

"Not when she's as important as you." He planted a dozen kisses across Winifred's face and swept her into his arms. Lowering onto the settee, he held her in his lap, eyes soft with love.

"You can't sit like that," I said.

"I can and I will—all night if needed to help Winnie feel better."

"Your uncle telephoned and said your visit is not to last more than one hour."

"Then I shall hold Winnie one hour."

She smiled up at him. "And recite to me?"

"Naturally. What are you in the mood for?"

"Romantic poems, but no heartbreak."

"We need the opposite emotion to feel the positive one. Did you know it was the great romantics who pioneered Gothic stories? We need the heartache to feel the joy and fear for the characters. Love and horror, the sublime experience. Did you not notice those themes in Mary Shelley's novel?"

I took a seat as Winifred shook her head. "You're much too smart for me, Sean. I just enjoy a good tale."

"But the best stories have both. You'd recognize them if you stopped to ponder it."

"I rush through, afraid to breathe in case I miss something."

"Learn to savor, Winnie. I'll help teach you."

His lips lowered to her mouth, breathtakingly slow. Each press of the succulent connection was broken with a slight retreat before he returned for another, longer kiss. Winifred's hands mussed through his hair, holding him to her lips so he could no longer retreat.

"That is more than enough," I said with as much force as possible.

Winifred clung to his neck and smiled. "He's teaching me, Merri."

"What good am I as a chaperone if you two carry on as if no one is here?"

Sean laughed and looked to me. "I consider this a lesson for the both of you. I'm sure you don't want to know what I'm capable of without a chaperone."

I ignored his wink and the images he invoked. "Separate a respectful distance or leave."

"Yes, ma'am!" He set Winifred on one end of the settee and straightened her skirt before taking the opposite corner, back erect in his orator posture. "Shall you hear Keats, Longfellow, or Shakespeare tonight?"

"Anything cheerful," she replied.

I relaxed in the armchair as I listened to Shakespearian monologues with rapt attention rivaling Winifred's. The mantel clock struck the half hour, then a quarter. Sean stood when he completed the next sonnet.

"I don't wish to push the limits now that Uncle Patrick has means to call me home in an instant. Goodnight, my dearest lady."

He kissed Winifred on the lips, but she didn't try to follow him. I went with him to the kitchen for the milk bottle, collecting a peck on my cheek before he slipped out the back door.

Twenty-eight

I woke in the rosy pre-dawn glow with my nightgown clinging to me. Sitting on the edge of the bed, I felt my body in an attempt to understand the moisture. Only the side closest to Winifred was affected. I touched a hand to hers and jerked back at the heat.

Fever!

Her face was whiter than the pillowcase, brow beaded with sweat.

I ran for Keziah's room with Tippet on my heels.

She wasn't there, so I ran for the stairs. "Keziah!"

A note rested on the kitchen counter by a fresh loaf of bread.

Miss Merritt,

I didn't want to tell you last night with Miss Winifred being tuckered out and y'all going to bed early, but a grand-niece of mine came to the kitchen door while Mr. Spunner was here. My sister is real sick and asking for me. I got up at two to fix y'all a loaf of bread and there's biscuits keeping warm in the oven for breakfast. I plan to return in a few days. I'm sure you'll do fine, especially with the menfolk checking in often.

Keziah

Tippet whined at the door. I let him out while tears ran down my face at the irony of the timing. Remembering the telephone, I raced for it. I picked up the humming earpiece and cranked the handle.

"Operator."

"I—I need a doctor. Dr. Sherard for the Eighth Ward. I don't know which street he's on."

"At this hour, I'll put you through to his house."

I never realized how annoying the buzzing ring of a telephone was until that anxious moment.

"The Sherards' residence."

"I need the doctor!" I blurted without manners.

"He's been called away, but I can take a message."

"Winifred Ramsay is severely ill and feverish. At the Allens' home. He'll know her."

"Yes, Miss. I'll give him word as soon as he checks in."

I hung the earpiece and rushed up the stairs. More sunlight coming in the window showcased Winifred's ghastly pallor. I gathered the remainder of the fever cloths Aunt Ethel had prepared and filled the pitcher for the dry sink in the bathroom. She didn't resist the cool cloth on her forehead or me tucking a fresh blanket over her. She made no response to anything at all.

Far in the distance, Tippet barked. Then the back screen snapped shut.

I didn't dare move, and I knew Sean wouldn't wait in the kitchen when his shout went unanswered.

He looked like a grown man in his navy suit and tie—ready for a day at the office—but was immediately at the side of the bed, hand on Winifred's cheek. "She's—"

"I know. And I *did* call for the doctor, but he was already out."

"And Keziah is gone. I saw the note."

I nodded, wringing a fresh cloth and replacing the now hot one.

"I'll call Uncle Patrick and tell him I'm staying here today, at least until the doctor comes."

"You can't do that, Sean. Mr. Finnigan counts on you, and Winifred could be contagious."

"I'd rather catch something from her than be kept apart. And if I leave you like this I'd be signing your own certainty for ill health. You'll be sick before noon, running up and down the stairs for supplies, telephone calls, and the door."

"I can't let you stay."

He grabbed my shoulders, eyes glowing with concern. "When Winifred needs me, you'll not be able to rid me from this house. But for now, you need to dress, and I'll set a place for her downstairs. I know what to do."

Choosing a functional calico dress, I brought it to the bathroom where I hastily washed and changed. I brushed and braided my hair, looping it into a bun at the back of my head before returning.

Sean clutched one of Winifred's hands in both of his, kneeling beside her as he prayed. I waited until he raised his head.

"Do what you need to, Sean."

Over the next quarter hour, Tippet barked, furniture scraped across floors, and the kettle whistled while I'd changed the cooling rag on Winifred's forehead several times.

Sean appeared bearing a tray with his suit jacket removed, sleeves rolled, and wearing an apron. "Eat, Merri. You'll need your strength."

He set the service with coffee, biscuits, and jam on the side table before disappearing again. Impressed with his domestic skills, I took a sip of coffee and had to keep from spitting it out. Laughing to myself, I reached for the little pitcher of milk to try to dull the overpowering bitterness. Sean might look like he knew everything, but he was a disaster in the kitchen.

Not knowing how much time I had, I hastily put jam on two biscuits and ate them. I drank as little of the coffee as possible, adding more milk after each mouthful.

Sean returned. "Her bed is ready."

I looked up from smoothing a fresh cloth on Winifred's brow. He was bare from the waist up. "What do you think you're playing at?"

"Since you're sending me off to work, I can't soil my clothing. As your nightgown showed, Winnie's perspiration does transfer. Not to mention potential germs you're always harking about. This way I'll be able to easily wash and redress without fear of spoiling clothes or transmitting infection."

"Fine." I huffed. "Carry her down."

"Not until you wash and dress her."

"I can't—"

"Why do you think I'm here?" He spread his arms, accentuating his bare chest. "I'll support her while you sponge bathe and dress her in a fresh gown."

"Sean Francis Spunner, you've got some nerve suggesting that!"

"She won't know I'm here, Merri, and you can't possibly support her yourself. With Keziah gone, what choice do you have?"

We stared, neither of us backing an inch. Or maybe I did.

"I won't wash her completely while you're here, but you must be blindfolded."

"Do it so we can get her comfortable."

In the bedroom, I took the sash from my Sunday dress and returned to Sean. He stood defiant before me, forcing me to touch his skin to turn him around.

"If you don't do exactly as I say, you'll never step foot inside this house again. Do you understand?"

"Yes, Merritt."

I pulled the sash tight, double knotting it around his eyes, before turning him back to face me and tugging the bottom hem down over his nose. I shivered at brushing his soft lips, and they quirked into a smile.

"I mean it, Sean. If anyone finds out about this I'll be disgraced—not to mention Winifred's reputation."

"We're being discreet, and I'd marry her no matter what, you know that."

"That doesn't mean you get a peek of her beforehand."

"I'm trustworthy, Merri."

I led him to the bed, pulled down the covers, and had him sit on the foot of the mattress.

"We're getting you cleaned and dry, Winnie." I unbuttoned Winifred's gown and then reached under her armpits to haul her upright. To Sean, I gave instructions. "Turn so you're facing the headboard. I'm going to lean her against you while I pull off the gown. It might take a minute to get free as it's under her backside."

"It would be easier to pull it off from her legs when I lift her."

"Good thinking."

Winifred's head fell against his shoulder, and he reached an arm about the back of her gown. I started with the side he didn't block, gently pulling her arm free of the sleeve.

"Switch sides, Sean."

He did so—hand on her bare back—with a sharp intake of his breath. I worked the other arm free and rolled the top of the gown around her waist. With a wet cloth, I washed the sweat from her neck and back.

"God, save me from myself," Sean muttered, followed by murmured Latin words that began with "*Sanctus.*"

In the moment I reached for the basin, I saw the precarious position I had placed us all in as Winifred's torso rested against Sean's—flesh to flesh. I laid Winifred back on the pillow. Sean bit his lip again, hands upon his chest where her breasts had pressed moments before. The sash about his eyes was darkened with moisture. When I looked back at him after washing her front, two rivulets ran down his cheeks.

"I'm sorry for allowing you to be in this situation." I placed a hand on his shoulder. "I need to fetch a new gown."

Half a minute later, I returned with the nightgown. Sean's hands were clasped in prayer.

"Can you support her again?"

"I'll support her my whole life if we survive this agony. I thought I loved her before, but now—if I didn't love her I wouldn't be fighting so hard against myself."

"Her summer would have been miserable without you." Hoping to keep him distracted, I prattled on as I brought her upright. "I'll put her head on your shoulder again, but you'll need to hold her lower about the waist so I can pull the gown over her head."

With Winifred situated, I reached for Sean's hands to guide him to her, but they were already skimming her mosquito-bitten legs. She shifted against him, chests fully connecting, his hands flexing around her hips until they met behind her back.

"God help me, she's wonderfully formed. Under any other circumstance—"

"Halfway there." I pulled the gown over her head and tugged the left arm into a sleeve.

Switching sides, I brought her right arm through the second sleeve and pulled her gown down between them. Sean gave a jagged half sigh, half moan.

I brushed through her hair and braided it before lowering her to the pillow. "The blindfold may be removed."

He yanked it over his head and shifted as though he was uncomfortable, exhaling a blast of air. "I'm sorry, Merri, but I'll need a minute before I stand. Gather what supplies you need and carry them down to the kitchen."

"Are you—oh!" I did my best not to look to his lap. "You'll be okay?"

"I pray I will be." He crossed himself. "If you had any idea what this feels like, you'd be a helpless wanton in a second. The books show the acts but they can't express the feeling of such contact. Tantalizingly intoxication doesn't give justice to this torture."

Blushing, I hurried from the room. I carried down an armful of fresh towels, cloths, and blankets, and then returned for several changes of nightclothes and underdrawers for Winifred, as well as a hairbrush and ribbons. The parlor was the same, as was the dining room and study. Where would Sean put a bed?

His dream! I was alone with Winifred so he set a pallet for her on the back porch.

I hastily organized the supplies on the counter by the wash basin and returned upstairs. "You did a lovely job with the bed. I'm sure she'll be comfortable."

"And you'll have water and food nearby. Plus Tippet will guard you."

"And you can look in on us whenever you wish."

His boyish grin broke across his worried face. "I will, several times a day and night."

"I don't doubt it, Sean. Let's get her settled."

He easily lifted her in his arms and held her steady so I could pull the soiled gown from her waist and properly adjust the fresh one. I dropped it on the bed and took the tray to the kitchen, Sean leading the way. He looked like something out of a fairy tale, a prince carrying a maiden to safety.

When I set the tray on the kitchen table, Winifred groaned.

"We're here for you, dearest," Sean whispered.

"Sean." Her lips scandalously met the skin of his chest before she slumped into exhaustion once more.

He carried her onto the porch and lowered her to the pallet with a row of crates beneath it to raise it off the floor. Respectfully smoothing her gown before pulling the blanket up, he tucked her in. Then, he straightened to do the sign of the cross over her.

"I love you, Winnie."

Sean disappeared inside. I thought he was putting his clothes back on, but he returned in his half-naked state, carrying all the linens from Aunt Ethel's room. He went straight out the door to the burn barrel, still situated beyond the satsuma trees. Fascinated with his level of concentration, I watched him light the fire.

Behind me, my cousin stirred restlessly. I fetched a glass of water from the kitchen.

"Winnie, try to drink a little." I pulled her upright, arm behind her shoulders to support her as I brought the drink to her mouth with my other hand. "Just a sip. It will help."

She took in three before she lost strength to swallow. I dabbed her mouth with the corner of the blanket and lowered her back.

"I'll be here for you," I told her as her eyes closed. "And Sean, bless him, has done more than I ever could have wished."

"Love." The word croaked like a broken dream.

"I know. You love each other, and I love both of you. Now rest until the doctor arrives."

Sean returned, and I followed him into the kitchen. Stopping at the sink, he turned on the water and washed his face, neck, and arms.

"The fire has burned below the rim." He spoke over the running water. "There's a full bucket by the farthest tree, so you could grab it if you need to run to put it out in case of an emergency."

"You're beyond thoughtful."

He turned off the faucet and stayed leaning over the sink, water dripping off his chest. "The only way I can walk away right now is to have thought out every possible scenario and provide you a ready help for each situation."

"I appreciate everything." After he straightened and toweled himself off with the dish rag, I threw my arms about him. "I wouldn't have survived the morning if it wasn't for you."

Twenty-nine

Whenever Winifred stirred, I forced her to drink. Her fever didn't worsen, but it never went away. A cold cloth on her head was constant, as was my persistent fear. I forced myself to eat bread and butter at noon and made a quick cup of tea.

Tippet didn't bark until Dr. Sherard came to the door.

"Miss Hall, I had hoped to see you under better circumstances."

I nodded. "This way, please. We've set up a sick room on the porch so I can better see to things. Keziah had to leave this morning. Her sister is ill and was asking for her."

"You're alone?"

"Just for a day or two, Dr. Sherard. You see, I have everything I need within a few steps. Even the telephone and half-bath is handy."

He harrumphed but took in the tidy space around Winifred's sick bed and Tippet sitting watch on the stoop.

"You've done well, but let me check Miss Ramsay. What are her symptoms?" He paused after feeling her forehead.

"She was tired yesterday, not herself, but she didn't complain. This morning she was burning hot and drenched in sweat. She's barely been conscious, but I've gotten her to drink water about once an hour since seven."

Pulse, temperature, and skin checks on her limbs resumed.

"With these symptoms and no rashes but numerous mosquito bites, I'll have to call it Yellow Jack, Miss Hall. I've yet to find a patient with it that didn't have at least half a dozen bites."

Arms crossed tight in front of my chest, I gritted my teeth.

"It isn't a death sentence. Your uncle was older and in failing health. Your cousin is in her prime. You have your wits about you. Keep her clean and cool. Continue to get her to drink and eat food if she revives enough to chew. She's a robust girl. Some rebound after only three days in bed."

"But Sean's friends—the Easton children—didn't make it."

"One of the girls did, but the boys were covered in bites. And little Rebecca. Those children ran wild in their yard. One of the blessings and curses of a large lot away from the business district— like this one here. Those old tales of Dr. Nott's are proving to be true with the mosquito connection. We're taking special note of it this time around."

"Sean warned us of mosquitoes weeks ago."

"He has a scientific mind. He'd make an excellent doctor, but his uncle has groomed him for law. Remember, when that flag goes up on the porch, no one comes in. Now that you have a telephone, I won't stop in unless you ring for me."

"Thank you, Dr. Sherard."

I saw him out, locked the front entrance, and closed my eyes as the hammering of the nails into the yellow marker sealed my fate.

Over the course of an hour, I made several trips upstairs, collecting more laundry. If yellow fever was transmitted by mosquitoes and not contagious, I could save the rest of the linens and clothes by washing what was used rather than burning everything. I laundered the used fever cloths, running them out to hang on the line by pairs so I wouldn't leave Winifred more than a minute. At five, I opened a can of soup and poured it into a pot on the stove. I strained a cup's worth of broth, hoping Winifred would drink it.

Sean found me with a stale biscuit and half a cup of mangled vegetable soup in the chair beside Winifred.

I met his concerned stare—even sterner paired with his suit and tie—with indifference in my exhausted state. "There's a yellow flag by the front door."

"Good thing I know my way to the back." He motioned to my homely meal. "What's this?"

"Supper. I didn't want to be away from Winnie too long and drained most of the broth for her."

"Althea is cooking extra beginning this evening. I'll be back with a supper plate for you, today and every day until Keziah returns. And Bart is bringing extra canned soups tomorrow, so you'll have plenty of easy meals during the day."

Tears in my eyes, I set my things down and stood to embrace him. "You're an angel."

Sean kissed my cheek. "I've been called worse—by you, actually."

I hugged him until the strength gave out in my arms.

"How is she?" He leaned over Winifred, fingering the hair that had gotten loose from her braid.

"No worse, slight improvement on the fever. Dr. Sherard didn't seem too concerned since she's been drinking."

"I'll be back in about two hours." He kissed Winifred's cheek before leaving.

I finished the soup and biscuit, and Winifred drank a few sips of the broth. Twilight fell, the green of the yard fading to navy as the minutes passed. Tippet barked, and the squeal of the gate hinge sounded from the front yard. Seconds later, Sean appeared at the door, a covered platter held before his jacketless white shirt.

"Sean is here," I said to Winifred as I stood.

I flipped the latch and held open the screen for him. "She's been mostly alert the last half hour. I even walked her to the bathroom."

He set the tray on the counter and rushed to the bed.

"Winnie!" He dropped the cloth from her forehead onto the floor and kissed all over her face. "You don't know how much I've prayed for you today."

"I've felt it." Her voice was thin, wavering.

He took the chair beside her, gathering her hands into his before turning to me. "You changed her gown?"

"I managed it in the bathroom. Dry clothes and a fresh pillowcase help her rest."

"Good. Now eat, Merri. I've got Winnie as my captive audience."

They grinned at each other—Sean with wonder and Winifred with a hint of fatigue. I brought the tray with the covered platter inside and started water to boil for coffee. When I sat at the kitchen table it was with blackened flounder, sautéed asparagus, and roasted potatoes. Not realizing how hungry I was, I had to slow my intake so I wouldn't inhale it all in two minutes.

Twice, Sean laughed and many times the rumble of his voice reached my ears, but it was mostly quiet.

Restored from the food and an extended sedentary rest, I washed the dishes and set them on the counter to dry before returning to the porch. Sean lay on his side on the edge of the pallet, attention fully on Winifred's profile. His folded arm acted as a pillow for his head and his other one was across the blanket covering her middle.

"Sean," I hissed in a whisper, for Winifred rested once more. "You shouldn't be so close."

"She's not contagious." He stretched to leave a gentle kiss on her pale jaw. "But she is beautiful, even when she's ill."

"If she's not contagious, why did Dr. Sherard hang a warning flag on the porch?"

"Changing public opinion in the midst of an epidemic isn't the most productive thing. The professionals would rather stick to the old standbys than try to cure people's misguided thinking during a time of fear." Sean chuckled and Winifred kept sleeping. "And he probably wants to safeguard you two, but don't worry. Bart will be here tomorrow. As will I—more times than you wish."

I poked his shoulder. "Then get home. Don't keep your uncle worrying tonight."

"You can't get rid of me that easily, Merri. I don't aim to leave for at least another thirty minutes." He grinned up at me. "I'm more than comfortable, so don't fuss over offering me my own seat. Go bathe and change for bed. I'll behave myself."

Twenty minutes later, hair neatly braided and garbed in a fresh day dress, I returned. Sean was still curled beside Winifred, but in place of the hard kitchen chair was one of the upholstered armchairs and ottomans from the parlor.

"I've never felt more cared for than I have under your attentions." I laid my hand on Sean's shoulder. "Thank you."

He stood. "Why aren't you dressed for bed?"

"Saving on laundry, for one thing. In case there's an emergency, I thought it best for me to be dressed."

"Are you ever *not* practical?"

"I was raised to be efficient and polite. My parents aren't highly demonstrative with affections, though I know I'm loved." I cupped his smiling face. "Thank you for showing me a new level of connection. I've never felt closer to friends than I do to you and Winnie. You're both open and carefree, even when worried."

"I believe the word you are searching for is vulnerability. Those who love with open arms expose their hearts and souls, for better or worse. Since I'm not afraid to show my feelings, I don't close my family and friends out of anything—even pain."

"It's a beautiful, although tragic, way to live."

"But it's the only way to truly live." He hugged me in a swaying embrace. "Is there anything else you need, Merri?"

"I hate to ask, especially because it's not proper, but Winifred needs another nightgown. Her one from last night was burned with the bedding and her other is hanging out to dry. She's wearing one of mine right now. And another pillowcase or two since those are being changed out so often. We're already short since Uncle Andrew's sickness. Hopefully her fever won't return, but should it—"

"You must be prepared."

"Exactly." I smiled with the relief of sharing my burden.

"Leave it to me, Merritt Hall."

Thirty

The comfort of the armchair Sean brought
to the porch helped me rest when I could, but Winifred's every
movement in the night jolted me awake. She accepted a bit of water
when I held her upright, but all she ever said was her beau's name.

"He'll be here in the morning," I always promised.

On the third interlude of wakefulness, Winifred refused to
drink. Trembling started, and I feared chills were upon her.

"I don't want to sleep," she shakily said. "Nancy is waiting
for me."

After laying a fresh cloth on her head, I smoothed her
blanket. "It's just a dream, Winnie. I'll keep you safe."

Winifred resettled, but I was restless. The next time she woke,
she drank and was back to muttering Sean's name.

Tippet's bark of greeting coincided with dawn, rousing me
from sleep.

Sean let himself in the unlatched screen door, set the milk
bottle on the counter, and leaned over Winifred to place a kiss on her
forehead. "She feels cooler. How is she?"

"She woke several times and drank, but she's complaining of
those nightmares."

"Poor Winnie. I know how disturbing dreams can be."

Not wishing him to dwell on his vision of her illness, I
changed the subject. "I'll need to get her to the bathroom when she
wakes. Maybe wash her if she has the strength. Her coloring looks
better." I smiled, stretching as I stood. "Thank you for the milk.
Hopefully Winnie will feel like drinking some this morning."

"And eating grits. That's what I was fed whenever I was sick.
Add some milk to the pot after it cooks to make it creamier."

"I know how to make grits, Sean."

"I'm used to young ladies who know nothing other than
ordering about the help. I'm glad you've taught Winnie some

domestic skills since you've been here. A woman shouldn't be helpless in her own home." He opened his arms to me.

Resting my head on his chest, I focused on the moment. It was different than when Bartholomew held me. Bartholomew's embrace had energy and breathlessness that made my body respond in new, exciting ways. Sean's arms were comfort and warmth—a place now as familiar and secure as home.

"Would you like some grits or have you already eaten breakfast?" I asked.

"I wouldn't say no if a bowl was offered."

I met his grin with one of my own. "Coffee?"

"Yes, please."

"Call me if she wakes so I can help her to the bathroom. And stay off the bed today."

"If I must."

I started to move away, but he took my hand.

"That driver my uncle hired returned yesterday evening. He saw your yellow flag and delivered a trunk to our house. I'll bring it later today."

"That means he found my family at home, right?"

"Yes," Sean said with a smile. "He said they fed him supper and allowed him to sleep in the barn."

"I'm glad they're home safe. That's one less worry for me. Hopefully there's a letter included in my provisions."

The kettle was ready and the grits added to the pot of boiling water when Sean carried Winifred into the kitchen.

I turned off the flames. "How do you feel, Winnie?"

"Better than I did yesterday."

"Let me get a few supplies right quick."

From my stash on the porch, I collected a towel and washcloth, plus a clean nightgown and underdrawers. Sean gently set Winifred on her feet in the doorway to the half-bathroom, keeping his hands about her waist for support.

"Give us a few minutes," I told him.

I stood by Winifred, offering a helping hand when needed.

"However did you manage me, Merri?" she asked as she held the sink for support while I pulled the fresh gown over her head.

"I couldn't have done it without Sean. He has a heart of gold."

As she could barely lift an arm to slip it into the sleeve, I took over for her and hollered for Sean. He flung open the door in a second. Finding me holding her upright, he whisked her back to bed.

"Do you need to lie down or could Sean hold you up so I can brush your hair?"

"Sean always has permission to hold me." The hint of a gleam brightened her eyes though the words sounded weak.

He kissed her and then sat in the armchair with her in his lap. I perched on the bed beside them, brushing through her tangled hair until it was smooth enough to braid. Hair completed, she asked to lie down until breakfast was ready. I hurriedly changed the linens on the bed and left Sean to tuck her in so I could finish cooking.

The three of us ate on the porch. Winifred in her bed, me in the armchair, and Sean on a kitchen chair he pulled in for the occasion. Winifred only ate a quarter of her bowl, but she drank the glass of milk before she asked to rest. Sean situated her while I cleared our dishes. Their lips were locked when I returned.

"Do you think that wise?"

"Wisdom from the heart, not mind," he countered as he straightened. "Winnie wants me to bring Father Quinn over to bless her. I'll schedule that with him and see you both in a few hours."

While Winifred napped, I kept busy with the household. Dishes done, I tackled yesterday's laundry ready for collection from the line, folding and storing them. Then I washed and hung the bedding and clothes from our latest changes. Tired from the physical morning after a night of restlessness, I rested in the chair a few minutes at noon before attempting dinner preparations.

Tippet barked twice and pawed to get out the screen, waking me from a sleep I didn't realize I was in. I opened the door and my dog ran for the stable. The kitchen clock said it was a quarter 'til one, and I assumed Bartholomew had arrived. I returned to the porch to check on Winifred. My cousin still slept, so I slipped into the yard, trying to keep the excitement over seeing Bartholomew for the first time after our tender moments.

Bartholomew exited the stable with a crate in his arms, sunlight glinting off his eyeglasses, and Tippet sniffing his ankles.

Unprepared for the physical response to seeing him after three days, I relished the uncontrolled smile on my face.

"Good afternoon, Merritt." He smiled and nodded toward the house. "If you could get the door, I'd appreciate it."

"Of course, but if you'd rather not go inside, I can unload the box from the stoop." I led the way around the house.

"Sean assured me it's safe, though taking medical advice from a law student might not be logical."

"Good thing Sean is intelligent." I held the screen door open, and he went straight for the kitchen.

Crate on the counter, Bartholomew's arms were free to open for me. I felt as carefree and safe as I did in Sean's arms—for a moment. Then the primal urge struck. Lifting my face from resting on his shirt, I welcomed his hot kiss. My hands migrated to his shoulders and his trailed my waist.

He broke the kiss first but held me, making me feel cherished. "How are you?"

"I'm doing well. I took an unplanned nap this last hour after getting all the washing done. I still need to heat up some dinner though. Have you eaten?"

"No, but I did bring you lots of soup, at Sean's request." He started stacking cans from the crate onto the counter.

"Thank you. I'll heat a couple cans and toast the rest of the bread."

"I brought something special for you as well." He held out a long rectangle the size of a bolt of fabric, wrapped in butcher paper.

"Bartholomew, you shouldn't have."

"The rest is charged to your store account at cost, but this is directly from me. I noticed you admiring it in the shop Thursday."

I peeled back the paper, revealing the green calico. "And I thought you were waiting on the customers while I looked at it."

"One eye was always on your beguiling form, Merritt."

I blushed and turned to the supplies, picking through the cans. "Don't start calling me a temptress, or I'll know you're full of falsehoods."

"Then I'll show you instead."

Bartholomew's kiss was the longest and deepest yet. I delighted in it as I sought to discover each muscle in his arms and back. His large hands made their way to my ribs. Hot through my simple cotton gown, I craved more—more of what I knew was part of the expression of love. Slowly arching in a timid invitation, I gasped as he cupped my breasts, rubbing them through the dress. I was slight of form and unbound, but his touch made me feel every bit a beautiful woman. His lips worked down my neck, one hand questing further up to undo the top button of my frock.

Shocked at my behavior, I straightened and met Sean's amused expression watching us from the doorway.

"Do I need to haul you both off to confession?" Sean asked with a smile.

Bartholomew laughed, arm about my waist to keep me close. "We're not even Catholic, Spunner."

"Have either of you eaten dinner?" I asked. They both shook their heads. "If you two can keep an eye on our sleeping beauty, I'll prepare dinner."

"I'd be happy to," Sean replied. "There's a package waiting on the porch for her to open when she wakes. And one for you on the stoop. Your trunk."

"Bartholomew, would you bring it to the hall for me?" I picked up two cans of tomato soup.

Bartholomew retrieved the small trunk, and then he and Sean carried kitchen chairs onto the porch while I heated soup and toasted buttered bread in the oven.

As I set bowls onto the serving tray, a floorboard squeaked behind me. Expecting Bartholomew, my eyes widened when I turned to face Sean.

"He loves you as you deserve, Merri. Your passion for each other is a beautiful thing, though you might want to be more careful where you indulge in your moments together. The kitchen is free range to household members."

"You're not—"

"Aren't I?" He quipped, eyebrow raised.

I smiled.

"I thought so."

Hugging him, I laughed. "Is Winifred awake?"

"No." His voice sounded dejected. "She's slept a long time, hasn't she?"

"Since you left this morning." I ladled the soup into three bowls and added the platter with the toast to the service. "I'll keep her chicken stock in the pot on the stove. You can carry this out."

He took the tray with a heavy countenance, his concern over Winifred increasing once more.

Settled in three kitchen chairs near the door so we wouldn't crowd the bed area, Sean blessed the food and prayed for Winifred's healing.

While we were eating, Winifred murmured for Sean.

He sprung from his chair. "I feared you would never wake."

"Is there something to drink?"

He helped her sit and reached for her glass. "Merri fixed chicken soup for you. Toast if you wish it as well."

"I think I'll try both, thank you."

Sean helped her to the bathroom and Winifred assured me she was fine. I waited with him in the hall, expecting a cry for help, but she opened the door a few minutes later. Reaching for him, Winifred conveniently went limp in his arms, and he carried her back to the porch.

Bartholomew stopped me in the kitchen. "I'll chaperone so you can get her dinner."

When I brought the food, Bartholomew leaned against the wash sink, watching the couple on the bed. Winifred sat against a pillow with her back to the wall for support, an opened box on her lap with Sean cross-legged on the mattress, facing her.

"I'll take it." Sean reached for the tray. "Today I'm Winnie's everything—from table to deliveryman."

"Isn't it beautiful, Merri?" She held a white nightgown with lace about the wrists and yoked neck, trimmed with sky blue ribbons the color of her eyes.

"Very beautiful."

"I knew when I saw it in Hammel's it was perfect for Winnie. There are four pillowcases as well." Sean balanced the tray in his lap and handed Winifred the teacup of chicken stock—small and light enough for her to handle alone.

Winifred finished the cup and ate a piece of toast. "I'm still tired. Is that normal?"

"Yes, dearest. Your body needs lots of rest to heal. Sleep as much as you wish. I'm just as happy watching you as chatting." He handed her the water glass. "Now drink a bit of this to wash it all down."

"Dr. Sherard thinks you should study medicine," I said as I took the tray from Sean. "You do have a soothing way with people."

"An excellent bedside manner." He winked.

"Spunner." Bartholomew's warning tone cooled the fire in Sean's eyes.

Winifred giggled, though it sounded strained. "I bet you could talk anyone into taking their medicine."

"And that's what lawyers need—the ability to sway people." Sean lifted Winifred from her seated position. "Merri, the pillow, please."

I fluffed the pillow, situated it at the head of the bed, and pulled down the blankets before stepping back. Sean lowered Winifred to the sheet and kneeled above her.

"Rest, Winnie. There's much we still need to share." He kissed both her cheeks, then her lips as the length of him dipped toward her innocent body.

Gasping, I stepped back from the evocative scene. Bartholomew grabbed Sean's collar.

The young man stood of his own accord, still smiling at Winifred, as he tucked her in. "I'll be right here if you need me, dearest."

After Winifred closed her eyes, Sean grabbed Bartholomew's arm and stalked into the kitchen with him. The two stared each other down.

Sean spoke first. "I don't appreciate you treating me as a threat."

"You had her below you on a bed. Merritt was shocked at your boldness."

"I would *never* force myself on Winnie or *any* young lady." Sean shoved at the other man. "Do you think that way because you do those things yourself? Did you have permission to grope Merritt the way you were earlier? Should I have yanked you away when I arrived?"

"Sean Francis!" I went for him at the same moment Bartholomew swung.

Sean ducked the strike and blocked me from coming closer at the same time with a smooth sidestep and outstretched arm. "I've been in the boxing club at school since I was thirteen. You don't want to mess with me, Graves."

Bartholomew pulled off his jacket, throwing it on the floor, and set his glasses on the counter while Sean rolled up his shirtsleeves.

"Get out of this house, the both of you!"

"You heard the lady." Sean went for the porch and turned back. "Or is this another example that *you* don't respect a woman's wishes?"

I stepped out of the way as Bartholomew lunged past. They both pushed out the screen door, causing it to snap back twice. I stood at the door to watch. I wasn't furious or even mad because I'd seen my brother get into enough physical fights with his best friends to know that's what boys did. Not to mention the brawls the grown men in my town had over politics though there were laughing together the next day.

Tippet whined to get to the yard, but I kept him inside, afraid he would distract them. Wincing each time one struck the other, it didn't matter which one walked away victorious because I'd patch up both.

Five minutes, a couple dozen headlocks, and countless punches later, they huffed their way toward the stoop with limping gaits.

"I'll clean and bandage the winner first. Which one of you is that?"

Bartholomew elbowed Sean, an exhausted smile on his battered face. "The scrappiest city dandy I ever met."

Sean's typically broad grin fell when it touched his swelling left eye. "A city dandy who treats women with respect."

"And I'd protect the two ladies here with my life."

"I never doubted you, Bart." Sean slapped him on the back and stepped through the door I held open.

My dog slipped out, licking Bartholomew's bleeding hand.

I pulled a chair close to the kitchen sink for Sean and set to washing his swelling face.

"What will your uncle say when you come home looking like this?"

Sean winced as I dabbed the cut on his left cheek. "He'll remind me of the importance of appearance for a man of the law, followed by asking how the other guy looks."

I smiled. "Sounds like this has happened before."

"And will probably again. No one can say I mistreat a girl and get away with the falsehood."

"I didn't fear your action, Sean. I gasped because it such an intimate position and—"

"You remembered the book!" He laughed, then flinched.

"If you don't hush about that book, Sean Spunner, I'll take it back and burn it." I pointed to the sink. "Now soap and water your hands, and then send Bartholomew in."

"And then I can wait by Winnie, right?" Despite the swelling and rising bruises, he managed to have a pleading expression.

"Yes, but stay off her bed."

Half a minute later, Bartholomew hobbled into the kitchen looking sheepish. "I'm sorry if I behaved poorly."

Smiling, I motioned to the chair. "I appreciate your willingness to physically step in, but I didn't question Sean's motives. I was shocked at the boldness of his movements."

Bartholomew settled in the chair and I brought a washcloth to his face. "Sean sure is something, isn't he? I haven't gotten into a fight like that in half a decade and I'm feeling it already. I might not be able to move tomorrow."

"How old are you, Bartholomew?" I rinsed the cloth in warm water and turned back to him.

"Twenty-three."

"That's hardly means for claiming aches of old age."

He laughed. "Aches from fisticuffs then. I'll look a fright to the customers in the morning."

"Just be your courteous self—you know, the one who doesn't try to flatten another man."

"I was a brute, but he was a bigger one." He touched my hand with a fingertip. "I'm glad you aren't upset over it."

"Ezra, my brother, is always getting into tussles with his friends. Of course, he's Sean's age, so that's to be expected. My father participated in his last brawl a couple years back. Hold still a moment." I brought a fresh cloth to his face to make sure I got all the grime. "My mother fussed at him so much, he hasn't done it again."

Sean must have gotten more strikes to the man's torso than his head because Bartholomew's face wasn't as swollen. Studying each contour and line from the blackening eye down, I finally focused on his mouth. He had a split lip but it didn't stop him from smiling when he saw me studying it. I broke the connection to toss the cloth into the sink.

"Will you kiss it better, Merritt?"

I laughed and placed my hands on his shoulders, leaning down to kiss him. "Now wash your hands. Your knuckles are busted something fierce."

"Sean has a hard head."

While Bartholomew soaped his hands, I collected a bottle of ointment from the medicine cupboard. Once again in the kitchen chair, I sat in another across from him, knees touching. He smelled of soap and earth and man. I concentrated on his medicinal needs, but my longing for his touch increased as I wrapped his knuckles with bandages to help the ointment absorb into his skin.

"Thank you, Merritt."

We stood at the same time, toe to toe between our kitchen chairs.

Bartholomew looked to me with tender brown eyes. "Is there anything I need to say or do to repair ill-feelings over the events of today?"

"I told you, I'm not shocked by the fight."

"What about how I was with you earlier? What Sean said about the liberties I took."

I reached my arms around him, nestling against his chest. "I wanted you to touch me, Bartholomew," I whispered. "Don't regret our experience—cherish it. You're the first man to have touched me like that."

"And hopefully the last."

His lips met mine as he embraced me. Surrendering my cares to feel every movement of lips and tongue left me drowning in the warm sea of Bartholomew's taste.

"You've quickly become my everything, Merritt. I know your hands are full here, and I'll help you all I can, but I won't push you to declare your feelings. Not that you're hiding them from me with these moments we share. Just know I won't ask you to put me before your family."

"Thank you, Bartholomew. That's just what I needed to hear."

Thirty-one

Winifred napped most of the

afternoon, but when she was awake, Sean read aloud from a copy of *Oliver Twist* he found in the study.

I kept busy washing laundry. Bartholomew carried the basket to the clothesline and held it so I could pin the items without bending. The late afternoon sun and dry breeze allowed me to gather the fresh linens before dark.

At six, Sean and Bartholomew walked to the Finnigan house to collect our Sunday supper. Winifred was awake, so I used the privacy to help her freshen. As we expected the priest that evening, I had her wear Aunt Ethel's lightweight blue dressing robe over her nightgown. Then I brushed and braided her hair.

"How do I look?"

"Pale and tired, but pretty. Sean can't stop looking at you."

"I can feel his love and prayers, even when sleeping."

Tippet barked, and I opened the door for Sean and Bartholomew. Sean immediately went for Winifred. Bartholomew carried the second tray into the kitchen, and I retrieved Sean's abandoned one. Under the silver lids, the trays held blackened red drum fillets, rice, sautéed green beans, and tiny cornbread muffins.

"It all looks and smells wonderful," I said.

"Winnie wants buttered rice and tea," Sean said as he joined us.

"Then you dish up the rice, and I'll prepare the water for tea. Who else wants some?"

The men agreed to tea, and Sean soon returned to the porch with a bowl of rice for Winifred. Bartholomew kept me company as I pulled plates out for the three of us while waiting for the water to boil. By the time I brought a cup to Winifred, she'd eaten the rice and drank a bit of water, though she happily accepted the teacup.

"Stay with me, Sean," she whispered.

"Of course, dearest. I'll sleep on the floor tonight if you wish it."

She smiled. "Merritt wouldn't allow that."

"You don't think I could talk her into it, even with my soothing manner?"

"Enough, Sean," I said as a means to cut their banter. "Go dish up and you can eat wherever you wish—except Winnie's bed."

He laughed and hopped off the edge of her bed where he'd been perched.

After dishing up my supper, I joined Bartholomew on the porch. Sean ate in the armchair by Winifred.

"Is there anything I can do for you tomorrow?" Bartholomew asked.

"I don't believe so, but thank you. I hope to keep things a bit quieter as Winifred needs more rest." I glanced across the porch before going for the kitchen, Bartholomew following. "I doubt I can keep Sean away, but he does sit calmly when she's sleeping."

"But more people around equals extra chatter and the opportunity to brawl."

I laughed. "Sean does tend to showoff for an audience."

"The shop has a shared telephone line with the feed store next door." Bartholomew paused. "Might I call to check on you?"

"I'd like that."

"And send word if you need me for anything—supplies or companionship."

"I will, Bart. Thank you."

Taking me in his arms, he gazed down at me. "May I kiss you goodnight, Merritt?"

"Please do."

Lips together in a tender dance, my hands roamed his shoulders as his locked about my waist, holding me close.

"I'll think of you every day," he whispered in my ear.

"Come back when you're able." I tucked against him once more.

He kissed me, quick and sweet, before going for the porch. He waved to Sean. "I'll see you soon, Spunner. Take care of that eye."

He raised his hand in farewell from his post by Winifred. Bartholomew scratched behind Tippet's ears, but left him on the shadowed porch when he went into the night. Gathering Sean's dishes, I paused to check on Winifred.

"She looks pale," I whispered.

Sean nodded, frowning. "Father Quinn will bless her. He should be here soon."

Father Quinn's knock came when I was halfway through washing the supper dishes. I skirted around the trunk from home in the hall and unlocked the front door.

The man in black looked tired, but he offered a smile. "Miss Hall?"

"Yes, Father Quinn. Sean told me you would come tonight. Thank you for helping." Tippet slipped out the door when he entered. I took the priest's hat. His dark hair was thick, face unwrinkled—younger than I expected. "Sean is on the back porch with Winifred."

"Is he behaving himself, Miss Hall? Young men can be precocious about girls."

"There's a shared attraction between him and my cousin, but he's thoughtful and kind. Without his help, the past few weeks would have been unbearable for all of us."

As soon as he stepped onto the porch, Sean dropped to his knees and kissed the man's hand. "Father Quinn, you must heal her and bless the house."

"Patience, my son. I can only do the Father's will, in His time."

"But you can try. She's troubled and needs rest."

He gripped Sean's shoulder. "Is your faith strong?"

"You know it is."

I ached at the desperation in his voice.

"Strong enough to *not* walk away from the Church if the prayers are not answered to your liking?"

Sean bit his lip and nodded, eyes sparkling with moisture.

The priest fingered Sean's brow. "What are you doing, getting into fights?"

"It was for a good cause, Father Quinn."

He shook his head. I followed them to the bed where Winifred shifted uncomfortably, a light sheen on her forehead in the half-light.

"Winnie, Father Quinn is here." Sean stepped to the foot of the bed and motioned the priest to Winifred.

"Do you seek a blessing, my daughter?"

"Yes, please, Father."

The priest retrieved supplies from a small satchel that hung about him crosswise, partially hidden by his left arm. He pressed a cross into her limp hand and Sean removed prayer beads from his own pocket. Winifred was anointed and the sign of the cross done over her before Father Quinn began speaking in Latin.

Beyond the healing words, an unrest built like a summer storm. Father Quinn began chanting Rites in Latin as he made his way toward the kitchen, blessing the house. His voice grew fainter, but Sean's grew louder.

"Heal her, O Lord." One hand cupped Winifred's cheek. "I need her loving spirit."

Leaning over Winifred, he kissed her, creating a curling smile as her eyes fluttered open.

"I love you, Sean," she whispered.

"And I you." He lifted her free hand with his, bringing it to his heart and then to his lips.

Following the priest, I silently waited for him in the hallway until he finished sprinkling Holy water about the rooms as he prayed.

"Do you need something, my child?" he asked as we returned to the kitchen.

"I'm curious about Sean. He says he has a second sight. He has dreams—visions. Is that part of your religion?"

The priest shook his head. "Superstitions from the old country. Some families pass down tales and seek to keep the folklore alive in the new generations. The girl has been blessed and also the house. I can do no more here."

On the porch, Sean accepted Father Quinn's hand and returned the cross Winifred had held. "Thank you, Father."

"Yes, thank you." I walked him to the front door. Tippet ran in when he went out.

"Don't allow Sean stay here too long. He needs the guidance of his uncle at this time."

I assured the priest I would before saying farewell.

Quarter of an hour later, Sean reluctantly trudged home.

Winifred still peacefully slept, so I collected clean clothes and washed and changed in the half-bathroom downstairs. Pausing in the hall, I lifted the lid on the trunk. My requested clothes and a few books from home were tucked inside. Grateful to have more clothing and reading options, I took the letter from the top of the pile and brought it to the porch.

I smoothed the blanket around Winifred, let Tippet into the yard, and settled on a chair in the kitchen doorway to read.

Dear Merritt,

I am sorry to hear about the issues plaguing Ethel's household. Andrew was a fine man and she was always a stalwart figure. Losing him must have cost her dearly. Stay as long as you are needed. I am grateful you are there to help in my behalf.

Our trip to Gladys's was pleasant. Yellow Fever is not an issue in the Jackson area, but it has been all that is talked about since we returned. Your father and Ezra are busy at the store but I have everything under control at home. If needed, you may telephone the store during business hours to speak to your father, but I do not think it wise to do without firm cause.

I have enclosed everything you requested, along with a few of your books you left on your desk. The untidy pile has been bothering me. Rather than attempt to place them in your bookcase, I am sending them on. Your room is now orderly.

You must try to keep house for Ethel better than you did your own room. Hopefully this man you are in love with will see you as efficient in the role of housekeeper during this trial run. Do not disappoint me by failing to showcase all I have taught you about domestic life.

Love, Mama

I sighed and folded the letter in my lap. After weeks with gushing Winifred and Sean, my mother's no-frills communication was disappointing. She loved me, but to show my love for her she wanted me to do a great job with my service at the Allens' house. Action spoke louder to her than flowery words, but I was beginning to see I now wanted gestures and words of love more than the obedience and servitude I was raised with. Finding the balance would be difficult.

I reset the kitchen chairs at the table and clicked off the lights. Giving myself a few moments to adjust to the darkness, I slowly made my way to the porch, letting Tippet inside, and latched the screen. Fluffing a small pillow, I tucked my head against it and curled into the armchair.

***

Midnight found me switching out fever cloths on Winifred's forehead. It could have been my imagination, but she felt hotter than she did when she first took ill. Out of her mind with delirium, she mumbled off and on. The only intelligible words were "Nancy" and "Sean."

The hours blurred as I tried to keep her cool. I dared not leave her to telephone the doctor. The laundry pile continued to grow. Winifred needed washing too, and the bed linens changing, but I hadn't the strength to tackle them alone.

Sometime later, Tippet barked and I jerked awake, rubbing my neck from where it had drooped in my exhaustion. I felt Winifred's burning cheek before going for the wash basin to rinse a clean cloth in cold water. The hairs on my arm tingled and I knew I was being watched from the darkness surrounding the house. Trying not to panic, I wrung the cloth and went back to Winifred to replace the old one.

Across the porch, Tippet's tail wagged and he pawed at the screen.

"Who's there, Tippet?"

"Me."

I nearly shrieked until it registered whose voice it was. "Sean, you scared me!"

He pressed a hand to the screen as I approached the door. "Merri—"

"I need your help. What time is it?" Tippet jumped at him when I opened the door.

"Four-thirty. I dreamt that you needed me."

"No matter that the priest doesn't believe in your dreams, I need you, Sean." I took his hand and led him to Winifred. "She's burning with fever again. I haven't left her side since before midnight. Stay with her while I telephone the doctor."

In the study, I asked the telephone operator for Dr. Sherard's house.

It rang a dozen times before she clicked back. "There's no answer, Miss."

I hung the receiver and hurried to the back porch. Sean looked up from praying over Winifred.

"No answer at Dr. Sherard's. I think we should bathe and change her. Are you up to helping with that again?"

He nodded.

"You're keeping all your clothes on this time, but let me fetch a blindfold."

"I'll be able to help you easier if I can see what we're doing. Time is important at this stage."

Even though Dr. Sherard had praised Sean's scientific mind, and the fact that he was already acquainted with the intimacies of the human body, I still hesitated.

"Merri?"

"We'll do it your way this time. I fear she's on her way out of this life." I had already failed too many people, beginning with cousin Diamond. But there wasn't time to mope. I handed a towel to Sean. "Keep the towel over your shoulder. We'll remove her nightgown and I'll wash her. Then you lift her, wrapping the towel around her, and I'll change the linens. We'll pull on the fresh gown and then I'll see to her hair if you can hold her a bit longer. And if she talks, don't reply. We work in silence."

I filled a pitcher half full while Sean moved the armchair out of the way.

With a nod, we moved as one to the bedside. I pulled the coverings to her middle and bunched her nightgown to her waist, over her underdrawers. I brought her upright, lifted the gown from her sweaty back, and then over her head, covering her chest with it as Sean laid her back. With a nod to me, he stepped away and held the pitcher with one hand and a stack of cloths in the other. I gently washed her face and neck. Gown fully removed, I washed her soft curves, using a clean cloth to pat her dry before leaning her forward to wash her back.

"Sean," she muttered, eyes closed.

"It's Merritt," I responded. "I'm getting you cleaned. It will just be another minute."

Sean spread the towel over her before lifting, and I quickly stripped the bed. Once it was remade, he sat on the edge with her in his lap. He lowered his face for a kiss and I waved my hands, shaking my head.

Bringing my white summer nightgown over her, I worked an arm through one short sleeve and then the other before tugging the towel out from under it. With a semblance of modesty in place, I undid her braid and brushed through her hair. When I set the brush aside, Sean ran a hand over the length of Winifred's brunette locks, a slight smile on his face as his fingers combed through the thickness. I elbowed him to stop and hastily braided it, tying a blue ribbon around the bottom.

After placing her on the crisp sheet, he took care buttoning the top half of the nightgown closed. He covered her with the quilt, sat beside her, and leaned over until his cheek was against hers.

"I could melt into you, Winnie. We'd be forged together forever." He kissed her cheeks and then lips. "You'll always be my first love, no matter what happens."

"Sean."

"I'm here, Winnie."

"Stay."

"I'll be here all day, dearest." He stretched out beside her as night crept toward dawn.

Thirty-two

At daybreak on that third day of fever,

I began washing laundry. Sean dozed beside Winifred as I worked. After feeding the fever cloths through the wringer, I carried the basket to the clothesline. I startled when Tippet barked three times and ran for the front.

Tippet faced the gate, tail wagging, as I rounded the house.

"Hello?" I stopped on the path ten feet from the gate and gave warning to the Black woman in a domestic's uniform. "The house is under quarantine for fever."

"Are you Miss Merritt? I figured my boy is here since he wasn't in bed, so I brought some food for y'all and came to collect the supper things."

"Oh, thank you, Miss—"

"Call me Althea like Sean Francis does."

"All right, Miss Althea. If you wait here I'll bring—"

"Sean Francis is smart, and if he's here, it's safe."

I smiled. "We tend to take his word as well."

"His word is as golden as his eyes, I always say."

I led the way to the back door and held the screen open. Althea paused and looked at the bed several seconds. Sean was on his side, head on Winifred's shoulder, arm about her waist, and his leg draped over hers.

Once we were in the kitchen, she spoke. "I've never seen a boy love a girl like he does that one. I fear for his true heart."

"He shares with you?"

"About everything since the day he arrived five year ago. He's always hungry and often sits in the kitchen, either reading or talking up a storm about everything on his mind while feeding his belly." She unpacked a loaf of bread, milk, and several parcels from her basket. "He told me all about his Winnie the day he met her—crying in the yard. I helped him figure out what to do to protect her from that spirit haunting her dreams."

"The bottles and painted ceiling?"

"Sure enough. And it kept her good for a bit, didn't it?"

"Yes, and thank you for the bread and milk."

"And cookies are in these packages. I figured he'd play hooky to be here all day. I don't worry about Sean Francis when he's with you as he says you take good care of him, but he'll appreciate the cookies if he's not too sad to eat. You too, Miss Merritt. Help yourself. I'll have supper ready for you all this evening. He'll have to fetch it though."

"Everything was excellent last night, Althea. Thank you. I wouldn't be able to keep up with Winifred and everything here if it wasn't for the help from your household. You don't think Mr. Finnigan minds, do you?"

"Mr. Finnigan might talk harsh, but he dotes on Sean Francis in his own way. He's working him hard now so he can have it easier when he's out of school. But I worry about that too. His talk of Mardi Gras societies and the unholy antics of those men aren't fit for Sean Francis. He needs a good girl and a well-stocked library, not fancy women and over-indulgences."

"Mr. Finnigan seems like a gentleman."

"He is for the most part, but come carnival season, society men turn into scamps. Bless their hearts. All the money in the city runs through them, but they don't have common sense between the lot of them." She took up her empty basket and packed yesterday's milk bottle and the washed supper dishes into it, then tucked the nestled trays under her arm.

On the porch, Althea peered over the couple.

Sean turned to her with a smile while keeping his arm about Winifred. "Isn't she the prettiest girl you ever saw, Althea?"

"She sure is, Sean Francis, and you two look fine together."

"I wish you could see her eyes, blue as the spring sky."

"I can image with that china doll complexion and dark hair. Be sure to fetch supper at six o'clock. Miss Merritt needs more meat on her bones, so save some cookies for her, you hear?"

"Yes, ma'am."

I held the door and then walked to the gate to open it for Althea, giving my thanks once more. Tippet stayed in the yard and I went straight to the telephone when I entered the house. This time, I got hold of the doctor.

"It's Merritt Hall, Dr. Sherard. Winifred's fever is back. She was doing better yesterday, but is hotter than ever since before midnight."

"Does she seem worse than before?"

"Without question."

"I had hoped she wouldn't relapse. I'll try to stop by midday to see her. Keep her cool and comfortable until then."

Feeling defeated and tired from the busy night and morning, I returned to the porch. "The doctor is coming midday," I whispered. "Would you like some toast, Sean?"

"Do you have butter, cinnamon, and sugar for it?"

"Yes, and coffee."

"Please, Merri." He smiled up at me from Winifred's shoulder. "After you eat, I want you to rest for a while."

"I need to wash the rest the laundry."

"I'll crank the wringer."

Winifred roused slightly. Sean was able to get her to drink half a cup of water, but she wasn't alert enough to eat. He snuggled back in bed with her while I prepared our simple breakfast.

Sean and I ate, and then washed and hung the laundry together—all while Winifred slept. Afterward, I stretched out on the settee in the parlor and allowed him to watch over the invalid. I fell asleep immediately and woke with Tippet's bark, followed by knocking on the front door. The mantel clock said it was half past eleven. Praying Sean and Winifred were decent, I let Dr. Sherard in the front door.

"She's still on the back porch?" he asked as I led the way toward the kitchen.

"Yes, it's working out well for us."

Sean sat in a kitchen chair near the doors, as far away from the bed as possible, but Dr. Sherard frowned at him. "What are you doing here, Sean?"

"I'm helping Merri by keeping an eye on Winnie when she's busy with chores."

"What does she need done? I've heard your uncle is sending her supper every day."

"Laundry—washing, drying, and collecting. Dishes because Merri is too polite to send things back dirty. Two other meals for herself, plus drinks and food for Winnie. Changing the linens and—"

"That's more than enough cheek, Sean."

He stood and looked at the doctor eye to eye. "I meant no disrespect, Dr. Sherard. Merri is the hardest working young woman I've ever seen, and she's doing it all while mourning her uncle and worrying about her aunt. How is Mrs. Allen doing?"

Caught off guard, the doctor looked from Sean's serious face to my surprised one. "She's holding steady with slight improvements. She spoke a full sentence when asked a question yesterday."

"And what was that?" I questioned.

Dr. Sherard tried not to smile. "She was asked if she wanted communion and said 'keep those pagan beliefs away from me.'"

Sean laughed. "You see, Merri? Being in a Catholic hospital will keep her fighting spirits up. That's a good thing."

I smiled at him and followed the doctor to Winifred. He examined her in his deliberate fashion, as though his mind was already made up and he sought to find evidence to support his theory. Winifred whimpered and squirmed though her eyes never opened.

"The infection is worsening, Miss Hall. If she seems uncomfortable, dose her with whiskey so she can sleep. Expect yellowing of her skin and possible vomiting as the days pass. If black vomit sets in, her chances of survival are next to none."

"But—"

"All you can do at this point is keep her comfortable." He washed his hands in the sink as I stared in disbelief. "Telephone me if you have questions, otherwise I'll stop in tomorrow. See me out, Sean, and then get yourself home. There's no need for you to witness this."

Sean disappeared with the doctor for several minutes. Upon returning, he took me in an embrace that let me know I was not alone.

***

While I washed the supper dishes, the telephone startled me out of my glazed stupor. I hurried across the hall and lifted the ear piece.

"Hello?"

"Good evening, Merritt."

My spirits rose. "Hello, Bartholomew"

"I called to see if there was anything you needed."

"No, but thank you."

"How's Winifred?"

"Not well. Her fever spiked during the night and she's been battling it since. The doctor's pronouncements weren't cheerful."

"I'm sorry to hear that. Do you need company?"

"Sean has been here since before daylight and has been a great help. I would love to see you, but coming would do nothing other than satisfy me temporarily."

"I'll be thinking of you, Merritt." He paused, the buzzing in the wires overtaking our conversation. "Stay in touch."

"Who was on the telephone?" Sean asked when I joined him on the porch.

"Bartholomew. He wanted to know how we were doing."

Sean pulled me onto his lap in the armchair and kissed my cheek. "And did you tell him I've been here all day, fulfilling your every need?"

"Half of that, you cad." I wriggled out of his grip and stood. "Now when are you leaving?"

Sean gave me an impish grin and kissed my nose.

A few minutes after Sean left with the empty supper tray, Tippet pawed the screen to be let out. I hurried to the door. At the sound of a horse, Tippet took off for the stable, and I followed. My heart raced at seeing Bartholomew holding the reins inside the yard, the gate already closed behind him. He looked handsome in all black—from his tall riding boots to his button down shirt, a mysterious visitor in the night.

"Sometimes temporary satisfaction is worth the effort," he said in answer to my unasked question. He led the horse toward the stable and I followed, slipping my hand into his free one.

"I'm happy to see you. Would you like something to eat or drink?"

"I'm here for you, not to be waited upon." He released my hand. "I'll be in as soon as I see to the horse."

Tippet stayed with Bartholomew, and I returned to Winifred. Her legs shifted and hands reached. Perched beside her, I felt her burning head before hastily going for the sink to prepare a fresh cloth.

Placing it on her forehead, I took her hand. "I'm here, Winnie. I stepped out for a minute, but I'm back."

She groaned.

"Tippet and Bartholomew are here too," I said as they entered the door. "He'll help you get some water."

I removed the cloth, and he held her upright so I could bring the glass to her parched lips. She drank several mouthfuls and began shivering.

"Winnie, I'm sorry I can't do more." I tucked another blanket over the others.

"Love. You. Merri." She spoke the broken words through chattering teeth.

"What can I do?" Bartholomew whispered to me.

"Whiskey! Dr. Sherard told me she could have whiskey. Run to Sean's house and beg some from Mr. Finnigan."

Bartholomew left without question. I spent the next minutes soothing my cousin as best I could. It was no surprise when Tippet barked a greeting, and Sean burst onto the porch.

"Winnie, I'm here." He crawled onto the bed with her, rubbing her shoulders through the blankets. "I'll warm you, dearest."

Bartholomew returned, holding bottle of Irish whiskey.

"How much do I give her?" I asked.

"A tiny amount," he replied. "What's the smallest cup you have?"

In the kitchen, I retrieved a quarter measuring cup. Bartholomew opened the bottle and poured enough to fill it halfway. Under the bright kitchen light the bruising on his face was pronounced a deep purple. I knew he'd do anything for me and took heart.

I brought the cup to Sean with renewed purpose. "Here it is."

Sean held Winifred upright while I got the whiskey down her throat. She immediately coughed and gagged, but Sean helped her relax, tucked her back in bed, and curled beside her.

With a sigh of relief, I turned to the kitchen to wash the cup. As soon as my chore was completed, Bartholomew opened his arms.

"It feels good to be held," I murmured into his chest. "Thank you for coming and getting help. I thought I could do it alone but I can't."

"Sean told his uncle he would stay with you as long as needed—to cancel his work for the week because he'd be here until Keziah returned."

"And Mr. Finnigan agreed?"

"He wasn't given the chance to voice objection. I'm sure Mr. Finnigan will show up at some point." Bartholomew hugged me tighter. "Shall I stay too?"

I kissed him, hoping he'd feel my want though I couldn't accept his offering. "You need your rest before work tomorrow, but I appreciate you coming."

He lifted me off the floor, hugging me and initiating another deep kiss.

"Don't hesitate to telephone. I'd close up the shop and be here within a quarter of an hour if needed."

Nodding, I clung to him another moment before we went to the porch.

Sean and Winifred were quiet on the bed, so I escorted Bartholomew to the yard with Tippet. I held the gate open for him to ride through, waving to him as he galloped into the night.

Thirty-three

The telephone was ringing when I got to the porch. Rushing through the house, I breathlessly answered.

"Miss Hall, I hope my nephew hasn't made a nuisance of himself."

"He's been an asset, Mr. Finnigan. Thank you for sending the whiskey. Mr. Graves stayed long enough to make sure it settled Winifred down—and it did."

"I'm glad to hear that. And Sean? Is he on his way home?"

"He…"

"Has he installed himself as Miss Ramsay's keeper?"

"Yes, Mr. Finnigan."

"I heard the grim report from Dr. Sherard and will allow Sean this indulgence. I do feel sorry for him—for you as well. Let me know whatever you need and I'll have it sent over. Speak with Althea if I'm not here. I know Sean is her pet, but I'll give her official permission to do whatever needs to be done for any of you in my absence. Don't hesitate to telephone."

"Thank you, Mr. Finnigan."

We ended the call, and I checked on my cousin. She was still sleeping peacefully, but Sean watched me.

"Who was it?" he whispered.

"Your uncle."

"Am I in trouble?"

"No, and we have permission to ask for anything we need—from him or Althea. You may stay as long as you wish."

"I was already going to do that." He grinned.

"Do you mind if I go upstairs and wash?"

"Please do. You're starting to stink, but I wasn't going to say anything."

I pinched him. "I have a few things to see to as well, but I won't take too long."

He nodded, still rubbing the spot on his arm where I goosed him.

I unloaded the trunk in two trips and tucked the empty container in the study before showering. It had been several days—how many, I'd lost count—since I had bathed properly. I washed everything twice, including my hair, and then buttoned on a simple blue dress my mother had sent in the delivery.

Feeling rejuvenated, I descended the stairs with my copy of *Sense and Sensibility*. I dropped the book in the parlor and I put the kettle on for tea. Sean and Winifred were cuddled together, whispering.

"How are you feeling, Winnie?"

"A tad better, but weak."

"I'm going to make tea. Would either of you want some?"

Winifred shook her head.

"We'll be fine, Merri," Sean said. "You enjoy your tea and rest for a while, somewhere you can stretch out for a bit."

"Then you need to sit up, Sean."

I waited on the porch until he moved to the side chair. Then I prepped my cup, took my treat into the parlor, propped my feet on the settee, and read while I ate two cookies and drank the hot tea.

The mantel clock read a quarter after midnight when I woke, still holding the open book in my hands. I picked up the teacup and set it on the kitchen counter. Tippet, stretched between the kitchen and porch door, looked at me with one eye before sighing and going back to sleep.

Eyes adjusting to the dimness of the far porch, I deliberately approached the bed. Sean was atop Winifred, moving in a carnal way that was obscene given the situation.

"Sean Francis Spunner!"

Tippet barked and Sean sat up, straddling Winifred. His clothing was still fastened except for the top few buttons of his shirt, but there was no mistaking the hunger in his eyes or Winifred's partially opened gown.

"You better be glad I don't have a shotgun handy because you'd be full of birdshot if I had my way!"

He scrambled off the bed, chin down with what I hoped was shame.

"No, Merri," Winifred said with labored breath. "I wanted him to make love to me, but he wouldn't. He was pleasuring me instead."

"Pleasuring! How do you even know about such things?"

"Sean explained to me the difference. I'm feeling better, but it won't last. I want to share as much as possible with Sean while I can."

She sounded five years more mature than she did the week before. Did looming death age a person? Was Winifred now my senior as she lay on death's bed?

I unleashed my pain and confusion. "You're drunk on whiskey. You don't realize you're going to get better and live a long, happy life!"

"We would be married, but I might not get that chance," Winifred spoke with conviction. "I want to share what I'm able to with the man I love while I can. There's no shame in that."

"I don't even know why I'm here when you two are more than happy to do as you please without thought of the chaperone."

"This isn't about you, it's between me and Sean. It will be my judgement, Merritt, not yours."

But weren't they all my follies, these terrible mistakes of my younger cousins? Each time I was the oldest—in charge. Diamond ran out in the middle of a thunderstorm to play at the creek because I didn't bolt the door when I knew she was set on proving her superiority. Winifred invited a man to bed her because I fell asleep during my chaperone duties. How are these things *not* my fault?

Sean brought Winifred's water glass to her lips.

"Thank you," Winifred told him. "Now please come back to me. I want to feel that exquisiteness again."

Without a glance my way from either of them, Winifred laid back and Sean climbed on top of her. He leaned over to kiss her and did a grinding motion where their hips met, causing her mouth to open as she arched into him. Trailing kisses down her neck, Sean tasted her collar bone within the opened buttons of my old nightgown. Winifred's hands tugged at his shirt, pulling it from his trousers. He straightened and yanked it over his head, dropping it on the floor. When her fingers met the sparse hair on his chest, an ache opened like a cavern in my middle.

They had been bare—chest to chest—two days before at my command, though Winifred was unknowing and Sean blindfolded. And he had held her earlier that day while I bathed her. But this erotic scene was lasciviousness unleashed. I was left bitter and scared and wanting.

Eyes blurry with tears, I stumbled to the kitchen and flopped into the nearest chair. I cried silently as Sean coaxed all sorts of sounds from Winifred's fevered body. How was it even possible without—I couldn't even think the word.

A hush settled over the house followed by a creaking floorboard, fumbling, and an uttered curse.

Sean's pants were kicked across the doorway and then the flash of his white buttocks met my view as he tied a blanket around his waist. He walked into the kitchen a moment later, carrying his pants and underdrawers.

"What do you think you're doing?" I demanded.

"I need to wash my clothes, but I don't want to turn on the porch light to do it out there. Winnie's sleeping again."

"You can't walk around the house naked."

"Well, I can't put these back on until I rinse them." He crossed his arms and glared at me with his blacken eyes, compliments of Bartholomew.

"What happened?" I crossed my arms too.

"Dammit, Merri, you know what happened!"

"The last thing I heard and saw from the two of you, you had your pants on and promised not to take Winifred's innocence. Then you're kicking off your clothes and flashing your derriere at me."

"You saw…" His face paled as white as his rear cheeks. "I'm sorry, Merri."

"Explain yourself, Mr. Spunner, or leave."

"I have book knowledge and heard a few firsthand stories from some people, but I've never been with a girl before. I…well, *you know.*"

"No, I don't."

"Oh, you might not." He reddened. "Please don't make me say it."

"Goodbye, Sean."

"I spent in my pants! There, are you happy?"

"You spent?" My furrowed brow lifted as understanding hit my brain. My face was surely as red as his, but I couldn't help laughing.

"You don't need to be cruel." He went for the bathroom, clutching the blanket about him.

I followed. "Serves you right, for your wicked ways!"

Sean shut the door in my face. Still laughing over his embarrassment, I went for the stairs. In the master bedroom, I found a pair of Uncle Andrew's trousers and left them folded by the bathroom door. Then, I lit the old wood-burning stove in the corner of the kitchen so we could dry his laundry quicker. The final step was putting the kettle on to boil.

Sean joined me a few minutes later, one hand holding up the too large pants and the other his soiled clothes.

I pointed to the chairs I placed before the stove. "Drape them over the back of those. There will be tea and cookies in a couple more minutes if you'd like to join me."

"Thank you, Merri." He went to check on Winifred and returned while buttoning on his shirt. "I'm sorry, but I couldn't deny her if it's one of her last wishes."

"If she recovers, how will you both go on having shared these moments when you know you can't marry for years?"

"Remember my dreams? Those premonitions have never been wrong."

Sean arranged two chairs in the rectangle of light spilling from the kitchen onto the porch so we could have our middle of the night snack while watching over Winifred. Once we were settled in the chairs with tea and the last of Althea's cookies on each of our saucers, we fell into companionable chatter of the most intimate type.

"What is it like to sleep beside Winifred?" I asked.

"A blend of comfort and exhilaration. I feel like I could sleep forever holding her, but I don't want to miss a minute of the experience by closing my eyes."

I nodded, imagining Bartholomew's embrace. "And how did it work—the two of you pleasuring?"

He gave an impish smile. "Friction, dear Merri."

"Did you touch her down there?"

"No, never. Remember the book—"

"You and that book!"

"Shh." He leaned closer. "Remember the way the bodies lined up, no matter the position?"

I nodded.

"Those areas are sensitive. Even through clothing, they can be stimulated. My hands never touched her sacred area, nor did they feel her bare breasts, though I ache to experience both." Sean took a sip of tea. "I'm haunted by thoughts of her—of what could be."

We finished our tea and cleared our seating arrangement. I sent Sean to sleep in the parlor and curled in the armchair beside Winifred's bed.

Several hours later, Winifred woke. I got her to drink water and held a cold cloth to her head, but she continued to shift uncomfortably. I hollered for Sean to bring the whiskey, and he helped me administer it. I allowed him to lie beside her until she fell asleep, then sent him back inside.

Thirty-four

I woke to Althea's "Good morning, Miss Merritt" spoken through the screen.

Winifred still slept under the effects of the whiskey. I stretched my stiff limbs as I crossed the porch to open the door for the cook.

"I hope my boy didn't give you too much trouble."

Images of Sean moving atop Winifred flashed through my mind. "Maybe a tad more than usual."

Althea set her baskets on the kitchen table. Taking in the sight of Sean's pants and drawers hanging on the chairs, she shook her head. "I'll take a switch to him if needed, Miss Merritt."

I laughed. "That's tempting."

"Where is he?"

"In the parlor." I pointed to the hall door. "I had to separate him from Winifred for a bit."

"That boy has one thing on his mind more than books, and it isn't food."

Not wanting to miss his talking to, I followed. Sean's shirt was folded over the side chair and he sprawled on his bare belly with his face turned away from the door. Uncle Andrew's pants were low about his hips, the fleshy top of his right buttocks exposed. Hand hanging over his backside a moment, Althea slapped his vulnerable rear with a smack that echoed in the room.

"Yeow! Mer—" Sean bolted upright as he turned, a hand gripping the waist of the baggy clothes so they wouldn't fall. "Miss Althea! What'd I do to you?"

"Obviously you did something to these girls if you figured Miss Merritt would wail on you like that, Sean Francis." She pointed to his legs. "What do you think you're doing in a dead man's trousers? I know Miss Estelle keeps you in clean clothes. Good thing I brought you a fresh outfit because those pants you tried to launder yourself look horrid. Do I even want to know what you did to dirty your clothes?"

"No, ma'am." Sean pitifully hung his head.

"Then you better get yourself to the kitchen and find the clean clothes and brushes I brought so you can get out of those big old things and tidy up before I get the shivers looking at you."

"Yes, ma'am!" He slowed enough to kiss my cheek on his way out. "Morning, Merri."

Sean grabbed his supplies from the kitchen and was in the half-bath before we made it to the porch.

"That boy needs a mama. Mrs. Finnigan is kind, but she knows nothing about boys. I do the best I can for him." Althea went to the bed, fingering Winifred's cheek. "Fever is high. Poor thing is putting up a good fight. Looks to be turning a bit lemon though. That ain't good."

I stepped closer. In the morning light, with Althea's brown hand next to Winifred's typically alabaster cheek, she did appear yellow.

"The fresh air here has been good for her, but I feel in my bones it's going to get chilly tonight. Have Sean Francis carry her inside before nightfall. If Keziah doesn't make it back today, I'll send him more clothes with supper."

"You know about Keziah?"

"I know all the domestics in the neighborhood. She's a good lady, but up in age. Not the same since her man died, but that's to be expected. Mrs. Allen did a fine thing bringing her in like she did, but now that she's with family, I wouldn't be surprised if she stays put."

"She said in her letter she was going to visit her dying sister."

"A family loses one and has room for another. They'd take her in, Miss Merritt. It would be good for her. She slaved her first thirty-some years, and worked daily as hired help more than the last three decades. She deserves some rest. I see you've got a head on those capable shoulders, but if she doesn't come back, and you're wanting a bit of help, let me know. I've got kin looking for steady positions."

"Thank you, Althea."

"Now fix some coffee and enjoy that cornbread before Sean Francis eats it all."

"I appreciate everything."

She collected Sean's laundry, emptied her food basket, and let herself out while I saw to a fresh cold cloth for Winifred.

Sean found me setting water on the stove and slipped an arm about my waist. "Is Althea gone?"

"Yes, and now I know who to call when you misbehave."

He flashed a sly grin and tucked his hands into the pockets his charcoal gray pants. "How did Winnie do the rest of the night?"

"All right, but her fever is still up and she's beginning to look like Yellow Jack kissed her all night rather than you."

Sean went for her, and I set about whipping up some honey butter for the cornbread.

Sean kept watch over Winifred all morning, and I saw to the laundry and kitchen.

Over lunch, we debated where to move Winifred.

"The parlor is large enough for all of us," I said.

"She'd be more comfortable in her bedroom," Sean insisted.

"What, so you can have privacy with her when I'm doing the wash? Besides, she hasn't slept in there for months."

"That was because of her nightmares." He stirred the vegetable soup in his bowl. "I want Winnie to be comfortable. In her room, you'd both have a bed to rest on."

"I can't allow you to stay with her if she's on a completely different floor of the house from me."

"You've done it before, but what happened last night was a rare window of opportunity. A gift. I doubt Winnie will feel half that strong and alert again, save for recovery."

I looked across the porch at Winifred before meeting his gaze once more. "I don't know what to think anymore, Sean."

He saw the defeat in my eyes and set both our bowls aside in order to take my hands in his. "Don't think, Merri. Feel. Grieve if you need to. You can cry on my shoulder all you want. But what you need is a good night's sleep. Let's set the sick room in your space upstairs. There are two beds and even two hammocks on the porch. You can get proper sleep at night, and I'll watch her, then I'll nap during the day. It will work out."

"You think so?" I asked.

"God, I hope so."

***

True to Althea's prediction, the afternoon cooled rather than warmed. Sean carried the dry sink basin and pitcher from Keziah's room to ours so I could keep fresh water handy. On my next trip upstairs, I couldn't help but look in Keziah's space. There were no personal items left beyond a few pieces of worn clothing. She truly could stay gone without losing anything beyond her job—but what worth would that be to a tired, old woman with a family willing to support her?

I brought in the morning's laundry from the line and made the beds while Sean watched over Winifred. Setting linens and cloths within easy access in the bedroom, I mulled over what Aunt Ethel would say about Sean living with us. Probably similar to her thoughts on being in a Catholic hospital. I prayed she would improve so she could come home, and for Winifred to heal or at least be comfortable. And forgiveness for myself if I was in error.

At five, someone knocked on the front door. I hurried down from my final touches—Tippet on my heels—and cracked the entrance.

"Mr. Finnigan, good afternoon." I opened the door fully.

Tippet slipped past him into the yard as though looking for more visitors.

"Miss Hall, I hope your cousin is improving."

"Winifred isn't any worse, but we've used the whiskey several times when she's restless. Thank you again for supplying it. Would you like to come in?" Seeing his hesitation, I gave him a polite way of refusal. "Sean is with Winifred on the back porch. I could meet you around there so you stay in the fresh air."

"Thank you. I'd like to speak with him."

I walked through the house quickly, but Mr. Finnigan was faster. He stared through the screen at Sean curled against Winifred, an arm resting just below her chest. Both slept and it looked innocent in the daytime compared to their snuggling in the dark, but I didn't like his uncle finding him like that.

Mr. Finnigan stepped lightly to the bedside and laid a hand on Sean's shoulder.

The imp groaned as though he didn't want to be bothered and stretched. His hand rubbed across Winifred until he cupped her generous breast above the blanketed mound.

"Do you truly think that's appropriate behavior given the circumstances?" Mr. Finnigan asked in a controlled whisper.

Sean sprang off the bed, turning midair toward the voice. "Uncle Patrick," he sputtered. "Forgive me! I was asleep and—"

Winifred whimpered from the loss of contact.

"Dearest Winnie." Sean leaned over to stroke her cheek. "I'm still here."

She immediately settled, nuzzling into his hand. He kissed her forehead and inched away until his fingers trailed off her jaw. Tiptoeing until he was on the far side of the porch, the men stepped outside. I braced for their heated discussion.

"What exactly is going on here that has you groping a young lady like that?" Mr. Finnigan demanded.

"I comfort her, nothing more. I didn't mean to—"

"Like hell you didn't. You've always known how to make a cat purr with the right strokes. If Miss Hall is too blind to see what's going on under her nose then she's not the capable young lady I thought she was."

My cheeks flamed with embarrassment.

"Merri is wonderful!" Sean's fists clenched, and I feared he would strike like he had Bartholomew. "She's a terrific chaperone, but I make mistakes. That's me, Uncle Patrick, trying to get as much togetherness with the girl I love while I can."

"You're too familiar with Miss Ramsay. It will only cause more heartache if she dies."

"She will. I saw it like I did with granny and my parents. I'm not leaving while she still breathes."

"God in Heaven help you, son. Why didn't you tell me?" Mr. Finnigan embraced Sean as he sobbed unashamedly. He stroked his nephew's mop of brown hair and patted his back. "You've had it rough, but the first love is always the hardest to lose, no matter how it happens. Hold her while you can."

I looked away from the intimate scene, studying the way Winifred's rosebud mouth twisted in discomfort.

Sitting beside her, I took her hand. "I'm here, Winnie. Do you want some water?"

"Sean."

"He's talking to his uncle."

She pulled away with a flash of strength and ripped her coverings off. "Sean!"

He nearly burst the screen door in his haste. I moved out of his way, and he fell onto the bed as he took her in his arms.

"Winnie, I'm right here. I won't leave you." He kissed her forehead and spoke over his shoulder to me. "Her fever is up. Pass me the glass."

I got the water from the counter and held it at the ready. Mr. Finnigan waited across the porch.

"Dearest, you must drink something." He settled her against him so he could hold her with one arm.

"Not the burning medicine."

"No, it's just water. You need that when the fever is high." He reached toward me and I passed him the glass. "I'll help you hold it, Winnie."

Stepping closer to Mr. Finnigan, I whispered. "He can always reach her. She'll calm for him, drink the whiskey or water, and anything else I can't get her to do when she's like this. I couldn't care for her without Sean. Thank you for allowing him to be here."

Mr. Finnigan nodded. "Dr. Sherard always told me I was doing the world a disservice by encouraging law when Sean would make an excellent doctor, but his heart wouldn't be able to take the pain of patients dying. He would want to grieve with the families. He'd make a good priest if he wasn't such a sensual creature. He quotes romantics like other young men know weapons or baseball. And his explorations. Miss Hall, I do apologize for his behavior toward your cousin."

"Winifred always welcomed his attentions."

"Now that I see how things are, I'll hire someone to do the deliveries if one of my household staff can't bring the supplies over. Sean may stay as long as you welcome him. I'll have the supper tray brought between six and six thirty each night—just a drop to the back porch. Same with pickup and the milk delivery in the morning."

"Thank you, once again."

"Althea told me she already arranged to deal with his laundry, so expect a parcel for that as well." He looked back at Sean cradling Winifred. "I had no idea he had another vision. I'll pray for them both. And you, Miss Hall. I'm going to see your aunt tomorrow. I'll send word as soon as I can about her."

"I'll never be able to repay you, Mr. Finnigan."

"Keeping watch over my nephew while he's here is enough." He glanced once more at Sean. "I've only had him with me five years, but he's a son to me, no matter our differences."

Althea arrived with a covered tray and a sack over her shoulders at precisely six.

"I've brought you more outfits and pajamas so you won't wear a dead man's clothes again, or worse yet, sleep in your drawers in front of these ladies."

"Thank you, Althea." Sean kissed her cheek as he took the canvas bag.

"Today is speckled trout, scalloped potatoes, greens, and some plain rice for your girl. Plus cookies and a couple pieces of pecan pie. Now fetch me that empty milk bottle and I'll be gone."

Sean and I ate, and then I cleaned our dishes.

"Now go on and get a shower and ready for bed," he told me as he buttered rice for Winifred. "I want to see you in a beautiful nightgown when I get up there with Winnie."

I rolled my eyes at him, but the thought of a nightgown and bed after four days sounded heavenly.

"I'll be up there with her as soon as she eats."

When I exited the bathroom after my shower, I crossed my arms over the thin white fabric printed with pink roses. Sean and Winifred weren't in the bedroom, so I stashed my laundry and pattered downstairs. They sat side-by-side on the porch bed, their backs against the wall and Winifred's head on his shoulder, her cheeks beyond the yellow looked flushed.

"I think it's time to get Winifred to bed."

She lifted her head. "Sean told me we're going inside."

"That's right. He'll carry you upstairs."

Tippet scratched at the screen and I let him in, latching the door before following Sean through the house as he carried his love to bed.

"Do you wish a quick bath or shower?" I asked Winifred. "A change of clothing at the very least."

"A quick wash, if you'll help me, Merri."

"Of course. Bring her to the bathroom and I'll collect her clothes."

Ten minutes later, I opened the bathroom door. Sean waited in the hallway, eyes darting between me and Winifred.

"How did I'd get lucky enough to have two pretty girls sharing a bedroom with me tonight?" His amber eyes glittered, and the smile on his face could have swayed me if I wasn't keen to his antics. "It's nice to see you wearing that gown again, Winnie."

"Where did it come from?"

"I bought it at Hammel's Department Store for you. I love the way the blue ribbons match your eyes." He lifted her into his arms and carried her across the hall. "We're keeping the sleeping porch door open, so I want you nearest the hall to be away from the draft."

"I'm sorry for being a burden."

"You're no burden, Winnie. There's nowhere else I'd rather be than holding you." He lowered her to the pillow on the turned-down bed.

"You'll sleep with me, Sean?" she whispered as he pulled her covers up.

"I'll hold you all night, but let me tuck Merri into bed first so she doesn't get jealous."

Winifred giggled, and I glared.

Lifting the sheet over myself by the time he turned to me, I ended up smiling at his grinning face.

"I'll wake you if needed," he whispered. Sean kissed my forehead. "Goodnight, Merri."

A moment later, Tippet jumped onto the foot of my bed. He circled three times and then curled into a ball. Enjoying the ability to stretch out, I felt my body relax into the mattress and then the world faded.

Thirty-five

The room was dark save for the glow of the hall light coming in the opened door. I lay still, unsure what woke me. The weight of Tippet just beyond my feet comforted me as I lay on my side, facing the sleeping porch.

"Get under the blanket with me," Winifred whispered.

"I'm still in my clothes." Sean.

"Change for bed. I won't be able to sleep without you."

"You've dozed off twice now. Relax or I'll have to get the whiskey."

"Get your pajamas instead."

The other bed squeaked, soft footsteps across the floor.

"Stand there. I want to watch."

Confused at what she wanted to see, I fought the urge to sit up. Pajamas, watching...*Winifred!* She must feel better, but watching him change clothes was unacceptable. But hadn't Sean had the same experience with her as he helped care for her? I squeezed my eyes shut and tried not to listen.

Giggling.

An answering chuckle.

Clothing dropping on the floor.

"You're so handsome."

"Am I what a novelist would call 'virile'?"

"Yes, but what is the proper term for that?"

"Shh, Winnie."

Giggles that elicited nausea.

Bedsprings protesting.

"You're burning with fever."

Water droplets falling into the basin.

"It's cold. Hold me."

"Forever."

Kissing.

A hum of relaxation.

Silence.

A lone tear on my cheek.

Oblivion.

The next time I woke, I was on my back and all was quiet. Tippet gave a whine of annoyance when I sat upright. The hall light illuminated Sean and Winifred—he curled on his side and nestled against Winifred's back. He was bare to his pajama pants, the sheet and blanket about their knees and his right hand cupping her breast through her nightgown.

Slipping from bed, I lifted their sheet and gently raised it to their shoulders. Neither moved, so I repeated the gesture with the blanket. I collected the cold cloth that had fallen onto Winifred's pillow. Holding it over the basin, I poured water from the pitcher onto it, wrung it out, and set it on her forehead. She moaned and shifted with the disturbance. Sean squeezed her chest and nestled closer.

I climbed back into bed and slept until daybreak.

Sean and Winifred were still spooned together, half covered. I led Tippet downstairs. The tray of supper dishes was gone from the back stoop. In its place were two milk bottles and an empty laundry sack.

Leaving the items in the kitchen, I returned to the bedroom to closer inspect Winifred. She appeared more yellowed than the day before and scorching to the touch. A layer of sweat had her nightgown stuck to her torso.

"Sean," I whispered.

No response. I poked his backside.

"Come on, you're both covered in sweat. Bathing and laundry are first on today's list." I went to Winifred's side. "Winifred, how are you feeling?"

Waiting for a response, I felt her fevered brow and opened her gown at the neck.

"Winnie?" Her hand lay limp in mine, breath shallow. I looked to Sean. "When is the last time you spoke with her? I heard you talking together when you changed clothes."

Sean blushed but held my gaze. "I think it was around eleven. Once she fell asleep, she never said a full sentence again."

"Then let's bathe her. She needs a cooling wash. Carry her like that. I'll take her clothes once we're in the bathroom."

He nodded and easily lifted Winifred from the bed. I stripped the linens in a flash and followed them into the bathroom. Standing beside the tub, Sean looked to me with eyes both fearful and earnest.

"I wish Aunt Ethel were here, but I'm grateful to have your help and support, Sean. All this care is taxing work and I know you're battling even more emotions and physical trials than I am. I love you and appreciate all you're doing for me and Winnie. I can't say it enough."

Sean bowed his head. "I love y'all too."

We worked as one after that, rarely having to speak. The objective to bathe Winifred as quickly and thoroughly as possible was accompanied by the unspoken explanation of doing so with as much dignity as well. Sean, being in charge of supporting Winifred while I washed her, had to touch her lemon-toned skin, but he carefully placed his hands and didn't leer. When I finally shimmied off her drawers, he even closed his eyes—though he practically bit through his lip.

Afterward, as the water swirled down the drain, I laid a towel over Winifred's torso and leaned over to kiss Sean's forehead.

"Watch her while I make the bed right quick."

When it was done, Sean laid her on top the bedspread. I toweled her dry, keeping her torso covered until it was time for Sean to hold her up so I could slip a fresh gown over her. Underdrawers seemed unnecessary—and cumbersome—so I skipped them. Once the blankets were opened and Sean laid Winifred in bed, I tugged her gown down as far as it would go and tucked the coverings around her. Sean plopped onto my bed face-first.

Giving him privacy to gain control of his urges, I stepped toward the door. "I'll dress and see to breakfast."

Winifred slept through our breakfast, which Sean and I ate picnic style in the bedroom. After eating, he carried the dishes down and I the heap of laundry.

"Call to me if you need anything and I'll come running," I assured him.

Sean took me in a tight hug and I found myself pressed against his naked chest. "Sometimes I think you trust me too much."

"You've proven yourself more times than not, Sean Francis Spunner. Though I do think it would be best if you keep at least the sheet between your bodies from now on. Rest if you can—atop the sheet, *after* you dress for the day. We might have visitors in the form of your uncle or the doctor. It will be shocking enough if they know we're all sleeping in the same bedroom."

***

At four-thirty, I stared at the telephone in the study for several minutes as I tried to decide if I should call Bartholomew or not. Its shrill ring vibrated the receiver as I watched, causing me to jump.

"Hello?" I said with a quake in my voice.

"Miss Hall, I hope all is well." Hearing Mr. Finnigan's voice rather than Bartholomew's brought a heavy weight of disappointment over me.

"As well as can be. Winifred is yellow now. She's barely woken today, but she's resting without the whiskey. How is our aunt?"

"Mrs. Allen recognized me and asked about the status of her husband's will, followed by questions about you girls. I assured her you're both well because the doctors don't think it wise to upset her with news of Miss Ramsay's illness."

"She'll have to know eventually, especially if Winnie doesn't make it."

"We'll cross that bridge when we need to, but as she cannot go home yet, there is no need to alarm her while she is still in a precarious situation with her nerves." He paused. "Now, is there anything you need I can have sent to you, beyond the agreed to supper?"

"No, thank you, Mr. Finnigan. That's more than enough."

"And my nephew? Do I need to speak with him about anything?"

"No, Mr. Finnigan."

"Very well. I'll check with you tomorrow."

Exhausted, I climbed the stairs and gathered fresh clothing from the bedroom.

"Who was on the telephone?" Sean followed my movements from his spot on the bed.

"Your uncle. He wanted to know if you were behaving."

Sean grinned. "Did you tell him the truth?"

"Mostly." I smiled back. "I'm going to wash and dress for bed. I already put the milk bottles out, but if you would be in charge of collecting the supper tray, I'd appreciate it."

"You wore yourself out with cleaning and the laundry, didn't you?"

I nodded. "I won't be doing anything extra tomorrow, but the day after, I should tackle the rooms up here. Do we need to change the linens before I wash?"

"Might be best. Her fever is down, but she was sweating this afternoon."

I washed Winifred's face and neck before switching her into a clean nightgown. Sean held her on my bed while I changed the linens, adding to the growing pile of washing for tomorrow. Feeling defeated, I left him to tuck Winifred back into bed and locked myself in the bathroom.

Sean sat at the foot of Winifred's bed when I emerged, my copy of *Sense and Sensibility* in his lap. "Are you going to rest before supper?"

"I don't know if I'll sleep, but if I do, please wake me when the food arrives."

"I promise—for food and only food. Dear Merri needs her rest." Sean held back my bed covering so I could climb in. Afterward, he kissed my forehead. "Sweet dreams."

The next thing I knew, a large hand fingered my cheek, then my loose hair. It stroked the silky wave of my tresses. Delicious food smells accompanied the touch, and I hated to ruin the moment by calling out Sean's too familiar ways in waking me, but it needed to be done.

"Winifred has hair too. I don't think you need to be touching mine," I said, eyes still closed.

"But I prefer your hair, face, and everything."

I yelped at Bartholomew's voice and sat up. Remembering my nightgown, I pulled the sheet to my neck. Sean, sitting on the bed across from me, laughed so hard I thought he'd wake Winifred.

"Forgive me for startling you, but Sean said I could wake you since supper arrived right before I did." Dressed in all black like his last visit, Bartholomew cupped my cheek as he moved in for a kiss. His lips lingered, making it more than a peck.

"I'm glad it was you and not Sean. I would have had to give him a lesson on propriety."

"Your hair, Merritt, is mystical. The thickness and rich coloring is gorgeous, especially with the auburn streaks. Merritt, my love." He held my face in both hands and locked his brown eyes on mine. "I'm glad we finally met."

His lips were warm and insistent. My arms went about his neck, pulling him to me. Had I already expressed too much with Bartholomew or witnessed more than I should with Sean and Winifred? Whatever the cause, I found myself on my pillow once more, Bartholomew kissing me from above. A moment of panic filled my mind as his body laid the length of mine—fear over his larger stature squashing me. Then warmth, excitement, and utter comfort filled me. Our kisses deepened and his pelvis nestled to mine with a movement that made me press against him in return as I gasped into his mouth.

"No you don't, old man." Sean had Bartholomew by the back of his shirt with one hand and removed my grip on his shoulder with the other. "There will be time enough for that another day."

He pointed Bartholomew to the rocking chair in the corner and then focused on me. "You looked dazed, Merri."

I nodded, but my head was spinning and the world felt more like a dream than reality. Sean helped me sit against the headboard and brought me a tray holding a supper plate, glass of iced tea, and silverware. After I ate a few bites of mashed potatoes, he turned to Bartholomew.

"If you can control yourself, you may sit at the end of her bed while she eats, but then you'll need to go because Merri needs her rest."

"You play a better chaperone than you do a suitor," I remarked between bites.

"I've learned from the best." Sean winked.

Bartholomew settled at the foot of my bed and adjusted his eyeglasses. "I was hoping to hear from you today. Sean caught me up with Winifred's news, but how are you?"

"I almost telephoned this afternoon, but I didn't want to disturb you."

Bartholomew placed a hand on the blanket above my knee. "Everything about you and what's happening here is of importance to me."

Smiling, I told him of my work the past two days, along with the news of Aunt Ethel.

"And Sean stays here all the time?"

I nodded, chewing my last forkful of fried fish. Bartholomew looked about the room and stretched a bit to see out the open door to the sleeping porch.

"I stay right here," Sean said from his position beside Winifred, facing us. "All day and all night, I watch over my girls."

Bartholomew's mouth turned down at the corners, but it wasn't quite a full frown. "How is the arrangement working out for you, Merritt?"

"I couldn't care for Winifred without Sean's help." I lowered my voice. "He helps with everything, Bartholomew. Changing, bathing, *everything* at his own peril, but please don't tell anyone. I don't want Winifred taken away. Aunt Ethel is already gone. I'd be alone."

Moving my tray, he took me in his arms. "I'm glad you have Sean and I understand how you all feel about each other." He continued to hug me. "I won't tell anyone, Merritt, and I don't judge you."

My arms went about Bartholomew as those words set me free. "I was worried," I spoke into his neck. "It must look scandalous, but there's a certain amount of decorum involved."

"I'd expect nothing less from you."

His warm mouth was on mine and we indulged until Sean cleared his throat.

Bartholomew's eyes lowered to the chest of my thin frock. Blushing, I took hold of the blanket and slowly raised it.

"Time to say goodnight, Bart," Sean said. "I'll clear the supper dishes and give you two minutes to say goodbye before I throw you out."

As soon as Sean was gone with the tray, Bartholomew helped me stand so he could look me over. "You're enchanting," Bartholomew declared as he walked me backwards until we were in the hall. Stroking my unbound hair, he smiled down at me. "I'm glad you relocated. I was worried about you staying on the porch where you didn't have a proper place to rest."

"I did sleep better last night. Having Sean here is a comfort I don't wish to lose."

"I look forward to being the one to care for you." Arms about my waist, his hands flexed about my slight hips and tugged me against him as our lips met.

Not wanting to be struck with that sensation almost returning, I pulled away before things progressed, but Bartholomew's glasses were already fogged over. He stood in the hall, looking at me with his dimpled grin as I climbed into bed. Then Sean was there, nudging him toward the stairs.

"Telephone or come back another day, old man."

Thirty-six

I woke in the semi-darkness to Winifred thrashing in the next bed.

Scrambling to rise, I joined Sean as he tried to calm my cousin. He held her, but she shifted restlessly and her forehead burned with fever.

Tippet whined from the doorway.

"I'll get the whiskey and let Tippet out."

I hurried down the stairs to the kitchen. Tippet dashed for the far yard as soon as I opened the screen. Not wanting to wait for him, I tucked a rolled towel between the screen and doorframe to keep it ajar so he could paw it open.

In the bedroom, I poured the whiskey into a small cup and set the bottle on the dresser so it would be near. Sean had to hold Winifred's arms so I could bring the liquid to her mouth while he spoke.

"You need your medicine, dearest. It might not taste good, but it will help you feel better. You must drink it all. Come on, Winnie. You'll get the biggest kiss after you take it all. Almost done."

As soon as I took the cup away, his mouth was on hers but she was too unsettled for the kiss to last.

"What can I do?" I whispered.

"Pray, Merri." Sean rocked her in his arms. "Pray for Winnie to feel comforted."

I went to my knees on the side of the bed, hands clasped.

Tippet ran into the room and jumped onto Winifred's bed. He stepped closer to her face cradled against Sean's shoulder.

"No, Tippet! Down!"

Tippet licked her cheek before leaving the bed.

"Oh, Tippet, you dear! He's trying to help." Tippet, sitting by the door, received lots of belly rubs.

Thanks to the whiskey, Winifred was soon slumbering beside Sean. Tucked behind her, Sean's right arm was where it typically was when they slept—slung over her middle and his hand at her breast.

"Goodnight, again, Sean."

"Goodnight, Merri."

I slept again until daybreak on the sixth day of Winifred's fever. Then I dressed, carried the laundry downstairs, collected the milk, and started on breakfast. My morning routine was the same as the previous day. When I was hanging fever cloths on the clothesline, Tippet sat up from where he was lying under the satsuma tree and looked at the house.

A split second later, Sean hollered my name.

I stumbled up the stairs and skidded to a halt at the sound of retching.

"Sean?"

"Help!"

He had Winifred on her side at the edge of the bed, holding the washbasin below her head with tremoring hands as she spewed black vomit.

The yellowed skin showed Winifred's liver and kidneys were shutting down, but this was proof there was internal bleeding.

There was no going back.

The end was near.

I rushed for another bowl and speedily returned.

"Go, Sean. I'll take your place."

"I can't."

Locked in fear and repulsion, he held his spot. I replaced the bowl just in time for the next round of retching. Crawling onto the bed behind Winifred, I better secured her hair and tried to hold her steady as she convulsed with the force of the vomit.

By the time she emptied her insides, I laid in tears beside her exhausted body. Looking at Sean over the side of the bed—the brokenness in his eyes and black bile splattered pajamas—I cried harder.

When I caught my breath enough to stand, I pried the bowl from him. "I'm going to clean these and then you're going to shower."

He motioned to the spots on the side of the linens and floor. "I did my best."

"You did more than expected, Sean. Give me a minute."

I gathered the top sheet and bowls, rinsing them in the bathtub before throwing the sheet in the basket and scrubbing the basin with soap. The second bowl I returned to the bedroom filled with soapy water so I could wash the floor.

Sean was still in a stupor, propped against the wall. I removed his pajama shirt without protest from him. Then I worked the fouled sheet out from under Winifred, shocked to see she had wet herself. I filled the tub with warm water and laid out a clean gown. When all was prepared, I crouched before Sean and took his face in my hands. Eyes bloodshot, he focused on me.

"I need you, Sean. If you'll help me for fifteen minutes, you can retreat after that. May I count on you once more?"

He nodded. Before I could give instruction, he went to the dresser, took a swig of the whiskey, and thumped his bare chest.

"She needs to soak in a warm bath for a few minutes if you will carry her in there and watch her while I scrub the mattress. Then the mattress will need to be set out to dry. The far corner of the sleeping porch should be fine as it gets afternoon sunlight. You could move my mattress to this bed, all right?"

He nodded and focused on Winifred. Distended veins marred her previously flawless countenance—angry, jagged lines like cracks in our breaking hearts.

"It took the remainder of her strength to expel all that," I whispered as he held Winifred upright so I could remove her nightgown.

Without word, Sean carried her to the bath and stepped into the tub, lowering until he sat against the back. Her unresponsive body nestled between his legs and her torso and head leaned back on his chest. He grabbed a nearby towel and tucked it over her shoulders and chest that were above the waterline, then hugged his arms about her. Swallowing the lump in my throat, I got the scrubbing supplies and set to work tackling the stains on the mattress so I wouldn't have to think.

When I returned to the bathroom, Sean stared at the ceiling, arms still about Winifred.

"Are you drunk?"

"It takes more than one shot to get me drunk, Merri, but I wouldn't mind another swig to try to numb the pain."

"Whiskey won't help you."

"'Let us eat and drink, for tomorrow we shall die.' Why be sober when pain is on the horizon?"

"I don't think she'll be awake much after that display." I kneeled by the tub and washed Winifred's face, neck, and a soiled strands of hair. "Move your arms, Sean. I might as well wash her fully before we get her out."

He released his hold, but she stayed solid against his length. "God in Heaven, I know she's meant for your realm, but don't allow her to suffer the remainder of her time here. Ease her pain, even if more is given to me instead. In the name of the Father and Son and Holy Ghost, Amen."

I was silent as he crossed himself. When Sean made no further movement, I spoke. "You pray while in a bathtub?"

"I pray anywhere and everywhere. God hears me and hears you. Did Tippet not bring comfort to Winnie when you asked for it?"

"Yes, but—"

"But that was more respectable because you were dressed and on your knees and I'm half-naked, lounging with my fully naked lover in a bathtub? God hears me especially loud right now, Merri, for the devil is here too."

I hurriedly finished washing Winifred, pulled the plug, and took a fresh towel from the nearby rack. Sean shifted forward and brought his right arm under Winifred's knees before standing. I draped the towel over her and collected another on our way out. After he gently placed her on my bed, I quickly dried her and then the floor from Sean's dripping while he brought the soiled mattress to the balcony and then dressed.

"Just leave her on this bed," I told him when he came back. "There's no need to shift her around, but I want to put a towel under her, just in case."

"Might as well put two down." He caught my eye. "I know what happened—what will continue to happen—as she loses connection with her body. Don't worry over sensibilities now, Merri."

"You're wise beyond your years."

"A blessing and a curse." He lifted Winifred once more so I could place the towels under her lower half.

I noticed for the first time Sean's undivided attention on Winifred's body when I lifted the towel once she was back on the bed.

"I've felt a difference the last few days. Her weight loss is more pronounced." He crossed himself and bit his lip as his eyes continued to roam. "Even yellowed and with the veins burst on her face, she's like a painting, discolored and cracked from age. She could be Eve in the Sistine Chapel or Venus gracing the wall of a majestic library."

Sean sat on the edge and hoisted her to sitting against him. Once I got her head through the neck of a nightgown, he stilled my hand. "Let me, please. I won't be able to undress her on our wedding night so allow me to dress her on her deathbed."

With tears in my eyes, I watched him place her arms through the sleeves. Sean gently pulled the gown over Winifred's body. Once her head was situated on the pillow without so much as opening an eye, he kissed her forehead.

"God knows I don't deserve you, but I'm glad we've had this time. I've loved loving you and will keep on loving you long after Merri kicks me out." He left a kiss on her lips and went for the whiskey with a glance in my direction. "You said I could, and I doubt we'll be able to get anything else in her besides a few drops of water."

He lifted the bottle and took several mouthfuls.

"Sean!"

"Don't be a teetotaler now. Give your ol' Baptist blood some Irish fire."

I nudged his offering away. "I have more laundry to do and dinner to make."

"I'm not hungry."

"Neither am I," I admitted.

"Tonight—supper and spirits. You might need it by then."

***

As I finished feeding the last of the laundry through the wringer, the telephone rang. I dried my hands on my apron as I hurried through the house.

"Hello?"

"Good afternoon, Miss Hall."

"Hello, Mr. Finnigan."

"You sound strained. Is everything okay?"

"Winifred had a bout with black vomit. She's been sleeping ever since. I haven't had a chance to telephone the doctor because I've been catching up on laundry."

"I will update Dr. Sherard, if you wish."

"Yes, please."

"I won't keep you long, but your aunt is continuing to improve. She's asking about you and Miss Ramsay. I assured her on my visit this morning you are fine." He asked after Sean and said goodbye.

Both Sean and Winnifred were still sleeping. Winifred's breath was shallow, but Sean snored as loud as a hurricane sprawled beside her. Concerned that the doctor might show up, I hesitated over Sean but decided to let him sleep as long as possible. I placed a quilt over him and returned to my work.

The next telephone call was Dr. Sherard.

"Mr. Finnigan informed me of Miss Ramsay's decline. Has she woken yet?"

"No, she's sleeping soundly."

"Comatose is the word, Miss Hall. She is liable to slip away without ever waking again. Was there much vomit?"

"Bowlfuls. It burst the veins in her face too. I'm still not recovered from witnessing it."

"Such a shame, that pretty creature. Do you wish me to examine her? Would that help you feel better?"

"If there's nothing you can do for her, I don't see the reason to pull you from helping those who could benefit. Just tell me how to keep her comfortable."

"Keep her mouth moistened. Squeeze a few drops of water from a cloth into her open lips whenever possible. If she relieves herself, change her and keep her skin clean."

"I've done that already, and placed towels under her after the first instance."

"Practical and resourceful, Miss Hall. You're caring for her as well as a trained nurse could. Telephone with any concerns or if you decide you wish a visit. Otherwise, I'll hear from you when it's time to collect her."

"Thank you, Dr. Sherard."

My relief at not having to hide Sean's cohabitation quickly turned to grief over the approaching loss of my cousin. I worked at collecting the dried laundry under the threat of a late afternoon thunderstorm, gathering the still-damp items off the yard line to hang them on the back porch. With everything caught up, I checked on my charges. Both still slept. I didn't want to lie down, afraid I would fall asleep and we'd miss supper. I went for the telephone and asked the operator for Allen's General Store.

The line crackled and I caught the words "Feed and Grain."

"I was trying to get in touch with Mr. Graves at Allen's General Store."

"We share the line but I got it first. Let me send my boy over to tell him to pick up."

I stared at the wall of bookcases for what seemed like minutes.

"You still there, Miss?"

"Yes."

"You in town?"

"Yes, on the west end."

"Is it raining there yet?"

"Not so far."

"It's headed your way. We've got a soaker."

"Thank—"

A *buzz* and *click*.

"Hello?"

"It's for you, Bart. I'll hang up."

Click.

"Hello?"

"Bartholomew, are you busy?"

"Never too busy for you, Merri. What's wrong?"

I shared my grief over Winifred's condition and the report from the doctor on what to expect. He listened intently, asking all the proper questions that reassured me that I was doing right for my cousin.

"And Sean is coping?" he asked.

I gave a dry laugh. "After we settled Winifred, he got drunk on the whiskey and has been passed out all afternoon. I'm letting him sleep until supper arrives."

"How you do it all is a wonder, Merritt. Is there anything I can do?"

"Listening to me is enough, but thank you. I plan to eat supper and go to bed early as I'm not sure how Winifred will do during the night."

The store front bell rung in the background. "Will you telephone me tomorrow?"

"Yes, Bartholomew."

"I'll count on it, Merritt. I love you."

The words—strong and matter-of-fact—struck my soul, renewing my energy with a simple joy that manifest as girlish giddiness. I spun away from the telephone box and took a quarter of an hour to wash and change into a clean day dress. Carrying the fresh laundry to its various locations for storage kept me busy until supper came.

I set the tray on the dresser and nudged Sean awake.

He groaned.

"You better be glad your uncle didn't stop by today, and that I talked Dr. Sherard into not making a house call."

His eyes opened wide as he sat up.

"Supper is here."

Sean rubbed his belly as he stood. "Did I really sleep all afternoon?"

"Snored like a bear. I don't know how Winifred slept through the racket."

He gave her a longing gaze, sighed, and scratched himself. "I'll be back."

When he was in the bathroom, I settled in the rocking chair with my plate. Tippet sniffed Winifred and then jumped onto the bed, settling at her feet.

Sean hurried through to the sleeping porch a minute later and came back with a frown. "It rained?"

"About an hour ago."

"The mattress is damp from it."

"I should have thought to pull it away from the screen. I did get the laundry saved though."

"It's my fault. I was in charge of the mattress. If I hadn't drunk so much, I would have been alert. Should I bring in one from another room?"

"No, come eat. I'll sleep in the hammock tonight."

Sean fixed his plate and sat in the little desk chair pulled close to me. "I'm sorry for being worthless this afternoon. Will you allow me to bless the food?"

"Of course."

While we ate, I told him of the telephone calls. He was introspective over the pronouncements from Dr. Sherard. The weight of not knowing if Winifred would ever wake dulled the light in his eyes. Hoping to cheer him, I returned to a conversation from earlier in the day.

"You promised me supper and spirits this evening. Can you do so without toasting yourself into another stupor? You're on night watch, remember?"

His mischievous smile nearly melted my heart when it shone on his face. "I dare not touch more today, so tonight will be for you, but only one shot. I have the feeling you'll lose all inhibitions under the spell of Irish whiskey and I don't want Bart accusing me of getting you liquored for nefarious reasons. Finish your supper. A full stomach is best. That was my mistake midday."

"*One* of them," I teased.

"One of many," he agreed.

"You'll see me to bed, clear the dishes, and set them out for morning pickup if I don't take well to the whiskey?"

"Naturally, but think of it as medicinal. You need help relaxing to be sure you sleep."

"Like Aunt Ethel before she—"

"None of that, Merri. I won't let you go into hysterics." He took my teacup and added a splash of whiskey. "That's even less than Winnie got. Drink it fast because it's going to burn like the dickens."

If flames in a throat were possible, there was a fire inside me.

Sean slapped my back when the coughing struck, but I could do nothing until I worked enough saliva in my mouth to coat my throat.

"Why do people drink that?"

"It puts hair on your chest."

"I don't want—"

Sean laughed. "It's an old saying, Merri. Your chest is perfect the way it is."

I went to pinch him but he jumped back. Returning to his chair, Sean finished eating.

"I feel warm all over." I leaned my head back and stretched my legs.

"Do what you need to do to ready for bed, Merri. When it fully strikes your virgin vessel, it's going to hit you hard."

"Virgin?" I giggled.

"Untouched by alcohol, you wicked creature." He held my hand. "And otherwise, though you gave a good show of enthusiasm with Bart."

I closed my eyes, head still resting on the chair. "He's told me he loves me several times now."

"And have you returned that favor?"

"I'm scared to."

"Don't be." He squeezed the hand he held. "A man needs to know for certain."

"Men have all the confidence in the world. It's women who worry."

"We pretend as much as anything. That or shake off indecision and blaze a trail without forethought and end up having to ask forgiveness, but it's better than regret for things left undone, unsaid." He sighed, his hand caressing mine. "Don't allow him to wonder over your affections. Time is short. Share your feelings with Bart."

"I already told my mother in the letter I wrote her last week. And Winifred."

"There's a girl for you! She tells everyone but the man."

I laughed. "Shall I tell him now on the telephone?"

"Please don't."

"Why?"

"You never giggle. He'll know you're drunk and will never be sure if it's the whiskey that made you say it."

"But you're sober."

"Very sober."

"And you'll watch Winifred?"

"Yes, Merri."

"Good. My head is spinning. I need to lie down."

"Come on." Sean took my arm and escorted me to the sleeping porch. "You sure you want to sleep out here? The hammock might give you trouble if you try to get out of it when tipsy."

"I'll holler if I need help."

"And I'll be here for you."

Thirty-seven

I slept deeply until daylight. Climbing out of the hammock, I found Tippet resting at Winifred's feet as he had the evening before, but there was a rumpled indention beside her where Sean had been. Winifred's face was hot to the touch, but not burning as she was the day before. She didn't move, even with my checking the pulse in her wrist and lifting the blanket to check the towels for soiling.

After my morning ablutions, I went to the kitchen where the odor of burnt bread permeated the room.

Sean looked at me from the stove with a sheepish grin. "Althea sent bread with the milk, and I wanted to make toast."

I shook my head. "Keep to wooing girls. I'll take over so you don't waste the whole loaf."

He kissed my cheek. "How's Winnie? I've been down here twenty minutes."

"And you destroyed this much? That's impressive."

He laughed and shrugged. "But Winnie?"

"She's clean and doesn't appear to have sweated much, though she's warm. Her pulse is slower today. Did she ever wake?"

"No." He looked solemn. "I watched her most of the night. I dozed off a couple times, but I've been thinking of what to tell her if she does wake. What words would I send her off with for a final farewell?"

"The words aren't important—it's that it will come from your heart that matters. Winifred will feel your love and be comforted. But don't wait for her to wake. Don't regret words unspoken, as you told me last night. Tell her while she sleeps. Her spirit will hear you."

Sean kissed my cheek. "Thank you."

We went about the morning with quiet reverence. Learning Tippet hadn't left Winifred's bed all night, I took him by the collar and forced him outside for a few minutes before noon. After eating with Sean, I cleaned the kitchen and then stood before the telephone box in the study.

Before I could think better of it, I held the receiver to my ear and cranked the machine to call the operator.

"How may I direct your call?"

"Local, please. Allen's General Store."

"One moment."

"Allen's General Store. Mr. Graves speaking."

A flood of warmth hit my chest at his deep voice. "Bartholomew," was all I could reply.

"Merritt, I hope all is well."

"Winifred is steady. She still hasn't woken up, but she appears comfortable."

"And you?"

"I slept well and have felt rested today, but I want to…wanted to tell you that…well…I love you, Bartholomew." My cheeks heated though no one could see me. "I didn't want to say it over the telephone, but I could no longer wait to let you know. I'll tell you in person when I next see you, I promise."

He laughed—a rumbly pure sound that sent a shiver up my spine. "I'll hold you to that. And you know I love you too."

"Yes," I whispered.

"Would you like me to visit this evening?"

"I would, but not if it's an inconvenience for you."

"Merritt, nothing would stand in my way. Is seven o'clock good?"

"I'll see you then."

I gathered the small collection of laundry off the line. Before I could put them away, I answered a telephone call from Mr. Finnigan. Then, I brought the pile of fever cloths and Winifred's nightgown upstairs. Sean squeezed water droplets into Winifred's mouth he held open with the thumb and forefinger of his left hand. He had taken all the instructions on caring for her to heart and her holding steady was proof of his attentions.

"Is that enough, dearest?" He sponged the moist cloth across her lips and kissed her jaw where he had held her.

"Sean, I'm done with chores for the day. Would you like me to read aloud?"

"That would be nice. But don't take it personally if I fall asleep." Sean settled on his side with his arm about his sweetheart.

"You need your rest and I can help Winnie if needed." I smoothed the blanket over her and then ruffled Sean's hair. "Bartholomew is visiting after supper."

He grinned up at me. "Kiss him good, but nothing more, Merri. Your chaperone will be on duty."

***

While I washed supper dishes, the screen door opened on the porch. Used to Tippet's telltale bark alerting me to visitors, I jumped at the noise. Bartholomew entered wearing another riding outfit. He didn't hesitate to wrap me in his arms. I set my soapy hands on his shoulders and accepted his kiss before tucking against his chest.

"Merritt?" I looked up at his smiling face. "Please tell me."

I touched his shadowy chin, fingers trailing down his neck and back to his shoulder. "I love you, Bartholomew Hutkee Graves."

His dimples winked as his mouth met mine with a gentle parting.

"Merritt, unless you want me doing more, we need to go visit Winifred." He took my hand in his and we walked into the bedroom where the second mattress was restored, the bed neatly made.

Sean sat beside Winifred, talking to her silent form, but looked up at us. "You have company, Winnie. Bart is here, and he's holding Merri's hand like a proper beau. Do you realize that if your cousin marries this old man she'll become Merri Graves? How's that for irony?"

Bartholomew and I laughed, causing Tippet to look at us from his sentry at Winifred's feet.

Sean waved us closer. "Come say hello, Bart. He looks dangerous, Winnie, all dressed in black to escape the notice of the quarantine officers."

Bartholomew smiled. "I cut through the backstreets and empty lots to avoid having to lie about where I've been."

"I didn't realize it took so much trouble to visit," I said.

"No trouble is too great to stop me from seeing you."

"Hear that, Winnie? Merri is looking at him like he's the only man in the world, but I'm right here. Can you imagine that, after all I've done for her?"

"You'll always have a part of my heart, Sean, and you know it."

Bartholomew pulled the desk chair to the bedside for me and stood behind it, hands gently kneading my shoulder and neck muscles. The three of us chatted, Sean including silent Winnie on occasion.

After half an hour, Bartholomew leaned over and kissed my cheek. "I don't want to keep you up too late. Allow me to say goodbye."

He stepped around me and took Winifred's free hand in his. The yellow of her skin was even more pronounced that night.

"You told me when you came to the store last week that you wanted us to hug in greeting and farewell as a symbol of our friendship. Since you can't return a hug at the moment, allow me to kiss you, Winifred." Bartholomew bent over her hand and kissed the back of it. "Merritt and Sean are taking great care of you. I hope you feel their love and prayers."

Sean whispered his thanks.

Bartholomew escorted me back to the kitchen where he enfolded me in his arms once more.

"It won't be long for Winifred, will it?" he whispered.

"No. Poor Sean. She's my cousin, but he's known her longer and loves her on a different level. I don't know what to do for him."

"You can continue to support each other like you've done, Merri." He lifted my chin. "I do like that name for you."

"Use it all you like, Bart." Smiling at him, I linked my arms about his waist. "I love you. Now kiss me goodnight so you can get home before a quarantine officer tracks you down."

Warm lips and little caresses brought us closer for several minutes.

"Telephone me."

He didn't need to add the words "when she passes" because I knew what he meant.

"I will."

"I love you, Merri."

"I love you too."

After he left, I finished the dishes and set the Finnigans' tray on the stoop for collection in the morning. Sean snuggled to Winifred, so I washed and changed for bed. When I returned in my nightgown, I stood in front of the dresser and undid my hair to brush it.

"May I brush Winnie's hair when you're done?" Sean asked from the bed.

"Of course."

He was silent a minute. "Her breathing is slow and shallow, about once every ten seconds."

"I'm glad you're with her, Sean. She knows you're here and there's no one else she would rather be with."

I braided my hair and sat beside Winifred's knees. Tippet nosed my back from his claimed post as foot warmer.

Sean folded down the covers, hoisted Winifred under the arms, and carefully sat her upright. Allowing her head to gently fall forward onto my shoulder, Sean positioned my hands at Winifred's sides then settled close behind her. He undid the ribbon at the bottom of her braid and fingered through the twists to loosen the strands. Then he worked the paddle brush through her dark locks, scalp to tip in a smooth rhythm of devotion as he murmured endearments.

"Let's trade positions so you can braid it," he said when he was done.

We did so in a dance of forbidden closeness as we shifted around her. Winifred's limp body was soon supported by Sean's capable arms as he hugged her. I braided her hair with precision and retied the ribbon at the bottom.

"All right, Sean." I stood. "You may lay her down."

And he did with a sensuous motion of lowering with her so he was tucked to her side, kissing her cheek when they were both horizontal.

"Winnie, I'll love you forever, but I know God needs you. You'll be the prettiest angel." He played with the lace at her neck and kept talking. "Happiness and joy is what you'll have in Heaven. And your parents and sister and Uncle Andrew. Look for my parents too, will you? Give my mom a hug, and tell my dad I'll make him proud. I'll look out for Merri and Aunt Ethel. You'll always be my first love and the first for many explorations."

His smile was bright, eyes twinkling with his memories as he caressed her. I sat on the edge of the second bed and blinked away tears.

"I've never touched a girl like I've touched you, Winnie. Never pleasured one or kissed with an open mouth. I'm not such a cad, am I? I shared with you—gave you almost everything you wanted—cared for your needs rather than my own. We had beautiful moments together and no one will take that away from us. It's ours, forever. You'll live on in my heart, dearest Winnie."

He kissed her hand and brought it to his chest, holding it there with his fingers clasped in hers, and tucked his head against her breast—quietly listening as her heartbeat faded.

I knew the moment it happened.

Tippet silently left the room, and Sean erupted into sobs.

The clock showed it nine minutes after nine as I reached across the space separating the beds and touched his arm. He laid Winifred's hand on her stomach and clasped mine instead. Several minutes later, he let go and knelt over Winifred to take her other hand and folded them on her middle. After doing the sign of the cross over her and leaving a kiss on her forehead, he stood beside me.

He wiped his sleeve across his wet cheeks. "They will have to come for her, my dearest Winnie.

'Lily-like, white as snow
She hardly knew
She was a woman, so
Sweetly she grew.'"

"Keats?"

"No, the third stanza of 'Requiescat' by Oscar Wilde." The softness left his eyes as he sniffed back his runny nose. "I'll call Uncle Patrick and wait downstairs."

Sean straightened his shirt and took a suit jacket from his stash of clothing in the wardrobe. He even donned socks, shoes, and a cravat. With a solemn nod, he went for the stairs. I was left wondering what happened to my friend. Did complete heartbreak instantly change him into a shell of himself that he passed me without a touch? Having been ready to hold him, I felt emptier than ever as I gazed at my dead cousin. I dressed, settled in the rocking chair, and waited.

A quarter of an hour later, Tippet barked and there were voices downstairs, but I didn't move. Half an hour after that, Sean showed strangers into the room. I watched the masked and gloved men wrap Winifred into a black blanket and carry her out the door.

"Merritt, my uncle would like a word with you."

Ready to accuse Sean of being heartless, I paused a moment to study him. There was a slight tremor in his hand, his mouth was a tight line, and his eyes were liquid with pain. He did everything in his power to hold himself together. I didn't dare touch him, and unleash the flood.

Mr. Finnigan stood from the armchair in the parlor. "Miss Hall, my deepest sympathies. What can I do to assist you?"

"I hardly know. I assume there will be no funeral, but is there a family plot with space for Winifred?"

"I plan on seeing to that in the morning, Miss Hall."

"Thank you. And my aunt—may I visit her?"

"That cannot be. With you in a house under quarantine, the hospital wouldn't allow it. I will tell her of Miss Ramsay's passing tomorrow, while medical professionals are in attendance should she need sedation."

"If she handles the news, will she be able to come home?"

"That's my hope, but it will be up to the doctors."

"Then should I go back to my parents in the meantime?" I looked to Sean, but he stared at the floor. "I feel lost, Mr. Finnigan. I came specifically to help with Winifred. With her gone, I feel like my time is up as well."

"You visited before your cousin moved in—several times a year as I recall. And don't forget this house will be yours. Without Winifred, God rest her soul, you are the sole heir."

"But Aunt Ethel is alive."

"She might be permanently labeled mentally unfit. We don't know yet."

I shook my head. "I'd rather not think of claiming the house until it's the only option, Mr. Finnigan. I'd like to see my parents and—"

"Quarantine officers will not allow you to leave the city within the next two weeks. The Allen family and this address now has two strikes against it. You can't return to your parents until you are cleared by a doctor after that timeline. You might as well make yourself comfortable. Spruce things up a bit—you have the funds at your disposal." Mr. Finnigan looked from Sean back to me. "I will telephone you tomorrow after I see to Mrs. Allen and arrange for Miss Ramsay's burial. Say goodnight, Sean. The young lady needs her rest."

"No."

We looked to Sean.

He raised his head and gazed straight at his uncle. "I'm not leaving Merritt alone."

"Miss Hall will be fine, Sean. She has her dog and is familiar with the house. I'll provide her milk delivery and supper for the next few days to see her through."

"No, Uncle Patrick. I'm not leaving her alone with her grief. It would be cruel."

"Come to your senses. You cannot stay here unchaperoned with a young woman."

"I've been here days and will continue to stay until her aunt returns or she's able to leave for Grand Bay. And don't give me any stories about chaperones. Winifred was in a coma, so technically there was no chaperone for me and Merri last night."

"If you're that concerned, we'll bring her home with us."

"It wouldn't be fair to the servants to bring someone from quarantine home. Everyone except Althea would treat her like a leper." Sean's voice strengthened. "Give me tomorrow. After that, I'll return to work and my studies, though I'll stay the nights with Merri."

"Do you hear yourself? You've got some nerve!"

"But you know I'm in the right, Uncle Patrick."

A staring match ensued.

Mr. Finnigan finally slapped Sean on the back. "You're going to be a damn fine lawyer, Sean Francis. Goodnight, the both of you."

Thirty-eight

Sean saw his uncle to the front door and then marched upstairs. I collected Tippet and followed. He had stripped Winifred's last resting space—and himself. A pile of linens were in the basket by the door but his own clothing and footwear were all over as though he'd thrown them off. He lay doubled over in only his trousers on the made bed, crying.

Tippet sniffed the air and walked through the chaos to the sleeping porch, but I climbed onto the bed in front of Sean and hugged him.

"Thank you for staying with me." I kissed his head and he snuggled to my breast.

We lay together, tears mingling with time in suspended rest.

Hours later, Sean got up to relieve himself and turned off all the lights on his way back. He tucked himself behind me and followed the curve of my body from knee to shoulder with his warm skin. His touch felt more alert—inquisitive. His fingers brushed aside the loose hairs at my neck and trailed over the length of my arm resting on my side all the way to my hip.

"Merri." His breath on the shell of my ear sent currents throughout my body. "I need to feel alive to know I'll make it through this pain."

I wrapped my hand around his, and he lifted our connected limbs to rest below my chest.

"Did you know the most common response humans have after dangerous situations or death is the urge to procreate? It helps insure survival of the species."

I turned onto my back and looked up at him as my eyes adjusted to the dark. "What are you trying to say?"

"I want to hold you and be held." He traced my shoulders.

I tilted toward him, welcoming his nearness I had previously enjoyed. "We've been doing that for hours."

"I need more, Merri. Loving attentions. Pleasuring." He pressed his forehead to mine, breath sweet on my face.

My lips brushed his cheek. "But we shouldn't."

"I know you're worried, but no one needs to know that we've done anything." His hand traced a hip, gently pulling me closer. "You're curious about many things, as am I. Why don't we learn together?"

Sitting up, he gave me the physical space I needed to think clearly. Winifred was right in saying Sean could talk anyone into taking medicine. He was earnest and logical. His mannerisms were innocent, his smile charming enough to melt anyone's heart. But the young man beneath the angelic exterior had the potential for devilry. Was I ready to tempt that fate? I thought I was.

"All right, Sean. I am curious, and I trust you." I stood and opened the buttons on my dress and stepped out of it. Gooseflesh pimpled my arms and my thin chemise didn't hide the small peaks of my unbound breasts.

But I knew I wouldn't be cold for long.

Sean was immediately before me, pulling me into his warm embrace. He wasn't as tall as Bartholomew, but I still felt protected within his arms. His hands caressed my back, feeling much too good to be the touch of my dead cousin's beau.

"Don't go too far," I whispered. "I don't—"

"I won't take that from you, Merritt. Not even if you begged me."

I knew he meant his words, but a part of me feared we were both capable of losing all sense of control.

"You're so petite and delicate. The difference in our frames makes me feel powerful. No wonder Bart took hold of you like he did last Saturday." His hands went to my chest. "It's a reminder of your gentle femininity, to cherish rather than ravish because it would be too easy to do that."

The way he stroked me had me wanting to climb upon him. I arched closer.

"You're as responsive as Winnie, but different." He pulled my hair free so it caped my shoulders. He laid on the bed closest to the open balcony door and patted his thighs. "Straddle me here—one of the positions from the book."

I lifted the chemise to maneuver onto my knees as I settled over Sean. His thighs and pelvis firm beneath me, with something extra pressing into the center of my underdrawers. When I made a tentative rocking motion, we both gasped.

"The pleasure can be exquisite without complete consummation, Merri, but it can be just as messy."

Feeling bold, I fingered the sprinkling of hair on his torso. "Are you going to spend in your pants again?"

"I have no doubt I will, but at least I have fresh clothes this time."

I laughed and then tensed as I felt something unexpected. "What is it?"

Shaking my head, I looked at his navel rather than meet his eye.

"No secrets, Merri. We're learning together."

Unable to speak the words, I poked my finger into his belly button.

"Hey!" Sean bucked, bringing to light more of my concern. "I'm sensitive there."

I went to do it again, but he caught my wrist and flipped us so he was on top.

"You have a naughty streak." He kissed me and sat up. "Now tell me your troubles."

"I'm getting damp. Down there. I can feel it."

"That's completely natural—the best thing for a woman."

"Why?"

Sean settled on his side, facing me. "It's your body's response to pleasure. The areas that will come into contact with the man moisten so he can slide inside without discomfort to you."

My eyes widened. "But you're not going to—"

"I know that, and you know that, but your body expects it to happen—*wants* it to happen—because of the stimulation."

He trailed a finger across my collarbone and down until it caressed between my breasts that were pressed together with my side angle.

"Does that make you feel more down there?"

I nodded and he brought his lips to my throat.

"And that?"

"Yes." I wanted to hold him to me and feel more.

"When your pleasure peaks, you'll need to change your under things too!"

I pinched his arm and Sean laughed. He moved on top and bumped his hips as I'd seen him do with Winifred. The feelings of electric euphoria returned as I replied to his rhythm with complimentary movements of my own.

"Oh, Merri, don't stop. Please let me experience this with you. We both need it. I'm about to—I need a moment. Get on top again."

I settled over him and he skimmed his hands under my chemise to grip my hips. Two of his fingers on each side touched the bare skin of my stomach, making me shudder.

"I don't want you under my clothes, Sean."

He pulled his hands free. "I'm sorry if I went too far."

"This whole thing might be too far."

"But you like it."

"Yes, more than I thought possible." I shifted until I felt the zing of pleasure from our contact and continued the stroking movement with my hips.

I grew lightheaded but couldn't stop until I reached something I knew I was supposed to feel, but wasn't sure what it was. I leaned forward to try a different angle. My loose hair draped us. Sean bucked his hips a few times, sending me higher on his length until his mouth met my collarbone. Kissing his way to the low neckline of my chemise, Sean devoured my meager décolletage. The sensations washed my body in heat that threatened to consume me.

I moaned, unable to speak clearly in my inflamed state. I froze as lightning bloomed from my womanhood out as I cried his name. Using my stillness in the aftermath to tug me higher, Sean tongued further into my drooping underdress.

"No, Sean, stop!" Fear heightened my voice.

Sean set me off him and sat on the opposite bed.

Limp from the new sensations, I flopped onto my side.

Tippet barked as the sound of crashing came from downstairs. There was a scuffle on the stairs between boots and the click of the dog's nails.

"Get out of my way, Tippet!" Bartholomew's words reached the bedroom a second before he turned the switch for the gaslight.

His eyes fell on Sean, half undressed and holding his groin. "What the hell is going on here?"

Then he noticed me curled on my side on the far bed and rushed over.

"Merritt, if he hurt you, I'll kill him." He smoothed my hair away from my face. "I heard you yell at him to stop."

"He did, right away."

"What was he doing?"

Unable to look at the concern and pain on Bartholomew's face, I closed my eyes. "I'm sorry, Bartholomew. You don't have to love me anymore."

"Merritt?"

I shook my head, refusing to say more while I was still reeling from the effects of my explorations. He moved toward the other bed.

"Spunner, you've got two seconds to explain yourself before I bust your face again."

"We needed physical contact—a scientifically proven human necessity after experiencing danger or death." Sean's shoulder drooped in defeat. "Merri and I both have questions about love making. She agreed to explore with me. It was completely mutual and agreed upon that there would be no consummation. She kept her underclothes on and me my pants."

Bartholomew forcefully expelled a ragged breath. "For all your book smarts, you have no common sense. You're both so deep in grief you don't know what you're doing!"

My eyes widened at the exasperation in Bartholomew's voice.

"I did get carried away," Sean said somberly, "but stopped when she told me to."

"You're a complete ass, but I can't even strike you because you're nothing but a hurting child right now. What are you even doing here this time of day?"

"I'm staying with Merri until her aunt returns or she goes home so she isn't alone."

"The hell you are! You might have shared the room with Winifred here, but not anymore. You're sleeping on the back porch, Spunner."

"Yes, sir." Sean bowed his head.

Bartholomew poked him in the chest. "And if you *ever* try anything like that on my girl again, I'll kill you."

"And what are you doing here this time of the night?" Sean countered.

"In case you haven't noticed, the sun is rising. You telephoned me last night to inform me about Winifred, and I wanted to pay my respects to Merritt before opening the store this morning. I didn't expect to hear her fighting you off."

Sean tilted his head. "You busted the door, didn't you?"

"I sure as hell did! You think I was going to stand in the yard and holler to see if Merritt needed help? Have fun rehanging the screen today."

"You're the one who ripped it off."

"Because you were acting like a dunce." Bartholomew hauled Sean to his feet and shoved him away. "I'm sorry for you loss, but you need to get everything of yours out of this bedroom—right now."

"Yes, sir." Sean crouched to pick up his shirt and other items on his way to the wardrobe.

"And you, Merritt, have no business trying to learn about sex from a younger man when you have me." Bartholomew sat on the edge of the bed and stroked my hair, soothing me as much as his deep voice did. "I'll show you everything when the time is right."

"I don't want to look like a fool with you."

"You never will, Merri." He leaned over and kissed me. "I worried about you most of the night. If I had known what you two would attempt, I would have rushed over when I heard the news."

"I felt so alone," I whispered.

Bartholomew pulled me into his lap. "You never need to be alone."

He held me while I cried, and then I fell asleep for half an hour. Waking in his arms brought a smile to my face.

"I love you, Bartholomew."

"And I love you."

Seeing daylight brought me fully awake. "You'll be late opening the store!"

"I had the forethought to leave a sign saying I would be late because of a family emergency."

"Family?"

"The sign says ALLEN'S GENERAL STORE, the family to which you and Winifred belong, and I do hope to make you part of *my* family in the future." He stood me on my feet. "Get dressed, and I'll see you downstairs for breakfast before I leave."

"Thank you, Bart."

He took me by the shoulders as I looked up at him. "Is there any wonder Sean lost control with you? You're a beguiling creature sent to capture my heart."

"I don't mean to tempt anyone. I never thought I would even be capable of it."

"And that makes you even more appealing."

Thirty-nine

By the time I descended the stairs in fresh layers of clothing, the scent of bacon and eggs filled the house. Bartholomew and Sean were laughing in the kitchen but stopped when I walked in. I blushed and shrunk back a step.

"Don't you dare go shy on me, Merritt Hall." Bartholomew took my hand and led me to Sean. "Or with this scoundrel."

"Do you forgive me, Merri?" Sean's countenance was mournful, though he'd just been joking with Bartholomew.

"Yes, even though you're a rascal."

Sean threw his arms around my black dress and pulled me close. "I hope to always be your friend. You have nothing to be shy about, Merri. Althea came with the milk and cooked breakfast for us. That's got to count for something on your path to forgiving me."

"Why should it? You didn't lift a finger."

"I'll clean up after. We've been waiting for you to eat—well, except for a few pilfered pieces of bacon."

The three of us ate in the dining room. There were periods of lighthearted conversations and melancholy quiet as Sean and I worked to process the reality of life without Winifred. After a solid week of worry and toil, a vast emptiness loomed before me.

After we ate, I walked Bartholomew to the stable while Sean started on the dishes.

"I'm going to telephone this afternoon to check on you," Bartholomew informed me. "And to make sure Sean fixed the door properly. I'm not a violent man, though you've seen me behave so. Do you think me a barbarian?"

"I understand, and I'm grateful. I'll look forward to your call."

"But rest if you can." He cupped my cheek in his hand. "I love you, Merri."

Tippet stayed outside when I entered the house. Sean was elbow deep in soap suds at the kitchen sink, so I settled on the piano bench in the parlor. Thinking of the times I spent singing with

Winifred while she played, I started singing "The Lord is My Shepherd." Cheeks wet with tears by the time I finished the tune, I collapsed on the settee and cried. Sean soon joined me, offering his shoulder.

"Merri," he said once my tears stopped, "let me bring you upstairs so you can rest."

"What if your uncle telephones with news?"

"I'm more than capable of taking a message if you fall asleep." He held my arm as we walked up the stairs. In the hall, he motioned to the bathroom. "Wash your face and I'll make sure a bed is ready for you."

When I finished, Sean stood beside the made bed closest the door, hands clasped behind his back as he smiled at me. I sat on the edge and then tentatively lay back.

"I see the fear in your eyes, Merri. I won't ever push anything physical with you again. It was wrong, even though we both liked it."

"Don't ever withhold your friendship. I love you and the comfort you give."

"As I do with you, more than you'll ever understand." He leaned over and kissed my cheek. "I might make a bit of noise as I fix the screen door, but I'll see to it right now so I don't wake you later."

I nodded and closed my eyes. A few minutes later, Tippet jumped onto the bed and settled at my feet, allowing me to drift into restful slumber.

The faraway ringing of the telephone roused me. Sitting up too fast, I dizzily looked to the clock. A quarter after one in the afternoon.

"Sean," I called, hoping he'd hear me and know I was awake so I could take the telephone if it was for me.

"Are you all right?" he hollered.

"Yes," I said as I went to the top of the stairs. "I'm just waking up. Is the telephone for me?"

"It's Bart this time. My uncle called earlier. Winnie is being laid to rest in the morning. He'll give us more details later."

I hurried down the steps.

Sean stopped me with a hug. "Your cheeks are rosy."

"They usually are after a nap." I went for the study and picked up the receiver that was on the telephone box's ledge and held it to my ear.

"Hello, Bartholomew."

"Did you get some rest?"

"Yes, thank you." I glanced to the doorway where my audience of one stood. "And Sean is being a complete gentleman."

"He's invited me to come for supper—said he'd inform his family's cook. Is that all right with you?" Bartholomew asked.

"You're always welcome, day or night."

"Just try not to tear anymore doors off their hinges!" Sean shouted.

"Did you hear that?" I asked.

"How could I not? He informed me he got the screen back up. I'll double-check it this evening."

"Thank you. I look forward to seeing you again."

I hung the receiver and turned to Sean. "Why don't you try to nap now? I'm going to clean the dining room and parlor as we have a guest tonight. I expect your uncle will stop in at some point as well."

Sean rubbed his stomach. "We need dinner first."

"You haven't eaten?"

"I'm not allowed to cook—not even toast."

I hooked my arm through his. "Come on. I'll fix something right quick."

After we ate, I helped Sean make the porch bed with fresh linens. Then I set to work on dusting, mopping, and waxing the furniture. The hours of manual labor worked my body and kept my mind from causing too much trouble.

"Merri?"

I jumped at the sound of Sean's voice and turned from the piano I'd been staring at.

He came to my side. "What is it? I watched you for five minutes and you haven't moved."

"I've been thinking about what my family will say when they hear I lost another cousin."

"Merri, neither event was your fault." He tucked me within his embrace. "You did all you were capable of at your young age with Diamond. And Winnie was touched by Yellow Jack. You went beyond caregiving for Winnie, loving her as you did. Her own mother couldn't have done a better job."

I nodded through my tears.

"You promise you'll stop? If you don't, I'll be forced to kiss the doubt out of you. Then Bart would beat me, and we'd never be able to see each other again."

I laughed and sniffled back my runny nose that always accompanied crying.

"Why don't you go shower and change into something extra pretty for supper? It will cheer you up and Bart and I will enjoy the scenery." He kissed my cheek. "You know I'm right."

"But you don't have to brag about it."

"I always tell the truth."

"And it will get you into trouble someday."

***

I took my time washing and preparing for supper, hoping to make a good impression. Thanks to the generosity of Uncle Andrew and Aunt Ethel, I didn't need a man to keep me, but I still wanted to put my best face forward to my beau, my friend, and my lawyer.

The white Easter dress Bartholomew admired in the photograph had arrived in the trunk from Grand Bay. Wearing it, I secured a black mourning band about my upper arm to show respect to Winifred and Uncle Andrew. I brushed my hair until the strands shone and then secured it with two silver combs, leaving the length of it down my back. Not wanting to overdress, I stayed barefoot.

Sean looked up from the book he was reading when I reached the parlor and grinned at me. "You look like an angel. It helps me imagine what Winnie looks like now."

"We look nothing alike. We aren't even related by blood."

"You both possess an air of passion and adventure, though it took you longer to find yours."

I sat in the nearest armchair and Tippet laid by my feet. "Do you think it bad of me to wear white?"

"I think it's a fitting tribute to pure, sweet Winnie."

A few minutes later, Tippet barked and there was a knock at the front door. Sean jumped from his seat to answer it.

"Where's the quarantine flag?" Mr. Finnigan asked as soon as he was inside.

"I burned that worthless scrap," Sean said with boldness. "Merri is no danger to anyone."

I stood by my chair when he returned with his uncle.

Mr. Finnigan's eyes went wide as he approached. "Miss Hall, you appear rested." He extended his hand, and I offered mine to which he bowed over with a kiss. "I hope you don't object, but I informed Althea I was joining your supper gathering here rather than eating alone—again."

Sean met his uncle's glance with a raised brow.

More grateful than ever that I had thoroughly cleaned the entertaining rooms, I smiled. "You're most welcome, Mr. Finnigan. Please have a seat."

"Even if I turn the meal into a business meeting of sorts?"

"Nothing too heavy over supper, Uncle Patrick."

"Merely a review and catch up of sorts. I hear Mr. Graves will be in attendance as well." His eyes roamed me and a slight smile met his kind mouth.

"*Sean* invited him this afternoon when he telephoned."

"Then I shall wait until all are in attendance to share the updates, for I know he'll be interested." Mr. Finnigan looked about and flexed his hands.

"There are no decanters in this house, Uncle. Merri cannot offer you a drink."

"There's the whiskey bottle you gave us. I have no need of it now," I said.

"A bit of my whisky would be just the thing, Miss Hall. Thank you."

I forced myself to walk calmly from the parlor.

"She really is most enchanting," I heard him remark as I climbed the stairs.

"Merri is wonderful," Sean replied. "Mr. Graves is blessed to have captured her affections."

I stopped in the dining room to add a fourth place setting before returning with the bottle and a glass. I walked in on a lecture of sorts that didn't stop with my presence.

"It isn't proper for you to stay in a house with an unmarried woman. It could harm her reputation."

"Merri and Bart are practically engaged. He knows I'm here. If he sees no issue, I don't know why you should." Sean's cheeks were pink.

"Thank you, Miss Hall." He accepted the glass and bottle of whiskey and slung back a shot before setting them on the side table. "What would Father Quinn say to you about the appearance of evil?"

"I'd like to think he would be happy I'm caring for a young woman in distress."

"This isn't one of your romances, Sean. Real life has consequences they don't always share in novels."

"I think you need to hear Merri's opinion on the matter. After all, it's her reputation." Sean pursed his lips and sat back with his arms crossed.

Tippet rose from the rug, sniffed the air, and went for the kitchen the same moment the back screen snapped shut. Sean was on his feet in an instant, crossing the room. He returned with Bartholomew. Mr. Finnigan and I both stood, but Bartholomew only had eyes for me.

Smiling, he opened his arms. "Merritt, you look even prettier than you do in the photograph."

"Thank you." I hugged him and lifted my face for his kiss on my cheek.

I sat back in my chair, and he approached the lawyer. "Mr. Finnigan, it's good to see you. Many thanks for allowing your cook to provide the supper here tonight."

"I've come to enjoy the food and company myself. There is a bit of business to attend to, but first is a more personal and pressing matter in regards to Miss Hall."

Bartholomew lifted an empty armchair and set it beside mine. Once seated, he leaned toward me and offered his hand. "What is the issue, and is it something I can help with, Merritt?"

I clasped my fingers through his. "Mr. Finnigan is concerned over my reputation with Sean staying here."

Sean met Bartholomew's quick glance with a cocky smirk I was glad his uncle didn't see.

"Do you want Sean here?"

"I'd rather not be alone at night. With no hired help at the moment and not knowing anyone else in town besides you and Mr. Finnigan, I think Sean is the best choice for someone to stay."

"And he sleeps on the downstairs porch, practically outside?" Bartholomew stressed the words.

I nodded, hoping Mr. Finnigan wouldn't ask Sean such a direct question.

Bartholomew turned his attention to the lawyer. "What is the issue, Mr. Finnigan?"

"It's a most unusual situation. I worry Miss Hall's reputation will be sullied."

"I—we—appreciate your concern, but the city is in the midst of an epidemic. Societal rules are bent, lives in upheaval. I doubt an unknown young woman visiting family would cause much alarm to the public when everyone has so much to worry about."

"Precisely!" Sean said with a relieved grin.

Mr. Finnigan looked between me and Bartholomew. "It might not be my business, but as I'm lawyer to you both, it would be helpful to know. Do you have an agreement, a promise, between each other?"

Bartholomew gently squeezed my hand. "I know Merri is grieving and burdened right now. I'd never ask anything of her at a time like this, but she knows how I feel and that I wish to make her part of my family in the future. For now, I'm providing her all the support I can."

The lawyer's eyes focused on me. I shyly leaned my head on Bartholomew's shoulder. "I love Bartholomew and hope to bring him happiness, but he's right in saying I can make no commitments at this time. I came here to help Aunt Ethel, and I must see that fulfilled before indulging my own affairs."

"Your dedication and sincerity is commendable. Have a bit of whiskey, Mr. Graves, as a toast to your good fortune in catching the eye of such a woman. Sean, get a glass for him."

"And Merri and myself?"

Remembering the burn, I declined. "No, thank you."

Sean returned with two glasses and the three men toasted my health with the remainder of the whiskey.

Althea arrived and the four of us were seated on the long sides of the dining table because I did not wish to place anyone at the head. I kept Bartholomew by my side, and Sean sat with his uncle across from us.

Annoyed with Mr. Finnigan's lack of sharing, I grew tense and found it difficult to eat. Seeing my distress, Bartholomew placed his hand on my leg beneath the table, caressing my knee.

Feeling brave, I spoke. "Mr. Finnigan, will we be allowed to attend Winifred's burial?"

"I'm afraid not, but I will give you directions so you may visit later in the day." He took another bite of fish. "I was able to secure a plot in Magnolia Cemetery. It isn't in the same area as the prepaid space for the Allens, but it isn't too far."

"I would like to pay my respects to both my uncle and Winifred."

He nodded. "An evening trip would be best. I'll show Sean the cemetery map at the office tomorrow. He may guide you at your convenience."

"Tell me the time, and I'll collect you with the buggy," Bartholomew said.

"Thank you. I'll let you arrange that with Sean." I looked across the table. "And Aunt Ethel, Mr. Finnigan. How did she take the news?"

He exhaled a long breath. "Better than expected, but she's now even more concerned about you. I explained the hospital won't allow you in after being with a yellow fever patient, so she says she will return home."

"Wonderful! When—"

Mr. Finnigan raised a finger to quiet me. "She cannot leave the hospital without a doctor's release. None were willing to give it to her at this time, as I'm sure you can understand. Her nerves seem settled, but with the news of her niece, they want to give it a few days to be sure the improvements aren't temporary, which is known to happen. Even the most insane can play normal for a few days at the chance of escape."

"Uncle Patrick, that's most insensitive!"

"I meant nothing against Mrs. Allen. I spoke of patients in general. Though she's improved from the state she was in when she was admitted, she is in no way the woman she was before." Mr. Finnigan held my gaze. "She is physically weak, and probably mentally as well. Ethel Allen will need a companion. Are you prepared to live here with her or hire someone so you can return to Grand Bay?"

Three sets of eyes were on me with scrutiny and concern. Though I knew this was now my home, I couldn't say the words just yet.

"I'll do what's best for Aunt Ethel, however that falls."

Forty

I woke surprisingly rested the next morning, though my dreams were filled with a jumble of scenes from the reports Mr. Finnigan gave over supper. Cemetery gates. Bartholomew at the store. Aunt Ethel's return as an invalid.

Washed and dressed, I let Tippet into the yard, collected the milk, butter, fresh biscuits, and a basket of eggs off the stoop, and set about preparing breakfast.

Sean stumbled in from the porch, shirtless and rubbing his eyes. "Morning, Merri."

"The bathroom is yours to prepare for your first day back to work. Food should be ready by the time you're dressed."

Sean kissed my cheek and went back to the porch for a change of clothes before disappearing upstairs.

Half an hour later, we shared biscuits and scrambled eggs at the tiny kitchen table. He promised to telephone with news before he left a goodbye kiss on my forehead.

I spent the morning washing and hanging the laundry. Sad to see Winifred's used clothes for the final time, I realized it was fitting that she had been taken away and buried in the nightgown Sean bought her—a keepsake too painful for either of us to want to treasure. As the day proved mild and sunny, I washed all the bed linens too—happy to not have this chore more than once a week after today.

Sean's absence was felt at dinner as I ate alone, though telephone calls from both him and Bartholomew brightened the midday doldrums. To keep myself busy for the afternoon, I baked a batch of shortbread cookies.

At five, I was by the driveway gate, dressed in black. I clutched two arrangements of lantana blossoms, each with a late blooming hydrangea. Sean ran up from my right the same time Bartholomew brought the buggy to a stop from the left. Bartholomew offered his hand to me from above and Sean kept a hand on my back as I climbed in.

Settled on the padded bench between the two, I watched the neighborhood go by as we rolled south. The world beyond the yard loomed large in the twilight. I scrunched closer to Bartholomew and he put his arm around me.

"Are you cold?" he asked.

Not knowing how to explain the chill in my nerves, I nodded.

"Here, take my jacket."

The cemetery gates were only half a dozen blocks away. We soon passed under the archway and Sean gave instructions to the Allens' plot first. The double headstone still only had the names and birthdates of Uncle Andrew and Aunt Ethel, but the little ones on either side showcased the full names plus birth and death dates of my cousins who passed when I was a baby. I said a prayer, Sean recited a few scriptures, and I left one of the flower bundles on the dirt below Uncle Andrew's name.

At the buggy, Bartholomew lit a second lantern and hung it on the right front hook before climbing beside me.

He fingered his suit jacket draped around my shoulders. "Are you warm enough now?"

"Yes, thank you."

Sean navigated us to the corner in use for yellow fever victims and got out first. Row after row of little mounds of dirt without headstones because the engravers were backlogged with work. He walked a direct path while Bartholomew escorted me through the field of broken dreams. Sean finished whispering over the fresh mound of earth and removed a polished rock from his pocket to weight the paper in the center of the grave.

Standing, he looked to me with a slight smile. "A poem I wrote for Winnie. I read it to her. Now, wind or rain or nosy gravediggers may claim it—my final words to my first love."

I placed the flowers beside it and reached my hand across the grave to hold Sean's. Bartholomew offered the prayer and Sean quoted scriptures, including some scandalous ones from Song of Solomon.

Rather than going home, Bartholomew drove us to the Finnigans' house for supper. The electric lights reflected off the crystals hanging from the chandeliers. Sadness filled my chest at the thought of Winifred having lost the opportunity to live like a princess that a union with Sean would have given her.

Feeling dowdy in my simple black dress amid the finery, I stayed quiet, though Mr. Finnigan assured me it was a pleasure to dine with a lady once more. Sean was subdued as well, leaving Bartholomew to attempt to be pleasant company to our host, but he declined post-supper drinks with the excuse to see me and Sean home.

At my front gate, Bartholomew tied the horse to the hitching post.

I gazed at him in the flickering of the gas streetlamp. "I'm sorry for being poor company."

I slipped out of his jacket and held it open for him.

"I knew tonight would be somber, but anytime with you is worthwhile." He put his arms in and turned back to me as he buttoned the jacket. "You have every right to grieve, Merri."

"I need some time to myself to try to understand where I am in the world and what's needed of me before Aunt Ethel returns."

Bartholomew nodded. "May I telephone once a day to check in?"

"Please do. And I might change my mind about company."

"I'll be ready whenever you are."

***

Sean and I spent the next several days in solitude. The ritual of cooking for him in the morning and kissing him goodbye was calming because I knew he would return come sunset. We spent a couple hours in the parlor after supper in companionable silence as he read or played the piano while I sewed the green calico fabric from Bartholomew into a day dress that would wear well through autumn and the mild winters we typically had.

During the long days alone, I cleaned and organized every inch of the house, familiarizing myself with the contents of all cupboards, closets, and drawers. I arranged the parlor in a layout I found more comfortable for a courting couple as my mind often fixated on Bartholomew. I spoke with both him and Mr. Finnigan daily, but never more than for a minute or two—enough to stay informed of Aunt Ethel's condition and assure Bartholomew I was well.

With the interior set to rights, the following Tuesday I turned my attention to the exterior windows. I washed the glass and dreamed of having the shutters fixed and the house painted.

Sean arrived hours before normal and shook the ladder I stood on. "What do you think you're doing, Merri?"

"Washing windows, you ninny!" Knuckles white around the highest rung, I looked down at him. "What do you think *you're* doing, besides trying to break my neck?"

"Enjoying the view up your dress."

His wide grin taunted me, and I climbed down to pinch him. He pulled of his suit jacket and ran. Feeling free as I chased him around the yard, I remembered Winnie did the same thing many times before. I slowed to a stop by the ladder we began at.

Seeing my hesitation, Sean came to me. "Are you all right?"

Eyes questioning, I held his gaze. "Am I? Are you? Will we ever be fine?"

He smiled in his disarming way and stepped closer. "I believe we'll both survive and have lives Winnie would be proud to see us live."

"I'm glad to hear that, Sean." I picked up my wash bucket. "This is from Winnie!"

I slung the soapy contents at him and ran for the back step where I had a second bucket at the ready. Falling into my trap, I met him under the satsuma trees with a cold rinse for his sudsy clothes. Water glistened off the colorful bottles hanging above him as he locked his arms about me.

"Thank you for washing the dirty thoughts from me, Merri." Laughing, he kissed my cheek. "Allow me to help you finish the windows. You'll want everything perfect for Mrs. Allen's homecoming tomorrow."

"She's being released?"

He nodded. "That's why I came. I wanted you to hear the news in person."

"Thank you." I hugged him. "What do you think about inviting Bartholomew to supper tonight? Would Althea be able to squeeze in another serving?"

"I already arranged it, Merri. I plan on making myself scarce after supper, allowing you time to discuss with old Bart what you came to realize this past week and what you need to decide as you move forward."

"I already know one thing of importance."

"What's that?" Sean asked as he squeezed water out of the hem of his shirt.

"I'll never be able to live without a friend like you."

THE END

Author's Note

This trilogy allowed me to explore several new aspects of Mobile history, as well as touch on things only hinted at in my other novels. While The Malevolent Trilogy can be read alone, it ties in with The Possession Chronicles, featuring and namedropping several characters you will recognize from the series, though it introduces new faces as well.

Writing about an epidemic during a pandemic wasn't an escape—which I prefer in my reading and writing hours. With such heavy topics mirroring real life, it took me over a year (Autumn 2019-December 2020) to wade through the first draft of *Malevolent Hearts*. Members of Dalby's Darklings were there for me, offering name ideas when needed, giving me a place to share bits of research (including my ever-present visuals), and more. Special thanks to Jennifer, Megan, Carmel, and Rebecca for sharing character name ideas that I adopted. I hope you're pleased with seeing them in print, no matter how large or small their roles are.

Once again, my Dial-A-Nerd and critique buddies had my back, no matter the hour or day. Candice Marley Conner, Joyce Scarbrough, Lee Ann Ward, and MeLeesa Swann are the best.

Much love to my family, for the love and support they give me, with a special shout to Angela for helping me make my dreams into a reality.

I owe much of this story's powerful presence to Sean Connell. It had been over six years, but it was great to work with him once more. Thanks for being an extraordinary editor, Sean. (And I'm sorry if your namesake is a bit of a cad.) May it be formally noted that I claim any lingering mistakes.

I was fortunate to have Mobile Bay area artist Amanda Herman capture the image of the real-life home that inspired the Allen house in an amazing watercolor for the cover. The looming presence of the structure helps set the tone for the quarantine prison Merritt finds within the property. Thank you for lending your talents, Amanda. See more of her work at instagram.com/amandawithmagic.

Read Next

Look for *Tangled Discoveries*, the second novel in the Malevolent Trilogy, to find out how their losses, friendship, and love shaped the lives of Merritt, Sean, and Bartholomew in the new century.

If you want more Sean Spunner, you can read about him chronologically by jumping over to *Mosaic of Seduction*, novella #1.5 in The Possession Chronicles.

To find out more, check Carrie Dalby's website for book news, sale links, and more. carriedalby.com

About the Author

While experiencing the typical adventures of growing up, Carrie Dalby called several places in California home, but she's lived on the Alabama Gulf Coast since 1996. Serving two terms as president of Mobile Writers' Guild and five years as the Mobile area Local Liaison for the Society of Children's Book Writers and Illustrators are two of the writing-related volunteer positions she's held. When Carrie isn't reading, writing, browsing bookstores/libraries, or homeschooling her children, she can often be found knitting or attending concerts.

Carrie writes for both teens and adults. *Fortitude* is listed as a Best Historical Book for Kids by Grateful American Foundation. The Possession Chronicles, a Southern Gothic family saga series, is her largest body of work for adults. She has also published several short stories that can be found in different anthologies.

For more information and links to her monthly newsletter, blog, social media accounts, and more, visit Carrie Dalby's website:

carriedalby.com